ALIX JAMES

MR. DARCY'S CHRISTMAS KISS

A PRIDE & PREJUDICE CHRISTMAS VARIATION

Blog and Website: https://alixjames.com/
Newsletter: https://subscribepage.io/alix-james
Book Bub: https://www.bookbub.com/authors/alix-james
Facebook: https://www.facebook.com/ShortSweetNovellas
Twitter: https://twitter.com/N_Clarkston
Amazon: https://www.amazon.com/stores/Alix-James/author/B07Z1BWFF3
Austen Variations: http://austenvariations.com/

Contents

Prologue	1
1. One	10
2. Two	17
3. Three	26
4. Four	35
5. Five	45
6. Six	54
7. Seven	62
8. Eight	72
9. Nine	81
10. Ten	88
11. Eleven	96
12. Twelve	103
13. Thirteen	112
14. Fourteen	120
15. Fifteen	130
16. Sixteen	137
17. Seventeen	148
18. Eighteen	159
19. Nineteen	171
20. Twenty	181

21. Twenty-One   188

22. Twenty-Two   198

23. Twenty-Three   207

24. Twenty-Four   217

25. Twenty-Five   225

26. Twenty-Six   232

27. Twenty-Seven   241

28. Epilogue   250

From Alix   255

Also By Alix James   257

About Alix James   262

How to Get Caught Under the Mistletoe   263

The Scotsman's Ghost   275

Prologue

May 1803, Paris
The End of the Peace of Amiens

The air in Paris had changed overnight. Ancient streets, once thrumming with lively conversations and the hum of commerce, had grown tense, crackling with unspoken threats. War again.

Darcy could feel it as a living thing—something unseen, hunting, shifting in the shadows. He tightened his grip on the walking stick he'd borrowed from the rooming house. Not that it would make much of a weapon if it came to that, but it gave his hands something to do.

He'd lost Richard. Of course, he had. His cousin had run off to meet with someone, a half-baked plan to secure papers. "Stay here, Darcy," Richard had barked, and then disappeared into the chaos. As if Darcy could stand by and wait for fate to collect him. That had been hours ago, and the rooming house was no longer safe.

Sir Thomas Ashford had been their lone voice of reason since yesterday. Originally in Paris on some vague business matter—Darcy and the others never knew what, nor did they care—the man was some twenty years their senior and a friend of half their fathers. Such a friend, a man who remembered Paris from better days, was a valuable ally when a young man embarked upon his Grand Tour.

But there was to be no Tour for them now. Ashford had held them all in check when the initial waves of panic struck, and reminded them who they were—Englishmen, not cowards. Wise counsel in a foreign land, and Ashford was someone with the right connections to get them all out of the middle of a war zone.

If only they knew where he had gone just now.

So, Darcy and the others—nearly a dozen British sons of wealth and privilege, not a one of them older than two and twenty—had turned out. They were a panicked lot, and three of them had promptly rounded the first street corner and marched right into the hands of the French.

Now, Darcy was navigating the streets alone, his mind half on the ships that might yet be waiting at Calais, half on the soldiers that seemed to multiply at every corner. All he wanted... he just wanted to go home. To hear his father's welcoming voice, catch Georgiana as she leaped into his arms, drink in the familiar air of Pemberley, and sleep in peace once more. But that did not seem likely now.

The rumors had begun flying as early as last night—British citizens detained by the dozens. Some dragged out of their beds, and some plucked from the street as they tried to leave. There was no rhyme or reason to it, just the thick tension of a city closing its grip, clenching its teeth as war loomed once more.

A noise behind him. Darcy's pulse quickened. He kept walking, slower now, glancing casually to the side—nothing. Just a couple of boys, no older than twelve, darting between stalls. Still, he had the distinct impression of being watched.

Then he saw them.

French soldiers. Four of them, walking with that casual swagger that made their purpose clear. A man in uniform could always be dangerous in times such as these, but these men were something more. Their eyes were hunting. Darcy turned his head forward, heart thumping now. He was wearing a French coat and a French style hat. Perhaps they noticed nothing odd. No need to rush. No need to panic.

He didn't need to. Not yet.

But they were gaining. He could hear their boots against the cobblestones, feel the weight of their gaze, and his stomach twisted into icy knots.

Keep walking, Darcy.

His shoulders straightened, spine taut with pride, as if he could outpace fear with posture alone.

"Vous, là-bas!" A voice, sharp and commanding.

Darcy didn't turn. Didn't flinch. He kept his pace steady. A marketplace was up ahead, thick with carts and milling bodies. *Blend in.* He'd make it into the crowd, lose himself for a few minutes, then slip down one of the alleys.

"Arrêtez!"

They were closer. He swallowed hard, muscles tightening. His instincts screamed at him to run, but there was nowhere to go. Panic bloomed at the base of his throat. This was it. They'd seen him, a British aristocrat, in a city that no longer had room for him.

A hand clamped down on his shoulder, jerking him back with enough force to spin him halfway around. Darcy staggered, heart lurching in his chest as the soldiers closed in. One, with a face like a bulldog, grinned in triumph, stepping closer, barking French at him—too fast for Darcy to catch.

They were trying to bind him, hands already tearing at his coat, when someone crashed into the soldiers from the side. A blur of movement, and suddenly, one man was knocked off balance, stumbling into his comrades.

Darcy blinked in shock. *What the devil?*

"Sorry, terribly sorry!" The voice was bright, too bright, a half-hearted attempt at levity in the middle of a disaster. Charles Bingley. One of the young twits from the rooming house.

Only, he did not seem such a twit now. What the devil was he doing?

Before Darcy could process it, Bingley was already grabbing his arm, dragging him sideways, feet stumbling over each other as they veered off the path. "Time to go, Darcy," Bingley panted, still grinning like a lunatic, eyes darting behind them.

The soldiers shouted—one swore loudly—but Bingley did not stop. He was pulling Darcy through the crowd, weaving between carts and startled vendors, knocking over a crate of apples with a crash that sent fruit skittering across the cobblestones.

Darcy ran out of air, and his heart pounded as if it were trying to escape his chest entirely. "Are you insane?" he managed, glancing back over his shoulder. The soldiers were giving chase now, fury in their faces as they shoved past the crowd.

"Quite possibly!" Bingley huffed, not slowing in the slightest. "This way!"

They darted down a narrow alley, the sound of boots hammering behind them. The smell of sweat and fear mixed with something metallic, sharp in the back of Darcy's throat. They were boxed in, walls too high, and there was no way—

Bingley suddenly stopped short, a hand on Darcy's chest. "Hold on." The alley turned sharply ahead. Bingley motioned for silence, gasping for breath as they pressed against the wall, barely concealed by a stack of barrels.

Darcy's pulse thundered in his ears, and his limbs trembled as he tried to flatten himself against the rough brick. This was madness. This was utterly—

The soldiers rounded the corner at full speed, just missing them, the sound of their pursuit fading into the next street. Bingley let out a low breath, turning with a grin, though his face was pale.

"That," he said, still panting, "was close."

Darcy swallowed hard, his mouth dry, but there was no time for gratitude yet. "We're not safe," he whispered. "Not yet."

Bingley nodded, and for the first time, Darcy noticed the blood. It was seeping through the shoulder of Bingley's coat, a deep crimson spreading fast.

"Good God." Darcy reached out instinctively. "You are wounded!"

Bingley glanced down at the gash as if it had just occurred to him. "Ah. Yes, well. It's not as bad as it looks." He winced, waving off Darcy's concern. "Bayonet, I think. Lucky it wasn't worse."

Darcy stared at him, his throat tightening. The man was an idiot. A bloody, reckless idiot.

And he owed him his life.

The thought settled in his chest like a stone. Darcy, who had always believed in careful planning, in prudence, had just been saved by a man who had leaped headfirst into danger without a second thought.

Bingley, the boy from trade, who Darcy had barely spared a glance for. And now—

Now he could not think of anything but the fact that this foolish, smiling young man had just thrown himself between Darcy and a blade without hesitation.

"Why?" Darcy heard himself ask, his voice hoarse. He did not mean to say it, but the question hung between them in the damp air. "Why would you do that?"

Bingley looked at him for a moment, blue eyes bright with a mix of pain and mischief, then shrugged. "Couldn't very well let them have you, could I?"

Darcy blinked, stunned into silence. There was nothing else to say. No one had ever done anything like that for him before.

And just like that, the world shifted, subtly but irrevocably, in the space of a heartbeat.

"We need to get to Calais," Darcy finally said. "But first—let us get that shoulder seen to."

Bingley smirked. "Don't suppose you know how to sew?"

Darcy, against all odds, felt a laugh bubble up through his chest. It was ridiculous. The entire day had been chaos, but somehow, standing in a filthy Parisian alley with a man who had just saved his life, it did not seem quite as dark as it had moments ago.

"No. But I will figure something out."

THE SALT-TINGED AIR WHIPPED across the docks at Calais, the sky a gray smear that promised either a dismal rain or a quick escape, depending on how fortune played her hand. Ships bobbed in the harbor, their masts swaying in the wind, and the dockworkers moved with frenetic energy, hauling crates, securing lines, and barking orders. It felt like the last breath before a storm.

Darcy stood with his cousin Richard, his eyes scanning the chaotic scene. Beside them, Sir Thomas Ashford was issuing brisk instructions to a clerk, who was scribbling furiously on a sheaf of papers. Every so often, Sir Thomas would glance up, his eyes flicking across the crowds, watching for familiar faces—anyone he might have missed. It was as if he carried the weight of every young Englishman stranded in France on his shoulders.

"That's the last of the names I've managed to track down," Richard said, holding up a small list. "We should have everyone on board within the hour."

"Good," said Sir Thomas without looking up. "But I am not finished yet."

Darcy frowned. "What do you mean?"

"I'm going back to Paris." He straightened, folding the clerk's notes and tucking them inside his coat. "There are still a few boys from the rooming house unaccounted for. I saw them arrested the night the peace broke."

"Watts, Pence, and Drummond?" Darcy asked. "I saw them, too. They were swept up near the Tuileries."

"Yes, them. I've a few contacts in Paris who might be able to help. Businessmen and diplomats. If there's a way to get those boys out, I'll find it."

"You cannot be serious!" Richard blurted. "You've done enough. More than enough. You've got us this far—"

"And those boys?" Sir Thomas cut him off. "Nineteen years old without a friend in the country? I'll not leave them to rot in some French cell because it's inconvenient for me to go back."

"But you've secured your own passage," Richard argued, like a man reasoning with a stubborn child. "Your name is on the manifest. If you're captured—"

"I am a baronet, Fitzwilliam. They shan't harm me. In the worst case, I will be held until someone can negotiate my release. And the French are not fools—they would rather trade me than keep me. I will be safe enough."

"You hope," Darcy said. "Sir Thomas, you would be a valuable hostage. They could hold you for months—years, even."

"Perhaps." Sir Thomas adjusted his coat, and for a moment, Darcy could see the faint lines of exhaustion around his eyes. "But those boys won't be. They're young, not a penny on them, I'd wager, and far from home. If we wait for the crown to act, it could be months before their families even hear a word, and much longer before anyone can secure their release. By then, who knows what condition they will be in? I have a chance to help now, and I am going to take it."

Darcy opened his mouth to argue, but Richard laid a hand on his arm. "You're sure about this?" Richard asked. "Going back?"

"I won't abandon them, not when there's something I can do. Besides," he added, a glint of wry humor in his eye, "someone has to keep these diplomats honest. They'll find it difficult to brush me off when I'm standing in front of them."

"You're risking everything," Darcy said. "For boys who aren't even your own."

Sir Thomas stepped closer, and when he spoke, it was as if he were addressing Darcy alone. "They're someone's boys, Darcy. Someone's sons, brothers—your friends, if I'm not mistaken. And that's reason enough."

Richard gave a stiff nod, his jaw clenched. "Then we wish you Godspeed."

Sir Thomas smiled—a sad, knowing smile—and took Richard's hand, shaking it firmly. "Take care of yourselves," he said, his gaze shifting between the two of them. "Get on that ship and get home."

As Sir Thomas turned to leave, Darcy reached out and grabbed his arm, the words tumbling out before he could stop them. "Don't do this alone. Let me come with you."

Sir Thomas shook his head. "No, Darcy. I need you on that ship. You've a clearer head on your shoulders than most. Get home and see that the others are accounted for. That's your duty now." He paused, his expression softening. "I need to know there's someone I can count on if things go wrong."

Darcy let go, his throat tight, unable to find a response that did not sound hollow. Sir Thomas clapped him on the shoulder and then turned, striding across the docks toward a waiting carriage.

Darcy watched as he climbed inside, the door closing with a soft click. The carriage driver flicked the reins, and within moments, the wheels were churning over the cobblestones, heading back toward the shadow of Paris.

The wind had picked up, a sharp, biting chill that sliced through the bustling docks. Around them, sailors and passengers hurried to and fro, shouts and whistles mingling with the distant clamor of waves crashing against the pier. The ship that would take them home loomed ahead, its hull swaying gently as it tugged against the ropes.

Richard's expression was tight, his mouth set in a grim line. "Sir Thomas will manage," he said, as if trying to convince himself as much as Darcy. "He's too stubborn to let the French keep him."

"I hope you are right." As they approached the gangplank, Darcy slowed.

Richard glanced over his shoulder at him. "Coming aboard?"

"In a moment," said Darcy. "I'll catch up."

"Don't be long. The tide won't wait for you." He gave Darcy a firm pat on the back before striding up the plank, disappearing among the clusters of passengers.

Darcy turned his steps aside. Charles Bingley, the fool who had saved him in Paris, was leaning against a crate by the rail, gazing out toward the harbor. His right arm was balanced in a sling and bandaged beneath his coat, the wound from the bayonet still soaking through the linens when he moved too much. But Bingley wore the same easy, half-smile he always did. As if the world had not just turned upside down.

Darcy crossed the dock and came to stand beside him. "Bingley."

Bingley turned, his eyes brightening. "Ah, there you are, Darcy. You looked rather conflicted a moment ago. Thought you might've decided to stay in France and keep Sir Thomas company."

"I nearly did. But I had to see you before we boarded. I... wanted to thank you, properly. You did not have to do what you did back there—saving me from those soldiers. If you had not..." He trailed off, the words catching, before he forced himself to continue. "I owe you a debt. Anything you need, at any time, I am at your service. Just say the word."

Bingley's expression shifted, a flicker of hesitation passing over his face. "Funny you should say that," he began, with a hint of nervous laughter. "While we were in Paris, I had this idea. Bit of a mad one, perhaps, but... bother it, the notion kept rattling around in my head, and I thought, well, if I made it back to England, I'd give it a try."

Darcy's brow furrowed. "Go on."

"Beeswax candles," said Bingley, the words tumbling out in a rush. "You see, they're far superior to tallow. Cleaner burn, longer lasting, less smoke. The French were using them everywhere, and I thought—why not bring them to England? But I'd need capital. More than I can scrape together on my own." He glanced at Darcy, his smile hopeful but tentative.

"You want a loan?"

"Oh, no! No, not merely a loan. I need someone sharp—someone who knows how to create order of things and is clever with money. I am dashed cunning with the ideas and... well, I am a fair hand at forming partnerships, seeing opportunities, that sort of thing, but no man has every skill. It's a lucky fellow who finds a perfect complement to his own talents, they say. I... Well, I was hoping *you* might consider partnering with me."

For a moment, Darcy was silent, his eyes fixed on Bingley's. This was not what he had expected. He had assumed the young man might ask for help in climbing London's social ladder—a polite introduction here, a whispered recommendation there. He was used to such favors and had learned to dispense them with a kind of detached grace.

But this... this was about business, a venture that would require Darcy to step into a world he had always kept at arm's length.

"Bingley," he began, choosing his words carefully, "I am grateful for what you did, more than I can say. It is no exaggeration to state that I may owe you my very life. But you must understand... I do not engage in trade. It is not... well, it's not the way of my family."

Bingley's brow furrowed. "Well, of course, I am not entirely simple. But surely you have investments?"

"I do," said Darcy, with a nod. "Shares in established companies, certain... ventures that ensure steady returns. But I do not speculate. My family has always preferred to collect interest on capital, not risk the principal. And I am to inherit my father's estate someday, so employment of that nature is... well, I can see you understand."

For a moment, Bingley's shoulders sagged, and Darcy felt a pang of guilt twist in his chest. He had expected Bingley to be disappointed, perhaps even hurt, but instead, the young man simply gave a resigned nod and rolled his bandaged shoulder, wincing slightly as he did.

"I understand," Bingley said, his voice light, though there was a strain beneath it. "No hard feelings, of course. It was a silly idea, anyway. Just thought I'd ask."

Oh, blast. How could he refuse such a cheerful request? Good heavens, Bingley had hardly stopped bleeding! Could he not find some decency in himself to return such a favor? Darcy opened his mouth to speak, but before he could find the right words, the ship's bell rang, loud and clear. The call for boarding had begun, and the crew shouted for the passengers to make their way on board. The tide was shifting; they had to move.

Darcy hesitated, the urge to walk away battling with a nagging sense of obligation. *"Anything,"* he had promised, and now, faced with the opportunity, he was recoiling. Egad, he was a blackguard and a coward. He owed the man his life!

He took a deep breath, glancing up at the ship, where Richard was already waving impatiently. Then he looked back at Bingley, who had turned away slightly, already preparing to board, cradling his right arm and listing somewhat to the starboard as he walked.

"Wait."

Bingley paused, turning back.

Darcy swallowed, tasting the bitterness of his own words. "I'll do it. I'll... I'll back you on the candles."

Bingley's eyes widened, surprise flickering across his face, followed quickly by a broad, disbelieving grin. "You'll back me? Or you will *partner* with me?"

"Partners," Darcy said, and despite himself, he felt a small smile tug at the corner of his mouth. "You saved my life, Bingley. The least I can do is... risk a little capital." *Social* capital that was... but could he truly do less?

Bingley's grin widened, and he stretched forth his right hand to pump Darcy's so hard that he nearly knocked him off balance.

"Well then, you won't regret it! We'll make a fortune, you'll see. And if we don't, well..." He shrugged, still smiling. "We'll have some very nice candles."

One

November 1811
London

"DARCY, FOR MERCY'S SAKE, when was the last time you smiled at something that wasn't an income ledger?"

Bingley was pacing again. Restless, no doubt. He had been like this for weeks now, fidgeting in meetings, sighing loudly over reports, and coming up with endless excuses to get away from his desk. Darcy found it mildly irritating, though he could hardly blame the man. Bingley had never been one for details, for the daily grind of keeping their empire running smoothly. He was explosions of brilliance, barely contained in his mortal coil—indeed, Bingley was the sort of man who left Darcy in awe of his energy and inspiration at times.

But at other times, it felt like he was trapped in a room with a moonstruck cat that was forever climbing the drapes and shredding the furniture.

Darcy glanced down at the report in front of him—a promising shipping forecast from Calais—pretending not to hear the question. Numbers, figures, logistics. These things made sense. They had always made sense. He was good at them.

Bingley had the instincts, the charm, the wild ideas that somehow—against all odds—worked. But it was Darcy who made it all run, who ensured they never missed a payment or a shipment, who turned Bingley's flights of fancy into something tangible, something profitable. Into the monster that was DarBing Enterprises—a name Darcy had mocked mercilessly until the business proved worthy.

"I smile," he said, keeping his voice even as his quill scratched across the paper. "Occasionally."

Bingley made a sound that was somewhere between a snort and a groan. "Ah, yes. You save those rare grins for particularly favorable shipping manifests. But even then, it's more of a grimace, if I'm being honest."

Darcy ignored him, flipping the page. They were seeing exponential growth from the new venture in India. That was satisfying, surely. But when he glanced up, Bingley had slumped into the chair across from him, looking for all the world as though he were down to his last penny without a friend in the world.

"We've built half of London's trade on our backs. You realize that, don't you?" Bingley said suddenly. "Grown this little empire of ours tenfold. Why, even the East India Company is feeling a bit threatened. All because I somehow guilted you into those beeswax candles. Which, I remind you, you thought was madness."

Darcy did not respond. He *had* thought it was madness, of course—at the time. The idea of smuggling French beeswax during a war seemed not only unseemly but unsustainable. And yet here they were, nearly a decade later, their fortune secured many times over, turning on the lynchpin of that bizarre, brilliant idea of Bingley's.

"I'm tired," Bingley said. "Are you not?"

"Then go home."

"Not *that* sort of tired. I need a change of scenery, Darcy! I'm tired of seeing only your infuriatingly perfect face across the desk from me. I'm tired of sorting all the invitations we receive by which ones will result in meeting profitable contacts. I'm tired of not even remembering what my sister's new husband's name is."

"He is not worth remembering."

"My *point*, Darcy, is that we don't live at all! We've all this money, success beyond even *my* wildest imagination—and you know exactly how wild that is—"

"Indubitably."

"And tell me, when was the last time that you enjoyed *anything?*"

Darcy paused his writing. "Just last week I enjoyed seeing that shipment arrive from Lisbon."

"There, you have proved my point! All the things you call enjoyment are to do with work! I say, tell me the last time you enjoyed the company of a lady, and if it was within the last year, I will eat my hat."

"I took tea with Georgiana last Friday." Darcy looked up. "Would you like some salt or perhaps a fine Hollandaise sauce to go with that beaver? We also have some excellent French Wine downstairs."

"Your sister does not count. I mean a *real* female. Egad, man, don't you have an estate for which you are meant to provide an heir? I don't know if your father ever told you this, but sons need mothers, and before a woman can become a mother, she must—"

"All in good time." The quill scratched against the page in a steady rhythm. "I will attend to that when we've perfected our position. The new numbers we had last quarter show a faint stagnation. If we do not capitalize on our latest opportunities, the business suffers. You know that."

"More growth," Bingley muttered. "More investments. More 'perfection.'" He sat up, leaning toward Darcy with an exasperated, almost conspiratorial grin. "When is it enough, Darcy? We've made our fortune a thousand times over, and yet—" He waved a hand, exasperated. "Here you are, chained to that desk as if it's the only thing keeping you alive."

Darcy didn't flinch. He kept his gaze on the numbers, on the precise, predictable columns of figures that laid out their success like a blueprint. "And where would you have me, Bingley? Pemberley?"

The word tasted faintly of dust, of something long abandoned. He had not set foot on Pemberley's grounds in more than a year. There was no time to waste on wool and wheat—not when his steward could manage just as well. *This* was where his talents shone. This was where he was needed.

"Yes!" Bingley slapped his hand on the desk, rattling a few of the carefully organized papers. Darcy looked up, more in surprise than irritation. "Pemberley! That's *exactly* where I'd have you. I'd have you on horseback, striding through the moors, or—better yet—lounging in a grand library with a book in one hand and a glass of wine in the other. You've forgot how to rest, Darcy."

Rest? The thought was almost laughable. Rest was for men who had finished their work, men who had reached their limit. But Darcy, as far as he could see, was nowhere near his. There was still *more*. Always more.

"Pemberley," Darcy repeated, his voice steady but faintly amused. "You make it sound like I am one foot in the grave already."

"You might as well be. You live like an old man who's decided that the only excitement left in life is—what?—balancing the books and managing shipments? Face it, Darcy, you haven't set foot in the country in years. And it shows. Look at you! Egad, you are nearly translucent."

Darcy flicked an eyebrow upward. "I wasn't aware that my pallor was of such concern."

"It's not the pallor," Bingley shot back, waving a hand in dismissal. "It's the soullessness." He gestured dramatically to the neat stacks of ledgers, the orderly maps of trade routes pinned on the walls. "You're drowning in this. And don't tell me you love it, because I know you, Darcy. You *endure* it. You thrive in it because it's predictable, and you can control it. But don't pretend you find joy in it."

Darcy leaned back in his chair, crossing his arms. His mouth twitched, just a hint, like he might be considering a smile but had not quite committed. "The world does not turn on charm and hunches, Bingley. I've other ambitions, and this is a means to achieving them."

"Ah, yes! It is not enough for you to kill yourself over a desk full of shipping manifests and profit forecasts. You must find new ways to do it in the halls of Westminster."

"You yourself thought it a capital idea," Darcy reminded him. "In fact, it was *you* who suggested it, just like every other hare-brained scheme I've found myself considering these last several years."

"That was before I realized I had created a monster," Bingley fired back. "And what do you mean, 'hare-brained scheme'? I should say you have ample evidence that my instincts are sound."

Darcy gave a small shake of his head. "I never said they were not. I simply—"

"No, no, no!" Bingley held up a hand, feigning horror. "Let's not walk back now. You've made it clear from the start. You thought the candles were absurd. You thought the wines were too risky. The silk trade, you swore, was pure madness. I distinctly remember the word 'madness,' Darcy."

"Yes, and you were fortunate enough to be right in all three instances. Somehow." Darcy's tone was dry, but the fondness beneath it was undeniable. He had never quite understood how Bingley managed to be so consistently lucky, so impossibly optimistic, and... so irritatingly correct.

Bingley grinned, looking as though he might bask in Darcy's reluctant praise. But the grin faltered as he stood and began pacing again, running a hand through his unruly blond hair. "That's exactly the problem! Don't you see? We've *done* it, Darcy. We've made our fortune. We've proved everyone wrong a thousand times over. Now, we should be enjoying it."

"Enjoying it how, exactly?" Darcy arched an eyebrow, watching Bingley's restless movements. "By... retreating to the country? Wasting away in idle conversation and bad brandy?"

"Wasting away?" Bingley laughed, though it was a bit sharper than usual. "Darcy, you make it sound as though taking a breath of fresh air might kill you. Yes, retreating to the country! Relaxing. Letting the world turn without us needing to crank its wheels and spindles for once. Buying a house, for Heaven's sake."

"Buying a house? I already own a perfectly sumptuous house, and so do you."

"In the city." Bingley's frustration cracked through now, his hands gesturing wildly again as he paced. "I'm talking about a house in the *country*, Darcy. Where things are green, remember? Fresh air, quiet—"

"I have one of those as well."

"Yes, a four-day drive from London. But since I can hardly get you out of Mayfair, except to go to St. James' or Pall Mall, what is the use of even saying you own the house?"

"Well, Pemberley itself brings in a rather tidy income..."

"Darcy!" Bingley laughed. "You are intentionally missing my point!"

Darcy put his quill away with a sigh. No point in trying to finish this now. "What would you have me do, Bingley?"

Bingley was pacing by now, his hands braced at his waist as he cast occasional glances at Darcy on his course across the room. "I want you to dip into that thing called 'living' once in a while. I want you to go... I don't know... shoot a brace of geese yourself and put them on your own table for a change. I want you to take a few fences, or gallop until your hat flies off your head on some of those valuable hunters you prize in your stables but have never seen. I want you to take your sister to a play or an opera where you are *not* trying to find an opportunity to make a business or a political connection."

Darcy scoffed. "Do not be naive. You know perfectly well I was only trying to be friendly to Lords Hastings and Meriwether."

"Hah! I jolly well know no such thing! You ascribe pounds and pence to every conversation. I have seen the ledger, Darcy."

"What, ledger? It is merely my notes, which have proved useful more than—"

"And what about ladies? What about marriage and a family of your own?"

Darcy blinked. Then swallowed. "I told you. All in—"

"The 'good time' is *now*, Darcy. Not when you are fifty. Egad, man, you were already five years old by the time your father was the age you are now! Look here. It is already November. You and I are full up of invitations to balls, soirées, Assemblies. I say we accept at least half of them."

"Why?"

"Because, Darcy, I want *you* out of my hair!"

Darcy frowned and glanced speculatively at the wall behind Bingley. "Well, you could have said…"

"I *have* said. Find a woman, Darcy. Find a hobby. Gad's teeth, run for office if it will keep you busy and get you out of here for a change!"

"Ah, so *that* is your motive. You are not seeking to make me 'happy,' as you claim. You want to be rid of me?"

Bingley went quiet, still pacing.

Darcy shifted in his chair. "Interesting. You *do* want to be rid of me."

"No, no! But… Darcy, for more than eight years, we've done nothing but work. I live like an old man. I've no friends who are not also business partners, I spend so much time at my desk that I am winded when I take the stairs to my own room, and I was trying to remember the last time I danced at a ball. Take a guess, Darcy."

"Two years, one month, and four days ago," Darcy answered flatly. "Lady Hansen's ball. Look, Bingley, if you are so tired of work, take a holiday. Go to the country yourself."

"Aha, as if I could! No, Darcy, I know exactly what will come of that. An urgent summons will find me the moment I've tried to start anything new, and I'll achieve nothing but wasted time and frustration. There is absolutely no point in me trying to do anything or go anywhere unless *you* are diverted elsewhere. That is why…" Bingley cleared his throat and turned around. "I have already accepted those invitations."

Darcy narrowed his eyes. "Which invitations?"

"All… all of them. We will have a merry time this winter, Darcy. We shall meet ladies and dance and smoke cigars with our friends—real friends, Darcy! I mean to go skating in Hyde Park and—"

"Bingley," Darcy interrupted. "I have no intention of prancing about like a fool. You want to attend four parties each evening and drink wassail and eat fig pudding until it comes out your eyeballs, you are welcome to do it alone."

"No good, Darcy. You have to come with me."

"I do not recall that as a condition in our business contract."

"Good, because I am not talking about business." Bingley strode closer, that insouciant grin widening on his face. "You *owe* me, Darcy."

Darcy crossed his arms and quirked a brow. "Here we go again. You saved my life. Got me out of French hands, took a bayonet to the shoulder. I have not forgot."

"Oh! How fortunate. I was worried I would have to remind you."

Darcy scoffed and shook his head. "Why would you hold back this time? That never stopped you before, when you tried to put the screws to me for some scheme of yours."

"And tell me when I was wrong, hmm?"

"I…"

"This evening, Darcy. Seven o'clock sharp. I shall have my carriage at your door for Lady Stanwick's dinner party."

Darcy squirmed in his chair. "I have my own carriage."

Bingley was already halfway to the door, but he turned back with a bright-eyed grin. "Yes, but I want to make sure you actually get *into* a carriage. I will see you at seven."

❦

Two

ELIZABETH FOLDED HER FAVORITE shawl and tucked it into her trunk with a precise little pat. "I believe that is the last of it. Are you quite finished yet, Jane?"

Jane swirled around and cleared her throat. "Ah... almost, Lizzy. Let me just..." Jane busied herself behind the propped-open lid of her trunk, then closed it quickly, turned the key, and hurriedly sat at the vanity to plump her cheeks.

"Oh, dear," Elizabeth sighed. "What is it now?"

"Hmm?" Jane turned on the stool. "Whatever do you mean?"

Elizabeth cocked a wary eye at her sister. "You have been behaving oddly since this morning, Jane. If I did not know better, I would suspect that we are *not* going home tomorrow as expected, and that you know something you are not telling me."

"Oh, Lizzy! Such a silly notion. I do wonder where Aunt is, though. She said she meant to come up and help us with all our new gowns. I think she just wanted to see them one more time, you know."

"Well, she deserves to. They were too generous to us, Jane. I daresay I have bought enough gowns and chemises and petticoats to last me five years." She braced her hands on her hips and surveyed the trunk with a frown. "Or at least until Mama decides we need wedding clothes because some tall, dark, and handsome stranger moves to town."

Jane glanced at Elizabeth through the vanity mirror. "Well, Lizzy, one thing you must admit is that Mama always likes us to be well-prepared."

Elizabeth's eyebrow quirked. "Oh, for a certainty. I wonder if she has my children named for me yet or if she has decided to put that particular preparation off until the next time I dance with someone more than once."

"Oh, she has a list of names. I have seen it—I believe Lydia has circled the top dozen to claim them for herself."

Elizabeth snorted. "Jane, I can almost believe that is true. Oh! That must be Aunt." She closed her trunk at the sound of a knock and stepped to open the door.

Mrs. Gardiner tipped her head cautiously from side to side, surveying the room as she walked in. "My goodness. How did you two manage to fit all those gowns into your trunks in such short order?"

"Mama has taught us well, Aunt," Jane said with a laugh. "Papa always says Mama could kit out an entire regiment if he gave her just two trunks and four of five stout lads to carry them."

Mrs. Gardiner chuckled. "That does not surprise me. Well, I see I ought to have come up a bit sooner. I had hoped to catch you before you put your party gowns away."

"Party gowns?" Elizabeth glanced at her sister, but Jane was already rising from the vanity to move toward her own trunk, and Elizabeth could not see her face. "Whatever for?"

"Oh, nothing much. Your uncle has guests coming this evening, that is all. Rather dull stuff—business contacts, I am afraid, but there was nothing else for it. Tonight was the only night everyone could manage."

"Business contacts?" Elizabeth echoed, a skeptical note in her voice. "And what, pray tell, do men of business want with a quiet family dinner? If Uncle Gardiner's partners are half as worldly as he, I should think they would find our company positively provincial."

Mrs. Gardiner waved a dismissive hand. "Oh, nonsense, Lizzy. A simple dinner is all. I am certain they shall be as dry as dust, but perhaps you will find it in your heart to entertain them a little. You know how your uncle does like to keep up his contacts."

Elizabeth narrowed her eyes. It was not the sudden announcement of a dinner party, nor the fact that her uncle would be entertaining business guests. It was the odd way Jane was pursing her lips and running her fingers over the rim of her trunk, and something in the way her aunt was holding her breath as she made the announcement.

"When was this arranged, Aunt?" Elizabeth asked casually.

"Hmm? Oh! Perhaps yesterday, I should think. I am sorry, Lizzy, I ought to have said something sooner. I hope it will not be too much bother to find your new blue gown. It is not at the bottom of your trunk, is it?"

"The *very* bottom," Elizabeth confirmed. "As I felt it would be positively the last gown I should have need of for the foreseeable future. What of my plum-colored one, Aunt? I think I can draw that one out with little trouble."

There it was again. The way Mrs. Gardiner caught Jane's eye, and the way Jane sucked her top lip between her teeth and looked innocently away.

"Ah... well, whatever you think, Lizzy," Mrs. Gardiner replied hesitantly. "Oh, but I did fancy the things that blue one does for your eyes. You have *such* rare eyes, you know. Not one in ten girls with hair of such rich ebony as yours also have blue eyes—like ice crystals they are, and that gown sets them off so dazzlingly well."

Elizabeth arched a brow. "I thought these were merely business friends of my uncle's. Why should they be looking at my gown at all? Assuming, of course, it serves its office of covering those parts of me which must be covered for decency's sake."

Jane coughed. "No reason at all, Lizzy. But... are you *sure* the new blue gown is at the bottom? I thought I saw you put it in close to the last."

Elizabeth crossed her arms. "Aunt, Jane, what *are* you two scheming?"

"Scheming! Why, Lizzy, you do me too much credit," her aunt laughed. "They are your uncle's guests, not mine. How should I have anything to do with the timing of their invitation?"

Elizabeth's mouth tugged to the side as her eyes slid to her sister. "Jane, open that trunk."

Jane swallowed. "Oh, but Lizzy, I have only just locked it. Let me see, what did I do with that key?" She slipped her hands into the pockets hidden in her day dress, then withdrew them to pat down her reticule, which lay flat on the bed. When that yielded nothing, she dropped to her knees to perform a quick search under the bed. "Oh, dear. What could I have done...?"

"Is it this key you are looking for?" Elizabeth asked, picking up the small brass thing from the vanity. "Truly, Jane, if you are going to put me on, you will have to try a *bit* harder than that."

Jane shot their aunt a shame-faced glance, then took the key from Elizabeth's fingers. "What was it you wished to see, Lizzy?" she asked innocently.

Elizabeth made a flipping motion with her hand and arched a brow.

Jane sighed, then turned to her trunk to unlock it and lift the lid on creaking hinges.

"Ah-hah." Elizabeth strode closer and plucked the very top gown out of the trunk. It was a frothy pink confection, perfectly suited to Jane's fair features and rosy blushes... but not at *all* suited for travel tomorrow or dinner at Longbourn once they arrived.

"How odd that, knowing we would be setting out in the morning, you chose to put this gown at the very top."

"Do not be silly, Lizzy! I simply put my gown in last because I like admiring it so." Jane's cheeks colored faintly, though she kept her head down, fussing with the silk ribbons on her gown. Elizabeth, however, caught it, and her suspicions only grew.

"I see," Elizabeth said slowly, her gaze lingering on her sister a moment longer. "And how many of these... business contacts should we expect, Aunt?"

"Oh, just two. Mr. Bingley and Mr. Darcy. Fine men, both of them, I believe," Mrs. Gardiner replied, her tone carefully even—as though Elizabeth had not already pieced together some bits of the puzzle. "Your uncle speaks quite highly of them, you know."

"Mr. Darcy and Mr. Bingley?" Elizabeth repeated, her lips curving into a faint smile. "These gentlemen sound... familiar. Why, I believe I have heard mention of them somewhere. Ah... yes, in fact, I have! At nearly every party we have attended with you and Uncle—"

"Oh, Lizzy, you must not make so much of—"

"—for the last *five* years." Elizabeth finished. "Two of the wealthiest bachelors in London, the ones half the females in Town are setting their caps for, whose reclusive natures have kept them largely out of the public eye since their meteoric rise to wealth. Have I got it right, Aunt?"

"Rise to wealth," Mrs. Gardiner repeated with a laugh. "You make it sound as if they were not already wealthy, which, I assure you, both were."

"A minor detail. Tell me, Aunt, why should such gentlemen wish to spend an evening with *us*? Surely, they have livelier options for entertainment."

"Oh, Lizzy, not everyone finds the charms of elaborate soirées or even gambling dens quite so irresistible as you seem to think. I dare say they might even find our company refreshing."

"Yes, so refreshing that they might fall asleep in their soup. And tell me, Aunt, should I be worried that you and Jane have taken it upon yourselves to secure me in the company of any gentleman who happens to be in town?"

Mrs. Gardiner gave her a reproachful look, though the twinkle in her eyes remained. "Why, Lizzy, what on earth could have given you such an idea?"

"Oh, I am certain I do not know," Elizabeth said, her tone innocent, but her gaze pointed. "Perhaps the way Jane has been mincing about her packing, looking over her shoulder every handful of seconds, and delaying putting that nice gown of hers up until it grew awkward."

"Oh, come now," Mrs. Gardiner chided gently. "Your uncle only invited them to dinner to sort out some new business, whatever you may suspect, Lizzy. But I daresay it will not be such a terrible duty for you both to put on a smile or two for the gentlemen. If you cannot manage to enjoy yourself for an evening, Elizabeth, well..."

Elizabeth laughed, shaking her head. "I am merely wary of how very eager you both seem to throw us in their path. Very well, I shall take my *plum*-colored dinner gown out, since it will not be as much bother as trying to get the creases out of the blue one. But Aunt, if I fall asleep halfway through the soup, I shall hold you entirely responsible."

"Indeed," Mrs. Gardiner said, smiling as she patted Elizabeth's hand. "I am sure you will find a way to endure it, dear."

As Mrs. Gardiner left the room, Elizabeth turned back to Jane, arms crossed and a knowing smile on her lips. "And you—you are not nearly as innocent as you pretend. What is it you know that I do not?"

Jane bit her lip, looking up at Elizabeth with a slightly guilty but thoroughly amused expression. "Nothing more than you, I am sure. I simply think that one evening among old friends—whether they are Uncle Gardiner's or not—will be rather pleasant. And perhaps even enlightening."

Elizabeth narrowed her eyes, her smile turning wry. "Enlightening. Yes, I am sure. And if by the end of the evening, I discover the whole affair has been a grand scheme between you and Aunt Gardiner, I shall demand full recompense."

Jane laughed. "Then you had best begin thinking of your price now, Lizzy, for I believe it shall be a most charming evening indeed."

Bingley's footsteps echoed impatiently against the gleaming floor of Darcy's study as he paced back and forth, casting the occasional exasperated glance at his friend. Darcy was seated at his desk, pen in hand, though he was currently more interested in issuing a mild scolding than in finishing his correspondence.

"Tell me, Bingley, just what possessed you to drag me to that... farce of a dinner party two nights ago? You assured me it was a mere gathering, but I counted no fewer than six young ladies strategically placed around the table, all of whom seemed ready to faint dead away if I so much as inquired after their names."

Bingley stopped his pacing long enough to flash an innocent grin. "Oh, come now, Darcy. You are being melodramatic."

"Am I?" Darcy arched an eyebrow. "Perhaps you failed to notice that the only other gentlemen present were married or otherwise engaged. Or did you think it was a coincidence that Lady Stanwick arranged her table so I was boxed in by not one, but two of her nieces?"

Bingley shrugged, utterly unrepentant. "The ladies were pleasant company, I thought."

"Pleasant company?" Darcy scoffed. "Bingley, one of them spent twenty minutes extolling her own embroidery, speaking of it as though it were the work of Michelangelo himself, while the other waxed poetic on the beauty of—what was it? —seashell collections."

Bingley stifled a laugh. "Seashells, Darcy. Come, they can be quite pretty! The lady was only being polite, filling the silence since you seemed determined to contribute nothing beyond the occasional monosyllabic response."

Darcy shot him a withering look. "Can you blame me? I agreed to attend a dinner, not a matchmaking symposium."

Bingley chuckled, unruffled. "You have always been impossible to please. You find the ladies vacuous. You find the company dull. Would it have killed you to smile a little?"

"Smile? Bingley, if I had smiled, the entire evening would have been declared a triumph, and I would find myself besieged by Lady Stanwick's relations for the remainder of the season. No, thank you. I am finished with these so-called dinner parties. From now on, you are to attend those affairs on your own."

"On my own?" Bingley threw up his hands in exaggerated despair. "Darcy, you cannot abandon me to these people. Besides, that would defeat the entire object!"

"Which is?"

"Getting *you* out from behind that desk once in a while and thinking of something besides *my* business all the time."

"Ah, I nearly forgot." Darcy dipped his quill again. "You seek to be rid of me."

"Not *rid* of you, Darcy, but perhaps... less of you. Egad, are you not weary of seeing hardly anyone but *me*, and the people who work for you?"

"You are mistaken. I speak with dozens of men each week who do not work for me."

"Yes, all contracts and business partners and the like. By Jove, I wish Fitzwilliam were in Town. I could bloody well use a bit of his cleverness just now to oust you from your study—for your own good, of course."

"Such a pity he entered the Army and made himself more useful to the crown than to us..."

"You speak as if all I do is use and manipulate you, Darcy." Bingley's tone sounded wounded. "It is not as if I have not exerted efforts of my own in this partnership."

Darcy glanced up and dash it all if Bingley was not massaging that old bayonet wound as he paced. Darcy sighed. "I never said you did not, but all these things you claim are for *my* benefit seem rather to be things that *you* want, not I."

"But how can you not want this? A little jolliness, a little pleasure in life! I know you do. You are a dull shell of a man suffering from desperately low spirits, not at all the fellow I knew in France."

"Good heavens, I should hope I am no longer a youth of twenty."

"You know what I mean, Darcy! You need to laugh, meet some ladies, dance a little."

"You mean drink myself into oblivion and embarrass myself with some female whose father will be at my door tomorrow morning..."

"I mean, we are expected at Almack's this evening."

"Then, by all means, go enjoy yourself. I, however, shall not be joining you."

Bingley gaped at him, genuinely bewildered. "Not going to Almack's? Darcy, that is practically unheard of. Half of London will be expecting you!"

Darcy gave a slight, almost imperceptible shrug. "Half of London will survive without me for one evening, I assure you."

"No, no. Not this time, Darcy. I mean to drag you from this house by main force if I must. Nearly everyone we know will be there, and *you*, Darcy, will enjoy yourself."

"I cannot go, Bingley, and for that matter, neither can you, so you had best put away your dancing shoes."

Bingley let out a huff of frustration. "And what could possibly be more pressing than Almack's?"

Darcy leaned back in his chair. "I had a letter this morning from Edward Gardiner. Remember him?"

Bingley blinked. "Gardiner? The merchant?"

"Yes. He was one of the first men to take a chance on us, back when we were starting out with that ludicrous scheme of yours to import French beeswax. We owe him a great deal."

"Oh, come now. Gardiner was just a good-natured fellow with a nose for profit. We made him wealthy, he made us wealthy, and then our needs diverged. We have hardly done any business with him these past five years. Surely, he does not expect us to drop everything and turn up for some business meeting when we were expected at Almack's."

Darcy gave him a pointed look. "He has requested that we speak on an urgent shipping matter. Apparently, he is in some straits and believes we can help. I am not one to ignore an old friend's request, especially one who took a risk on us when no one else would."

Bingley sighed, throwing himself into the chair opposite Darcy's desk with a dramatic flourish. "So, let me understand this. You would have me abandon the delights of Almack's for yet another dull business dinner?"

"Precisely," Darcy said with a slight smile.

"Oh, Darcy, I am beginning to think you derive some peculiar satisfaction from dragging me to the dreariest possible affairs."

Darcy gave a dry chuckle. "I derive satisfaction from keeping you out of trouble, which is precisely what you are bound to find at Almack's if left unsupervised."

Bingley shook his head, looking both exasperated and amused. "The 'trouble,' as you put it, is simply society. You really should try embracing it now and again, Darcy. You may even find it tolerable."

"I doubt that very much," Darcy replied. "And besides, this is not merely business. It is a matter of loyalty. Gardiner helped us establish our reputation, and I shall not brush off his request for the sake of... frivolity."

"Frivolity?" Bingley looked almost cut to the heart. "You think Almack's is frivolous?"

"I think *most* of the events you drag me to are frivolous. And given recent experience, any arguments you might make to the contrary have not a leg to stand on."

Bingley gave a resigned sigh. "Very well, Darcy. If you insist, I shall accompany you to this... thrilling business dinner. But mark my words, I shall hold you responsible if it proves as mind-numbing as I expect."

"Then it is settled. Now, shall we see what Mr. Gardiner wishes to discuss?"

Bingley gave one last, forlorn glance at the door, as if Almack's were a beloved pet he was being forced to leave behind. "Very well," he muttered, folding his arms with a good-natured grumble. "But you owe me, Darcy. You owe me a proper evening of enjoyment one of these days."

Darcy merely smirked. "I would hardly call Almack's 'enjoyment,' but if it will ease your suffering, perhaps we shall revisit the idea—after we have shown Mr. Gardiner the courtesy he deserves."

Bingley chuckled, rising to his feet. "Lead on, Darcy. But next time, you shall have to face the consequences of Lady Stanwick's nieces without me."

Three

"WHY ARE WE DOING this? Admit it, Darcy—you would rather be *anywhere* else in London tonight."

"Quite true," Darcy replied, adjusting his gloves. "Though my preference would be *anywhere* but Almack's. No matter how many times you try to sell me on its charms, I have yet to find a single one."

Bingley shook his head, chuckling. "You're insufferable. The ladies there are lovely—charming, eligible, exactly the sort you claim to want."

Darcy gave him a look, a half-smile tugging at his mouth. "If by 'charming,' you mean 'practiced in the art of fainting prettily,' then perhaps. But I have little interest in women who look ready to topple over at the sight of my bank account."

"So, you're after a lady who will ignore it?" Bingley shot back. "*Bonne chance.* Perhaps you'll find her down by the docks, far from the rarefied air of society."

"Not precisely. But there are qualities a woman ought to have if she is to be a companion worth the effort."

Bingley shot him an incredulous look. "I daresay you've become so particular you'll require her to quote Plato by heart and handle one of your mile-high ledgers over afternoon tea."

"Plato might be a bit much, but I would like someone who cares about more than the latest invitation to Almack's."

Bingley folded his arms, looking at Darcy with sudden interest. "And tell me, do you imagine this paragon of yours is simply waiting for you to stroll by? You want a veritable goddess, but you will not trouble yourself to look for her."

"No, Bingley, I am well aware. In fact, the very definition of the woman I seek is that she is not 'waiting' for me at all." Darcy cast a glance out of the window as they turned up another street, then back at his friend. "But neither will I find her in a room full of fortune-hunters and ambitious daughters of the peerage."

"Some of the best families in London frequent Almack's!" Bingley protested. "And what else would you have them do? Surely, it's not a crime for a lady to seek a worthy match?"

Darcy held up a hand, shaking his head. "It is not that simple. The more wealth I accumulated, the more... complicated society became. It was one thing when I was only Fitzwilliam Darcy of Pemberley. But now—"

"Now you're even richer," Bingley finished. "It is no secret that your name is at the top of all those party invitations and when you do accept one, the lady of the house brags to her friends for weeks about it. I have it on good authority that at least four families are waiting with bated breath on your sister's come-out just so they have an excuse to call at Darcy House."

Darcy grunted. "And that is why she will be entertaining all callers at Matlock House instead. The matter is already settled."

"Oh, Darcy, you will spoil their fun! That puts everyone back to hoping you will turn up at a ball or two, poor things. Not that I can blame anyone for wanting a bit of security."

"Security is one thing. But London is overrun with women who think wealth and eligibility are all that is required of a gentleman. To them, I'm a bank draft that can walk and talk. It is not exactly flattering."

"I suppose you would like them to faint for nobler reasons?"

Darcy sighed, giving his friend a long-suffering look. "If you must know, yes."

Bingley sighed, shaking his head. "You are impossible, Darcy. You say you want a lady of breeding, but you will not go where they are. You want a woman of intelligence, yet you mock them for their accomplishments. Is there nothing that would please you?"

Darcy hesitated. "As terrified as I am to confess something like this to you—for I know you will run with it as if it were marching orders—I *would* like to actually enjoy a lady's company someday. But men of our position must be... particular."

"Particular?" He raised his eyebrows, laughter brimming behind his look of disbelief. "If you're any more particular, Darcy, I'll have to drop you off on some mountain where you can live like a hermit."

"I am serious. If I am to marry, it will be to someone who can be a partner in every sense. She must be intelligent, able to manage the pressures of her place in society, for it is no easy precipice. She must be reliable, not a changeful miss blown about by the caprices of gossip and fortune. And for my own pleasure, she must have some warmth—some gentleness. Not ambition, not social climbing. That... that would ruin everything."

For a moment, Bingley was silent, his expression thoughtful as they drove. "You speak of a precipice... do you ever worry that entering trade has... changed your place? In society, I mean."

Darcy's mouth flickered in an almost-smile. "Of course it has. The old families no longer see me as one of their own, for I bear the 'stench of trade' now. My own uncle still grimaces whenever he is obliged to introduce me anywhere. But the new sort of man sees me as an interloper—a 'gentleman' who would not stay in his own sphere. I am a man of both worlds now, yet a master of neither."

Bingley's mouth twitched downward as he shuffled his boots on the floor of the carriage. "I'd never any thought of what it would cost you when I asked you—surely, you must have some regrets."

"Not for a second. I made my decision eight years ago in Calais, and I have never looked back. But it has... complicated things."

Bingley nodded slowly as he looked up once more. "So, you feel you are even further from the kind of woman you'd like to marry."

Darcy shook his head. "No, it is just... she will be harder to find, and no amount of your manipulation and wishful tactics will make her surface any sooner. The woman I seek must see past the money *and* the name, Bingley, or none of it is worth a farthing."

Bingley was quiet for a moment. "I don't think I've ever heard you speak quite like this."

"Then consider it a rare confession." Darcy gave him a small, wry smile. "Perhaps the result of your influence. You were, after all, the one who got me into all this in the first place."

Bingley laughed. "And you've thrived in it, just as I knew you would. But let me make my own confession." He took a deep breath, eyes thoughtful. "One of these days, I'm hoping you'll meet this impossible woman of yours. Not just so you can spare me some of this moralizing, but maybe, for once, allow yourself a bit of happiness."

"And on that day, Bingley, may she also distract me enough to save you from my insufferable standards."

Bingley grinned. "A man can hope."

Darcy shook his head as the carriage pulled to a halt in front of Gardiner's residence. "For now, I'll settle for a quiet dinner with a man I can trust—a simple meal without society's expectations breathing down my neck."

"Ah, yes," Bingley sighed, straightening his jacket as the footman came to put down the step. "Trade routes and exchange rates and shipping delays... why did we even bother to leave our studies?"

"Come, now!" Darcy chided as they stepped down. "It will not be entirely disagreeable. Gardiner always kept a fine sideboard, and you used to get on well with Mrs. Gardiner."

"That is because an elegant, beautiful lady is a delight at any table. You ought to try it yourself sometime, Darcy."

Darcy shot his friend a pointed look, but there was no time for more conversation. The door swung open, and the butler stepped aside to let them in. Darcy crossed the threshold, feeling a rare sense of relief at the thought of a private evening with talk he could understand. No dancing or fear of offending ladies, no worry that every word out of his mouth would be parsed and printed in the gossip rags the next day. Just ease and...

And then he saw *her*.

She was standing near the staircase, her back half-turned, speaking to another lady with an ease that looked entirely unselfconscious. Her gown, a deep plum, set off her dark hair, which was swept up in a way that highlighted her cheekbones. But more unfussy ringlets were left to curl softly at her temples, framing her face in a way that lent her a certain gentle elegance. Her expression was animated, her eyes bright with intelligence, as if she were engaged in some private amusement.

But it was her eyes that struck him—clear and direct, and an unexpected, vivid blue. She flicked them over him with a look that held neither fluster nor expectation, and then her gaze moved simply to Bingley with the same lightness.

For a second, he felt caught, as though she'd just swept him into her awareness with the same curiosity he felt now, entirely against his will.

"Darcy?" Bingley murmured, nudging him.

"Right," he muttered, shifting his gaze back to Mr. Gardiner and extending his hand, though his focus remained strangely split.

ELIZABETH ADJUSTED THE LACE cuff of her sleeve, casting a sidelong glance at Jane, who was smoothing the drape of her gown with altogether too much care. It was apparent to anyone watching that Jane was concealing some small amusement, though she seemed determined not to let it slip. Across the drawing room, Uncle Gardiner stood with his hands clasped behind his back, shifting slightly from one foot to the other as if balancing on deck in a storm.

"Are you quite well, Uncle?" Elizabeth asked. "It seems as though the floorboards are conspiring to keep you in motion."

Her uncle gave a start and laughed, though it had an awkward edge. "Yes, yes—just restless. We... we do not often host visitors of such... stature."

"Uncle, I hardly think the gentlemen bite. Besides, I thought you were well acquainted with them already."

"Oh! To be sure. Though it has been some time since we spoke, and our paths do not often cross these days. Still, I..." He tugged at his cravat as he cleared his throat. "Yes, well, I was honored that they accepted the invitation." But as he shot a fleeting look toward Aunt Gardiner, who was inspecting the room with an air of pleased accomplishment, Elizabeth's suspicion took root.

Whatever the supposed purpose of this dinner, there was no doubting that her aunt was behind it. Mrs. Gardiner had the air of a seasoned general, surveying the setup and positioning herself just-so, leaving Elizabeth feeling that the timing of this particular invitation had much more to do with her own travel plans than anything related to her uncle's business.

Moments later, the butler appeared and announced their guests. "Mr. Darcy and Mr. Bingley, sir."

The gentlemen entered, offering greetings with the smooth polish of men accustomed to society. Mr. Bingley was all warmth, his smile widening as he took in the room with clear pleasure.

But Mr. Darcy, after glancing at his host and hostess, faltered slightly when his gaze fell on her. Elizabeth noted the pause, watching as Mr. Bingley looked faintly alarmed, nudging his partner and murmuring something under his breath. Mr. Darcy quickly regained his composure, but his hesitation struck her somewhat oddly. His pupils dilated far too quickly to be entirely natural, and he was suddenly holding his breath—a mark of a man who would probably much rather be elsewhere.

The reason was not difficult to decipher. Doubtless, the gentlemen had anticipated only seeing her uncle and perhaps her aunt this evening. Elizabeth clenched her teeth slightly behind her polite smile and slid a glance toward Aunt Gardiner, as if she could shuffle the blame for her very presence onto their hostess without having to utter a word.

Mr. Gardiner stepped forward. "Mr. Darcy, Mr. Bingley—thank you for joining us this evening. It is a pleasure to welcome you again. I daresay it has been far too long."

"Thank you, sir," Mr. Darcy replied with a measured nod. "We were pleased by the invitation."

Elizabeth caught the briefest flicker of tension in her uncle's stance, just before he glanced at his wife, who gave him a quick, encouraging smile. Mr. Gardiner cleared his throat, turning to Jane. "And I do not believe you have yet had the pleasure of meeting my nieces, Miss Jane Bennet, and Miss Elizabeth Bennet. They have been visiting us these last two months."

Mr. Darcy's gaze turned to them with polite interest as he nodded to each of them. "It is an honor."

Mr. Bingley, all brightness and ease, followed suit, his smile widening by the moment. "Indeed, Miss Bennet, Miss Bennet. I cannot think of a more pleasant surprise than meeting fair faces in good company."

Elizabeth smiled, meeting his enthusiasm with a polite nod. Meanwhile, she noticed Mr. Darcy's gaze flickering between Mr. and Mrs. Gardiner with a faint look of bemusement, as if he sensed the evening's unspoken motives. If only she could sink through the floorboards...

Mr. Gardiner cleared his throat and turned back to the gentlemen. "Ah, yes, well, please, do be seated, sirs. I must thank you again for accepting our invitation. It is not often I have the chance to host two of the brightest minds on Change Alley. And... of course, we might discuss that recent matter of..." Uncle Gardiner hesitated for an instant, glancing again at his wife. "The, ah... the Lisbon shipments."

What was that? Elizabeth's attention shifted between her aunt and Jane, noting the shared, almost conspiratorial look between them at the mention of "Lisbon shipments." The entire setup felt like a rather elaborate pretense.

Mr. Darcy seemed to catch some nuance as well, his gaze drifting toward her with an almost imperceptible glint of amusement. "Indeed, sir. I am now... exceedingly curious."

"Oh, but we need not assault the gentlemen with your questions all at once, my dear," Aunt Gardiner protested. "Can we not begin with the usual pleasantries? It is always delightful to have friends from Derbyshire in London."

"Ah, yes—Derbyshire," Mr. Bingley said with a grin. "I had forgot you hailed from there, Mrs. Gardiner. And yet I wonder if Mr. Darcy himself would even recognize it, as long as it has been since he saw it."

Mr. Darcy gave him a mildly reproachful look. "I remember Derbyshire well, thank you, Bingley. It is simply that business in London has required my attention."

"Required?" Bingley scoffed. "You might as well admit you have buried yourself in ledgers, Darcy, and barely come up for air!"

Mr. Gardiner laughed. "Ah, a man dedicated to his pursuits—Mr. Darcy, you must know you are in good company here."

Mrs. Gardiner cast her husband a look. "And yet, Mr. Darcy, it is still a fine thing to revisit one's home and take a bit of leisure now and again. You may recall that some years ago, we were able to purchase a bit of property that included the cottage where I grew up, and have scarcely had an opportunity to see it since. We intend to journey north next summer for just that purpose. Perhaps we can hope to see you back in Derbyshire one of these days?"

Mr. Darcy's gaze softened slightly. "I would not deny Pemberley has its appeal, Mrs. Gardiner. But my friend here"—he gestured to Bingley with a faint smile— "seems intent on keeping me tethered to every venture in London."

"Which is, naturally, to everyone's benefit," Mr. Bingley replied with mock solemnity. "You know Darcy. He is a fearsome creature when he has nothing whatever to do, so he invents things to keep himself occupied and create the illusion of being indispensable wherever he goes."

"As I recall," Mr. Darcy returned mildly, "each of those 'things to keep me occupied' originated in *your* imagination, not mine."

"Only because you were starting to get that 'look' in your eye again, old man, and I feared I, myself, would be your next project," Mr. Bingley laughed. "Better to try to keep up with you than to have to stay a step ahead of you, I say."

Elizabeth chuckled and nearly forgot her place—the words simply came. "I daresay, Mr. Darcy, that business cannot be so consuming that you never find time for your home in Derbyshire. We *make* time for those things that are important to us, do we not?"

He turned to her, a faint look of surprise flickering across his face. "Perhaps I have... forgot the charm of certain places."

"I would not have thought the charm of one's home could be such a fleeting memory, sir."

There was a tug at the corner of his mouth. "You have caught me out, Miss Elizabeth. You are quite right. There is nothing amiss with my memory, nor is anything wanting from the charms of my home. I have simply persuaded myself that I am more useful elsewhere, and for the most part, I have been proved right."

She pressed her lips and tilted her head. "That is an interesting condition you added—'for the most part.'"

"Indeed, Miss Elizabeth," Mr. Bingley interjected. "The only person Darcy has ever lied to is himself, and having so little practice at it, he is not at all skilled in the art. He scarcely believes half the things he tries to persuade himself of."

Elizabeth laughed. "Mr. Bingley, I cannot decide whether you mean to compliment or insult your friend with such a remark."

"Both, I imagine," Mr. Darcy replied, but there was a spark of humor in his eyes. "I will own my flaws openly before any man... or woman, if I may," he added with a deferential dip of his head. "But Bingley is partially in jest, for a frank appraisal of his words would have you assuming that I am not entirely in touch with reality and that I fancy the world is a place more to my own liking than it truly is. I assure you, that is not altogether the case."

"Then, on what matters *do* you deceive yourself?" she asked.

Mr. Darcy shifted in his chair, and his eyes flicked briefly to Mr. Gardiner. At that, Elizabeth sucked in a breath. Somehow, she had managed to monopolize her uncle's guest. It had not been her intention, and yet... something in her was terribly curious how he would answer.

"It might be said that sometimes I..." he hesitated, "... I suppose my friend's assessment is correct. I permit myself to believe that I am the only one who can accomplish what is needed."

Elizabeth arched her brows. "A failing, indeed, but not a very interesting one, Mr. Darcy."

A flash of laughter brightened his face. "Indeed! I must ask, then, Miss Elizabeth, what sort of faults you find 'interesting.'"

"Oh, all the nefarious ones. Gentlemen who own too many watch fobs to be entirely decent, ladies who wear ostrich feathers out of season, and anyone who insists that the violin is more pleasant to the ear than the piano."

His brows ticked together in what appeared to be slight bewilderment. "Then perhaps you will find me 'interesting,' after all, Miss Elizabeth, for while I have never worn an ostrich feather, I am afraid you will find me guilty of the other two faults."

"Excellent! We shall have something to talk about, after all."

Four

THE BUTLER ANNOUNCED DINNER, and Darcy offered his arm to Mrs. Gardiner, leading the others to the dining room. He was determined to keep his focus on the matter at hand, but found his attention straying, almost of its own accord, to Miss Elizabeth Bennet as she walked beside her uncle. There was something disarming about her, something he could not quite put his finger on. And she had the most remarkable eyes—a rich, cerulean blue with shards of silver splintering through them, and even shafts of turquoise when the light struck them. But it was more than their color, although that was what had first taken his fancy. It was the sharp intelligence mirrored there that sent prickles down the back of his neck.

As he helped Mrs. Gardiner into her seat at the foot of the table, he glanced up and discovered Bingley escorting Miss Jane Bennet, taking both seats on one long side of the table. That would, necessarily, place Darcy beside Elizabeth Bennet during the meal. It was all arranged rather too neatly, and to his increasing dismay, he was not nearly as offended as he ought to have been by the false pretense that had brought him here tonight.

Bingley caught his eye and smirked as he claimed his seat. At least one of them was clearly pleased with how the evening had developed. Darcy returned his friend's look with a quick glare, silently warning him to keep any notions to himself.

As they settled at the table, Mr. Gardiner cleared his throat. "Gentlemen, I must thank you again for joining us tonight. I know matters of business can be time-consuming, but I trust your insight on the recent issues will be invaluable."

Darcy inclined his head. "The pleasure is ours, Mr. Gardiner. We are always happy to be of service."

Mrs. Gardiner smiled warmly, a glance exchanged with her husband, though Darcy could not help noticing the slight hesitation before she turned her attention back to Bingley and Miss Bennet. There was something amusingly purposeful about the Gardiners' insistence on Lisbon—he knew they were likely hoping for a discussion of some substance, though he suspected it was a thinly veiled excuse.

Elizabeth Bennet sat beside him, unruffled and observant. Darcy noticed a quick glance between her and her aunt, the faintest hint of a smile she kept to herself. Interesting. He would have expected her to be preening and putting on a display of beauty and wit just for his benefit, since he was well and truly caught for the evening. But she seemed instead to be summoning her patience and trying to make the best of it. The usual artifice he had come to expect was missing here; instead, her presence was... refreshing.

Mr. Gardiner picked up that thread of business talk with renewed determination. "Of course, Lisbon is not our only concern, but given the importance of trade in these times, well..." He trailed off, looking between Darcy and Bingley. "With all the delays, I've needed a reliable perspective... though I have tried several avenues myself."

Darcy had to tear his eyes off Elizabeth Bennet—a chink in his armor that he was mortified to discover so quickly. The evening had scarcely begun, and he had known the lady for under a quarter of an hour, but he could hardly look away. "Of course, Mr. Gardiner. Where, specifically, are you seeing delays? We have seen nothing of the kind, and we had two large shipments arrive this very week."

Gardiner's composure fractured somewhat. "Ah... well, the port wine, naturally. They tell me that there was some trouble with the grape harvest this year."

Darcy frowned and glanced at Bingley. "Odd. We have heard quite the opposite. In fact, our prices were lower than last year, as producers were trying to compete to sell the overage."

Gardiner blinked. "Indeed!" He cleared his throat. "Well, I... I shall have to write to my man in Lisbon. Perhaps he can shed some light on the matter. Ah... what of cork, Darcy? I do not suppose you have had any... delays?"

Darcy shook his head, again glancing at Bingley, but his friend was already distracted by his dinner companion. Darcy hid a grimace. "None whatever."

"Indeed." Gardiner sipped his wine, his forehead creasing. "Devilish unlucky for me, I daresay. And... ah... well, what of your olive oil imports? Any misfortunes there?"

Darcy set his own glass down, hesitating a moment to see if Bingley would actually join the conversation. When he did not, Darcy cleared his throat and nodded. "Yes, in fact, we have."

Gardiner's face washed in relief. "Oh, jolly good. I feared I was the only one!"

"Well, I doubt you would have been affected by the same troubles as we have had. It was one of our own vessels, and as it turned out, the captain was not the loyal fellow he was made out to be. He left Lisbon with his cargo and sailed promptly for Marseille."

"Oh!" Gardiner stared at his plate, his jaw working. "That... that is unfortunate, Mr. Darcy."

"It would have been even more unfortunate if he had not been apprehended by a British frigate just south of Cádiz. Otherwise, we would have lost the whole lot—ship, cargo, all of it. As it was, we were merely delayed, and there was a rather heavy 'tax' to pay at the port. But all in all, we have little to complain of, and I am curious that you do. You are a man of experience, and you have no shortage of competent advice to guide you."

The man coughed, and was it Darcy's imagination, or did he spear his wife with a slightly accusing look? But he quickly composed himself and pasted a smile back on his face. "Well, now, Darcy, I should not say that our troubles have been outsized, not by any means. I was simply looking for..." His brow furrowed, and Darcy was sure of it this time—the man was looking to his wife for some sort of inspiration. "...I suppose I was hoping for some little push or some extra measure of expertise to see us through the next season."

Darcy grunted and leaned back as a footman placed a bowl before him. "I understand. It might help if you told me what measures you have already undertaken. Perhaps there is a way to help your company weather the coming storms."

Mr. Gardiner hesitated, glancing at his wife before replying. "Well... truthfully, I have explored nearly every option I could think of—secured new contracts, invested in my shipping enterprise, hired new help. There have been improvements already, but I felt... well, another set of eyes might see something I had missed."

Darcy tilted his head. "And you say the situation is improving?"

"Yes, indeed. Slowly, but steadily," Gardiner admitted, his gaze shifting to the table-cloth as if the damask could reveal more than crumbs from the bread. "It may well be that my concerns are resolving themselves, but one cannot be too careful, you understand."

Just as Darcy opened his mouth to ask why Gardiner still felt in need of assistance, Bingley cleared his throat, cutting in with an easy smile. "Forgive me, Darcy, but I would hate to see you monopolized on business all evening. Perhaps, as Mr. Gardiner's situation seems to be under control, you might spare a moment for more pleasant conversation."

Darcy arched a brow, glancing between Bingley and Gardiner. "What conversation did you have in mind, Bingley?"

"Hmm? Oh, nothing particular. I daresay we've any number of things to speak of. Ah, Miss Bennet, where did you say you were from again?"

Darcy arched a brow and turned his attention to his soup as Bingley lost himself speaking to Miss Bennet. She *was* a pretty creature. Fair, with flaxen curls tumbling about her temples and the same starry eyes as her sister. But, if a man had a right to judge on expression and posture alone, there was something rather less fetching about her. He could not say precisely what it was, for he was similarly at a loss to describe exactly why Elizabeth Bennet had caught up the scattered threads of his imagination the moment he walked in the door.

"It seems you have solved my uncle's 'serious dilemma' for now," came her low voice at his elbow.

Darcy tried not to start, but his hand quaked somewhat on the spoon as he tried to bring it to his mouth. He darted her a quick glance, but then his eyes lingered of their own accord. "It does not appear there was much 'dilemma' to solve."

She brought her napkin to her lips to hide a chuckle. "I see you have judged the matter rightly, sir. I hope you were not kept from more pressing matters this evening."

"Not unless you consider an evening of dancing and drinking and more dancing and drinking with the elite of London's *haut ton* to be 'pressing.'"

She blinked, lowering her napkin slowly back to her lap. "Oh. Oh, dear, I did not realize—"

"You need not apologize, Miss Elizabeth. You see before you a man vastly better pleased away from Almack's. Bingley might have been somewhat disappointed when I informed him of our evening plans, but..." Darcy glanced across the table at his friend, who was so engrossed in conversation with Miss Bennet that he never even looked up. "Well, as you can see, he seems to have recovered from his disappointment."

She offered him a thin smile as she looked away to spoon her soup. "Mr. Darcy, I—"

"Oh, Lizzy, dear," Mrs. Gardiner interrupted. "Did you know that Mr. Darcy was the one who introduced your uncle to John Broadwood several years ago? It was he who is responsible for that lovely pianoforte sitting in the drawing room."

Darcy smiled tightly at the compliment as Miss Elizabeth turned an appreciative gaze on him. "Then, sir, I must offer my gratitude, for that poor piano has withstood many hours of my rather lackluster practicing, and yet, it has kept tune all the while."

Darcy laughed. "Well, then, I hope you will do us all the honor of playing something on it after dinner, Miss Elizabeth."

"Oh, no, you do not. I am no fool, Mr. Darcy. My aunt may attempt to burnish my pride with praise of my abilities, but I am merely competent, no more. I've no intention of humiliating myself in front of a man who, no doubt, has heard the best musicians London can boast."

"'Best' is a relative term, is it not?" he countered. "The 'best' musician may have dazzling technique, and his fingers may move with such speed that my eye cannot even keep up, but if I cannot appreciate his taste or his delivery, then I should hardly call him the 'best,' now, should I?"

"And what do you consider to be good taste, sir?"

He frowned and tilted his head. "I should think it begins with a performer who is aware of his... or her... limitations. One who plays merely to impress with the volume and speed of their fingering is completely intolerable."

"I shall keep that in mind, sir. And what else qualifies as a 'tolerable' performance in your eyes?"

He pursed his lips, and, for a moment, allowed himself the indulgence of meeting her gaze. "One who understands that the *pleasure* of listening to music is enhanced by a *pleasing* countenance and a *pleasant* manner. I care not if they play the most difficult piece ever composed without a single mistake. I would prefer to hear a musician who is enjoying themselves, as well as the music."

Her brows arched. "How very interesting, sir. Well, in that case, perhaps you might prevail on me to play something for you. But only on the condition that you promise to look at my face rather than my hands, for I fear my fingers will fumble rather too much for my liking."

Darcy cast an appraising glance over that face—a heart-shaped rose, really, with little chocolate whorls framing it that offset the veritable sapphires burning in her eyes. "That," he vowed in a voice suddenly grown somewhat husky— "is a promise I can readily give, Miss Elizabeth."

A UNT GARDINER PUT HER up to it.

Not that she was surprised—the little hint at dinner about Mr. Darcy helping to secure the Gardiners' Broadwood was sufficient to warn her that she would be expected to play later. The coffee service had hardly been brought when her aunt begged her to entertain them all.

It ought to have been Jane. Jane was the eldest. She was the one who should catch a suitor and marry first, and she was the one who seemed to be behind this entire evening. But no—Jane had never learned to play, and besides, it looked as though Mr. Bingley was perfectly happy to sit beside her and just stare at her, even if she was not making a sound. And so, it must be she.

Elizabeth took her place at the piano, trying to maintain a semblance of poise as she arranged the music in front of her. She had not expected Mr. Darcy to be quite so prompt to join her, but there he was, already seated beside her, his posture straight and his expression surprisingly warm. He gave a polite nod, his hand poised to turn the pages, and she noticed that even his movements carried a kind of restrained elegance she'd been determined not to find impressive.

"Well, Miss Elizabeth," he said, "I hope I have not made myself out to be a more critical audience than you anticipated."

"Critical? No, not at all. Though I am prepared to deliver my modest performance to even the highest standards of... 'tolerance'."

"Then I shall summon all the 'tolerance' I can muster," he replied with a glint of amusement. "I am certain it will be scarcely needed."

"Oh, I would not be so certain, Mr. Darcy." Elizabeth settled her fingers on the keys and played the opening notes with deliberate simplicity. "You see, I am not one to shy from humility when it is warranted."

"Humility is often overstated," he said, watching her hands with careful attention. "Particularly when one has a skill worth displaying."

Elizabeth threw him a sidelong glance. "I hope, sir, that is not flattery meant to divert my nerves."

"If it does divert your nerves, then it is purely accidental," he replied, turning the page smoothly. "I would be remiss if I did not assure you of my honest admiration—of your playing, that is."

A small laugh escaped her, and she managed a little trill on the keys before returning to the melody. "Well, then, I shall do my best to avoid any sour notes and secure your approval, Mr. Darcy."

They continued in this vein for a few measures, Darcy's remarks growing bolder as she grew more comfortable with the piece. He had a surprisingly adept hand at easing the tension she had anticipated, and Elizabeth found herself smiling as they traded comments under their breaths between the measures. She half-wondered if he was as determined to keep her distracted as he was to turn the pages.

As she neared the end of the piece, she stole a glance at him, her curiosity getting the better of her. "I must say, Mr. Darcy, it did not take you long to discover the... shall we say, *finer* points of this evening's invitation."

A flicker of amusement crossed his face. "Oh? And what finer points might those be, Miss Elizabeth?"

She pressed a hand to a few soft chords. "I should not like to presume, of course, but it occurs to me that my aunt and sister may have been more invested in tonight's company than they let on."

He turned the next page with a barely-there smile. "You mean to say your uncle did *not* send me an urgent summons regarding olive oil imports?"

Elizabeth's shoulders shook with laughter. "No, indeed, he *sent* it. But I would imagine the hand that *wrote* it had a peculiar way of forming its 's's, as well as a rather feminine loop to the 'l's."

"I would not be surprised."

She thinned her lips into a forced smile. "I suspect your Lisbon expertise was merely a convenient excuse to lure you here for a private evening of... conversation."

"A captive audience, as it were."

She winced. "I see you understand."

He gave a faint nod, his expression one of mock solemnity. "Indeed. It might shock you to hear, Miss Elizabeth, that this is far from the first time that Bingley and I have been the unwitting victims of a most elaborate ruse."

Elizabeth's fingers stilled for a moment before she resumed the melody, heat rising in her cheeks. "I assure you, Mr. Darcy, my aunt and sister are not in the habit of concocting schemes. Jane, in particular, would typically be mortified to think she had caused you any trouble."

"Mortified?" he echoed, a skeptical arch of his brow hinting at amusement. "She appears to be so far from 'mortified' that if I had to stake a guess on matters, I would make the assumption that she was in league with Mrs. Gardiner. Would that be an accurate guess, Miss Elizabeth?"

She blinked. The heat was crawling down her neck now, and she knew from experience that her cheeks were probably such a flaming pink that they almost looked painted. "It... would not be *in*accurate. But if you think my sister and I are the sort to manipulate people for our own gain—"

"You needn't become defensive, Miss Elizabeth. The letter was sent, and here we are, false pretenses or not."

One of her eyes narrowed skeptically as she tilted her head at him. "And missing out on better amusements at Almack's, apparently."

Mr. Darcy had... *oh*, he had a terribly nice smile. She fancied that he used it but rarely, but when he did, it was enough to turn her stomach to jelly. "Yes, I hardly know how I shall bear the loss. In fact, I daresay I have been greatly inconvenienced by this... ruse. How fortunate that you happen to be seated by the piano and in a position to repay the debt."

"Is that so?" she replied, striking a light, playful chord. "Then I must continue playing to make amends."

"Indeed, Miss Elizabeth. And I do not intend to let you stop until I am fully compensated for my suffering."

"Well, then," she replied, arching her brow, "What would you like best to hear? You ought to know that I have been practicing diligently this week, and I am capable of mangling at least four pieces by Clementi, two by Mozart, and I can make a perfect hash of the first half of a piece by Haydn. I am glad I came prepared with several pieces, Mr. Darcy, as it appears your requirements are quite exacting."

"Only fair, for a gentleman so gravely deceived," he replied, turning the page just as she neared the end of another measure.

By the time Aunt Gardiner was serving a second round of coffee, Elizabeth finally declared her fingers to be done in. Mr. Darcy was gallant enough to pronounce the "debt" satisfied, and he extended his hand, escorting Elizabeth back to where the others were already settled. Elizabeth took her seat beside her aunt, who looked positively delighted by the entire evening.

"I hate to turn us all back to the dull prospect of business," Mr. Bingley said after setting down his cup. "But Mr. Gardiner, something you said earlier just struck my fancy."

"Indeed?" Uncle Gardiner inhaled the steam from his cup and set it aside, fixing his attention on Mr. Bingley. "And what is that?"

"Cork. A marvel, is it not?"

Uncle Gardiner blinked and frowned. "Cork, sir?"

"Darcy, you know," he said, gesturing to his friend. "We were just saying something like this earlier."

Mr. Darcy was seated in the chair nearest Elizabeth's corner of the sofa, and he straightened in his seat. "We were?"

"Oh, indeed. How short your memory is! It really is a rather unique thing, cork. Remarkably durable under all kinds of pressure."

Elizabeth glanced at Mr. Darcy, then back at Mr. Bingley. What a peculiar subject!

"You see, Miss Bennet," Mr. Bingley continued, as if this were an entirely usual topic of conversation, "Darcy and I were speaking of how certain things—sometimes the most unassuming things from the most unexpected places—can prove to be so valuable. Cork, for instance, is not only prized for wine but for... well, a multitude of things. Its resilience is truly unmatched. Holds up to pressure, keeps everything secure—it is dependable. Essential, really, for I challenge you to find another substance that is half as good."

Mr. Darcy's expression shifted, and Elizabeth caught an unmistakable flicker of something—discomfort? Bemusement? Whatever it was, Mr. Darcy clearly wasn't enjoying the topic as much as Mr. Bingley.

"Reliable materials, like cork, are often underestimated," Mr. Bingley pressed on, now directing his attention to Darcy with a glint in his eye. "Would you not say, Miss Elizabeth, that dependability is one of the most valuable qualities a material—or person—can possess?"

Elizabeth's curiosity deepened as she looked between the two men, fully aware that this conversation was not simply about cork. "You make it sound as if cork is a model of virtue, Mr. Bingley," she said lightly. "What admirable qualities it seems to have."

"Absolutely," Mr. Bingley agreed, glancing at her. "The finest things are often unassuming, and their true value only reveals itself under scrutiny." He paused, his gaze sliding back to Darcy. "Would you not say, Darcy, that finding such qualities is... quite rare?"

Mr. Darcy met Elizabeth's gaze, then cocked an eyebrow and regarded his friend once more. "I believe, Bingley, that you have made your point, and rather less eloquently than you think."

Mr. Bingley leaned back, looking altogether too pleased with himself. "There you have it, Darcy. No need to search far and wide when what you have in front of you is already perfect to the task."

Five

Darcy stared at the papers on his desk the next morning, but his focus drifted in a way he had not felt in years. That woman... the one who teased him and talked to him as if he were any other man...

Elizabeth Bennet.

She was a singular woman, that much was clear, though he knew precious little else. Her uncle was a man of trade, which explained why she had never been paraded about in any of the Society balls Bingley had dragged him to. But her father, he had gathered, was a gentleman of some modest property. In some ways, Elizabeth Bennet was much like himself, a person whose connections straddled the worlds of trade and gentility.

Yet, for all this overlap, she was entirely unlike anyone he had ever met.

Her wit, her unpolished honesty, her unshakable poise even when she was teasing him—it was... well, he was not entirely sure *what* it was. She had made it plain that while her aunt had orchestrated the evening—likely with an eye to benefiting *her*, Elizabeth Bennet was a lady perfectly capable of voicing her reservations over such ploys.

That alone had turned the whole manipulation into something he could not quite resent.

The door to his study swung open with a bang, and Darcy did not even need to look up to identify Bingley, strolling in with a bounce in his step and a whistle on his lips. He slapped a document down on the desk on top of the page Darcy was already trying to read.

"Here," Bingley declared. "My solution to your exile here in Town."

Darcy glanced at the document, lifting a brow. "And what, exactly, am I looking at?"

"A holiday for both of us, if I have any say in it," Bingley replied, folding his arms and grinning. "It is a lease. For a property in Hertfordshire."

Darcy picked up the document, glancing over the lines. "You have leased an estate?"

"Not entirely leased. Not yet. That paper is the offer. All you have to do is lend your hearty agreement, and I shall secure it."

"And why would you need my agreement? You have money of your own, do you not?"

"Because—" Bingley stepped forward to tap his finger on the page— "as I have said before, it avails me nothing at all to try to do something for my own pleasure without gagging and hamstringing you first. You will find some urgent business that entangles me here before I've even set foot in the carriage. I drag you along with me, or I do not go."

Darcy frowned and scanned the paper, cocking an eye at Bingley every few seconds. "Why a lease? It is like throwing money out with the rubbish bin. You could certainly afford to purchase."

"Oh," Bingley said with a dismissive wave. "I can buy property any day of the week. But what I cannot readily do is find something so happily situated. This estate is not offered for sale, only a lease, but it is close enough that we can reach it in less than a day's ride, and far enough from Town to afford us a true escape. It has fine grounds, the agent reports excellent shooting—although we missed most of that for the season—scenic views, and even a pleasant lake. If I cannot to drag you all the way to Pemberley, then, at the very least, I will get you out of London."

Darcy smirked, setting down the paper. "And you think I will go quietly."

"Not at all." Bingley's grin widened. "I am prepared to drag you by your cravat if it comes to that."

"I am half a head taller and at least a stone heavier than you are," Darcy murmured, scanning the lease details. "Good luck in your attempt, though."

"Then I will write to the War Office and have Fitzwilliam sent over here at once with his sword and pistols to force you into the carriage."

Darcy frowned and pushed the lease paperwork back into Bingley's hands. "Now is not an opportune time to leave London."

"Oh, no. I will not hear that excuse. There has never *been* a more opportune time! Your sister is staying with Lady Matlock and requires absolutely nothing from you until next year when she prepares to come out. Your estate—you know, the one you never visit—has already put up the season's harvest and is slipping peacefully into hibernation for the winter. We are not expecting anything but routine business for the next month at least, and for whatever does arise, we can be reached by express in just a few hours."

Darcy blinked and released a slow exhale. He had fancied, at least for a few moments there, that he might... well, perhaps he might call again on Mr. Gardiner. Just to see that those port wine and olive oil imports had straightened out. He swallowed and was just reaching to examine the lease document again when Bingley plucked them up from the desk and rolled them up.

"You owe me, Darcy," he said, tapping those rolled papers on his shoulder where that old scar was.

Darcy sighed. It was pointless to argue once Bingley decided to play his trump card. "Very well. A week. I will go for a week."

"A month, and not a day less."

Darcy's jaw shifted. "A fortnight."

Bingley laughed. "Do you know, you always managed to catch me with that sort of bargaining before, but I shall not be moved this time. A month, or I will start canceling some of our contracts, so you truly have nothing to do for weeks on end in this great cavernous room here."

"You would not dare."

"A month, Darcy. Through Christmas and Boxing Day, at least. You could do with an escape from Town—admit it, you hate all the parties, anyway, so we shall enjoy a quiet Christmas in the country. And you had best go upstairs to dress now, because your valet already has your trunk packed, and my carriage is waiting outside."

Darcy's jaw dropped. "You... What the devil? You said you had not even signed the lease yet!"

"Come, come, you do not think I have worked alongside you for eight years and learned nothing, do you? I would not sign the lease without seeing the property first. Tick, tock, time to go, Darcy."

Darcy gaped for a few seconds more. There seemed to be no getting round this. Bingley would have his way—at least, for today. Darcy had no intention of letting himself be stranded in Hertfordshire for all of December, but perhaps a few days... a week... might satisfy Bingley's thirst for adventure and the outdoors.

"You will have to give me at least a quarter of an hour to change and another half hour to gather some paperw—"

"Tut, tut. Off with you, now. I will gather up these important documents for you to bore yourself over while you dress. The carriage leaves in a quarter of an hour, and you will be in it, Darcy."

THE CARRIAGE ROCKED THEM side to side over the icy road, and Elizabeth rubbed her hands together for warmth, stealing a glance at Jane. Her sister was peeking through the curtain covering the window, her cheeks flushed from the chill air seeping through the seams of the carriage.

The carriage slowed, and Elizabeth peered out the window to find herself looking upon the bustling courtyard of The Angel, their first stop to change horses. A weathered sign swung gently overhead, painted with a faded angel in flight, while stable hands dashed about, leading horses to and from the stalls with practiced haste. A few travelers lingered by the entrance, adjusting their cloaks and gloves as they chatted in low voices against the crisp December air, clouds of breath rising like smoke.

Elizabeth wrapped her shawl more tightly, preparing to sit through the stop as usual, assuming their driver would see to the horses without delay. But as soon as the carriage jostled to a halt, James surprised her by stepping down and coming to the window. He tapped on the glass, his hat tipped low against the wind.

Elizabeth lowered the window. "Yes, James?"

He cleared his throat, casting a quick glance over his shoulder. "Begging your pardon, Miss Bennet, Miss Elizabeth, but it seems there's a bit of a concern with the wheel. One of the spokes has worked loose, I'm afraid, and I'd not feel right setting off again without a blacksmith's look at it. I'll see if he's available straight away."

Elizabeth leaned forward, craning her neck to peer at the carriage wheel herself, but even with her best scrutiny, she saw nothing particularly amiss.

Elizabeth squinted, peering at the wheel in question. "A loose spoke, you say? I'm no expert, James, but it appears sound to me."

"Aye," he said, scratching the back of his neck. "Well, it's not always visible, miss, but I've been at this work a fair bit, and I can tell you—it'll need a blacksmith to see to it."

Elizabeth tilted her head, but before she could speak, she caught the curious look that James cast at Jane. Her sister looked away at once, smoothing the cuffs of her gloves and gathering her reticule as if she had almost expected this.

"Very well, James," Elizabeth replied, a spark of suspicion lighting her gaze. "If it must be done, it must be done. You may see to it. We will wait inside."

"Much obliged, miss," he said, and with a final tip of his hat, he strode off toward the blacksmith.

Elizabeth cast a knowing glance at Jane with no small degree of suspicion as they stepped out of the carriage and started for the inn's door. "Our wheel, perfectly sound all the way from Gracechurch Street, now decides to endanger our lives? Dear Jane, do tell me if you have any notion as to why we have so suddenly developed carriage troubles."

Jane blinked. "What an odd question, Lizzy. Are we not on our way to Longbourn, precisely as planned?"

"We are, yes. But I am suddenly possessed of the strangest suspicion that you and Aunt Gardiner might have had a quiet word with our good driver."

Jane gave a light laugh, perfectly composed. "To what end? What, you think Aunt schemed for us to drive five miles from her warm home just to see us stranded at a coaching inn? Rubbish! James has always been quite dependable. And if he says there is trouble with the wheel, well, then I suppose there is."

Elizabeth arched a brow. "Very well. Then, let us go inside and 'suppose' our way into a comfortable seat while the blacksmith attends to his 'work.' I believe I could do with a cup of tea."

They made their way into the inn, where Elizabeth took a seat by the window, offering a prime view of the yard. Jane joined her, her manner so casual and pleasant that Elizabeth could hardly stand it. After they ordered tea and a light meal, Elizabeth turned her attention out the window, watching for any sign of actual work on the wheel. She was just contemplating the lack of activity when another carriage pulled up, and to her utter surprise, none other than Mr. Bingley and Mr. Darcy alighted from it.

Elizabeth felt a sudden jolt of panic. She could hear Mr. Darcy's voice carrying through the glass pane, his tone clipped with mild annoyance. "Really, Bingley, this is unnecessary. The horses can be changed in a matter of moments. I do not see why we must retire here."

Mr. Bingley only smiled back at his friend as he dusted off his coat. "A momentary repast, Darcy, is hardly a sin. You could do with a breath of air, you know."

Mr. Darcy crossed his arms. "I am quite capable of breathing within a moving carriage."

"Ah, but you miss the point, my friend." Bingley turned, his hands on his hips. "'Tis not the destination, but the journey you must learn to appreciate. You wouldn't deprive me of a moment of genuine country charm, would you?"

Elizabeth snorted, glancing at Jane, who had turned her attention resolutely to her tea.

"Jane Bennet," Elizabeth hissed, "do you have anything to do with this charming little coincidence?"

"Coincidence?" Jane asked, her tone all guileless and pure, though her cheeks had taken on a decidedly pink hue. "Whatever do you mean?"

Elizabeth scowled and chucked her thumb toward the glass as the gentlemen drew closer to the inn door. "Do not play innocent with me."

Jane lowered her cup and, clearing her throat, pinched absently at her cheeks and smoothed the way her skirt laid over her knees. "Why, Lizzy, what a preposterous accusation. How could I possibly have known Mr. Darcy and Mr. Bingley were traveling today, or have any notion that they might stop here?"

"Indeed. So, this 'loose spoke' that I cannot see, and *their* sudden whim to take tea precisely when our carriage faltered... They are pure happenstance, then?"

Jane took another sip of tea, her gaze fixed firmly on the cup. "I am as mystified as you are, Lizzy."

"Mystified!" Elizabeth said with a soft laugh. "Then you must have no objections if I... ah, check the air outside?"

"Lizzy," Jane protested, her voice a low whisper, "we cannot simply... approach them!"

"Oh, can we not?" Elizabeth countered. "We have been introduced, and this is a public place. Surely, we may take the air in company. And besides..." She glanced pointedly toward the men as they made for the door of the inn. "It seems they intend to come to us."

Darcy was looking impatient, his brow furrowed and his gaze fixed on the ground as he muttered something to Bingley. But Bingley, grinning widely, opened the door and guided Darcy inside with the air of a man entirely too pleased with himself.

As they entered, Bingley's gaze landed on Jane, and his entire expression brightened. "Why, Miss Bennet! Miss Elizabeth! What a surprise to see you both here."

"A surprise indeed," Elizabeth mumbled, glancing at Jane, who had turned an even brighter shade of pink.

Darcy's brows rose, the barest flicker of surprise in his dark eyes. "Miss Bennet. Miss Elizabeth." He glanced sharply at Bingley, then back at the ladies, and his tone held a touch of disbelief. "I had not expected to encounter familiar faces here."

Elizabeth met his gaze with the faintest hint of challenge. "Nor did we, Mr. Darcy. Though it seems fate has taken a rather lively hand in our travels today. That—" she gestured toward the window, looking outside– "is our carriage, and, as you can see, it has been beset by some woeful trouble."

Mr. Darcy slanted his head to the side to afford him a view through the window. "Indeed," he replied, his gaze flickering between her and the driver, who was now intently inspecting the carriage wheel with more scrutiny than seemed entirely necessary. He folded his arms, casting a skeptical look toward Bingley, who was rather pointedly avoiding his eye. "I trust your journey has otherwise been without incident?"

"Oh, entirely smooth," Elizabeth replied, her tone dry, "until this unexpected mishap. James assures us it is merely a matter of prudence to prevent a loose spoke from causing any... disruption."

"Prudence, indeed," Darcy murmured, a faintly amused glint in his eye as he observed the driver's exaggerated inspection. "One would not wish to overlook a matter of such importance."

Elizabeth allowed a slow smile. "Quite so. And yet, how fortunate that we find ourselves so unexpectedly... well-accompanied."

"Yes," he said, his mouth twitching. "It does seem that chance has conspired most efficiently." He shot Bingley a sidelong glance.

There seemed little else to do—the gentlemen ordered refreshments, and moments later, a round table near the fireplace was prepared for them all. Darcy and Bingley took seats on either side of the ladies, a configuration that felt both perfectly casual and slightly strategic to Elizabeth. She settled herself between the gentlemen, amused at the coincidence—or the seeming coincidence, rather—and the hint of curiosity she noted on Darcy's face.

He turned to her with a polite, if slightly quizzical, expression. "I must say, Miss Elizabeth, I was unaware that you and your sister intended to travel. No one made any mention of it to me last evening. Are you returning to your family home?"

"Yes," she replied. "To Longbourn, near the town of Meryton, in Hertfordshire."

There was a quick, sharp glance between Darcy and Bingley that did not escape Elizabeth's notice. Darcy's expression tightened, and Bingley chuckled, the sound somewhere between sheepish and triumphant.

"A fine coincidence, indeed!" Bingley declared, looking far too pleased with himself.

Elizabeth tilted her head, puzzled. "A coincidence? I believe you have caught me at a disadvantage, Mr. Bingley. What, exactly, is this coincidence?"

Darcy gave Bingley a look that seemed to convey some unspoken reprimand, but he answered Elizabeth, all the same. "We are traveling to inspect a property that my friend intends to lease—an estate called Netherfield, which, I am given to understand, is also in Hertfordshire."

Elizabeth's expression brightened. "Why, Netherfield is only three miles from Longbourn!" She glanced at Jane, who was biting her lip and looking down at her lap. "Then... it must be true that the baronet is leaving, after all. Jane...?"

Jane helplessly shook her head. "Charlotte mentioned something in passing in her last letter, but I know no more than you do."

Bingley and Darcy exchanged confused looks, and Bingley leaned forward, intrigued. "Baronet, Miss Elizabeth? Do you mean to say Netherfield is currently owned by one?"

"Yes, for some years now. And you say it is for lease?" Elizabeth asked.

"Indeed, I have the documents in the strongbox of my carriage." Bingley spared Jane a quick glance, and Elizabeth had the distinct impression that the gentleman was holding his breath. "I—well, a dashed fine coincidence, that," he said. "The papers came to me only this morning. Tell me, what is this you were saying about a baronet?"

Elizabeth opened her mouth, then hesitated. "It is not our place to say," she replied carefully. "We would not wish to put such a good man in a poor light or assume anything about his affairs."

Darcy inclined his head slightly. "Quite understandable, Miss Elizabeth. I respect discretion in such matters." He paused before adding, "It seems, however, that the 'coincidences' are multiplying."

She offered a tight smile and slid her gaze toward Jane, but her sister was already saying something to Mr. Bingley. "It certainly does. I hope, sir that you do not think either of us manipulated—"

He cut her off with a shake of his head. "I have been in company with Bingley for too long to suspect *you*." He followed this with a faint arch of his brow in Jane's direction and lowered his voice to a soft murmur as he leaned closer. "Your sister, however, does bear some scrutiny."

"Sir, I—"

"Never mind that. Tell me, how large of a town is Meryton? What is the town like in the winter?"

Elizabeth's chest eased at Darcy's strategic change of topic. "Oh, it is delightful! There is a small lake just outside of town that freezes over every winter, and the whole village gathers there to skate. The local children have already started counting the days. We have dances in the assembly hall every month, and the best merchants travel from London to set up stalls in the square in December. On Christmas Eve, there is a great bonfire, and nearly everyone comes with food and mulled wine to share, singing all the carols they can remember."

Darcy listened, glancing at Bingley, who was visibly charmed by Elizabeth's descriptions. Darcy cleared his throat, inclining his head in Elizabeth's direction. "It sounds, indeed, like a rather charming way to pass Christmas—in the country."

For some reason, Mr. Bingley's face reddened, but he grinned widely. "I could not agree more, Darcy."

Six

DARCY SETTLED INTO HIS seat as their carriage rattled over the icy road, a bright December breeze keeping the windows clear of frost. Bingley, beside him, had barely contained his restlessness from the first mile since they left The Angel, glancing out the window at every bend in the road with that barely-hidden eagerness Darcy knew too well. And every time the horses needed to be changed, somehow Bingley found an excuse to pop out of the carriage.

"Another inn?" Darcy asked as their carriage began to slow again. "Surely you do not need 'refreshment' so frequently, Bingley. At this rate, we will not reach Netherfield until Easter."

Bingley smirked. "I am merely a considerate traveling companion, Darcy. I would not wish for the ladies to suffer from... neglect, shall we say? What if they need new hot bricks for their feet or their gloves suffered some dampness from moisture in the carriage?"

Darcy rolled his eyes. "Yes, quite selfless of you. I commend your devotion."

As they stepped down from the carriage, Bingley darted immediately to Miss Bennet, offering his arm even as the lady's foot had scarcely met the paving stones. Darcy's gaze drifted, almost of its own accord, to Miss Elizabeth, who was adjusting her cloak against the cold before she stepped out. She caught his eye and raised an eyebrow.

"Mr. Darcy, do you approve of such frequent interruptions? I was under the impression that gentlemen preferred a more straightforward journey."

He allowed himself a small smile. "I prefer efficiency, yes. But I am amenable to the alteration. At least, within reason."

"Yes, but is getting out of the carriage every five miles 'within reason'? This is our third stop, and somehow, our drivers and fellow passengers have contrived to find some reason for us to warm ourselves in the coaching inn for at least half an hour each time. It will be dark by the time we reach Meryton."

"I think you underestimate Bingley's powers of diversion."

"Or Jane's," she sighed. "She may look sweet and innocent, Mr. Darcy, but I am beginning to fear that under that modest pelisse beats a heart that is pure conspiracy."

"It seems we have met our match, then, for we are about to be waylaid again." He nodded, turning her attention to the driver who was approaching them.

"Pardon, miss, but it'll be a few more moments than expected. Horses are a touch fussy today, what with the ice. I'd like to get this fresh team settled in to be sure they are not surprised by the slick road."

Her brows lifted, but she merely smiled. "Well, that is only to be expected, I suppose. Mr. Darcy, shall we wait inside?"

He offered her his arm. "Better than staring at the driver as he pretends to fuss over the animals, I suppose."

Inside, the inn was modest but warm, with a fire crackling away in the large hearth at the back. The smell of freshly baked bread mingled with the warmth of the place, and Darcy found himself strangely pleased to settle into the quiet corner table Elizabeth had chosen by the window. He sat across from her, their proximity allowing him a close view of her expression as she glanced out over the frosty countryside.

"Are you familiar with this part of the country, Mr. Darcy?" she asked.

"Not particularly," he admitted, his gaze following hers out the window, where snowflakes began to drift lazily down. "I never stopped any more than necessary when I was traveling to Pemberley."

"And when was the last time you were there?"

He toyed with a funny little ridge on the table. It stuck up and caught the edge of his thumb as he passed his hand over the surface, and it gave him something to look at besides those eyes of hers. "I assume what you mean by that is 'the last time I was there for more than a day.'"

"As you please," she replied. "But why go all the way to Derbyshire for only a day?"

He swallowed and shifted his feet under the table. "Five years ago, my father died, leaving me the estate, my family name, and a young sister who was, at the time, only ten years of age and could not reasonably travel to London alone."

Her brows arched. "So, you are avoiding painful memories?"

"You might say..." His brow pinched, and he dug into that ridge of the wood with his fingernail, as if the effort and mild destruction of prying it loose would distract his mind from the sting of memory. "Father disapproved of my ventures with Bingley."

"Hardly surprising," she mused. "I confess to wondering at it myself, after everything my aunt told me about the Darcy family and Pemberley. Why did you do it?"

He lifted a shoulder. "Because I gave my word. I owed a debt—a debt that money alone could not repay. And so..."

He trailed off, clamping his teeth shut as Bingley arrived beside him, helping Miss Bennet into the seat nearest her sister and plopping into another himself.

"I say, Darcy, this is indeed capital! Fresh air, the trees along the way laden with snow, the jingle of harness bells—I always did fancy harness bells. Why do we not use them in summer?"

"Would you like them half as well if you heard them constantly?"

Bingley's brow puckered. "Do you know, I've not the least idea, but I would not mind finding out."

Jane Bennet laughed. "I imagine you will have your fill of them in Meryton, for by now, everyone will have them out, along with their sleighs. The main streets in town do not see so much traffic as those in London, so the snow tends to build faster and linger longer."

"Just as I hoped!" he declared. "Something so fresh and clean about snow, is there not? Far better than slushy paths and gray streets. Tell me, Miss Bennet, what else have we to look forward to in Hertfordshire?"

"Oh, if you are looking for lavish entertainments, I am afraid you may be disappointed. We are a simple town."

"Just so!" Bingley enthused. "That will suit Darcy admirably, eh, chap?"

Elizabeth Bennet slanted a sly smile at him. "Are you saying, Mr. Darcy, that you would not miss the stifling ballrooms and endless parlor games you would face in London?"

"Not at all. In fact, I believe I would much prefer frostbite."

"Then, why do you never leave London?"

Darcy's face fell. *Why, indeed...* He darted a quick glance to Bingley, whose expression had also sobered. But in an instant, Bingley had shifted back to his eager charm as he gestured toward Miss Bennet.

"Darcy here is putting you on a bit. Why, he is just as dapper in a ballroom as he is in a drawing room or a study."

"Oh!" Miss Elizabeth surveyed him with teasing approval. "Adaptable, are you, Mr. Darcy?"

"More so than he will admit," Bingley declared. "Why, you should have seen him in France at Madame De Courcy's—"

Darcy cut him off with a sharp clearing of his throat, and Bingley colored and fell silent.

Miss Elizabeth raised a brow, her eyes dancing with intrigue. "I imagine that must be quite a story."

Darcy shot Bingley a warning look, but it was already too late.

"Oh, quite! He had this new waistcoat, do you see, and it happened to be the same color as—"

"I am sure Miss Elizabeth would not be interested," Darcy interrupted.

Bingley wilted, but what did Darcy in was the disappointment in Elizabeth Bennet's... rather astonishing... eyes... He swallowed and almost recanted his objection. After all, the story was not *that* inappropriate. Just embarrassing. But he was saved when the driver appeared at the door just then, calling out that the horses were ready.

Darcy took the opportunity to stand, feeling as though he had narrowly escaped a rather humiliating exposure before the first woman whose good opinion he had ever cared about. As he glanced over, however, he saw Elizabeth watching him. He thinned his lips and offered to help her rise, but he said no more.

They returned to the carriages, but as he climbed into his seat across from Bingley, Darcy found himself glancing back out the window, catching a last glimpse of Elizabeth Bennet before the door closed.

Bingley stretched his feet out as far as the carriage would allow, sighing in satisfaction. "Well, Darcy, I must say, Miss Bennet and Miss Elizabeth have made this journey far more enjoyable than I could have anticipated."

"You anticipated much, then?" Darcy replied, arching an eyebrow.

"Oh, come now! You cannot deny it has been a welcome distraction." Bingley's grin was far too knowing. "And for you as well, I think. I have seen you conversing more today than in all our outings last month."

"Politeness demands it." Darcy looked away, feigning interest in the passing scenery. "Miss Elizabeth has... an engaging wit."

"An engaging wit, yes. And a smile that could thaw the River Thames, no doubt?"

Darcy shot him a glare. "Do you ever cease, Bingley?"

"Not when I am on the scent of a good story." Bingley laughed. "And I think there is one here. Tell me, Darcy—when was the last time you spent so much time in conversation with a lady without a single obligatory dance or card game to sustain you?"

Darcy turned sharply. "Is this your new occupation then? Chronicling my interactions?"

Bingley merely grinned, unrepentant. "I find it endlessly fascinating. And I suspect the young ladies do, as well. Miss Elizabeth seems quite... well, I think you know what I mean."

"If you're referring to your habit of being absolutely transparent, I think everyone knows what you mean, Bingley."

"Admit it, Darcy," Bingley said, crossing his arms with smug satisfaction. "This journey has been entirely worthwhile."

Darcy gave him a warning look. "I have never denied the advantages of a rural setting, but if you insist on reading more into a polite conversation—"

"Oh, I insist on nothing," Bingley interrupted with a grin. "It's you, Darcy, who seems determined to read nothing at all."

Darcy said nothing, but his gaze flickered once more out the window, watching the landscape change as they neared Meryton. He had no idea what lay in store for him at Netherfield, or how often he might see Miss Elizabeth. But he could not deny a strange, heady anticipation settling in his chest, making him almost eager to reach their destination.

THE CARRIAGE SLOWED AS it drove through Meryton. Mr. Bingley and Mr. Darcy's coach rolled to a stop outside the inn, where they meant to pass the night, while Jane and Elizabeth's rumbled on toward Longbourn. Elizabeth glanced at her sister just in time to catch Jane's hand drifting up toward the window, her fingertips brushing the glass as she gave the faintest wave to Mr. Bingley. She blushed deeply, lowering her hand with a bashful smile, but Elizabeth said nothing.

As they neared Longbourn, the house came into view, its windows ablaze with warm candlelight against the growing dusk. A soft flurry had begun, dusting the fields and trees in white, making the familiar sight of home look almost magical. But before the carriage had even come to a full stop, the front door flew open, and Mrs. Bennet, with her bonnet askew and shawl hastily tied, bustled out, wringing her hands as she squinted through the twilight.

"Jane! Lizzy! Oh, *where* have you been? I thought you'd fallen into a ditch, or else that the coachman had run away with my girls!" she fretted, waving wildly for them to hurry out of the carriage.

"Oh, Mama," Jane soothed, stepping down and greeting her mother with a warm embrace. "The journey was longer than usual owing to the roads, but we are perfectly well."

Roads, indeed. Elizabeth followed, laughing as her younger sisters Lydia and Kitty came rushing out of the house, their skirts flapping and faces aglow with excitement.

"What took you so long? I thought you'd be here hours ago!" Kitty exclaimed.

"Did you bring anything back for us?" Lydia demanded, her eyes bright with anticipation.

"I daresay, we have been spoiled thoroughly by Aunt and Uncle Gardiner," Elizabeth replied, holding her hands up in mock surrender. "Yes, there are gifts for each of you, but you will have to wait until my trunk is taken up before I can dig them out."

"Oh, then hurry!" Lydia pleaded, tugging at Elizabeth's cloak as if to hurry her along.

Before Elizabeth could respond, Mr. Bennet appeared in the doorway, one eyebrow arched in his usual sardonic amusement.

"Welcome back, my dear girls," he greeted. "Tell me, should I be bracing myself for any heartbroken suitors chasing you back from London, or have you both been so ruthless as to leave all your conquests thoroughly crushed and are now looking to wreak fresh havoc on Hertfordshire?"

Jane's cheeks turned a lovely shade of pink, and Elizabeth gave her father an arch look. "Papa, I can assure you that we have not left any gentleman in ruin. As for the gentlemen of Hertfordshire..." She gestured around them at the merry chaos. "I think they shall have to brace themselves once again."

Mr. Bennet chuckled, waving them inside. "Well, be gentle with them, at least for my sake. Now come, both of you, before your mother's fretting shakes the rafters loose."

As the girls made their way inside, their mother peppered them with questions, asking for every last detail of their stay, though Jane excused herself to go upstairs and change for dinner. Elizabeth reassured her younger sisters once again about their gifts, laughing at their excitement as she pried their hands from hers to start for the hall.

Finally, as Mr. Bennet turned to head toward his library, Elizabeth made good her efforts at escape, glancing over her shoulder before following and quietly slipping in after him.

Elizabeth waited until the door had clicked quietly shut behind her, then crossed to her father's desk, folding her hands in front of her. Mr. Bennet had already settled back into his chair, spectacles perched on his nose, a hefty volume open on his lap. He glanced up, eyebrows lifting in mild surprise at her hesitation.

"Yes? What secret is trembling upon your lips, my dear, that you could not speak before your mother and sisters?"

"Papa, Jane and I heard... well, there is a rumor that Netherfield Park is to be let."

Mr. Bennet's brow furrowed as he slipped off his spectacles, tapping them thoughtfully against his book. "Let, you say?" He seemed to weigh the notion, glancing toward the window as though the news had drifted in from the grounds outside. "It is news to me, though I cannot say it is entirely unexpected. There has been gossip for some time, but I had heard nothing certain. Things may not be as rosy for the baronet as they once were."

Elizabeth hesitated, her fingers curling together. "Do you suppose it could have anything to do with... his activities?"

A grim smile tugged at the corner of her father's mouth. "That would be a fair assumption. When one chooses to shoulder such burdens, there is always a cost." He let out a long breath, his gaze distant. "He had ample resources, or he did at one time, but perhaps he has encountered more setbacks than he anticipated."

Elizabeth sank into the chair opposite him, her stomach suddenly twisting into a sick emptiness. "It would be a terrible loss if he is forced to shutter Netherfield," she murmured. "To... everyone."

"Yes," Mr. Bennet agreed, his tone softening. He watched her for a moment, then leaned forward, his voice taking on a gentler edge. "But let us not dwell on such morose matters, Lizzy. You've only just returned from London. I expect some sort of tale to entertain me, as long as it does not involve dancing or lace or any description of the endless gowns and bonnets."

Elizabeth managed a small smile, clasping her hands in her lap. "Very well, I shall do my best to spare you tales of ribbons and feathers, though you will miss hearing about the most extravagant hats on Bond Street. Aunt Gardiner and I agreed one in particular could serve as a garden trellis."

Mr. Bennet chuckled, his eyes twinkling. "Indeed, I am most grateful to be spared. What else occupied your time? Surely, not all of it was spent gawking at outlandish headgear."

Elizabeth leaned back, glancing at the fire. "Not at all. Uncle Gardiner took us to the British Museum, where Jane and I saw a curious collection of Egyptian artifacts, including a very stern-looking statue that Aunt said resembled a distant cousin of ours. And I had the pleasure of introducing Jane to an unexpected admirer."

Mr. Bennet's brow arched. "Oh?"

She smiled, suppressing a laugh. "A young poet—one who recited a verse for her on the spot. Aunt Gardiner quite feared he would follow us all the way back to Cheapside."

He shook his head with a wry smile. "I see it was a most eventful journey, indeed."

"Very much so." Elizabeth was suddenly beset by a yawn and found her eyelids growing heavy as the long journey finally seemed to be catching up with her. "Papa, I fear I am far more fatigued than I realized. Perhaps I should tell you more of London in the morning."

He patted her hand in a gentle dismissal, his eyes crinkling with affection. "Yes, yes, off with you, Lizzy. Go rest your weary head—you have given me enough amusement for one night."

Elizabeth rose, turning toward the door, but just as her fingers brushed the handle, her father called after her, his tone sly.

"Oh, Lizzy. You missed quite the spectacle while you were away. I suppose you are sorry to have missed my cousin Collins's visit. Believe me, my dear, you would have found him vastly amusing."

She stopped, glancing back at him, a slow grin creeping over her face. "Such a pity," she said, her eyes gleaming with mirth, "that Aunt and Uncle invited Jane and me to London just as Mr. Collins was expected."

Mr. Bennet chuckled dryly, his smile widening. "Yes, a pity indeed."

Seven

"THIS IS SILLY," BINGLEY announced as the footman put down the step in front of the Meryton inn. "We've still almost an hour of daylight left. I say we drive on and have a look at the house this evening rather than putting up at the inn to do nothing."

"We do not have an hour," Darcy countered as he regarded the horizon. "Half an hour, at best, and you propose to drive three or four more miles, look about the property, and then return before nightfall?"

"What care we for whether it is dark when we come back? The horses can see the road well enough, what with the lanterns, and besides, I am quite too restless to simply cool my heels in a taproom. Driver! Take us to Netherfield, please."

The footman took back the step and closed the door, the carriage lurched, and they were in motion again. Darcy leaned back, tapping his foot on the floorboards. Bingley was fairly bouncing in his seat, glancing out the window at every bend with an almost boyish eagerness that Darcy could not quite fathom.

Some while later, they made a turn at a brick-layered post that probably once bore a sign of some sort, but now stood as a mute, unmarked sentry. They must be on Netherfield's lands now. Twilight was settling over the landscape, casting long shadows that swallowed most of the finer details of the property.

"Tell me, Bingley, you did inform the owner of our impending arrival?" Darcy asked, already dreading the answer.

Bingley shifted, a sheepish grin spreading across his face. "Not... exactly. The agent only gave me the specifics about the property this morning. By the time the lease terms reached me, there was hardly a moment to spare before we set off. The agent assured me that I could call at the property directly, leave my card, and speak with the owner—who is, I might add, quite desperate to secure a tenant. Surely, he will not object to our presence."

Darcy's eyebrows shot up. "You intend to knock on the door of a man's home at dusk, completely unannounced, and discuss tenancy? Have you lost all sense of propriety, Bingley?"

Bingley's smile didn't falter, though he did pull his coat tighter. "I may not have scheduled an audience, but the agent seemed quite confident that any prospective tenant would be most welcome here."

Darcy huffed in disbelief. "Perhaps next time, you will simply post an invitation for him to host you to tea on your terms." He gestured to the sky, already deepening to a dark slate. "And you expect to view the property before nightfall?"

"Oh, yes!" Bingley said, undeterred. "The driver spoke to some fellows from Meryton, and he says the grounds are easy enough to survey from the front lawn, at least well enough to form an opinion. Besides, we have lanterns, and we can return to the Meryton inn after we have had our look around. It will be quite safe."

Darcy crossed his arms, unimpressed. "This from the same man who finds excuse after excuse to stop at every inn along the road? If you had not delayed us so thoroughly with all these... social niceties, we might already be comfortably situated at an inn now, with a fire and a meal."

"Social niceties? I only stopped to ensure Miss Bennet and Miss Elizabeth had adequate comfort! Fresh hot bricks for their feet and proper protection and all. It would have been ungentlemanly to allow two ladies to travel unaccompanied for so long."

"'Unaccompanied'? They had their driver, Bingley," Darcy retorted. "And Mr. Gardiner's private carriage, which is far more than most ladies can lay claim to. I should not need to remind you of what 'accompanied' entails. And I suppose your eyes were also filled with 'neighborly interest' every time you so much as glanced Miss Bennet's way."

Bingley gave a huff, waving off the suggestion. "Interest? I should hardly call it that. Miss Bennet is simply a most pleasant companion—and a new neighbor, as we hope. Can you imagine me so ungallant as to neglect a lady in need?"

"A lady in need, she was not. From where I sat, she looked remarkably content with her lot."

Bingley raised his chin, feigning indignation. "I have no idea what you mean. Besides, need I remind you that our acquaintance with the Bennet ladies is thanks entirely to *you,* Darcy? It was *your* insistence on dining with Gardiner that led to it all."

Darcy frowned, momentarily silenced. Yes, he had been the one to press for that evening, but it *had* been a practical matter of business, nothing more. Yet here he was, at Netherfield, in the very same county as the Bennet sisters, for no other reason than Bingley's nagging persistence.

"And *you* did not seem altogether displeased with the arrangement. In fact, I think you found something rather... diverting about Miss Elizabeth."

Darcy looked away, focusing on the dim outline of Netherfield beyond the carriage. "Bingley, you would do well to contain such suppositions."

Bingley chuckled. "Oh, come now! You cannot deny that she is remarkably clever, charming, terribly pretty, and altogether pleasant to be around. It is a rare combination, even you must admit."

Darcy's gaze lingered on the dark windows of the house, though his thoughts were far from Netherfield. "It is... unusual," he allowed after a moment, his tone careful. "Almost... unsettling."

Bingley's eyebrows rose. "Unsettling? How so?"

Darcy hesitated, choosing his words. "Miss Elizabeth Bennet is almost... too perfect a combination of qualities. Her intellect, her wit, her forthrightness... It feels... manufactured."

Bingley laughed outright at that. "Manufactured! My dear fellow, it sounds as though you're suggesting someone conjured her to suit your tastes. Admit it—you are smitten."

Darcy narrowed his eyes, refusing to indulge his friend's amusement. "Smitten is a strong word, Bingley. One I do not intend to apply here. My experience has taught me that anything seemingly perfect deserves a measure of caution."

"Deserves caution? My friend, only you would approach the prospect of charm with trepidation!"

Just then, the carriage rolled to a stop, and Darcy grimaced at the outline of Netherfield dimly silhouetted against the evening sky. Might as well have done with it, for Bingley would not rest until he had made footprints in Netherfield's snow. They stepped down from the carriage, Bingley pacing about with enthusiasm, while Darcy paused a moment longer, the flicker of lamplight casting odd shadows on the estate ahead.

The chill evening air seeped through Darcy's coat as he watched Bingley swinging the lantern about, casting faint, dancing shadows across the snow-covered gravel of the main drive. Netherfield house loomed in the dark, several of the windows lit as its residents no doubt moved about inside. Darcy cast an exasperated look at his friend.

"Bingley, this is improper. We were not announced, and it is unthinkable to wander about the grounds uninvited. They will think we are housebreakers or some other nonsense."

Bingley waved off his concern with his usual cheerful confidence. "Come now, Darcy, no one even knows we are here! It is hardly as if we're peering through windows. I only wanted a glance at the property—a man ought to know what he is leasing, after all."

Darcy sighed. "A matter you could have taken up by daylight, after notifying the owner. Egad, the landscape is covered in snow. What do you expect to see?"

"But it's just too splendid to pass up." Bingley moved the lantern to one side, inspecting the grounds with a pleased nod. "These fields, the woods to the west—there's game here, I'll wager."

"Wonderful," Darcy replied flatly. "Now, if you have satisfied your curiosity, perhaps we can return to Meryton for the night before we embarrass ourselves further."

"Oh, very well," Bingley said, relenting with a grin. "I would not want to risk offending your delicate sense of propriety."

Just as they turned back toward the carriage, a voice called out. "Evening, gentlemen. May I ask your business?"

Darcy froze, his stomach sinking with mortification, while Bingley, unperturbed, swung back around with his ready grin.

"Ah, good evening!" Bingley hailed the man approaching them. "Charles Bingley, sir. My apologies if our presence here startled you. Forgive me—we had not thought we were near enough to the house to cause any alarm. I came at the recommendation of Mr. Sutton in London—he is the estate's agent—and I wanted to leave my card with the owner."

The man stepped closer, close enough that the lantern's glow revealed his features—a weathered face, a patch over one eye, and a gait that dragged noticeably. Darcy's gaze caught the hint of an old scar along the man's jaw, and he felt a flicker of respect. This was no ordinary servant; he had seen combat, that much was certain.

"I am Jackson, head coachman here," the man said, his tone respectful enough, though his visible eye flickered cautiously between them. He held Bingley's gaze for a moment, then turned to survey Darcy. "Mr. Sutton, you say?"

"Yes, precisely," Bingley replied, nodding eagerly. "I understand the owner is interested in a potential lease?"

The coachman's eye narrowed, glancing back toward the house. "You said you were leaving your card at the house. But... you looked as though you were returning to your carriage. Where would you go at this hour?"

Bingley shifted, glancing at Darcy before answering. "Er—yes, well, we were, actually. We meant only to see the grounds, and thought we'd lodge at the inn in Meryton tonight. It was, perhaps, a bit of... curiosity. We meant to return for a proper call in the morning."

The coachman's expression did not change, but he nodded slowly, as if mulling over the answer. "Hm. Curious or no, my master would not care for it if he knew visitors from London were left to the cold. Best you have your driver bring the carriage up to the house."

Darcy stiffened. "We would not want to impose upon the master, unannounced as we are. I am sure he would prefer our call to be arranged through the agent at a more suitable hour."

Jackson's eye glinted, the faintest hint of amusement. "It's late, sir. Best to come inside, as the master would want."

Bingley, already eager, took Darcy's silence for agreement. "Then, by all means, let us come up! I thank you, Mr. Jackson." He signaled to the driver, who guided the carriage up the main drive as the coachman led the way toward the grand entrance.

Darcy followed, thoroughly unsettled. He leaned toward Bingley as they walked, keeping his voice low. "You realize this is the sort of boldness most men would avoid."

Bingley gave him a cheerful nudge. "Well, it is fortunate I am not most men, then, isn't it?"

"REALLY, DARCY," BINGLEY SAID with a chuckle, "you look as if you're headed to the scaffold, not an evening call. Relax a little! The coachman assured us, remember? The master would welcome visitors."

Darcy raised a skeptical brow. "This is the very height of impropriety, Bingley, and you know it. Arriving unannounced—practically trespassing in the dead of night—"

"Hardly trespassing when we have a man of the house's own staff escorting us to the door," Bingley countered.

"Perhaps the master is rather like something out of the German folk tales and devours would-be guests as soon as they let down their guards."

"Now, Darcy, that is an outrageous thing to say, even for you."

Darcy pressed his lips into a thin line, determined to maintain his disapproval. "Perhaps, but if we are held up for money or, more likely, sent away on the spot, you will have no one to blame but yourself."

"Not to worry," Bingley replied, grinning as he adjusted his gloves. "If I were the master, I would be positively thrilled to greet prospective tenants, especially in such a dismal economy. And if we are turned away, well—we'll have tried. You cannot say we did not have a pleasant drive today."

The carriage slowed to a halt before the grand entryway, and Darcy sighed, resigning himself to the inevitable as the footman opened the door. The two men climbed out, Darcy taking a moment to assess the front of the house. It was imposing in the dark, the stonework faintly visible under the glow of lantern light, casting long shadows across the weathered steps.

As they climbed the stairs, the heavy front door swung open. A man with neatly combed hair and a serious expression appeared, bowing in greeting. His left sleeve was pinned up to the elbow, and Darcy noticed with some surprise that he was missing his right hand.

"Good evening, sirs," the man said with an amiable nod. "The master awaits you. If you would be so kind as to follow me to the drawing room, he will join you shortly."

They stepped inside, and as the man led them down a hallway, Bingley shot Darcy a sidelong glance. After the man departed, closing the drawing room door behind him, Bingley raised an eyebrow. "Well, that was unexpected. Do you suppose the fellow lost his hand in battle?"

"Perhaps," Darcy murmured, glancing around the room, though he couldn't quite shake his unease. "From what I gather, this 'baronet' has a rather singular approach to staffing his estate. It would seem he employs those... who may find it difficult to secure work elsewhere."

"Admirable, I'd say." Bingley strolled to the plush sofa in front of the fireplace and sank into it, stretching his arms out along the back. "He's clearly not a man to shrink from bestowing a bit of goodwill. In fact, I rather like the fellow already."

Darcy, however, remained standing, hands clasped behind his back as he surveyed the room. He was about to speak when the door opened again, and a voice echoed from the hallway.

"My apologies, gentlemen, if you have been kept waiting."

Darcy had just turned his gaze to a painting over the mantel, but at the sound of the voice, he froze. His stomach dropped, and a strange tightness gripped his chest. He *knew* that voice.

Spinning around, his heart pounding in disbelief, he found himself face to face with Sir Thomas Ashford. Sir Thomas stopped in the doorway, his shock registering as his face paled slightly.

"Darcy! And... and Bingley! Why, is it really you? This is a pleasant surprise, indeed."

For a moment, Darcy was too stunned to speak, his mind scrambling to reconcile the tall, familiar figure before him with the very different setting around them. It was Sir Thomas—his old benefactor from Calais, the man who had once risked his own security, fortune... even his life to see them safely across the Channel. But the last Darcy had heard, Sir Thomas had retired to Bath, far removed from the responsibilities of country estates.

Bingley broke the silence, clearing his throat as he stepped forward, his voice faltering just slightly. "Sir Thomas! It is a pleasure, truly... though, I confess, an unexpected one. We were not aware Netherfield was yours."

Sir Thomas smiled, his eyes brightening with genuine warmth. "And this is certainly the last place I ever expected to encounter either of you again. Fate has an interesting way of arranging things, does it not?" His gaze softened as he looked between them. "But please, sit. I trust your journey was pleasant?"

Darcy and Bingley exchanged a quick glance before Bingley gathered himself enough to nod. "Indeed, very pleasant," Bingley replied, easing the words out with his usual charm. "Actually, we... we came with a purpose, though it feels rather forward now. We hoped to inquire about leasing Netherfield for a time."

"Leasing it?" Sir Thomas's expression shifted for the briefest moment—something uncomfortable flickered there, but he quickly recovered. "Ah. I see. Yes... yes, that is indeed the purpose my agent set forth."

Bingley gave a quick, awkward smile. "Well, yes. I hope you don't find it too presumptuous. We simply wished to see the property ourselves and, if suitable, to arrange some terms."

"Not at all, Mr. Bingley," Sir Thomas replied, though his tone was a touch graver than before. "In fact, I should be quite pleased if Netherfield found such occupants." He glanced away, as though contemplating something beyond the room. "It... appears that managing the estate is somewhat beyond what I had anticipated when I acquired it. Bath suited me well enough for a time, but, as they say, a man sometimes feels the pull of the country."

"When did you come to Hertfordshire, sir?" Darcy asked, noting the pensive cast to Sir Thomas's features. "I recall you once mentioned a preference for the life in Bath."

"Ah, yes." Sir Thomas gave a half-hearted smile, his eyes clouded as he looked toward the tall windows, where the last of the evening's light had faded. "It was about five years ago. I was taken by a notion, perhaps a foolish one, that I might... er... make something of it. But I did not foresee all the... particulars of managing such an estate. Bath was, indeed, simpler."

Bingley shifted, a flicker of sympathy crossing his face. "So, it has proved more of an undertaking than expected?"

"Yes, you could say that," Sir Thomas admitted, his tone carrying a subtle but unmistakable note of regret. "One takes a fancy to certain prospects, you understand, and... Well. Perhaps we shall discuss the details later." He paused, then his expression brightened again, as if determined to set aside any concerns. "You both look in need of rest after such a journey. Let me have you shown to some rooms. I cannot think of anything less hospitable than letting you return to Meryton in the dark to suffer a night at that drafty old inn."

Darcy opened his mouth to protest, but Sir Thomas raised a hand, his voice warm and final. "Come now, Mr. Darcy. It would please me beyond measure to be your host. Think of it as a small token of my pleasure at renewing a previous acquaintance, if you will. Daniels?"

Darcy and Bingley both turned as Daniels, the footman who had let them in, stepped back into the drawing room. But he was not alone, for just outside the open door, a maid was hovering, her expression troubled. She appeared to have been speaking with Daniels in hushed tones, and she quickly fell silent as he straightened and turned his attention to Sir Thomas.

"Roberts," Sir Thomas said, nodding at Darcy and Bingley, "see to it that Mr. Darcy and Mr. Bingley's trunks are brought up by some of the others. They shall stay with us tonight."

Roberts inclined his head with almost military formality. "Of course, sir."

Sir Thomas then turned to the maid with a gentle smile. "Miss Flora, would you arrange to have tea sent up to their rooms, and perhaps a light supper if the kitchen has anything ready?"

The maid nodded as her eyes shifted uncertainly to Darcy and Bingley. "Yes, sir. Right away, sir."

Sir Thomas turned back to them with a smile that, though polite, seemed faintly wistful. "My people here will ensure you are well looked after. And I should be honored to show you over the house myself in the morning. Rest well, my friends." With that, he inclined his head in a farewell bow and slipped quietly from the room.

Darcy and Bingley watched him go, glancing curiously at each other until Roberts spoke again.

"If you would follow me, gentlemen," he said, gesturing toward the hall. Darcy's gaze trailed to the doorway where "Miss Flora" had been, but she had already disappeared, leaving only Daniels waiting for them. As they ascended the stairs, Darcy noted the quiet, almost reverent stillness in the house, and an uneasy feeling settled in his chest.

Bingley, however, appeared unfazed, leaning close to Darcy as they climbed the stairs. "How very peculiar! I'd no idea of blundering into Sir Thomas's house. What luck, eh, Darcy?"

Darcy only tightened his jaw as they followed the footman. At the top of the stairs, they followed the man down the corridor, passing several closed doors. Darcy's eye snagged on one that had a ribbon tied to the handle. He thought it odd at first, but two doors later, he saw another. What could be the meaning of that? He glanced over his shoulder at Bingley, whose eye was roving the ceiling beams and carpet and nearly everything but the odd little ribbons on the doors.

"These will be your rooms, sir," Roberts said, pausing before an open door. "The sitting room is for your private use, and there is a bedroom on either side. The maids will be here soon with tea, and I will see that your trunks are brought up directly."

Darcy nodded. "Thank you."

Roberts bowed shortly and left them. Bingley turned to watch the man go, then looked back at Darcy with his brow quirked. "Odd. I do not think he is quite a proper footman, is he?"

Darcy shook his head and wandered into the sitting room, motioning for Bingley to close the door behind him. "No. Polite enough, but perhaps he is... new." His gaze swept the room—soaring windows that might have done Pemberley proud, covered by drapes at least a decade out of fashion but still quite serviceable. The furnishings were of a similar style—outmoded, perhaps, but solid.

Bingley was wandering the room with a similar fascination, looking about at everything. He swept his hand over an old mahogany writing desk, and, as was his wont, could not pass by without tugging open the drawer. However, instead of the usual pens, sealing wax, and pounce pots contained in most desk drawers, he plucked out a roll of linen bandaging strips.

He held it up to show Darcy, his brow furrowed in confusion. "How very singular."

Darcy frowned and drew closer. "Indeed."

"Well," Bingley murmured, casting another glance about the room, "our first night at Netherfield, and I daresay it already feels as though we have entered something... intriguing."

Darcy cast a wary glance at his friend. "Intriguing? I would use a different word, Bingley."

"Oh? What word might that be?"

Darcy shook his head, but his frown deepened. "Unsettling, perhaps."

Eight

"Y OU MISSED ALL THE fun, Lizzy." Lydia leaned over the table, banging her spoon accidentally on her glass. "Mr. Collins tripped on his way out of church last Sunday. Mary King said he nearly took old Mrs. Goodwin down with him."

Kitty snickered. "And I heard his hat flew off into the mud. It took him three tries to pick it up."

Mary frowned and reached for the butter. "Perhaps he was merely offering Mrs. Goodwin assistance in walking," she said. "One should not jump to conclusions."

"Oh, Mary, do pass the jam," Lydia said, rolling her eyes. "And do not defend him! It was devilish funny. You would have laughed, too."

Mr. Bennet glanced over the top of his spectacles, his gaze flickering from daughter to daughter. "And is this the most scandalous news our little town can boast of this week?"

Mary put up one hand as she was passing the teapot to Elizabeth. "Actually, I think Mrs. Lucas mentioned that the Wilkinsons are painting their front door bright green."

Elizabeth poured herself a cup of tea, raising an eyebrow. "Bright green? How shocking. What will Meryton do with itself?"

"A fine joke, Lizzy, but you did not hear what *shade* of green. Kitty and me think it looks exactly like horse dr—"

"That will do extremely well, child," Mr. Bennet sighed. "We are still at table, Lydia."

Elizabeth and Jane traded amused smirks over their teacups. Ah, but it was good to be home again. London had certainly possessed its charms, but there was nothing to the loving chaos of Longbourn.

A few moments later, Hill entered quietly and made her way to Mrs. Bennet, bending down to whisper in her ear. Mrs. Bennet's hand flew to her chest, and she gasped, looking over the table with wide eyes. "Oh! Girls—Mr. Bennet! Such news!"

Elizabeth's eyes slid to Hill as she made her hasty exit, then she regarded her mother with open curiosity. "What is it, Mama?"

"Oh, it is everything splendid! Hill tells me she learned from Perkins, the stable boy—who, I might add, had it from the butcher when he went to Meryton this morning, and he heard it directly from Mr. Jackson at Netherfield—that two wealthy strangers arrived late last night asking to lease the property!"

Jane's face lit up at once, and her eyes met Elizabeth's across the table. Elizabeth raised an eyebrow and returned Jane's gaze, nudging her own food with her fork, determinedly feigning disinterest. Jane sat straighter, her lips parting as if she were about to explain the "strangers" in question. Elizabeth shot her sister a swift shake of her head, silently pleading for restraint. Jane's mouth closed again, though a glimmer of delight remained in her eyes.

Mr. Bennet paused mid-bite, his mouth twitching in faint amusement. He looked between his wife and his two eldest daughters, chewing thoughtfully. Then, his eyes settled on Elizabeth, who caught his wry gaze and returned it with a look that all but begged for his mercy. He took his time finishing his mouthful, then finally spoke, his tone dry as he set down his fork.

"Well, Mrs. Bennet, I daresay these two mysterious strangers must be quite elderly and, quite probably, married as well. I see no reason to raise my blood over so little inducement."

Mrs. Bennet clucked her tongue and fixed her husband with a fierce glare. "Nonsense, Mr. Bennet! You are always so quick to dismiss matters of importance. Why, Hill was told they are quite handsome, and there was no mention at all of wives. If they are, in fact, single and wealthy, I insist that you ride over to Netherfield and introduce yourself at once!"

"Introduce myself?" Mr. Bennet raised his eyebrows, his voice laced with mock astonishment. "Why should I importune them so? They have been in the country less than a day. At least give them a sporting chance at leisure before I go knocking on Netherfield's door."

"Nonsense," Mrs. Bennet replied with conviction. "No one comes to a house and does not expect to meet new acquaintances! A proper gentleman would not leave the matter to chance. Think of our daughters, Mr. Bennet! If you introduce yourself first, why, our girls will have the advantage over all the other families in Meryton!"

Elizabeth stifled a smile and glanced at Jane, who had taken to delicately nibbling on a piece of toast. She raised a brow, and Jane took the hint, clearing her throat to change the subject.

"Did any of the militia officers dine here while we were in London?"

Lydia's head snapped up, her face alight. "Oh, Jane, you cannot imagine! Captain Carter was here nearly every day, was he not, Mama? And Mr. Denny! He has the most charming waistcoat, and his buttons, la! Oh, and how well he looks in his white breeches—"

Kitty sighed dreamily. "And he asked me, personally, if he might take a second cup of tea."

"Oh, yes, because Mr. Denny asks for seconds at every house!" Lydia shot back with a giggle.

"Such handsome officers!" Mrs. Bennet interrupted with a delighted clap of her hands. "I daresay we must invite them all to dine here next week. Who knows, perhaps we might soon see one of you settled, and with a husband in uniform, no less!"

Elizabeth hid a smile behind her teacup as the conversation spiraled from who had looked best at tea, to the color of the officers' horses, to who had nearly tripped in the snow outside Meryton's assembly hall. She shared a quick look with Jane, and after a few more rounds of tales, they each pushed back their chairs and excused themselves from the table.

"I believe I shall take a walk in the garden, even if it is snowy and cold," Elizabeth announced lightly, as they started for the hall. "I could do with a bit of fresh air."

Jane followed her, and the moment they were alone, Jane caught her elbow, forcing Elizabeth to turn around.

"Lizzy, why did you not let me speak of Mr. Bingley and Mr. Darcy? Surely, everyone will hear of them soon enough."

Elizabeth grinned, barely holding back a laugh. "You heard what Papa said. It is not sporting."

"**G**OOD MORNING, DARCY!" BINGLEY greeted him with an almost indecent amount of cheerfulness, fastening his cuffs with quick, efficient movements. "I trust you slept well?"

Darcy glanced up from adjusting his coat, his expression carefully composed. "Quite well, though I might have slept better had we arrived before midnight. And if I had brought my valet."

Bingley only laughed. "Ah, there it is. I know you are putting me on when you exaggerate like that. I say, this place—it is remarkable, is it not? A bit more... character than I anticipated."

"That would be one word for it," Darcy replied, casting a glance around the faded appointments in the sitting room. Despite the estate boasting "good bones," as Bingley had put it last night, something about Netherfield felt slightly off-kilter, as if each item were meticulously selected but lacked the cohesion one expected in such a house. "Though I might prefer my adventures to occur at a reasonable hour."

"Still so particular, I see," Bingley teased, clasping Darcy's shoulder with a friendly pat. "Come now, let us find breakfast. After last night's welcome, I am more than ready to see what else the place has to offer."

With that, he strode out the door, leaving Darcy to follow with a faint sigh. As they descended the staircase, Darcy took in the quiet morning light spilling through the tall windows, casting shadows across the walls and down the corridors.

When they reached the hall, a maid awaited them—a slight girl of no more than fifteen or sixteen, but she held herself with an almost startling composure for one so young. Her expression was one of polite reserve. "Good morning, sirs. Sir Thomas asked me to wait on you and show you to the breakfast room."

"Oh, capital," Bingley replied. "I daresay a bit of biscuit and cheese would not go amiss just now."

The girl bobbed a curtsy and then led them down a hallway. As they entered the breakfast room, Bingley took an appreciative breath, his eyes lighting up at the sight of the long table laden with cold meats, cheeses, and pastries. With his usual buoyant enthusiasm, he immediately reached for a plate, piling it high with bread, ham, and a generous wedge of soft cheese.

"Do you know, Darcy, I am beginning to think this place has been waiting just for us," he remarked cheerfully, adding a flaky pastry to his plate for good measure.

Darcy murmured a polite agreement, though his mind was elsewhere, taking in the quiet but unusual efficiency of the room around them. The young maid paused a few paces from the door, exchanging a few words with another servant—a girl who looked scarcely older than herself.

"Would you advise the master that his guests are at breakfast?" she said with an understated authority that Darcy found remarkable. Her tone was calm, almost... managerial.

The second maid responded with a quick nod. "Yes, Mrs. Jackson," she replied, and hurried from the room, leaving Darcy blinking after her.

Mrs. Jackson? Darcy found himself looking back at the young girl who had led them here, assessing her with sharper scrutiny. Could she truly be married at her age? Or had he mistaken her age altogether? He could hardly keep himself from watching her, studying her demeanor for clues.

But if she noticed his attention, she gave no sign. With a brief curtsy, she left them to their meal, closing the door with a quiet click behind her.

Bingley didn't seem the least bit perturbed by the unusual encounter, lifting his glass in a silent toast to the food before him. He took a hearty bite of ham, humming appreciatively, while Darcy approached the table more slowly, selecting smaller portions than usual, still feeling oddly unsettled.

"I must say, the hospitality here has exceeded my expectations," Bingley continued between bites, his eyes twinkling as he glanced around the room. "It's as if they anticipated our arrival all along."

Darcy merely nodded, his thoughts spinning. He took a small bite of bread, chewing absently as his gaze drifted to the large windows overlooking the grounds. Something about Netherfield—or rather, something about the entire establishment—seemed... out of place. Every servant they had encountered thus far held an air of competency, even pride, that struck him as both unusual and strangely admirable. Yet it felt almost as though he were seeing everything through the wrong end of a telescope, the familiar shapes and functions of estate life slightly distorted, though the essence remained the same.

"Is it just me," Bingley said suddenly, looking over at him with a grin, "or have you never been quite so preoccupied at a breakfast table before?"

Darcy tore his gaze from the window, giving his friend a faint smile. "I cannot quite put my finger on it, Bingley, but there is something... unusual about this place."

"Unusual, perhaps, but in a refreshing way, I think. Everyone is positively delightful, and I've not yet seen one thing amiss." He leaned in conspiratorially, dropping his voice. "Perhaps it is simply the presence of such agreeable company yesterday that has left you in this pensive state."

Darcy gave him a quelling look, but Bingley only chuckled, undeterred, as he continued enjoying his breakfast. Darcy cast one more look around the room before quietly returning to his plate.

Perhaps five minutes later, Sir Thomas entered the breakfast room with a warm smile, his eyes lighting up as he greeted his guests. "Mr. Darcy, Mr. Bingley! I trust you both rested well?"

Bingley stood briefly to greet their host. "Very well, Sir Thomas, thank you. And might I say, we have not had such a breakfast spread since... well, since London, I daresay."

Sir Thomas laughed as he filled his plate with some cold meats and bread. "I am glad to hear it. I must confess, this is the most pleasant company I have had in quite some time. My household tends to be... more reserved." He took a seat, raising his coffee cup with a glint of genuine pleasure in his eyes. "It's the bitter stuff for me. I trust you found a decent pot of tea, Darcy? You always were particular."

"Indeed, very fine. My compliments on your selection."

"Very good. Come, tell me—how have you both kept yourselves busy since I last saw you? I hear things now and then, of course, but my own time in London has been sparse these several years."

Darcy inclined his head politely. "Bingley and I have... delved into business, as it happens. Investments, partnerships—keeping us both rather occupied."

Bingley cut in with a grin. "Occupied? Good heavens, Darcy, don't undersell us! Sir Thomas, Darcy is something of an alchemist. He has a talent for turning the driest of business contracts into gold." He winked. "And I do my best to keep up with him."

Sir Thomas's eyes crinkled with interest. "Is that so? Trade, Darcy? I expect your father was... pleased with that."

Darcy cocked an eyebrow at his friend. "I place the blame squarely at Bingley's feet, Sir Thomas. Whatever fool notion he takes into his head, somehow, he obliges me to muddle through with him."

Sir Thomas laughed heartily. "I suppose I should not be surprised. You were the clever chap of the whole lot in France. And Bingley, you always were both quick to seize an opportunity, even under the most trying circumstances."

Darcy allowed himself a faint smile, leaning back slightly. "You have judged him rightly. But I must say, our ventures these days have been rather satisfactory."

Bingley laughed, nodding in agreement. "True enough. But all this talk of business—I am certain you must have a hundred other stories to tell, Sir Thomas. You left us so quickly in France. Other than hearing you removed to Bath when you returned to England, I hardly know what you have been about."

Sir Thomas sipped his coffee, and his expression seemed to flicker with a touch of something pensive. "Ah, I fear my stories would pale in comparison. Besides, I am an old man, and my efforts these days are mostly confined to this little estate." He set down his coffee and turned his gaze toward them with a curious smile. "And speaking of estates—may I ask what brought you to Netherfield? You must have started for Hertfordshire the moment you heard of it; even my agent had no chance to send word ahead."

Bingley blushed and cleared his throat. Darcy leaned back, gesturing for his friend to take the lead. "Yes, Bingley, what *did* bring us to Netherfield, of all places, and on such urgent timing? I should like to hear that confession as well."

"Oh, well..." Bingley managed a sheepish grin, finally gathering himself. "It is rather a... ahem, unique story. I heard of Netherfield through a lady I met recently in London. She happened to mention her neighborhood and mentioned that a house nearby might soon be... That is..." he cleared his throat again.

Sir Thomas's eyes sharpened with interest, though his tone remained mild. "And the lady's name?"

"Miss Jane Bennet," Bingley admitted, looking slightly abashed.

At that, Sir Thomas's face brightened. "Ah, Miss Bennet! I understand perfectly, then, Mr. Bingley. A gentleman could hardly fail to take an interest in an estate that so neatly suits his wants."

"Well, yes," Bingley replied, clearing his throat yet again and recovering his cheer. "And I had been looking for a chance to get Darcy away from London's bustle, but the stodgy fellow would stir no farther than a half day's drive or so from Town. I thought a country estate so near would give us a pleasant refuge without... complete exile." He shot a quick smile at Darcy, who rolled his eyes.

Sir Thomas studied Bingley for a moment, his smile slipping into something more wistful before he sighed and set his fork aside. "Well, you heard rightly, I am afraid. I *am* rather desperate to find a tenant." His gaze drifted toward the window as though he were seeing something far beyond the frosty garden outside. "I had hoped... very much desired, that is... to stay on at least through Christmas. But I realize that might be asking too much."

"Oh." Bingley blinked, clearly taken aback, but he quickly gathered himself. "Well, I am sure we can consider any terms that might be agreeable to you, sir. I would not wish to... inconvenience you."

Sir Thomas inclined his head gratefully. "Thank you, Mr. Bingley. I appreciate that consideration."

Just then, Miss Flora—the maid from the previous night—appeared quietly in the doorway and inclined her head toward Sir Thomas. "Pardon, sir," she murmured. "The master is wanted."

"Of course, of course." Sir Thomas rose, his gaze lingering warmly on Darcy and Bingley. "Please, continue your breakfast. I shall return shortly, and we can discuss any details you might wish to go over. My people will see to your comfort." He turned to Flora, gesturing for her to lead the way, and slipped out, leaving the door ajar behind him.

Bingley took a hearty bite of his toast, completely at ease. "Well, Darcy, I must say—this has been a most satisfactory beginning, wouldn't you agree? I could hardly have anticipated the master would be Sir Thomas himself!"

Darcy, however, frowned, glancing at the door through which Sir Thomas had just exited. "Did you not find him... altered?"

Bingley looked up, surprised. "Altered? He seemed perfectly genial to me. And clearly pleased to see us."

Darcy shook his head slowly. "I remember Sir Thomas as a man of conviction—a decisive, powerful figure. The sort who could turn a room to his will with a single word. When we escaped to Calais, he commanded every detail with precision. Yet now..." He trailed off, his expression thoughtful.

Bingley tilted his head, considering. "You may have a point. He does seem quieter—more subdued than I recall." He tapped his chin thoughtfully. "Did we not hear that he had some trouble after his return to Paris? Something about being held for some months?"

"Yes." Darcy squinted as he tried to recall. "That was the rumor, though few enough real facts reached us. My father and others rallied to support him, but it was all in the hands of the diplomats, you remember. And there was talk that he had suffered deprivation... perhaps even worse, until his full ransom was paid."

Bingley set his fork down, his good humor momentarily faded. "So, you think... that he might have been mistreated?"

Darcy nodded slowly. "It would explain a great deal. If he suffered... or worse... It is a hard thing to return from, especially for a man of his strength." He fell silent, thoughts churning as he tried to reconcile the once-unbreakable figure of Sir Thomas with the man he'd just seen.

Nine

CHARLOTTE ARRIVED AT LONGBOURN just after noon, her cheeks rosy from the cold and her eyes bright with curiosity as Hill showed her into the sitting room where Elizabeth and Jane were enjoying a rare moment of quiet. Charlotte barely had time to exchange greetings with Jane and Elizabeth before Mrs. Bennet swept in, delighted to see the daughter of her good friend Lady Lucas.

"Oh, Charlotte, how good of you to visit! And how convenient, too—now that we have such news to share!" Mrs. Bennet's eyes danced with glee, her voice dropping to a conspiring hush. "Have you heard, Charlotte? Two wealthy gentlemen arrived at Netherfield just last night, asking after the property! Perhaps we will, at last, have some valuable neighbors there. I am sure Mr. Bennet will drive over this very afternoon to call on them, and it is only a matter of time before we know everything. I daresay I shall have a daughter settled before Twelfth Night!"

Elizabeth cleared her throat. "Mama, please, we have only just returned from London. Perhaps Charlotte is here to see us for reasons *beyond* gentlemen."

But Mrs. Bennet waved this off with a laugh. "Oh, nonsense, Lizzy. *Everyone* knows why we are all interested in Netherfield these days, and I daresay it is a far sight better than that nonsense that is carrying on now. Oh! I must ask Hill to order some ham."

With a mutter of excuse, she hurried off, leaving the three young ladies alone. Elizabeth settled back in her seat and raised an eyebrow at her friend. "I trust you're here to offer congratulations on our return," she said dryly, "or perhaps to share news of the latest scandal in Meryton?"

"Oh, certainly," Charlotte replied, "for you must know, the whole town has been in uproar since the latest rumors about Netherfield began this morning. Mrs. Long said she was 'sure' she saw your uncle's carriage yesterday, closely following a strange one with two wealthy-looking gentlemen inside. Almost as if you were traveling *together*, hmm?"

Elizabeth shot her sister a wry look. "Almost."

Charlotte grinned. "Well, I thought it prudent to come and hear your side of the story, since I could hardly trust anyone else's."

Jane coughed. "What is being said? We have not heard much of Meryton's opinion yet, only that there seem to be some concerns about Sir Thomas's... ability to keep the estate."

Charlotte leaned forward, lowering her voice slightly. "More than concerns, I am afraid. Some things have worsened substantially in the two months you were away."

A knot formed in Elizabeth's stomach. "Tell us, Charlotte."

"Some of the townsfolk—most, in fact—have been saying for some time that surely Sir Thomas will have to leave Netherfield soon. Good riddance, they all say."

"Oh, but that is old stuff. You said as much in your last letter," Jane replied. "What *more* is there?" She emphasized this with a significant widening of her eyes and an odd tilt of her head that drew Elizabeth's notice.

Charlotte cleared her throat. "Yes. Ah... Mr. Archer—you remember, my father just brought on a new man of all work, and he came to us directly from Netherfield—he verified it all last week. He insisted it was only a matter of time."

Elizabeth's brows furrowed, a pang of disappointment prickling her. "So, the rumors *are* true, then? Sir Thomas will lose Netherfield?"

Charlotte hesitated, glancing between Elizabeth and Jane, her expression a mix of sadness and sympathy. "It is very likely. Mr. Archer heard it from Mr. Jackson himself, the head coachman. The estate is simply too costly for Sir Thomas to maintain alone, especially with all the... expenses he has there."

"I imagine the vicar is pleased," Elizabeth grumbled, shaking her head.

"Oh, yes," Charlotte sighed. "Most in Meryton think he should abandon his efforts, or at least keep his affairs *much* more discreet. A few have even gone so far as to say that if he cannot afford his own household, he certainly cannot afford all his *other* endeavors, and they think very ill of him for it. I am sorry to say that most are wishing for his failure."

Elizabeth folded her arms and glanced out the window. "It is a shame that kindness and good sense should not be enough to secure him a welcome in this town. What a miserable state of affairs."

Charlotte gave a small, sad smile. "Perhaps that is why he will be grateful if some other gentleman should be interested in taking on the lease. It might give him some relief—though I will be sorry to see him abandon Netherfield entirely."

Jane tilted her head, a frown tugging at the corners of her mouth. "It is all so terribly sad. I cannot help but wish there was something more to be done."

"Oh, Jane," Charlotte sighed. "Sad, yes, but hardly unusual." She turned her gaze to Elizabeth. "Even if he could afford to stay at Netherfield, Papa says he believes Sir Thomas was going to be forced to remove eventually. The town simply does not wish for him to stay—some talk of refusing to take business from Netherfield, although I believe there is nothing in it... yet. If Sir Thomas was not so diligent about paying his debts, I am sure they would do more than just talk about turning away his business."

Jane's brow furrowed. "Oh, dear. I hope that Mr. Bingley and Mr. Darcy are not turned away by such talk."

Elizabeth gave a nonchalant shrug, though her interest was piqued. "We can hardly assume they are aware of all the gossip just yet. Perhaps they merely wish for a bit of land and peace. Not every gentleman has such a sensitive constitution."

Charlotte smiled at that. "Then let us hope they are made of stern enough stuff, for the welcome they are likely to receive from Meryton is not a warm one."

As Darcy and Bingley finished the last of their breakfast, the maid who had been tending the room approached with a slight curtsy. "Mr. Roberts will be along shortly to conduct you on a tour of the house, sirs."

"Oh, jolly good. Thank you," Bingley said.

They waited several minutes, during which Bingley polished off a second helping of cold ham and cast frequent glances toward the door. Finally, Roberts appeared, a little out of breath as he paused to straighten his coat before stepping into the room. His posture was impeccable, though his expression looked somewhat overwrought.

"Good morning, gentlemen," he greeted them, nodding politely. "I trust you found breakfast to your satisfaction?"

Bingley rose with an easy smile. "Very much so, Mr. Roberts. I am sure we have our work cut out for us if we mean to match such a spread at Netherfield."

"Sir Thomas takes pride in his hospitality," Roberts replied. "If it suits, I am here to guide you through the house as you requested."

"Indeed, lead on," Darcy said, rising as well, his gaze drifting back to the maid who had announced Roberts. As she lingered near the door, Darcy found himself wondering about the curious assortment of staff he had encountered thus far. The mix of youth and experience, each person marked by something distinct, something unusual—it was hard to ignore.

Roberts gestured for them to follow as he led the way down the hall. "Here we have the library," he said, opening the double doors to reveal a beautifully appointed room, lined floor-to-ceiling with volumes on polished walnut shelves. "Sir Thomas has taken care to maintain the library in fine order. I believe it is one of his favorite rooms."

"Remarkable," Darcy murmured, his gaze sweeping over the room. It was evident that Sir Thomas's library had been amassed with both care and ambition. Each shelf was immaculately organized, volumes arranged by subject and era, the collection spanning from Greek and Roman histories to modern studies on agriculture and estate management.

Well-bound classics mingled with leather-bound first editions, and here and there, Darcy spotted a few rare titles that he himself had sought for his own collection, with only occasional success. The polished walnut shelves spoke of attentive maintenance, their surfaces gleaming in the morning light, yet the library bore signs of true use—small bookmarks protruding here and there, a brass inkwell freshly filled, and a ledger left slightly askew on the writing desk, as though Sir Thomas had only recently abandoned it.

Darcy's hand itched to pull down a book or two, to examine Sir Thomas's interests more closely. Libraries, he had always believed, offered a window into a man's mind, and this one suggested both discernment and intellect. He was about to step further inside when Roberts gave a slight cough, drawing his attention back to the tour.

"If you will, sirs, this way," Roberts continued, guiding them to the adjoining door. "Through here is the master's study. Sir Thomas often finds himself here in the mornings, particularly when matters of estate require his attention."

The study was more intimate than the library, with a sturdy oak desk, well-worn and ink-stained from years of use. A map of the estate hung on the wall, and an array of ledgers and correspondence were stacked neatly in trays. Darcy took note of the fine leather furnishings, softened with age, and could easily imagine Sir Thomas here, working late into the evening.

As they proceeded down the hall, Roberts paused outside another set of doors. "The second drawing room," he announced, opening the doors to reveal a spacious, elegantly furnished room. "Sir Thomas uses this room but rarely, but I am given to understand that the previous owners, Mr. And Mrs. Bromley, favored this room for receiving guests, particularly in the evenings. It has a window facing westward and a fair prospect of the fields at sundown."

Darcy noted the faded, though once-splendid damask drapes and the slight layer of dust along the edges of the carpet. Indeed, the room had not been used in some time, though its grandeur would be easy to resurrect.

As they turned to leave, a maid approached, glancing at Roberts and leaning in to whisper something to him. Darcy could not hear the words, but he noted a brief, almost imperceptible frown on Roberts's face before he turned back to them, his voice carefully neutral.

"It seems the weather is holding steady for now," he said. "But snow is expected later, so perhaps you might enjoy a walk around the grounds before it arrives. The stables are well worth a visit, if you are so inclined."

Bingley paused, looking across the hall at another set of double doors that stood silent sentry near the main entrance. "What about the ballroom?" he asked. "It seems we are already nearby."

Roberts hesitated, glancing from Bingley to the doors, his demeanor stiffening. "The ballroom is currently shrouded, sir. Some repairs are needed, and it may not be suitable for viewing at present."

Darcy raised an eyebrow. "All the more reason for us to have a look, surely? We would wish to know the extent of any repairs before making arrangements."

Roberts's jaw tensed, and he cast a quick glance at the maid, who was watching him closely. "If you would not mind, sirs," he said after a pause, "Sir Thomas is best suited to discuss the specifics of any necessary repairs."

Bingley and Darcy exchanged glances, and Bingley gave a light shrug. "Very well, Roberts. I shall speak with Sir Thomas himself. I trust you will show us the grounds, then?"

Roberts's shoulders relaxed slightly, and he gave a nod. "Yes, sir. If you would allow me a moment, I will see that your coats are brought to the door so you may view the stables and grounds comfortably."

He turned to the maid, who curtsied and hurried away to carry out the request. Darcy watched Roberts closely, still puzzling over the reluctance he sensed in him, as if there was something more than just "repairs" behind the closed doors of the ballroom.

The estate grounds were pleasant, if not extravagant. Paths wound through modest gardens lined with bare winter trees, their branches arching over pathways that would surely be charming in spring. Darcy noted the well-kept hedges and the scattering of berry-laden holly bushes, adding a touch of color to the otherwise frosted landscape. As they moved along, Roberts pointed out a well-maintained kitchen garden and a small orchard, currently dormant in the winter chill. Bingley, clearly enjoying the fresh air and open space, remarked on the tranquility of the grounds, and Darcy had to admit the landscape had a pleasing, unpretentious quality.

They arrived at the stables to find a tall man with an eye patch just brushing the flanks of a cart horse. Mr. Jackson, the coachman from last night. Jackson nodded a polite greeting, but his brow was slightly crumpled with suspicion as he watched Darcy and Bingley surveying his domain.

His broad shoulders and firm stance were unmistakably those of a soldier, which Darcy noted with quiet approval. The man had a steady air about him, though, in the daylight, Darcy was struck by his relatively young age. Late twenties, perhaps? Darcy recalled the girl in the house—a maid, he'd presumed—who had been addressed as "Mrs. Jackson." Could she truly be his wife? There was something strangely incongruent about it.

After examining the stables, well-kept and efficient if modest in size, they concluded their tour of the grounds and returned indoors. Roberts offered them an opportunity to "refresh" themselves before continuing, an offer that struck Darcy as unusual, though he could find no polite way to decline.

"Why not, Darcy?" Bingley chuckled as they climbed the staircase. "A bit of country leisure, I daresay! It is not as if we are in any rush."

They were halfway down the corridor when a distinct, unmistakable sound caught their attention—a baby's cry, clear and shrill, from somewhere down the hall. Darcy and Bingley exchanged a wide-eyed look, stopping in their tracks.

"Did you just hear...?" Bingley trailed off, staring toward the door marked with a ribbon from which the sound had come.

Darcy nodded slowly, staring at the door with raised brows. He had heard nothing about other guests, nor had there been any indication that Sir Thomas was married or had children. A brief silence stretched between them, only to be interrupted by the opening of the door.

Sir Thomas emerged, stripped down to his shirtsleeves and waistcoat, his forearms bared, looking markedly less formal than he had earlier. Beside him, a short, plump woman was speaking in hushed tones, but both stopped abruptly when they spotted Darcy and Bingley in the hall. Sir Thomas's face paled as his gaze met theirs, and a flicker of unease passed over his features.

Bingley, who had never been one for circumspection, blurted, "Was that a baby, man? I say, er... congratulations?"

A resigned sigh escaped Sir Thomas, and he murmured something to the woman at his side, who quickly nodded and excused herself, casting a brief but respectful glance toward the two gentlemen.

Sir Thomas took a steadying breath and addressed them. "Indeed, it was. Perhaps... we should have a word in private. My study?"

Darcy set his jaw. At last, they were to have some answers. "Certainly."

Ten

S IR THOMAS LED THEM into his study, the heavy door closing with a soft but
definitive thud. With a slight, apologetic gesture, Sir Thomas reached for the brandy
decanter on his desk and poured a glass for each of them. Darcy observed with a trace
of unease as the decanter ran dry, just as he poured the last drop into Bingley's glass. Sir
Thomas himself took none, instead sinking wearily into the large chair behind the desk.

He took a moment, his fingers tapping restlessly on the arm of his chair. "This is... not
an easy thing to explain. Nor a simple story."

Darcy leaned forward—alert, but holding his tongue. Bingley, beside him, watched
with unguarded curiosity.

"After France," Sir Thomas began slowly, "I had some modest fortune—well-invested,
enough to live comfortably. More than comfortably, I suppose. I believed that I would
retire to a quiet life, perhaps in Bath. But... well, you both know as well as I how such
notions change when the weight of war settles on a man's conscience."

He looked at Darcy and Bingley in turn, his eyes keen, searching. "Shortly after returning, I became involved in assisting wounded soldiers—some of whom I had been
imprisoned with. Men who had seen horrors that would make the strongest of us shudder.
It started as simple relief efforts, helping them find doctors, lodging, employment when
possible." He sighed. "But the need grew, and I knew I could do more than just play a
supporting role."

Darcy sensed where this was going, and his gaze sharpened, waiting.

"Five years ago," Sir Thomas continued, "I took the rather mad notion of purchasing Netherfield. The house was large, with ample land, and it seemed to be a perfect place to offer... refuge."

"For soldiers," Bingley murmured, his tone admiring.

"Yes. For those wounded in body and soul." Sir Thomas's eyes grew distant, his voice softening. "I employed two full-time nurses, with a physician and more nurses on retainer. I set aside the ballroom as an infirmary so those in most fragile health could receive the care they needed—round the clock, if necessary." He gave a faint smile, though there was little humor in it. "It was my hope that it would be a place for recovery, dignity, perhaps even some degree of peace."

Darcy and Bingley exchanged a quick look; the ballroom explained at last.

"Of course," Sir Thomas continued, "not all wounds are physical. Some of these men..." He trailed off, a shadow darkening his face. "Some had been damaged so deeply by the war that they could scarcely function. They'd have ended up in the streets or worse without intervention." He hesitated, then shook his head. "Most recover well enough to leave, to start new lives. But some—like Roberts and Jackson—have stayed on. I have been fortunate enough to find them work here."

Darcy nodded slowly, feeling a twinge of respect for Sir Thomas that went beyond their shared past. It was noble, undeniably so, and the clear-eyed dedication in Sir Thomas's gaze said more than any words could have.

"Originally, it was a cause that had widespread support," Sir Thomas said with a bitter smile. "Meryton's residents were proud to say that one of their neighbors was aiding the war effort in such a way. I'd donors—wealthy philanthropists who funded our efforts generously from afar. Everyone spoke glowingly of Netherfield and its occupants."

Darcy's eyes narrowed. "I sense a 'but' in there."

Sir Thomas's frown deepened. "*But...* three years ago, I... found myself in a position to help another... group of people."

He paused, collecting his thoughts, and Bingley leaned forward, almost quivering now in eagerness to hear more.

"I learned about a young woman in a certain predicament." His voice grew softer. "An 'unfortunate,' if you will. She was... alone, with nowhere to turn. There was... nothing I could do to help her then—or so I thought—and to my eternal regret, I learned she was sent away. I never knew where. A workhouse, most probably."

Sir Thomas's voice was tight with guilt. "I did not help her, and she was... lost. The shame of it nearly destroyed me. I thought to myself that Netherfield could do... more. It had the capacity to take in more than just wounded soldiers. So, I made a decision."

He looked up, and Darcy could see the raw determination in his eyes. "I began offering shelter to young women in similar circumstances. Women with nowhere to go and no one to turn to."

Bingley blinked, taken aback. "Young women?"

"Most of them," Sir Thomas answered, his voice barely above a whisper. "Girls, really. Girls in their 'interesting' condition—young, lost, and in need. Most other shelters demand that such women give up their children. But here, I allow them to stay and raise their children if they wish, or, in some cases, I've found families willing to discreetly adopt." He paused, a flicker of sadness crossing his face. "The youngest we ever took in was but th irteen."

Darcy felt his stomach twist as he processed Sir Thomas's words. He looked toward Bingley, who had gone pale with astonishment.

Bingley swallowed, his gaze dropping to the glass in his hand. "The... the maids... those are they, are they not? They are all so young!"

"Yes," Sir Thomas said, his tone heavy with resignation. "Several of them are those I once took in. Not all stay, of course, but some remain on, even if their children are weaned or placed elsewhere. And, well, you can imagine... some have even found companionship among the men who also needed shelter." He offered a wan smile. "Mr. and Mrs. Jackson were married just last month. A man once broken in body, a woman once broken in spirit. They've found healing here."

For a moment, silence reigned in the study. Darcy and Bingley were both struggling to absorb the magnitude of what Sir Thomas had done, and the weight of it hung between them like a silent, undeniable presence.

Finally, Bingley spoke, his voice filled with approval. "Sir Thomas... there was no need to be secretive about this! No wonder you did not wish to give up the house until after Christmas. All those people who would be displaced... Nay, I would never ask such a thing! What you have done here, it... It is admirable beyond words."

But Darcy's mind was already working over the more practical implications. "How," he asked slowly, "have you financed all this, Sir Thomas? Surely, this could not have been supported with your own funds alone. And would your supporters in London... be aware of these other endeavors?"

Sir Thomas sagged visibly, the proud set of his shoulders softening as he leaned back in his chair. "You are right, Darcy. At first, I had plenty of support. But yes, when word began to spread about my sheltering unwed mothers... and in the same house as all those unmarried young men! —well, my benefactors were swift to withdraw." He shook his head. "These days, I am barely able to make ends meet. My personal fortune is all but exhausted, and Netherfield's upkeep... it is well beyond my means now."

Darcy felt a surge of anger—anger at the small-mindedness of society, at the cruelty of those who would judge and condemn without understanding. But he tempered it, glancing at Sir Thomas with a steady gaze. "And... your neighbors? Surely they know—they *must* know about all this."

Sir Thomas's expression grew bleak. "Most of the town would like nothing better than to see me gone. The vicar decries my work as shameful and a black disgrace upon the town, and several local businesses have threatened to refuse service to Netherfield. Even if I could afford to stay, I do not believe I could continue my work here, not with such mounting hostility. It is not fair to them—my friends here—to know they are so reviled whenever they take an errand into town." He exhaled heavily. "The burden has grown too great. I do not see how I can carry on, even if I were to somehow secure the funds."

A heavy silence fell between them, the bleakness of Sir Thomas's confession hanging thick in the air. Darcy looked at Bingley, who appeared equally at a loss, his usually bright expression shadowed with dismay.

Sir Thomas rose, straightening his waistcoat with an air of finality. "I understand, gentlemen, if these revelations change your minds about the lease." He forced a smile that did little to conceal his sadness. "Please, excuse me. You'll no doubt wish to confer with each other, and I am... expected in the infirmary for my rounds."

With that, he turned and left, the soft click of the door closing behind him, leaving Darcy and Bingley alone in the silence of the study.

E LIZABETH CLOSED THE DOOR to their room with a firm click, her gaze sharp as she turned to her sister. "Jane, what did you mean when Charlotte was here—about what she wrote to you in her last letter?"

Jane seated herself at the vanity and began to fuss with her hair—for no need, since it already looked perfect—and avoided Elizabeth's gaze in the mirror. "Whatever do you mean, Lizzy? Did she say nothing in the letter she sent to you?"

"Not a word beyond Maria's terrible piano practicing with Lydia and John sneaking sweets from the larder."

"Oh, surely, she wrote more than that. Perhaps you overlooked it." Jane pinched her right cheek, then turned her head from side to side to compare the effect.

"Not a chance. And you can give up the act at the vanity, for you are putting on airs like Kitty when we both know plain and well that is not your way. You have been remarkably evasive since before we left London. What *is* going on, Jane?"

Jane sighed, then twisted around in her seat, clasping her hands in her lap as she stared at the floor. "Elizabeth, I... Well, yes, I do know more than I let on. Charlotte... she wrote to me about it while we were in London, saying the same thing she just told us below. That it is beyond certain that Sir Thomas is pockets to let."

Elizabeth folded her arms. "Why would she not write the same to me? Or why would you 'forget' to mention it? That is far more than a simple oversight, dear sister."

"Because..." Jane worried her lip between her teeth before looking up with a frank expression, shedding her initial reluctance. "Because Charlotte and I agreed it would weigh on you too much. You have always had such sympathy for Sir Thomas and what he has tried to do here. Charlotte knew that if you heard the state of things, it would only make you miserable and ruin your time in London."

"That is the most preposterous thing! Ruin my time in London? What, was Charlotte expecting me to dance at balls every evening until I snagged a husband? I know Mama thought two months in London were sufficient to the task, but Charlotte could not be such a fool."

"No, not..." Jane frowned. "There was nothing you could do. It would have simply outraged you until you were tugging the sleeve of every wealthy gentleman we met and making uncomfortable demands that would have placed Uncle in an awkward position. You would have tried to mend the thing yourself, thinking that our time in London might afford us the opportunity to bang on doors and drag unwilling gentlemen along on some crusade. It would have—"

"It would have ruined your little holiday in London?" Elizabeth finished.

"Made you a laughingstock," Jane corrected.

Elizabeth narrowed her eyes. Her pulse was drumming through her limbs until her very veins pounded. "What else would you have me do? Just... *watch* while so many people lose the only home that is open to them?"

"Lizzy, some things are beyond our control."

Elizabeth covered her mouth with her hand and paced around the bed, finally sinking onto it and clutching a pillow to her stomach. She wanted to shake and cry, and... and just make it all go away. But then, something pricked her as sharply as a pin to the back of her neck.

"Tell me something, Jane. How *did* Mr. Bingley hear about Netherfield?"

Jane's eyes widened, and she sucked in a breath. "Oh, I am... I am quite sure it was a coincidence."

"What part? The part where he was nearly oozing into a puddle at your feet in Aunt's drawing room, or the part where he just 'happened' to stumble up to the same coaching inn yesterday?"

Jane swallowed. She opened her mouth, and Elizabeth put up a finger to silence her. "No more excuses, dear sister. The truth—*all* of it. When did you conspire with Mr. Bingley to send him to Netherfield?"

"Conspire! You make it sound very devious, indeed."

"Convince me, then, that it was not. What were you and Mr. Bingley talking about while I was playing the piano with Mr. Darcy beside me?"

Jane's face flushed, and she shifted uncomfortably. "Perhaps... I did *mention* Netherfield, yes."

Elizabeth pressed a hand to her forehead. "Why would you do such a thing, Jane? You knew Sir Thomas could lose his home, and yet you practically delivered it to strangers. How *could* you?"

"Lizzy, please." Jane took a shaky breath. "Not bringing anyone would not change Sir Thomas's position. He cannot keep the house."

Elizabeth shook her head, incredulous. "Then why *them*? Why tempt Mr. Bingley and Mr. Darcy here, knowing that, of all people, they might very well take possession of it right away? They are richer than Croesus! They have no need of circumspection or diligence and probably no patience, either!"

Jane hesitated. "Because... Oh, very well. You may as well know the whole of it. I told Aunt about Sir Thomas, Lizzy. She was adamant that we not say anything to you until it was unavoidable, but she did consider it possible that something might be done."

Elizabeth's jaw dropped. "She invited them on purpose. Just for this!"

"We thought that the *right* tenants might help Sir Thomas. If someone kind, someone with influence and means, were to lease Netherfield, perhaps Sir Thomas's work would continue. Perhaps they would be willing to... offer support."

"Jane! How could you..." She drew a shaking breath. "You deliberately withheld everything from Mr. Bingley and Mr. Darcy, and you knew—*knew*—they might be drawn into all of this against their knowledge. That they might find themselves trapped in a mess they never intended! You even used..." She struggled for the right word, her voice trembling. "Your charms! You *tempted* him into this!"

Jane flushed deeper, but kept her head high. "I did what I thought was best. Aunt Gardiner has known them—or known of their reputation, at least—for years. Lizzy, they have influence, they have wealth. She says the Darcys were always involved in charitable ends, and Mr. Bingley has a reputation for doing the same—surely, if they understood, they might wish to help."

"Help?" Elizabeth's voice was nearly a hiss. "Or are they just to be used? To say nothing of Sir Thomas! He is in a desperate enough state already without being dragged into some scheme where everyone will be in for a rude surprise." Her face was flushed with anger, but she caught herself, staring at her sister in disbelief. "And to think you would involve *me* in it as well! I thought it was all some odd coincidence, but you put me—both of us—forward to tempt the gentlemen here."

"It was not like—"

"Oh, hang your excuses! Do you know how this looks? They may see through your little scheme and even connect this manipulation to our uncle. Jane, they have the power to utterly ruin him if he offended them! How could you not see that?"

Jane's voice wavered, her eyes wide and pleading. "Lizzy, Mr. Bingley is too good to be offended. He would never retaliate against Uncle. I am sure he would forgive us."

Elizabeth turned away, her expression set. "Perhaps Mr. Bingley. But Mr. Darcy?" She shook her head. "Mr. Darcy is not a man whose resentment one should cultivate. He might not be so quick to forgive." She drew in a long breath, shoulders tense. "No. I cannot let this go. I will take the carriage to Netherfield myself and explain—somehow."

"Lizzy!" Jane cried, reaching for her arm. "Please, that is too bold. Surely, they will understand."

Elizabeth shook her head. "Mr. Darcy deserves honesty, even if it is delayed beyond reason or the cause stretches all credulity. Perhaps he can forgive some of it if he sees that I am willing to be truthful. And if it is too late... well, I would rather meet that disappointment head-on than live with the shame of being thought deceitful."

And with that, she left the room, heedless of Jane's protests as she scrambled downstairs and reached for her wrap. There was no time to lose.

Eleven

"S TEADY, GIRL." ELIZABETH LEANED forward, patting her horse as she guided it down the narrow lane toward Netherfield. No time for a carriage. She had barely managed to get the mare saddled and away without her mother questioning her departure—or suffering some sort of mishap, for she was no accomplished rider—and now, here she was, riding alone across half-frozen fields, her breath misting in the sharp morning air.

The house rose over the ridge, and Elizabeth's body tingled with a jolt of nerves—an odd twist of anticipation and dread. She was not entirely certain what she would say, but she knew she could not leave it unsaid.

She guided her horse around the side of the house rather than up the main drive, hoping to avoid drawing unnecessary attention. As she approached the rear entrance, she caught sight of a familiar figure bundled in a thick shawl. Miss Flora was crouched beside the back steps with a large brass bucket, disposing of ashes from the morning's hearth cleanings. Her cheeks were flushed from the cold, and she looked up as Elizabeth dismounted, pushing a stray strand of hair back under her cap.

Elizabeth wasted no time and raised her voice to call out, "Miss Flora!"

"Miss Elizabeth?" Miss Flora straightened, her posture cautious. "What brings you here?"

Elizabeth dismounted and led her horse closer. "I need to speak with Mr. Darcy and Mr. Bingley. Are they... here?"

"Yes, miss, they have been here since last evening," Miss Flora replied, her brows lifting slightly.

Elizabeth swallowed, nerving herself up for what must be done. Oh, dear… "Do you think there is a way I might speak with them?"

"A-alone, Miss?"

Elizabeth glanced over her shoulder as if her father could hear her even now, asking for a private audience with two unmarried men in a house most considered disreputable. "Please. It is urgent."

Miss Flora hesitated, her gaze shifting back toward the house. "If you'll give your horse to Mr. Jackson and come in to wait in the drawing room, miss, I shall see what I can do."

Elizabeth exhaled, watching as the maid disappeared through the door. She had not yet considered exactly how to explain this mess, but with each passing moment, she felt the words taking shape. She let a stable boy take her horse and made her way inside toward the drawing room.

As soon as the door closed behind her, she immediately began pacing, her mind in a feverish whirl of thoughts and half-formed explanations. Every way she imagined putting the matter to Mr. Darcy felt inadequate—either too forward for any "lady"—such as she ought to be—to consider, or too restrained considering the magnitude of the offense.

At last, after what felt like an eternity, the door opened, and Mr. Darcy entered alone. Her eyes darted beyond him in some panicked disbelief. Where was Mr. Bingley? Mr. Bingley might soften the blow. He might lighten the room or be persuaded to understand…

But it was only Mr. Darcy. His expression was grave, his gaze steady but darkened with something that looked very much like disapproval. Or resentment.

So, he knew. He had pieced the puzzle together quite without her and had already formed his opinion.

She took a deep breath, steeling herself as she stepped forward. "Mr. Darcy, I hardly know where to begin, but I… I felt it necessary to speak with you directly." She paused, hoping he might say something to soften his cool expression, but he remained silent, watching her with an unyielding gaze. Her pulse quickened, and she clasped her hands more tightly. "You have been… terribly used, I am afraid. You and Mr. Bingley both."

His face betrayed nothing. The words tumbled out of her mouth faster than she could temper them. "I have only just learned that my sister—my sister and Aunt Gardiner, in their hope to do some good, have misled you most unfairly. I am mortified beyond measure. It was wrong, very wrong of them to deceive you so—to tempt you into coming here under false pretenses."

She chanced a glance up at him, searching his face for any sign of forgiveness or understanding, but he stood resolute, his expression unreadable. Her voice faltered, and she dropped her gaze again, feeling the heat rise to her cheeks. "Please, do not blame my uncle," she added. "He is innocent in this—only doing what he was asked because he... he loves my aunt, and seeks to please her."

She fell silent, helplessly watching his stoic figure, her heart hammering as she waited for him to respond.

Mr. Darcy's face was black as a storm. "And you, Miss Elizabeth," he said, his voice low, though not unkind. "Did you have no inkling of their intent when you encountered us yesterday? You knew well enough of our plans to tour Netherfield."

Elizabeth's cheeks burned. "I... I knew that it was your intent, yes. But I did not know, at the time, that Sir Thomas's situation was so desperate as it has been since revealed to me. Nor did I know what manner of communication Mr. Bingley had with Sir Thomas's agent."

"But you knew about the house. You knew what was carried on here and chose to say nothing."

She swallowed, and her gaze faltered. "I did not feel it was my place to interfere in what I thought might be a simple viewing of the estate. I had no way of knowing that Sir Thomas himself did not hope to speak with you." She let out a shaky breath. "But once I learned of my sister's... intent... and the fact that it was truly *she* who arranged this... deception... I could not rest until I spoke to you, in the hope that I might somehow make things right."

Mr. Darcy said nothing for several leaden seconds, and his eyes were like molten coals, searing her conscience. *Oh, dash it all!* Elizabeth wanted to sink through the floorboards, to never hear the names Darcy or Bingley again, such was her shame. And Jane! Oh, the words she meant to have with her sister and her aunt...

At last, Mr. Darcy gave a slow nod. "Indeed, Miss Elizabeth, you are correct—this must be put right."

She closed her eyes. "Sir, I am quite prepared to accept whatever censure you—"

"And what, Miss Elizabeth, do you think your apologies will accomplish? We are here, are we not? We have seen the truth of the matter for ourselves and cannot un-know what we have learned. Is that how you go about affairs in your family, Miss Elizabeth? Setting unwitting gentlemen into unbidden circumstances for your own pleasure? Or did you seek something else? Hoping some wealthy man falls into your trap?"

Her jaw worked in shame, but at his last words, her ire flashed, and she met his eyes. "I did no such thing! Nor did my sister, truly, for all her underhanded scheming. If you choose to believe that, then I shall withdraw both my apology and my presence, for I see that nothing could sway you from your opinion. I only wished, as I said, to set the matter right to the best of my ability."

"I have agreed, if you remember, that it *must* be set right."

She regarded him with a skeptical look. "Yet your resentment makes that improbable."

Mr. Darcy's rigid stance softened all at once, and he turned to pace the length of the rug, rubbing his jaw... but she could have sworn that his hand concealed a faint smile. "Though I cannot deny that I feel used in this affair, I must admit that I had already resolved to help Sir Thomas, regardless."

Elizabeth blinked, her breath catching in surprise. "You... you had? But why?"

Darcy turned to face her, but his gaze remained unfocused, distant. "Because, Miss Bennet, Sir Thomas Ashford is no stranger to me. We have met before—in France, under very different circumstances. I owe him my life, as surely as Bingley does. And upon learning of his work here, I find that, regardless of what the world might think of it, he is engaged in a cause both noble and necessary."

Elizabeth's heart swelled with a mixture of relief and disbelief. "Then... you mean to support him?"

"'Support him'... such a vague phrase, with so many meanings."

She frowned and dared to step closer. "And which meaning do you choose?"

"So long as he continues in his charity, Sir Thomas shall not want for a penny."

Her eyes rounded. "You... you would go so far?"

Such a confession—seemingly complete and total affirmation—ought to have produced an expression of satisfaction on the gentlemen's face upon her acknowledgment. But Darcy's features remained carefully neutral. Elizabeth watched the flickering of his gaze as he seemed to be thinking, weighing his words.

"You consider that 'far,' Miss Elizabeth?"

"Well, it is... it is a hundred miles more than any other has done."

Mr. Darcy smiled faintly and huffed a short laugh as he turned to pace the room once more. "And who else should do it but I?"

Elizabeth swallowed, one hand tugging uncomfortably at the fingers of the other hand. Was this a test? "What of Mr. Bingley, sir? I should imagine that anything one of you undertakes would quite naturally affect the other."

"Such understated phrases do you no credit, Miss Elizabeth." He turned to glance at her again. "What you actually mean is that by me entering into a commitment to support Sir Thomas, I could be entirely alienating my business partner unless he is equally willing to suffer the consequences with me."

She pursed her lips and arched her brows. "Well?"

That faint smile returned. "I think you underestimate Bingley's impulsiveness, as well as his generous nature, if you could have any doubt of his answer."

She let go a breath in relief. "Sir, that... that is wonderful! Why, that means..." She was trembling head to foot as the dear, familiar faces she had come to know from Netherfield tumbled through her mind. So many of them—most, if not all, driven here by circumstances not of their choosing—and now, they would be able to stay in their home, in the little "family" they had founded here, through Christmas and beyond. "Sir, that means more than you can possibly imagine."

He drew in a long sigh. "No, I know precisely what it means. But I have come to realize that money alone will not suffice." He hesitated, his eyes narrowing thoughtfully. "The censure of public opinion is as dangerous an enemy as any financial hardship. If his work is to continue... well, that must be addressed as well."

Elizabeth blinked, and then slowly, almost involuntarily, a smile broke across her face. "And you think that can be done?"

"Not a chance in the world."

Elizabeth's smile fell. "But then... why did you say...?"

A faint smirk tugged at Darcy's lips as he met her gaze. "Do you think Bingley will let me back down now? No, no, that is unfair. I have got used to him carrying his way until I hardly knew which direction I was pointed. But I would not have you think I have no will of my own."

"On the contrary, sir, I think rather that you find Mr. Bingley's form of 'persuasion' to be rather convenient."

His eyebrow edged upward, and he took a step closer to her. "How so?"

"I think there is not a creature on earth capable of bending your will—that is my impression, at least. But letting yourself *appear* to be persuaded against your wishes due to some perceived obligation permits you to seem to object to the very course you had already set your mind upon. Thus, you save face—at least, in your own mind—and you still carry on with the 'irresponsible' or 'imprudent' thing you truly wished to do in the first place."

His lips were twitching now with restrained amusement. "I see I shall have to be exceedingly careful around you, Miss Elizabeth. But, back to the matter at hand. I have not yet begun to consider how to see Sir Thomas's little... project here... to security. I almost quail to ask, but do you have any ideas?"

Elizabeth's smile now threatened to split her face, and her stomach was turning a riot of delighted butterflies. "Oh, I am certain I can think of something."

DARCY LEANED BACK, EYEING Bingley across the low-lit study, a glass of brandy held idly between his fingers. "If we are serious about this—about helping Sir Thomas in a meaningful way—then it seems I must go back to London. There are people there, influential men, who could be persuaded to endorse his efforts. A single letter from certain quarters would do wonders." He swirled his glass thoughtfully. "William Wilberforce, for one—he has spoken publicly about reform and the importance of supporting charitable work among the poor. If he gave his blessing..."

Bingley shook his head. "But that is just it, Darcy. He might give his blessing to charitable work in general, but would he say to this? We are talking about a venture far more... particular than some of the other causes London has taken up. Sir Thomas's work extends beyond the merely unfortunate; it invites those with... colorful reputations, does it not?"

Darcy inclined his head. "I grant that it does. But still, if we could persuade men like Wilberforce, or perhaps the Earl of Shaftesbury—"

"They *might* support it, yes," Bingley cut in, "in drawing rooms full of expensive pipe smoke, miles away from the real problem, where no one soils their hands or their reputations by involving themselves. But London's opinion matters only so much here in Hertfordshire. We need to start with Meryton. It is the town itself that is against him, Darcy. Those who see him every day are the ones to sway. If we could win Meryton over, that support would radiate outward, wouldn't it? That way, anyone who questioned the worth of Sir Thomas's venture would have an entire community to answer to."

Darcy frowned, staring into his brandy. He could not deny the truth of it. There would be no real victory for Sir Thomas until he gained acceptance here, from the people of Meryton themselves. London might lend him prestige, but Meryton would give him safety.

After a long moment, Darcy set his glass down. "Miss Elizabeth suggested something yesterday," he said slowly. "She mentioned that Netherfield is the only house for miles around large enough to host a ball."

Bingley looked intrigued. "A... a ball, you say?"

"Not in the formal sense. She suggested a Christmas party—one large enough to include the entire community. Apparently, the town assembly hall here is modest, and Netherfield's ballroom would make a far grander setting."

Bingley leaned back with a grin, his eyes lighting up. "She is clever, that Miss Elizabeth. What better way to persuade people to change their minds than to welcome them in? It would be a jolly gathering, and we could introduce Sir Thomas's household in a way that lets the town see their humanity." He paused thoughtfully, glancing back at Darcy. "But you—well, you do realize what you are taking on. Hosting something like that is no simple affair. And you! You are hardly an experienced host. Egad, whenever we have a dinner party, *I* have to manage the affair, even if you are the one hosting."

Darcy gave a dry smile. "Indeed. But if it is the best way to change public opinion, I am prepared to take it on." He tapped a finger on the side of his glass, watching Bingley carefully. "We could make it not just a party, but a celebration of goodwill. The season would be an excuse for generosity, to invite everyone, not just the gentry. The whole town would have a reason to attend."

Bingley nodded slowly, his eyes alight with interest. "There could be a supper, some small entertainments..." He trailed off, his mind clearly turning over ideas. "We shall have to make it worth their while—something so irresistible that nothing would stop even the most... judgmental among them from coming, for fear of being left out."

Darcy allowed himself a small, approving smile. "And by the end of the night, with any luck, they will wonder why they ever opposed Sir Thomas at all."

"By Jove," Bingley said with a grin, "if all goes well, we shall have everyone on Sir Thomas's side by Christmas."

Twelve

SIR THOMAS BLINKED, HIS baffled gaze shifting from Darcy to Bingley as if he had not heard them correctly. "Stay on? You... both of you wish to remain at Netherfield?"

Bingley nodded. "Yes, precisely. We thought we might stay a while longer, come to know the neighborhood, see a bit more of the house."

Sir Thomas's eyebrows drew together. "Stay on... Well, now, I *did* hear you properly, did I not? I had assumed—well, I assumed that once you understood the state of things, you would be more eager to... distance yourselves from my circumstances."

"On the contrary," Darcy replied. "There is much to recommend the area, and for ourselves, it would be time well-spent. We will pay handsomely for your trouble, of course. You've no idea the bother you would save me by letting Bingley exhaust this bit of a whim. Forever trying to get me out of London, he is, and now, you see, he *has* got me out of London, and I am quite terrified to return too soon, lest he scheme up something far more inconvenient."

"Besides," Bingley interjected, "we rather like it here. The neighborhood has a... a lively atmosphere. You would be doing us a favor, really. Come, man, look at my friend here. Have you ever seen a fit man of eight and twenty with such a pallor? I daresay, any moment I can get him out of his study—and away from his plots and plans to grow our little empire—well, I shall not be the man to turn that opportunity down."

"But to stay *here*, as if I were any other host and you were any other guest..." Sir Thomas cleared his throat. "Forgive me, Mr. Bingley. I would not have you think yourselves unwelcome—far from it! It gives me immeasurable delight to see you both again. But...

well, I say, sir, you would not find many people here willing to accept my hospitality. Not without... reservations."

"That is precisely why we want to stay!" Bingley exclaimed, nearly rising from his seat. "Good heavens, man, do you know what a fearful bore Darcy can be when he thinks he shall be set upon by mercenary ladies? He shall have a natural sort of protection here. I might even get him out of doors for some skating or sleighing or something even more sociable like dancing and wassailing."

Sir Thomas's face paled. "Wassailing! You mean to stay on through Christmas?"

Darcy sighed. "What my friend is so clumsily trying to say is that, indeed, we would be deeply obliged if you found it within your means to permit us some... liberties. No expense is too great, sir. I would not have you put to the slightest inconvenience on our behalf, and nor would we wish to displace even a single one of your... ahem... what do you call them? Residents?"

Sir Thomas blinked vaguely. "I... we simply say, 'the household.' I was not aware I needed a formal name for the persons who inhabit my home."

"And so, you do not. Very well, we would not wish to inconvenience you or your household. In fact, we hope to make ourselves welcome by more means than simple good manners and cheerful characters."

Bingley made a snorting noise. "As if Darcy knows what a cheerful manner even is. I daresay, I thought he had nearly forgot how to smile at all until the other day, when—"

"I am sure Sir Thomas can have no interest in *that*," Darcy interrupted.

"I... I still do not understand," Sir Thomas protested. "What is your intention? You mean to secure the house for... what? A temporary stay? A long-term lease?"

Darcy frowned and arched a brow at Bingley.

"Oh, I should say a deal more than that!" Bingley enthused. "Why, does it not strike you that this house is nearly the most scenic setting one can imagine for a bit of winter revelry? Why, apart from Pemberley—and you will not get Darcy that far from London just now—I never saw a happier situation for a grand party."

Sir Thomas shook his head. "Scenery, it has in abundance. A party... why, that requires people."

"With all due respect," Bingley returned, "DarBing Enterprises never lacked for people willing to join their cause."

Sir Thomas closed his eyes for an instant, and when he opened them, it was with a long-suffering sort of resignation. "You may be wizards in business, the both of you. But

I think you will find that the stench of associating with Netherfield will cling to you no matter what 'revelries' you attempt to indulge in in Meryton."

"And *I* think you will find that when a single man of good fortune declares himself in want of a party, there tends to be no lack of applicants," Darcy replied.

Sir Thomas kneaded his forehead. "Darcy... Bingley... I know—or, at least, I think I know—what you are trying to do here. I assure you, the effort is not unappreciated, but I think you underestimate the difficulties. You will find not even one family who would stoop to accept the invitation."

Darcy and Bingley shared a glance. Bingley, for once, gave the faintest shake of his head, as if to beg Darcy to speak first. Darcy thinned his lips and turned to address Sir Thomas.

"People simply do not know your intentions here. The good you have accomplished. If they did—if they had any notion of what you do and why—I am sure the town would not remain so distant."

"They do not wish to know," Sir Thomas replied. "I cannot force their understanding."

"True," Darcy said, "but we might *tempt* them into a better understanding, if given a chance. Mr. Bingley and I have discussed it, and we thought... perhaps a large Christmas party—too large to be ignored, for *all* of your neighbors. To give Meryton's residents a chance to come into your home, see things for themselves."

Sir Thomas stared at them. "A Christmas party! At Netherfield. For *all* of Meryton?" He sounded as though Darcy had suggested inviting the House of Commons for tea.

"Oh, indeed, yes!" Bingley jumped in. "It would be festive, welcoming, and no one would wish to miss it!"

Darcy nodded, glancing at Sir Thomas's incredulous expression. "A large affair would serve many purposes. The season alone would excuse it, and every corner of Meryton could feel invited."

Sir Thomas was silent for a moment, his eyes searching each of theirs. "Meryton would never agree to it. They would not attend."

"They would," Darcy countered. "If it were open to all—if everyone knew they were welcome, if the food were abundant and the, er, libations flowed freely, and it were held at a house as grand as Netherfield. They would come because... well, because they would not wish to be left out."

Sir Thomas folded his arms, watching them carefully. "And you believe this will change their opinion of me and of Netherfield?"

"It may not happen overnight," Darcy replied, "but it would be a start. It would give the people a chance to see the house and meet those who live here—see them, not as rumors or as threats, but as... as neighbors."

Sir Thomas exhaled slowly, shaking his head. "Meryton has always been wary of me, but this..." He paused, his gaze sharpening. "They will think me mad! Where is the money to come from? You know everyone will talk. It is hardly a secret that I can hardly keep my own board from being bare."

"That, Sir Thomas, shall not be a problem." Darcy nodded toward his friend. "Bingley and I will see to every expense, down to the very particulars and beyond. It is, after all, the least we can do for inconveniencing you so by asking to host a party in your home."

Sir Thomas gaped at each of them, something like hope flashing in his eyes, quickly replaced by a shadow of doubt. "Darcy! You are the least likely fellow I ever saw to be hosting a party. I have not forgot how you used to find the most private nook in the house when your fellows were drinking and carrying on. You would sit in the corner with a book and watch it all, hardly letting yourself be drawn in. And you wish to convince me that this is *your* idea, for *your* pleasure?"

"I take pleasure in a great many things besides reading," Darcy said, a little defensively.

"He is lying about that last bit," Bingley put in, "but I am not. Come, man, what of it?"

"Bingley, it all seems improbable." Sir Thomas shook his head. "And how are we even to plan such a thing? I have no wife to serve as hostess. I would not know where to begin. I am an old bachelor, gentlemen; I am no expert in local customs or social niceties. I would not know how to make such an affair palatable to the town."

Bingley grinned. "That, sir, is easily solved. We had thought—well, that is—Darcy and I had discussed it, and we wondered if there might be a particular family... some respected local household, with social standing..."

"Someone the people already trust," Darcy continued, finishing Bingley's thought. "And someone, perhaps, whose family already views you in a somewhat more generous light than others. If you had their support, they would bring others along by association."

Sir Thomas raised his eyebrows, waiting for them to continue.

Bingley leaned forward. "The Bennets, sir. You know them, do you not?"

Sir Thomas considered. "By reputation only. I believe Mr. Bennet keeps somewhat to himself. But the family is respected, yes. Their elder daughters are quite well-regarded by those who speak of them, both for their beauty and their characters—the elder two, at least—and I..." He cleared his throat. "Well, that is, I have my suspicions that they have done a kindness or two for the girls here. My maids certainly seem to know who Miss Bennet and Miss Elizabeth are."

Bingley nodded eagerly. "Exactly so! They are sensible, practical women. We have spoken to them at length, and they seem to have a good understanding of the town's... sentiments."

Darcy added, "And Miss Elizabeth mentioned that the Bennets are well-acquainted with the social scene here. Their family has lived here for years, and they are nearly the center of the neighborhood."

Sir Thomas looked between them, a faint smile growing. "So, you would enlist the Bennets to help manage this gathering? What gives you the impression that they would agree?"

"Call it a hunch," Bingley said.

"Well," Sir Thomas sighed, "what do I know of such things? It is not as if I have something to lose in the affair, so you may as well please yourselves. And I suppose..." He glanced thoughtfully between them. "It would give you the chance to make the ladies' acquaintance."

Bingley cleared his throat, glancing sideways at Darcy. "Yes. We thought that, if you were to invite Mr. Bennet... perhaps he might bring his family to call. After all, what gathering could be successful without the right ladies to guide it?"

Darcy gave him a measured look but said nothing. Sir Thomas only chuckled. "Very well. If this is the approach you both believe will sway Meryton, I shall send Mr. Bennet an invitation. He may think me mad, but I doubt he will refuse outright."

ELIZABETH HAD SETTLED HERSELF with a book in the drawing room, curling up in her favorite chair by the hearth while Jane worked at a bit of embroidery on the sofa. It was an exceptionally cold afternoon, and the fire scarcely kept pace with the chill seeping into the room from the windows. As a consequence, their mother and younger sisters had returned upstairs directly after nuncheon, claiming the comforts of thick quilts and downy beds for the rest of the day.

Elizabeth's gaze had drifted off the pages and into the dancing flames. She had fully intended to read a bit more of *The Vicar of Wakefield*—at least through the part about the Primroses being forced to move from their home—but her attention felt thin and fickle as the wisps of fire flitting about the brick. Thanks to that one particular—

"Lizzy, you look five miles away," Jane observed from the sofa. "Or... perhaps only *three* miles."

Elizabeth cleared her throat and drew her shoulders back. "Sorry?"

Jane's mouth turned up on one side. "You were very coy about what the gentlemen said when you went to Netherfield. You must have seen them, I assume."

"Only Mr. Darcy."

"Oh! Why, that is... oh, dear, that does not sound very promising."

Elizabeth shot her sister a glance. "If you had left well enough alone, I might not have had to anger the gentleman when I went to explain everything to him."

Jane sucked her lip between her teeth. "Truly! Oh, I feared as much. I had thought... well, bother what I thought. Was he *very* angry?"

Elizabeth closed her book and set it on a table beside her. "Not really, but the fact that you feared he might be ought to be enough to chastise you properly on the matter. I still cannot fathom what you were thinking, Jane."

"Thinking! Why, I was thinking that Aunt had a dazzling idea."

Elizabeth blinked, her expression deadpan. "To trick two wealthy, single gentlemen into pairing off with her nieces at dinner?"

"Oh, pish-posh, Lizzy, do not be so silly. She has known both those gentlemen for years—both personally and by reputation. She knew very well that they *might* come to Netherfield—"

"After you tempted them."

"—*and*," Jane continued without missing a beat, "that they might be induced to do something for Sir Thomas—"

"After you put them in a position to feel guilty for imposing on the man."

"Now, Lizzy, you know very well that I never... or *hardly* ever do anything unseemly. This was just a *bit* of a push. And if the gentlemen truly are offended, what have we lost, hmm? Sir Thomas will hardly be worse off than he was before."

"What have we lost?" Elizabeth arched up in some incredulity. "What about our dignity?"

"Mine is perfectly intact. I took the advice of our aunt, a lady I respect, to bring a good man with a good cause to the notice of two supposedly kind and *very* wealthy benefactors."

Elizabeth sighed and kneaded her brow. "I cannot brush it off so easily as that."

Jane lifted her shoulders and looked as though she meant to invent some other outlandish bit of reasoning when their father entered, a sealed note in his hand and a skeptical look in his eye. Without ceremony, he settled himself in the chair nearest the fire and cleared his throat.

"A note from Sir Thomas Ashford," he announced, flicking his gaze between Jane and Elizabeth. "He invites me to dine at Netherfield this evening."

Elizabeth felt a flutter of something—not quite hope, but certainly curiosity. "Dinner at Netherfield?"

"Indeed, I've no idea what occasioned it, but it appears our 'scandalous' neighbor has decided to make a formal attempt at civility." He unfolded the note and squinted at the contents as if to reassure himself that he had read them aright. "Though why he would wish to waste an evening on me, I cannot imagine. He already claims to have two other visitors at present—now, let me see. A Mr. Bingley and a Mr. Darcy, both of London. Never heard of them."

Jane smothered a beam of triumph behind her prim smile. "Oh, perhaps he does not consider it a waste at all, Papa," she said, her voice a little too light. "It may be just a friendly attempt to strengthen ties with the neighborhood."

"Perhaps," Mr. Bennet agreed with a wry look, "but I hardly think your mother would approve. Though I daresay I could benefit from a change of scene. I wonder if Sir Thomas still has any of those Havana cigars he used to be so celebrated for, or if he has parted with them over the years."

Jane folded her hands, her voice taking on a tone of practiced innocence. "Papa, I cannot help but think how inconvenient this dinner might be for you. Who will manage all the proper social pleasantries? Surely you do not expect Sir Thomas and his soldiers—assuming some of them are at table with you—to endure your wit without some form of softening influence?"

Mr. Bennet snorted. "My dear Jane, do you suggest I am incapable of carrying a conversation with a baronet? My ego hardly knows how to survive such a blow."

Elizabeth stifled a laugh and turned to her sister. "Jane, truly, if you mean to manipulate Papa, you ought to be subtler. He is, after all, the master at the art. This is as transparent as glass."

Jane ignored her, leaning slightly toward her father, her smile unwavering. "Not at all, Papa. I simply mean that if there are other guests present—Mr. Bingley, perhaps? Mr. Darcy? —a lady's touch could be of service in balancing the conversation. A well-prepared hostess, after all, ensures the success of any evening."

Mr. Bennet stroked his chin as if considering the argument. "Hmm. And do you propose that I cannot manage these gentlemen alone, without being overshadowed by their youth, fortune, and charm?"

"Not at all," Jane said sweetly. "But surely even you cannot deny that Elizabeth and I might make the evening more... agreeable. For everyone."

Elizabeth rolled her eyes and shook her head. "Jane, you are as subtle as a sledge-hammer. We have not been invited! Jane, this is not an evening with the Lucases. It is Netherfield. A formal invitation, with Sir Thomas, Mr. Bingley, and Mr. Darcy—"

"Oh, that is what makes it so interesting," Jane replied. "Surely it would not hurt to expand our acquaintance?"

Mr. Bennet held up a hand. "Elizabeth is quite right, Jane. For my part, I hardly think Sir Thomas is in a position to refuse company, and though I ought to put my foot down, I find the prospect vastly amusing."

"Of course, you do," Jane wheedled. "And it is *you* who are inconvenienced by this invitation, after all. What possible grounds has Sir Thomas to protest?"

Their father grunted. "Your mother says often enough that I care too little for forwarding the interests of my daughters, and I ask you, what more promising opportunity than meeting these two gentlemen he speaks of? Perhaps they are wealthy and in search of wives, eh? Would not your mother be pleased?"

"Too pleased, Papa," Elizabeth protested. "How do you propose to just leave with us, with no explanations?"

"Indeed, indeed. You would have to find a way past your mother. A feat which, I need hardly tell you, is beyond most mortal men."

"But it would be easy enough if we were clever about it," Jane insisted, turning to Elizabeth with a sparkle in her eye. "We need only tell Mama that we are dining with Charlotte. That ought to suffice."

Elizabeth could only gape at her sister. "At Lucas Lodge! Jane, there will be snow this evening, and Papa will surely take the carriage himself."

"As if Mama will even notice Papa is gone! She shan't even know that he left, but will assume he is in his library like always."

"Jane!" Elizabeth hissed. "Why, you are at it again! Papa, you see what she is attempting, do you not?"

Mr. Bennet braced both hands on the arm of his chair. "Oh, I see it plainly, Elizabeth. And yet, I find myself curious to see if she will manage to convince your mother to let you out of the house in the first place. That, my dear Jane, will be the true test of your persuasiveness."

Jane's lips curved in triumph, and she shot Elizabeth a look of quiet satisfaction. "I shall take that as permission to try."

Elizabeth groaned, throwing her hands in the air. "Papa, you are encouraging her."

"I am encouraging entertainment," Mr. Bennet replied, folding his note again to slide it into his jacket pocket. "And Jane's attempt promises to be highly diverting."

"Jane, I beg you not to tell Mama," Elizabeth began, shooting her father an imploring look, "it is highly inappropriate for young ladies to join gentlemen for such an affair."

Mr. Bennet snorted, shaking his head. "Well, well. If you can devise a scheme that will satisfy your mother, I am prepared to be impressed. But mark my words, you are in for a task."

"Then it is settled!" Jane said cheerfully, rising from her chair and clasping her hands. "Elizabeth, we have much to plan."

Elizabeth stared after her sister, half in admiration and half in dismay. As Jane swept from the room, she turned to her father, who was already rising from his chair with an amused grin.

"You are encouraging this," she said, exasperated.

"Only because I believe it shall end in magnificent failure," Mr. Bennet replied with a chuckle. "But you may surprise me, my dear. Now go on—I expect you will need the whole remainder of the afternoon to contrive an escape."

Thirteen

S IR THOMAS PACED THE length of the drawing room, his hands clasped behind his back. Darcy and Bingley sat nearby, Bingley's leg bouncing with what could only be described as restrained eagerness. Darcy, for his part, looked immaculately calm, though his fingers tapped lightly against the arm of his chair.

"It is unusual," Sir Thomas said at last, breaking the silence. "Most unusual, in fact."

"Sir?" Darcy asked, arching a brow.

Sir Thomas paused, his face troubled but faintly amused. "Mr. Bennet replied to my invitation almost at once. That in itself is unexpected—he is known, I gather, for being a rather... unhurried correspondent."

"Perhaps he is a man who values good company," Bingley offered.

"Perhaps," Sir Thomas allowed, though his expression suggested otherwise. "But more curious still is the request he made. He asked if his two eldest daughters might accompany him to dinner this evening."

Darcy blinked, straightening slightly in his chair. "His daughters?"

Sir Thomas nodded, his brow furrowing. "I can only surmise that the Misses Bennet wish to call upon some of the ladies of the house. They have shown kindnesses to our... residents before, albeit discreetly. I expect they see this as an opportunity to extend their sympathies more openly."

Bingley sat forward, his grin widening. "Miss Bennet and Miss Elizabeth? Truly? How splendid! What remarkable foresight of Mr. Bennet to bring such delightful company."

Sir Thomas glanced between the two men, his brow lifting slightly as if recalibrating his assumptions. "Remarkable, indeed," he murmured, though the faintest of smiles tugged at his lips. He turned to Darcy, who met his gaze with a long-suffering expression before rolling his eyes and leaning back in his chair.

"Of course," Sir Thomas continued, his tone light but his eyes shrewd, "it could be that their father simply wished to ease the evening's discourse. Young ladies often enliven such gatherings, do they not?"

Bingley nodded vigorously. "Quite so, Sir Thomas! And as we are but a small group tonight, their presence will undoubtedly make the evening all the more pleasant."

Darcy said nothing, though his silence was eloquent enough.

Bingley caught it and his manner darkened somewhat. "You fear some ill consequence, Darcy?"

Darcy glanced at Sir Thomas, who dropped his gaze the instant Darcy's eyes touched his. "What do you think, Bingley?"

"Well, I... I hardly know, I suppose. Their father is escorting them, so there must be nothing improper—"

"If... only it were that simple, Bingley," Sir Thomas sighed. "But Darcy is right. The Bennet ladies risk their reputations by being allied with this house."

"But that is the very point of this party," Bingley protested. "They shall be no different from any other who comes to delight themselves in the joys of the season."

"You are ignoring the salient point that nothing has changed *yet*," Darcy replied. "And a gentlemen's dinner with no present hostess is hardly the time and place to begin."

"Oh, well, I am sure—"

The conversation was interrupted by the sound of harness bells jingling to a halt outside the house. Sir Thomas moved to the window, glancing out. "That must be them."

Bingley was already on his feet, smoothing his coat and adjusting his cravat. Darcy rose more deliberately, brushing an invisible speck from his sleeve as they all filed out into the hall.

The front door opened with a brisk creak, allowing a gust of cold air to swirl into the hall, accompanied by a murmur of voices. Footsteps rang sharply on the stone floor before Mr. Bennet emerged in the doorway, his smile curling beneath his neatly trimmed grey whiskers. His eyes, keen and sharp as a hawk's, surveyed the room with an air of detached amusement, as though he found the company—Darcy and Bingley included—a source of quiet mirth. Darcy noted the worn but dignified cut of his coat and the way his frame, still sturdy despite his years, carried a hint of impatience, as though the man had stepped into the company of others largely for his own amusement.

But Darcy's attention wandered almost at once, drawn irresistibly to Elizabeth as she stepped lightly into the room behind her father. The faint flush on her cheeks from the cold heightened the brightness of her crystal-blue eyes, and the dark tendrils of hair peeking from beneath her bonnet seemed to beckon the firelight. The cloak draped over her shoulders, dusted with melting snowflakes, framed her figure with an elegance so effortless that Darcy momentarily forgot the others in the room. It was not merely her beauty that held him; it was the energy she carried, a vibrant contrast to the gray day outside.

Elizabeth's gaze flicked to his—brief, fleeting, but enough to send a warmth coursing through him that the fire in the hearth could never rival. He straightened slightly, as though to meet her challenge, but the moment passed when Mr. Bennet cleared his throat, his wry expression suggesting he had missed nothing.

"Good evening, Sir Thomas," Mr. Bennet said, bowing. "And may I present my daughters, Miss Jane Bennet and Miss Elizabeth?"

Sir Thomas stepped forward with an amiable smile. "Mr. Bennet, a pleasure. Miss Bennet, Miss Elizabeth, welcome to Netherfield."

Jane curtsied gracefully, her serene expression warming the room. "Thank you, Sir Thomas. Your home is lovely."

Elizabeth followed suit, though her gaze flickered briefly to Darcy before she quickly looked away. "You are most kind to host us."

"Not at all," Sir Thomas replied. "Your father spoke so highly of you both that I could hardly refuse such company." He gestured to Bingley and Darcy. "You already know my guests, I believe—Mr. Bingley and Mr. Darcy."

Bingley bowed and stepped forward, his face lit with unmistakable delight. "Miss Bennet, Miss Elizabeth, this is an unexpected pleasure! We did not expect that we would have such charming company tonight."

Miss Elizabeth's lips twitched, though her expression remained polite. "The pleasure is ours, Mr. Bingley."

Darcy inclined his head in a reserved bow. "Miss Bennet, Miss Elizabeth."

Miss Bennet returned his bow with a slight curtsy, but Elizabeth simply nodded, her eyes fixed on him with the curious light of one who is in on a secret.

Sir Thomas gestured toward the drawing room. "Shall we all sit? Dinner will be ready shortly, and I trust the warmth of the fire will be welcome after your journey."

As they moved into the room, Sir Thomas glanced briefly at Darcy, his brow raising as if to say, *You are sure there is nothing of interest here for you?* Darcy returned his look with the barest lift of his chin before settling into his seat, deliberately positioning himself farthest from Elizabeth.

The evening was off to a curious start.

T HE TABLE WAS LAID with quiet elegance, the silver catching the glow of the candles as Elizabeth tried to focus on the soup before her. She dared not look directly at Mr. Darcy, who was seated across from her, but she was keenly aware of his presence. Every movement—his deliberate gestures, the quiet assurance in his voice—seemed to draw her attention like a compass needle to the north.

She risked a glance. He was speaking to her father, his low, even tone carrying across the table. There was nothing rushed about the way he spoke, nothing uncertain. The words fell from his lips with the weight of someone accustomed to command, and yet, there was no arrogance in his manner. For reasons she could not quite name, her fingers tightened on her spoon.

"It is an opportunity, Mr. Bennet," Darcy said, "to bring the community together. Sir Thomas has expressed a willingness to host the gathering at Netherfield, which, given the season, seems a most fitting location."

Her father's brow rose ever so slightly, but he made no immediate reply. Elizabeth had spent enough time watching her father deflect serious conversation to recognize the signs of amusement simmering beneath his expression. She turned her attention back to her soup.

Mr. Bingley leaned forward, his enthusiasm poorly contained. "And we thought, what better time than Christmas? A celebration to uplift everyone's spirits, rekindle old friendships, and perhaps even mend some unfortunate misconceptions. There could be music, a grand supper, maybe even—"

"—an opportunity to foster goodwill and unity," Mr. Darcy interrupted, his tone deliberate, clearly an effort to rein in Bingley's unchecked zeal. "Sir Thomas has graciously offered the use of Netherfield's ballroom."

Elizabeth caught the faintest twitch at the corner of Darcy's mouth as he glanced at Bingley, smoothing his expression before turning back to her father. She bit back a smile. The dynamic between the two men was fascinating—one brimming with unchecked energy, the other moving through the conversation like a careful chess master. For all of Darcy's composed exterior, she could sense his subtle effort to keep things dignified.

"And what sort of celebration, exactly, are you envisioning?" her father finally asked, setting down his spoon and leaning back in his chair.

"A Christmas party," Mr. Bingley said, leaning forward slightly. "Open to everyone in the neighborhood, of course—families, the gentry, even tradespeople—innkeepers, haberdashers, blacksmiths. It could be splendid! There could be music, dancing, a grand supper—perhaps even some entertainment or—"

"—a chance for the neighborhood to come together," Darcy said, cutting in smoothly, steering the conversation back to his controlled narrative.

Elizabeth glanced between them. Mr. Bingley seemed poised to overflow with ideas, while Mr. Darcy reined him in with the steady hand of someone well-practiced at tempering excess. Their dynamic, she thought, had a rhythm almost too perfect to be entirely accidental.

Jane, seated beside her, attempted to join the conversation. "It sounds like a lovely idea, does it not, Papa? A chance to bring some much-needed warmth to the season."

Elizabeth nearly rolled her eyes. Jane's tone was too sweet, her suggestion too transparent.

"And you, Miss Elizabeth?" Mr. Darcy asked suddenly, drawing her attention. "What is your opinion? If you were not sitting here listening to plans—if you were a disinterested party, would an event of this nature meet with your approval?"

Elizabeth blinked, the directness of his question leaving her momentarily unmoored. There was no disdain in his expression, no mockery. Only the sharp, unwavering focus of someone who genuinely wished to know her thoughts.

Her pulse quickened, though she forced herself to keep her tone light. "Approval?" she echoed. "I hardly think my opinion should matter in such an undertaking, Mr. Darcy."

"It matters to me," he replied without hesitation.

Elizabeth felt her breath hitch. There was no artifice in his words, no attempt to flatter. She could feel the heat rise to her cheeks, and though she managed to keep her composure, her spoon trembled slightly as she set it back in her bowl.

Her father snorted quietly, though he said nothing. Elizabeth, catching his glance, narrowed her eyes slightly before turning back to Darcy. "I think it is an admirable idea, though it is rather ambitious. Perhaps too ambitious?"

Sir Thomas, who had thus far remained silent, cleared his throat. "The success of such a party would depend greatly on its execution. I must confess, I have not hosted anything of this scale before. It is fortunate that Mr. Bingley and Mr. Darcy seem to have given the matter so much thought."

"They have, have they?" Mr. Bennet interjected, his tone as dry as tinder. "It is almost as though this plan had been contrived well before this dinner conversation. Though I wonder if I might suspect there has been sleight of hand occurring long before tonight?"

Elizabeth froze, her glass halting halfway to her lips. She glanced quickly at her father, only to find him looking directly at her, one brow arched in faint amusement. Her stomach dropped.

Bingley, oblivious, forged ahead. "Oh, Mr. Bennet, I assure you, it is all in the spirit of the season. Nothing underhanded, I promise."

Her father's gaze shifted to Bingley, his smile deepening. "I do not doubt that, Mr. Bingley. But I am becoming increasingly aware that *some* individuals"—he chanced a glance at Mr. Darcy, then looked pointedly at Elizabeth— "are more adept at orchestrating events than they let on."

Elizabeth felt the heat rise to her cheeks. She cast a sharp glance at Jane, who was studiously avoiding her gaze by inspecting her plate with great interest. Of course, her father had seen the glances she traded with Mr. Darcy, and he was just obstinate enough to misread her role in this. He probably blamed her, as though she were the one pulling all the strings!

Darcy's eyes flicked toward her, and there was something faintly amused about the way his gaze lingered. Elizabeth forced herself to pick up her spoon, pretending to focus on her meal, though her mind churned with indignation—and perhaps a trace of mortification.

Across the table, her father lifted his glass, a glint of humor in his eyes as he addressed the gentlemen. "Well, then. A Christmas party, you say? If nothing else, I am sure it shall be an event to remember."

D ARCY HAD SCARCELY TAKEN his seat in the drawing room when the door opened, and the footman with the missing hand stepped inside. He inclined his head respectfully, though his expression was tight.

"Sir Thomas," he began, "Mr. Bennet's coachman has asked me to deliver a concern. The snow is falling harder now, and he fears the roads will soon be impassable."

Everyone paused. The light conversation they had carried over from the dining room dissolved into silence as all eyes turned toward Sir Thomas.

Darcy rose from his chair almost instinctively, glancing toward the tall windows. The snow that had begun so softly earlier was now swirling heavily against the panes. "It may already be too dangerous," he said.

Miss Elizabeth stood as well, her face set in that familiar blend of determination and practicality. "Surely it is not so dire yet? If we left at once—"

"Let us have a look," Sir Thomas said, motioning for everyone to follow.

Darcy was at Miss Elizabeth's side as they moved toward the front door. Close enough to feel the gentle sway of her skirts brushing against his leg, close enough to catch the faint scent of vanilla and cloves that seemed to linger around her. It was entirely distracting—and entirely unfair.

The footman held the door open for them, and a gust of icy air swept inside. Miss Elizabeth wrapped her shawl tighter around herself as Darcy stepped forward, standing just a little ahead of her to shield her from the worst of the wind. He looked out into the darkness, where the snow fell in thick, relentless sheets, blanketing the ground faster than he would have thought possible.

"Well, that settles it," Mr. Bennet said behind him. "I shall have to take up permanent lodgings here until the thaw."

Sir Thomas smiled faintly, though he looked far from amused. "I am, of course, prepared to offer you shelter for the night. However..." His gaze flicked toward Miss Bennet and Miss Elizabeth, his face growing serious. "There is something you must consider, Mr. Bennet."

Miss Elizabeth frowned. "What do you mean?"

Sir Thomas hesitated. "Staying here overnight... may not be without consequence."

Miss Elizabeth stiffened. "You mean... because of the rumors?"

"I am afraid so. I would not have you or Miss Bennet unaware of the potential harm to your reputations. I have been called many things in this neighborhood, as you well know. If word spreads that you spent the night here, even with your father as a chaperone, I cannot guarantee the damage will not be lasting."

Miss Elizabeth exchanged a glance with Miss Bennet, whose pale face betrayed a flicker of unease. But their father seemed unbothered, a sardonic smile tugging at his lips.

"Well, if it means surviving the night, I think we shall just have to take our chances. Snowstorms, I believe, care very little for reputations."

Miss Elizabeth's lips pushed into a pout so delicious, Darcy was suddenly overtaken with visions of kissing those plump lips. "Indeed, Papa. If we do not stay, it seems we may not survive to hear the town's gossip anyway."

Darcy glanced toward her. Her gallows humor in the face of such an unflattering prospect was admirable—and so distinctly *her*. Yet beneath her words, he thought he caught the faintest thread of uncertainty. The idea of her being subjected to the harsh judgment of others stirred something protective deep within him.

Sir Thomas nodded, his expression heavy. "Very well. It is settled, then. Rooms shall be prepared for you and your daughters, Mr. Bennet."

"Thank you," Mr. Bennet said. "Now, if it is all the same to everyone, I should like to return to that drawing room and finish the glass of brandy I was so unceremoniously pulled away from."

The others laughed softly, the tension easing slightly as they turned back toward the warmth of the hearth. Darcy lingered for a moment, holding the door as Miss Elizabeth passed.

"Thank you, Mr. Darcy," she said quietly.

He gave a short nod, watching her retreat with her sister down the hall. He was meant to feel concerned for the awkward situation the storm had created—but instead, he found himself secretly, selfishly pleased. Miss Elizabeth Bennet would not be rushing away tonight.

Fourteen

E LIZABETH SAT ON THE edge of her bed, smoothing the folds of the nightgown Sir Thomas's housekeeper had so generously offered for her use. She and Jane had chosen to share a room, for it seemed that Netherfield was home to more people than either of them had realized, and they feared somehow displacing someone who would have kept silent out of politeness. As it was, Elizabeth was not altogether certain that someone had not already given up rooms for their comfort.

Jane leaned back against the pillows, still flushed from the warmth of the fire. The room Sir Thomas had provided them with was snug and quiet, the muffled sounds of the house winding down for the night and an occasional baby cry filtering faintly through the walls.

A soft knock came at the door, and at Elizabeth's welcome, a young maid stepped inside, her apron slightly askew and her cap slipping over her brow. She bobbed a curtsy. "Begging your pardon, miss. I'm Clara. Sir Thomas said I'd be looking after you, and asked me to see if you needed anything before settling in."

"That is very thoughtful of him," Jane answered. "I think we have all we need, thank you."

Elizabeth hesitated. The evening had left her restless, her thoughts tumbling over everything that had been said at dinner. She glanced toward the bedside table, conspicuously bare, and an idea struck. "Actually, I wonder if there is something to read. A book, perhaps? I often read before bed. Is there anything you might recommend?"

Clara shifted uncomfortably, her gaze flickering toward the floor. "The library is well stocked, miss, but I..." She trailed off, twisting her fingers in her apron.

Elizabeth's breath caught as understanding dawned. Like enough, this girl had never learned how to read. She quickly rose, shaking her head. "Oh, no, please, there is no need to trouble yourself. I can fetch it myself."

The maid looked up, startled. "I could show you the way, miss, but..." She hesitated again. "It is just that most of the household is abed by now, so you might find the corridors a bit dark."

"Is it improper for me to go alone?"

"Oh, no, miss! Sir Thomas always says the library is for any guest who wishes to use it, night or day."

Jane, who had been silent until now, sat forward with a faintly conspiratorial air. "Do go, Lizzy. A little walk might do you good. You were so pensive at dinner."

Elizabeth shot her sister a suspicious look. "And you? Will you simply sit here, perfectly content, while I wander about the house?"

"I am perfectly content, yes. But you are not, and I shall not rest knowing you are lying awake all night brooding."

"I do not brood."

"You most certainly do. Fetch your book, Lizzy. Perhaps Mr. Darcy was right—you do have a sharp understanding of what appeals to others, but you will never convince me you are not a brooder."

Elizabeth groaned, grabbing her shawl. "Why bring Mr. Darcy into the conversation? But very well—I shall fetch a book to avoid further accusations. That is all."

Jane's eyes twinkled. "Of course, Lizzy. That is all."

The maid led Elizabeth down the hall, her lantern casting warm circles of light against the walls. At the entrance to the library, she curtsied again. "Here it is, miss. You will find plenty to choose from. Shall I wait for you?"

"No, thank you, Clara."

"Then, I'll not disturb you further, miss."

Elizabeth thanked her and stepped inside, her steps muffled by the thick rug beneath her feet. The room had a settled quiet to it, as though it had been waiting for someone to disturb its stillness. The furniture, arranged with thoughtful symmetry, invited her to linger, while the faint gleam of lamplight on the polished surfaces gave the space a tranquil, almost watchful presence. The fire in the grate had been banked low, but enough light remained to illuminate the rows of shelves and the grand, sweeping space.

She scanned the titles along one wall, her fingers grazing the spines. It was a lovely collection—nothing particularly modern or eccentric but carefully curated. She could almost hear Mr. Darcy's voice echoing in her memory from the dinner conversation: measured, deliberate, and maddeningly thoughtful. Her lips twitched at the thought.

And then a sound—a soft rustle, like the turning of a page—came from deeper within the library.

Elizabeth froze, her heart dropping with a thud in her chest. Surely the maid had said the gentlemen were abed? She glanced toward the faint light pooling at the far end of the room. Her curiosity prickled. Taking a careful step forward, she peered around the edge of a tall shelf—and nearly gasped.

There, seated in a wingback chair by the fire, was Mr. Darcy himself, his profile cast in warm shadow, a book open in his hands.

D ARCY HAD COME TO the library intending to think.

The dinner conversation still echoed in his mind—Elizabeth Bennet's quick wit, the arch of her brow when she challenged him, the way her lips curled, half in jest, half in defiance. It unsettled him, how easily she lingered in his thoughts. He had retreated here with the intent to bury himself in a book, to distract his mind with the precision of well-crafted words, but every line he read dissolved into her voice.

Darcy turned another page, the faint rasp of paper breaking the library's quiet. He shifted slightly in his chair, letting his eyes skim the lines of text. The fire in the hearth glowed faintly, the warmth diffusing into the stillness of the room.

Then he heard it—a soft rustle, a step too light to be mistaken for one of the footmen. His hand paused on the edge of the book as he listened, his senses narrowing in on the sound.

Elizabeth Bennet stood within the glow of the firelight, her shawl loose around her shoulders as though she had paused mid-thought. Her gaze swept the shelves and furnishings with quiet purpose before landing on him. Surprise flickered across her features, but it faded quickly, leaving only that unmistakable spark of self-possession he had come to expect from her.

"Oh! Mr. Darcy."

Darcy rose, setting the book carefully on the chair behind him. "Miss Elizabeth," he replied, inclining his head. "I was not expecting company this evening."

Her pause lingered just long enough to quicken his pulse. "Nor I," she admitted, her fingers tightening over the edge of her shawl. "The maid assured me the gentlemen had retired, or I would not have intruded."

"Not at all," Darcy said swiftly. "This is Sir Thomas's library. It is yours to use as much as mine."

She nodded, but her expression was cautious, her lips pressing together as if unsure whether to stay or retreat. Darcy found himself hoping—foolishly, desperately—that she would stay.

"May I?" she asked, gesturing toward the shelves.

"Of course."

He watched as she moved toward the nearest row, her fingers brushing lightly over the spines of the books. She hesitated at one, tilting her head as she read the title. "My father has a volume like this."

"Does he?" Darcy's voice sounded far too formal, even to his own ears. He stepped closer, unable to help himself. "He must have an impressive collection."

Her lips curved faintly. "Impressive in size, certainly—especially when one compares the number of books to the number of shelves in his library. But I suspect you might find his tastes a bit... eclectic."

The humor in her tone sent a flicker of warmth through him. He studied her profile, the delicate line of her jaw, the way her lashes swept down as she considered another title. There was a quiet grace about her, a strength that only made her beauty more arresting.

"I imagine there is something rather charming in that," he said.

She glanced at him then, her brow lifting in surprise. "You would think so?"

He felt the corner of his mouth lift—unbidden, and so uncharacteristic of him that he almost startled himself. "I would."

For a moment, he simply watched her—the light play of her fingers over the book spines, the faint crease beside her mouth when she caught him gazing at her. He could feel the heat of the dying fire at his back, but it was nothing compared to the awareness that hummed through his limbs just in watching her. He knew he should step away, retreat to a safer distance.

And yet... he stayed.

At last, she pulled a title from the shelf and turned to face him, her gaze dropping to the book in his own hands. "What were you reading, Mr. Darcy?"

He glanced down, realizing he still held the volume. "An essay on goodwill and charity. One I have read many times before."

"You do not strike me as someone who revisits books often. Am I wrong?"

"You are not," he admitted. "But there are certain works worth returning to. Familiar words can offer new insights, depending on the reader's state of mind."

She drew a step closer, tilting her head to see the title of his book. "And what is your state of mind tonight, sir?"

Darcy hesitated, holding his book up for her inspection even as he groped for words. Joseph Addison's *The Spectator*—he had been both pleased and utterly unsurprised to discover it in Sir Thomas's library. "There are nights when sleep eludes me, Miss Elizabeth. This is one of them."

She read the book's title, her gaze softening with obvious recognition. "A restless mind can be a burden, I suppose. What keeps yours so occupied?"

Darcy turned his eyes to the fire, the flames casting flickering shadows across his face. "Obligations, mostly. Business, yes, but that is but a piece of it. The responsibilities of maintaining my family's estate, of seeing to its tenants and lands... they are unending, though I mostly manage them through my steward these days. It is still a duty, but one I accepted willingly when my father passed."

She studied him carefully. "And yet, I hear something more than mere duty in your tone. You said before that not all memories of your family home are pleasant—that you have kept away because of that. But you still miss your family home, do you not?"

"I... I do." Darcy forced a tight smile. "Yes, I do."

"Then why ever do you not return? There is no one to stop you, is there?"

He lifted his shoulders. "Well, if you listen to Bingley—and I caution you in that endeavor because listening to Bingley can be hazardous to one's peace of mind—"

He broke off when she laughed aloud. "Oh, dear, he sounds very much like Jane!"

Darcy chuckled. "You are not the first to trace a resemblance there."

She shook her head and made a shooing motion with her hand. "Forgive me for interrupting. Go on. If I listen to Mr. Bingley...?"

He had to give himself a good shake and suck in a breath because that smile of hers was enough to reignite the fire in the hearth. "Oh, nothing. It is only that he has been trying to get me out of London for ages, and... well, you know the rest. Always, I have an excuse—some contract that needs my personal attention. Some duty to my sister, which is entirely false because she went to live with our aunt, Lady Matlock in London when she left school. I have a thousand excuses to stay away, and I suppose too few real reasons to return."

"Or too few reasons that you will confess," she offered.

He dipped his head. "You are more right than you know. Ah... would you... care to join me, Miss Elizabeth? I know it is late and far from prudent, but..." He gestured to two empty chairs that graced either side of the still-warm hearth.

Her brow creased for a moment. "Oh, that is a dreadful idea. Which chair do you prefer?"

He laughed. "Whichever one you like the least, I suppose."

"Well..." She paced around both chairs, then, casting a glance toward the open door of the library, chose the seat facing away from the door. "There. Now, if someone should happen by, they will only see a very stern man reading by the fire and not the wayward 'lady' seated opposite him."

"Unless they hear your voice," he cautioned.

"I fear it is too late to worry about such things." She settled herself in the chair with a self-deprecating smile. "It seems that we are now doubly invested in this scheme, Mr. Darcy, for if Sir Thomas and his household do not gain favor in Meryton, Jane and I may well be ruined as well."

Darcy swallowed as he claimed the opposite chair. She was right. It did not matter if she sat alone in the library with him or with twenty men, for the fact that that library was in *this* house, and she was now a guest, made her somehow inculpate. The matter was easy enough for a gentleman to shrug off, but not a lady.

And that was the moment he made the determination—she would not be permitted to suffer for this. Whatever that meant... and he already held some notions of what the costs might be... on this, he would not be moved.

"Now, then, Mr. Darcy." She leaned forward in her chair, resting her chin on the backs of her knuckles as she smiled that knowing sweetness at him. "Before you so cleverly diverted me, you were about to tell me all the reasons that have thus far failed to draw you back to your family home."

Darcy could not help but grin as he sank further into his seat. "You seem to think it some great secret I am keeping from the world."

"Because you are not a man to waste time in evasive answers unless there is truly something you wish to hide. And as you could have no possible reason to fear what little *I* might be able to do to you, and as we are situated so comfortably here with little to do but talk, then I say, out with it, Mr. Darcy."

He laughed and crossed his thighs. "Then you must prepare yourself for a very dull story, indeed. My father instilled in me a profound sense of stewardship, of preserving what was entrusted to us. I suppose..." He sighed. "There are days when I wonder if I have lived up to his expectations—or if I have fallen short."

Elizabeth's brow furrowed. "Surely you do not believe that."

He gave a short, rueful laugh. "There are moments when I do. My father was a man of purpose and tradition, a man who saw the world in clear lines. I... I am not always so certain. He prepared me to carry on his legacy, yet there are parts of his vision I have left behind. Choices I have made that he would not have approved of."

"It sounds as though you have carved your own path, Mr. Darcy. That is not failure—it is strength."

"Hmm. Perhaps," he admitted. "There are ambitions I hold now that my father never imagined for me. For years, I dismissed the idea of a seat in Parliament. It seemed impractical—something better left to others. But it lingers."

"Why Parliament?" she asked. Her tone was curious, not prying.

"Why not? The opportunity to make changes, real changes, beyond the borders of my own estate or the influence of our business. The injustices one sees when traveling, the inequalities..." He paused, catching her eye. "Surely, you see them, too."

"More often than I would like." She tilted her head. "But Parliament? That would be no small undertaking."

"Indeed." His mouth twitched. "Endless debates, ceaseless correspondence, and public speeches—which I loathe."

Elizabeth's brow arched, her lips curving faintly. "I cannot imagine you faltering at public speaking."

"Perhaps not faltering," he conceded, "but hardly enjoying it. Yet the thought persists, as though refusing to be dismissed. My cousin, Colonel Fitzwilliam, believes it would suit me. And then, of course, there is my uncle, who sits in the House of Lords. They encourage it... even as I hesitate."

Elizabeth's brow lifted, and a smile tugged at the corner of her mouth. "I struggle to conceive of you hesitating over anything, Mr. Darcy. From what I have seen, you are a man of conviction."

Darcy leaned forward, setting the forgotten book on the small table beside him. His gaze lingered on Elizabeth's face, her features softened by the glow of the hearth. "Conviction is only as strong as the courage to act upon it, Miss Elizabeth. And there are times when I question... if mine is truly sufficient."

Elizabeth tilted her head, a glimmer of both curiosity and challenge in her expression. "If *you* lack courage, Mr. Darcy, then what hope is there for the rest of us?"

A reluctant smile tugged at his lips. "You give me far too much credit."

"And you give yourself far too little. You have courage enough to entertain great ambitions. That alone sets you apart from most men."

He leaned back slightly, her words settling over him like a balm. "You are kinder than I deserve."

"Oh, I shall remind you of that the next time you disagree with me."

Darcy chuckled softly. "I do not recall disagreeing with you so often."

She arched a brow. "And yet, you are disagreeing with me now."

"Touché, Miss Elizabeth."

She smiled fully now, and the moment felt suspended, as though the rest of the world had been painted over in soft strokes of firelight and shadow. "And what of peace, Mr. Darcy?" she asked after a beat, her voice gentler now. "Do you find it anywhere, amidst these obligations and ambitions?"

His gaze dropped briefly to the floor before returning to hers. "I try. I remind myself that no man's life is without flaw, and that failure—though inevitable—need not be defining."

Her brow furrowed slightly, as though turning over his words. "Wise counsel. And does it work?"

"Occasionally," he admitted, his voice lighter now. "But not always. Still, it is enough to carry me to sleep on most nights."

Elizabeth's expression shifted into something teasing. "I wonder, Mr. Darcy, if you might have missed your calling. Philosopher of Pemberley sounds rather grand."

He laughed again, the sound quieter this time, more intimate. "It lacks the practical application I value in life, I fear."

Her lips drew into a thoughtful frown. "You are a curious man, Mr. Darcy."

"Curious?" He raised a brow, leaning just slightly forward again. "How do you mean?"

"You hold yourself with such confidence, and yet you speak as though you are constantly at odds with yourself." She gestured vaguely toward the book he had abandoned. "It is an interesting contradiction."

He regarded her for a long moment, his voice quieter when he finally spoke. "Perhaps it is not a contradiction, Miss Elizabeth, but equilibrium. Certainty and doubt are not opposing forces; they are what keep us from falling too far in one direction."

Elizabeth blinked, her lips parting just slightly as though caught off guard. "I never thought of it that way."

"And you," he said softly, his tone laced with something unspoken, "never fail to inspire thought."

Their gazes held for a beat longer, the room growing still but for the fading crackle of the dying fire. Elizabeth shifted slightly, her fingers brushing the edge of her shawl as though she had forgot it was there. She glanced toward the window, where the darkened panes reflected the faint glow of the hearth, and her brow lifted slightly.

"I did not realize how late it must be." Her gaze returned to him, a small, almost rueful smile forming. "But I believe I shall be able to sleep now."

Darcy inclined his head, rising from his chair with deliberate care. "I am glad to hear it, Miss Elizabeth."

She stood as well, adjusting her shawl. Darcy took a step closer, his movements measured as though giving her space to retreat. She did not.

"Miss Elizabeth," he said, his voice low, "if I may..."

He reached for her hand, and she gave it. Slowly, he bent his head, pressing a soft kiss to her knuckles. The warmth of her skin against his lips sent a thrill through him that he dared not acknowledge aloud.

Elizabeth's breath caught, but she did not pull away. Instead, her gaze remained fixed on him, her features unreadable save for the faint curve of her lips.

"Goodnight," Darcy said, his voice quieter now, tinged with something that felt precariously close to longing.

She nodded, stepping back slowly, her hand slipping from his as she turned toward the door. "Goodnight, Mr. Darcy," she murmured before slipping away, the faint rustle of her skirts disappearing down the hall.

Darcy remained where he stood, his hand still warm from hers, the memory of her presence vivid and inescapable. Whatever the night might bring, he knew sleep would not come easily—not with the lingering echo of her smile in his mind.

Fifteen

"Lizzy, where are you off to so early?" Jane's voice broke the stillness, and Elizabeth paused on the stairs, startled.

She turned, drawing her shawl tighter around her shoulders. "Enjoying the quiet."

Jane raised an eyebrow as she descended to meet her. "And pacing the halls at dawn is how you achieve that?"

Elizabeth gave a quick shrug and continued down. "Perhaps I find peace in movement."

"Hmm," Jane murmured, slipping her arm through Elizabeth's when she reached her. "Or perhaps you find peace elusive this morning. Shall we sit by the fire and discuss it?"

Elizabeth hesitated, the thought of unburdening herself tempting but precarious. They reached the morning room, where a soft light filled the space. Elizabeth moved toward the window without answering, her gaze caught by the icy glaze shimmering over the surface of the snow.

Jane followed, but stayed a step back, observing her sister's reflection in the glass. "Goodness, Lizzy, but you seem preoccupied. Does it have anything to do with your late visit to the library?"

Elizabeth stiffened slightly but did not turn. "You're imagining things."

"Am I?" Jane crossed to the settee. "I know you too well for that."

Elizabeth sighed. Mr. Darcy's voice echoed in her mind again—so measured, so sure, but with that flicker of vulnerability she could not quite shake. She turned from the window and faced Jane, forcing a smile.

"It is nothing, truly."

"Of course," Jane said, folding her hands neatly in her lap. "And your restless night, your early rising, your current silence—none of those are anything, either?"

Elizabeth's smile faltered, and she pressed her lips together. "You are relentless."

"Because I care."

Elizabeth moved to sit beside her with a sigh. "I only wonder," she said, "what to make of someone who is not what they first seem."

Jane's brow furrowed slightly. "And you do not know yet if they are better or worse than you thought?"

Elizabeth hesitated. "Perhaps better. Possibly a vast deal better. Though I am not yet ready to say."

"Ah. And that troubling notion is what cost you so much sleep?"

Elizabeth gestured vaguely toward the stairs. "The house was too quiet, and I thought I might enjoy some air and see a bit more of the house."

Jane tilted her head, her expression knowing. "And perhaps run into Mr. Darcy?"

"Jane Bennet!" Elizabeth lowered her voice, glancing down the hall. "You know perfectly well that I—"

"Admire him?" Jane teased sweetly.

"Am trying to escape your matchmaking."

"Then perhaps you should avoid the breakfast room. I would imagine Mr. Darcy and Mr. Bingley are already there, and I would be shocked if Papa is not with them."

Elizabeth coughed. "Papa? He, ah... he seems to like Mr. Bingley and Mr. Darcy, would you not say?"

"I daresay he does. I saw Miss Flora in the hall, and she said the gentlemen were all up early, talking about the details for Sir Thomas's Christmas gathering." Jane's tone grew more serious. "Lizzy, I think it is a wonderful thing they are doing—for Sir Thomas and for his... residents."

Elizabeth nodded. She had suspected as much last night, though hearing it confirmed sent a ripple of warmth through her chest. Mr. Darcy's intentions seemed genuine, though she could not help but wonder what drove him to care so deeply about a cause that many others would dismiss outright.

"Shall we join them?" Jane's voice broke through her musings.

Elizabeth hesitated. But then she squared her shoulders. "If Mr. Darcy and Mr. Bingley are plotting how best to charm Meryton, I should like to see how they intend to manage it."

Jane chuckled as they made their way to the breakfast room. "Lizzy, you know very well that Mr. Darcy's charm lies in his reserve."

Elizabeth arched a brow. "His reserve or his glare? The distinction is subtle."

T HE BREAKFAST ROOM WAS alive with warmth. Mr. Bennet was seated near the fire, a cup of coffee in hand as Mr. Bingley gestured toward a sheet of paper spread before them. Mr. Darcy stood beside the table, his expression calm but attentive as he listened to Bingley's ideas.

"Ah, my dear girls!" Mr. Bennet greeted them as they entered. "You see, Mr. Bingley has concocted a plan to win over every heart in Meryton, while Mr. Darcy prepares to scowl them into submission."

Bingley laughed good-naturedly. "I shall take that as high praise, sir."

Darcy's lips quirked slightly, though he said nothing.

"Good morning," Jane said warmly, taking a seat beside their father.

Elizabeth hesitated, feeling Darcy's gaze on her as she chose a chair. "Mr. Bingley, I must say, you are taking this project very seriously."

"Of course!" Bingley exclaimed. "A celebration is no small thing, Miss Elizabeth. And Sir Thomas deserves nothing less than our best effort."

Darcy nodded. "We aim to show the neighborhood that he and his household are deserving of respect—not pity."

Elizabeth glanced at him, startled by the conviction in his tone. "That is a delicate balance, Mr. Darcy. Respect is not easily won, particularly in a place as entrenched as Meryton."

Darcy met her gaze, his expression thoughtful. "Which is why we must approach this carefully. The event itself must be flawless, and more than that, it must leave an impression strong enough to shift opinions."

"Flawless," Elizabeth echoed with a small, teasing smile. "And do you consider yourself an expert in such matters, Mr. Darcy?"

"Not an expert," Darcy admitted, the corner of his mouth twitching. "But I believe in thorough preparation."

Bingley clapped his hands together. "Then let us prepare! Miss Elizabeth, Miss Bennet—what advice might you offer? Surely you know your neighbors better than we do."

Jane hesitated, but Elizabeth leaned forward, her mind already turning. "If you wish to win Meryton's favor, you must appeal to their pride. Make them feel involved, important even. Invite the key families to contribute something—a dish, a decoration, a piece of music. Let them feel as though they are part of the celebration, not merely guests."

Darcy's eyes narrowed slightly, not in displeasure but in focus. "A sound strategy."

Mr. Bingley nodded eagerly. "Yes, yes, exactly! And what of the entertainment? Should there be games, carols, perhaps a bit of theatrics?"

"Certainly nothing too grand," Elizabeth said. "Something familiar, comforting. People like what they know."

"Then it is settled," Darcy said, his voice quiet but firm. "We will begin inviting the neighborhood at once and ensure they feel invested in the event."

The rest of the morning passed in a flurry of conversation and planning. Elizabeth found herself oddly drawn to Darcy's quiet competence, the way he listened carefully to every suggestion and offered thoughtful solutions. There was a steadiness about him that was so... opposite of anyone else in her life. A sense that he would see this endeavor through no matter the obstacles.

When Darcy caught her eye as they finalized the guest list, she felt her heart stutter. She quickly looked away, but the warmth of his gaze lingered, stirring something within her that she wished she could savor forever.

By the time the morning was over, Elizabeth felt both invigorated and unsettled. This Christmas party was shaping into something far more significant than she had anticipated—and Mr. Darcy, she realized, was shaping into someone far more intriguing than she had imagined.

T HE REMNANTS OF BREAKFAST still lingered on the sideboard as the company gathered in the drawing room. Sir Thomas had taken a chair near the hearth, his cup of coffee resting on the arm as he listened to Miss Bennet and Mr. Bingley exchange ideas for festive entertainments.

"No dancing," Bingley decreed. "Much as I enjoy the activity myself. Darcy and I felt... well, you know, the intent is for everyone to find something to enjoy, and dancing..."

"There are some who cannot, even if they wished to," Miss Bennet finished. "A game of forfeits might be suitable. It is always popular, especially among the young."

"And charades, perhaps?" Bingley added, his smile growing. "Something to involve both the children and the adults."

Sir Thomas gave a thoughtful nod. "Both are excellent suggestions. Simple yet engaging."

Darcy stood near the window, his arms crossed loosely as he watched the others. The snow beyond the glass had softened to a light dusting, though patches of ice still clung to the shaded edges of the garden paths. He shifted his gaze to Elizabeth, who was leafing through a book from one of the smaller shelves, her movements purposeful despite her apparent distraction.

The fire crackled, punctuating the exchange as more ideas for the party were proposed. Miss Elizabeth lifted her head and glanced toward the window, the faintest frown creasing her brow. Darcy pushed himself away from the sill and crossed the room, compelled to draw her into the conversation.

"Miss Elizabeth," he said, his voice low enough to avoid disturbing the others. "May I trouble you for a moment?"

She turned, her expression shifting from thoughtfulness to mild surprise. "Of course, Mr. Darcy."

He inclined his head slightly, suppressing a smile. "I wondered if your father had any further thoughts on the plans. It was rather bold of us to present them so decisively. I hope we have not caused him any annoyance."

Elizabeth cast a glance toward Mr. Bennet, who was seated in a corner, apparently engrossed in a book but with a faint smirk tugging at his lips. "Papa is not easily annoyed, sir. At least not when something entertains him."

"Then I am relieved," Darcy said. "Though I confess, what I value even more than your approval is your honest assessment of our chances."

Elizabeth tilted her head, curiosity flickering in her gaze. "Our chances, Mr. Darcy? Of pulling the whole affair off without incident—or of persuading the neighborhood to join hands and sing carols in perfect harmony?"

"Both."

She let out a small laugh. "If you wish for perfect harmony, I fear you may find disappointment. But if the goal is goodwill and a measure of unity, I believe it is not so hopeless as it might seem."

"Not hopeless," Darcy repeated, as though testing the phrase. "Do you truly believe so?"

"I do," she said. "Though it will require effort—and perhaps a little cunning—to overcome the town's natural... wariness."

His brow lifted slightly. "And do you count yourself among the cunning?"

Her lips curved, her voice gaining a playful edge. "That, Mr. Darcy, is for you to judge. But I will say this: the people of Meryton are not so hard-hearted as they might appear. Beneath all their gossip and judgment, they long for a reason to feel proud of their community. If this party gives them such a reason, I believe they will come."

Darcy regarded her for a moment, the quiet conviction in her voice drawing his admiration. "You make it sound almost simple."

"Simple?" She laughed. "Not at all. But then, nothing worth doing ever is, is it?"

"I am gratified to hear that," Darcy said. "You do not think it too ambitious?"

"Oh, it is ambitious. But ambition is often the hallmark of a worthwhile endeavor. Or so I have heard."

A small smile touched his lips. "Then I shall take that as encouragement."

"See that you do, Mr. Darcy."

Before Darcy could respond further, Bingley's voice rang out. "Darcy! You are monopolizing Miss Elizabeth."

Darcy turned toward his friend. "I had not realized I was doing so."

"Well, no harm done," Bingley replied with a grin. "But Miss Bennet has just received word from the coachman. It seems the roads may be passable sooner than expected."

"Mama will be relieved to see us home at last," Miss Bennet said.

"Yes, she will," Elizabeth replied, though her tone betrayed no particular joy at the thought. "But I fear we may have all manner of questions to answer."

Darcy stepped closer, his hands clasped behind his back as he considered her words. "Your mother is not so amenable as your father to... keeping certain company?"

"That depends." Elizabeth's lips curved faintly. "I imagine word that there were two single gentlemen staying here will go some way toward comforting her."

Darcy frowned. "I imagine."

"You must know how quickly rumors spread in small towns, Mr. Darcy."

His brow furrowed. "If such questions arise, I hope you will allow me to take responsibility. It is the fault of the weather, not your family."

She shook her head. "That would hardly silence a curious neighbor—or my mother."

"I cannot speak for your neighbors, but I would hope Mrs. Bennet might find some satisfaction in knowing her daughters have lent their assistance to a worthy cause."

Elizabeth gave him a sidelong glance, her expression teetering between amusement and disbelief. "You are an optimist, Mr. Darcy."

"Rarely. But I suppose one must allow for exceptions."

Their conversation was interrupted as the coachman entered the drawing room to announce that the carriage would soon be ready. Miss Bennet rose from her seat near the window, smoothing her skirts, and Mr. Bingley immediately moved to her side, murmuring something that made her smile.

Elizabeth reached for her shawl, feeling a mix of relief and something less easily named. Darcy, who had remained at her side, watched her for a moment before speaking again.

"Miss Elizabeth, might I hope to see you again soon? To help in planning the party, of course."

Her gaze flickered to him, a touch of warmth breaking through her guarded expression. "I expect you shall."

Darcy inclined his head. "Safe travels, Miss Elizabeth."

"Thank you, Mr. Darcy," she said, dipping into a slight curtsy before moving to join her sister.

Darcy's eyes lingered on her retreating figure, the warmth of the fire paling in comparison to the presence of the woman who had so thoroughly unsettled him. The day's tasks called for his attention, yet he found himself reluctant to let the moment slip away entirely.

Sixteen

THE BENNET CARRIAGE ROLLED into the Longbourn drive just as the weak winter sunlight broke through the clouds, gilding the frost-dappled hedgerows and glittering across the windows of the house. Elizabeth felt an odd mixture of relief and regret as the familiar sight came into view. Home, at last—but she could not help casting one last glance back toward the road as though Netherfield might linger just beyond the horizon.

Inside, they were greeted by a flurry of activity. Lydia and Kitty dashed into the hall, barely pausing to give their father a polite nod before peppering Jane and Elizabeth with questions.

"Oh, Jane, you must tell us everything!" Lydia exclaimed, her cheeks pink with curiosity. "Mama has been in a state ever since Hill said you spent the night. Everyone says it is the greatest scandal!"

Kitty was clutching at her sister's arm. "We heard Mrs. Long tell the butcher that you must have been kept against your will. Is it true?"

Elizabeth raised a brow, brushing snowflakes from her shawl. "Kept against our will? How thrilling. Were there also accounts of gallant rescues and daring escapes, or have you left those out for dramatic effect?"

Jane stepped in quickly. "Now, now, you must not believe everything you hear. The snowstorm made the roads impassable, that is all. Sir Thomas was kind enough to offer us shelter."

Lydia's expression darkened. "But Mama said—"

"Mrs. Bennet," Mr. Bennet interrupted from the doorway, "would do well to remember that discretion is the better part of wisdom. Come, my dear daughters, before your mother descends with tales of captivity and ruin. Let us all go to the drawing room and sit by the fire like civilized people."

The party moved toward the drawing room, where Hill had already laid out tea. Mrs. Bennet's voice floated down from upstairs, calling for Hill with increasing urgency. Elizabeth exchanged a glance with Jane, who smiled faintly but said nothing. It was only a matter of time before their mother joined them, full of questions and complaints. Seated by the fire, Elizabeth stirred her tea absently, her mind wandering. The warmth of the library at Netherfield still lingered in her thoughts, along with... *him*.

She had scarcely finished her first sip when Jane leaned closer, her voice low. "Lizzy, do you suppose we ought to let Mama help with the Christmas party?"

Elizabeth blinked, startled out of her reverie. "Mama? We are bracing for her histrionics even now. Why on earth would we invite her to meddle further?"

"Because we will need her help."

"Help?" Elizabeth arched a brow. "Jane, I doubt Sir Thomas would survive an hour of Mama's 'help'."

"Oh, Lizzy," Jane replied, shaking her head with a soft laugh. "You are being unfair. Mama is very good at certain things."

"Certain things like matchmaking and gossip?"

"Certain things like planning grand affairs," Jane corrected. "And you know it. If we mean to make this Christmas party a success, we must draw on every available resource. Mama included."

Elizabeth sighed, leaning back in her chair. "You *are* relentless."

"I am practical. You know she will agree, especially if we present the idea just so. Mention the officers. Lydia and Kitty will clamor for it. Mama will be won over before she even realizes what she is agreeing to, and once we have Mama, we have Aunt Philips, Mrs. Long, *and* Lady Lucas."

Elizabeth couldn't suppress a laugh. "You have a devious streak, Jane."

Jane's eyes twinkled. "Only when necessary."

A moment later, their mother entered the room in a flurry of lace and indignation. "Girls! Girls! What is this I hear about you staying at Netherfield overnight? With all that riff raff present! How could you, Jane? And you, Lizzy? Do you think I have no care for your reputations?"

Elizabeth opened her mouth, but Jane spoke first, her tone calm and sweet as ever. "Mama, the snowstorm made it unavoidable. Mr. Darcy and Mr. Bingley were both perfect gentlemen, and Sir Thomas was the soul of propriety. You must not worry so."

Mrs. Bennet's expression softened slightly, though her hands fluttered over her shawl. "Mr. Darcy and Mr. Bingley—who are they, I ask? More ne'er-do-wells, come to darken the shades of Netherfield, I'll wager. Well, I shan't have my girls mixed up with it!"

"Mama," Elizabeth broke in, "Mr. Darcy is an earl's grandson."

Mrs. Bennet blinked. "What was that, Lizzy?"

"And they are very wealthy businessmen. Uncle Gardiner knows them well," Jane added. "They have sterling reputations, and Papa liked them very much."

"Oh, your father would like a grub if it left him alone in his library. You must consider what people will say!"

Elizabeth's eyes widened. "That the Bennet ladies had the first intelligence of two handsome, single, *wealthy* gentlemen come to the neighborhood?"

"But *Netherfield*? Do you not hear yourself, Lizzy? Everyone will say you are loose. How will we answer such accusations?"

"By inviting them all to Netherfield ourselves," Jane said smoothly.

Elizabeth nearly choked on her tea, staring at her sister in disbelief. Jane continued without missing a beat.

"We were just discussing Sir Thomas's idea to host a Christmas party, Mama. Everyone in the neighborhood will be invited. It will be the perfect chance to show our gratitude for his hospitality—and to put any silly rumors to rest."

Mrs. Bennet's face lit up at the mention of a party. "A Christmas party? At Netherfield? Oh, my Jane, what a splendid idea!"

Elizabeth set her cup down with deliberate care. "Indeed, Mama, a splendid idea. Jane has thought of everything."

Jane smiled serenely, but Elizabeth caught the faintest flicker of triumph in her sister's eyes. She was not the only Bennet skilled in subtle manipulation, it seemed.

T HE BRISK WINTER AIR was biting as Elizabeth and Jane set out for Meryton. The cobbled streets glistened with frost, and the town hummed with quiet activity—shopkeepers arranging wares, matrons bustling between errands, and the occasional red-coated officer strolling past, tipping hats to passersby. Elizabeth tucked her gloved hands into her muff, her cheeks numbly flushed from both the cold and the anticipation of their task.

"Who shall we call on first?" Jane asked.

"Lady Lucas, of course. As you said, we have Mama's support now, and she has already gone to see Aunt Philips. Charlotte will help us, I am sure, and if we can bring Charlotte's family around, others will follow. The Lucas name carries weight—though not, I fear, due to Lady Lucas herself."

Jane gave a small laugh. "You are dreadful, Lizzy. But yes, Mama's closest friend is as good a place to start as any."

They were ushered into the drawing room by a servant, where Lady Lucas sat embroidering with Charlotte at her side. Both women rose to greet the Bennet sisters warmly, though Lady Lucas's expression carried a hint of curiosity, as if suspecting ulterior motives.

"Jane, Lizzy, how lovely of you to call!" Lady Lucas exclaimed. "I heard the most curious thing—you *must* tell us all about your night at Netherfield. I have always wondered at your father for his... eccentricities, but a thing such as this! Indeed, I do not exaggerate when I say that the entire town is simply aflutter with speculation."

"Speculation," Elizabeth echoed innocently as they took their seats. "How amusing. I had not thought a snowstorm worthy of gossip."

Lady Lucas gave her a knowing look. "Not just the snowstorm, my dear. It is the company you kept. Two eligible gentlemen, under the same roof with you and Jane? Why, tongues are wagging from Purvis Lodge to the market square, and there are some who might say I ought not to have received you today."

"Ah, yes, Mr. Darcy and Mr. Bingley," Jane said lightly, pointedly ignoring Lady Lucas's slights. "Charming gentlemen, both of them. We had the most delightful dinner conversation."

Elizabeth hid her smile behind a cough. "Indeed, and speaking of charming, Netherfield itself is simply beautiful. The ballroom alone—have you seen it, Lady Lucas?"

Lady Lucas blinked. "The ballroom?"

"Oh, you must have," Elizabeth said, feigning surprise. "We were just looking it over to be sure that it is suitable, and it is far beyond that."

"Suitable?" Lady Lucas glanced at Charlotte, who was eyeing Elizabeth with unbridled curiosity. "Suitable for what? A whelping room for ruined trollops?"

Elizabeth had to bite her tongue to keep from protesting Lady Lucas's vulgar language. She simply smiled all the brighter. "Surely you have heard of the Christmas party. It seems everyone in the neighborhood is abuzz about it."

"Christmas party?" Lady Lucas set down her embroidery hoop with deliberate care. "What Christmas party?"

Jane clasped her hands together, her eyes bright. "Why, the one at Netherfield, of course! Sir Thomas is hosting a grand gathering. A feast fit for a king, parlor games to last the night long, and I heard they are bringing in musicians from London. Lizzy and I were just discussing what we might wear."

Lady Lucas's brows knit together. "I have heard nothing of this."

Elizabeth gasped softly. "Nothing? Oh, how peculiar. Surely, Sir Thomas meant to include you. Everyone seems to be going. Have you not yet had your invitation?"

Charlotte looked up from her stitching, her gaze flickering to Elizabeth's with sudden understanding. She cleared her throat delicately. "Mother, perhaps the invitation is simply delayed. It is not like Sir Thomas to be remiss."

"Indeed," Jane added smoothly. "He spoke so warmly of you when we were at dinner. I imagine he values your opinion greatly."

Lady Lucas's lips pursed. "I should hope so. Though I confess, I have my doubts about that household."

Elizabeth leaned forward slightly, her tone light and conversational. "Oh, Lady Lucas, I cannot help but wonder what you will think of it. Netherfield's ballroom is quite grand. The musicians, the decorations—it promises to be quite the spectacle."

Lady Lucas's brow lifted, her curiosity piqued. "Spectacle, you say? I was not aware Sir Thomas had much interest in such displays."

"Perhaps not in the past," Elizabeth replied with a faint smile, "but Mr. Darcy and Mr. Bingley have been most enthusiastic in their planning. They are staying through Twelfth Night, of course, as they are old friends with Sir Thomas. And you know that Sir Thomas's generosity knows no bounds. I am sure he wishes for his friends to meet *everyone*."

Lady Lucas's eyes narrowed.

Charlotte glanced up, catching Elizabeth's sly tone. "It is said the flowers will also be brought in from London," she added innocently. "Very grand indeed."

Lady Lucas adjusted her shawl, clearly debating the matter. "Well, I daresay such extravagance would be worth seeing. It is not often one has the opportunity to attend an event of such scale in Meryton."

"Never in my lifetime," Elizabeth said smoothly. "I suspect the entire neighborhood will be talking about it for weeks afterward."

"Entirely possible," Lady Lucas murmured. "I suppose it would be foolish to form an opinion without... proper observation."

"Quite," Charlotte interjected, her cheek twitching as she focused on her stitching. "It would be remiss not to investigate, Mama."

Lady Lucas nodded with growing determination. "Yes, I suppose you are right. As chairwoman of the parish Benevolence Society, it is my duty to see things for myself."

Elizabeth and Jane exchanged the briefest of glances—satisfaction flickering between them like sparks in a hearth.

"Will you not join us on our calls today, Charlotte?" Elizabeth asked. "I expect Mr. Bingley and Mr. Darcy will be in town making orders, and we *might* have the pleasure of introducing you."

Charlotte looked up with a sly smile. "How could I refuse? Besides, I would not want to miss any of the theatrics."

Lady Lucas sighed. "I am sure this will be the talk of Meryton for weeks. I only hope Sir Thomas and his... household behave themselves."

Elizabeth rose, her expression perfectly pleasant. "Oh, I am certain they will, Lady Lucas. Sir Thomas is a gentleman, after all."

As the Bennet sisters and Charlotte made their way to the door, Elizabeth cast one last glance at Lady Lucas, who was already fluttering toward her writing desk. "She will spread the word before tea," Elizabeth murmured to Jane. "And if we work quickly enough, we will be ahead of her."

Charlotte chuckled. "Lizzy, you are positively ruthless."

"Not at all," Elizabeth replied with a grin. "Merely... efficient."

"Efficient," Jane agreed sweetly. "And perhaps just a little bit devious."

Darcy stepped down from the carriage first, his boots slipping faintly against the frosty cobblestones of Meryton's main street. Beside him, Bingley bounded out, nearly bumping shoulders with Roberts, who stood by the carriage, his eyes roving the town with a hint of wariness.

"Roberts," Bingley said brightly, "you have the list, I trust?"

"Yes, sir," Roberts replied, holding up a neatly folded sheet of paper.

Darcy surveyed the bustling street with a practiced eye. The draper's shop lay just ahead, its windows filled with bolts of fabric in muted winter tones. To the left, the butcher's had hung garlands of holly, though Darcy doubted it was enough to hide the shop's distinct, earthy smell.

"Well," Darcy said, "let us get to it. No sense in wasting time."

The trio strode toward the draper's shop, Bingley leading the way. He pushed the door open with gusto, setting the little bell above it jingling. Inside, a middle-aged woman behind the counter blinked in surprise as they entered.

"Good day, madam!" Bingley began. "We are in need of two dozen... no, make that three dozen table linens. Finest quality, naturally. And do not skimp on the measurements—every table at Netherfield's ballroom must be dressed to perfection."

The woman's eyes widened at the mention of Netherfield. "The ballroom, sir?"

"Yes!" Bingley exclaimed, spreading his arms. "For the Christmas party, of course. You have heard, have you not?"

Darcy edged his shoulder in before the poor woman fainted. "Not three doezen. We shall require cloths for no fewer than twenty-eight long tables, as well as napkins and perhaps a bolt or two for other embellishments."

The woman gaped. "Twenty-eight tables?"

"More, if we find the guest list grows," Bingley added with a grin. "And the flowers—oh, Darcy, we must speak to the florist about those orchids from London."

"Right," Darcy replied. "Roberts?"

Roberts stepped forward, handing the list to Darcy. "Here are the quantities we discussed, sir.".

Darcy reviewed the list briefly before addressing the shopkeeper. "These measurements have been confirmed. We will need enough to accommodate the specified arrangements."

The woman behind the counter nodded, though her gaze flickered momentarily to Roberts's empty sleeve. Her hesitation was brief, but Bingley filled the gap effortlessly.

"Excellent work as always, Roberts," he said with an easy smile. "I daresay you have kept us all in line this morning."

Roberts inclined his head slightly, stepping back to let the gentlemen complete their order. The shopkeeper's demeanor softened when Bingley drew out his coin purse to make a deposit on the order, and she quickly began jotting down their request.

"Er... will there be anything else, gentlemen?"

"Not yet," Darcy said. "We shall send word if we require anything further."

T HE BUTCHER'S BELL GAVE a sharp clang as they entered, the warm, savory scent of cured meats filling the air. A rotund man with a ruddy complexion greeted them with a nod, wiping his hands on his apron.

"Gentlemen," he said, his eyes flickering over them with interest. "What can I do for you?"

"We require roast beef," Bingley announced with a grin, "and plenty of it. Enough for... oh, let us say a hundred fifty guests?"

The butcher stared. "A hundred fifty?"

"No, no, at least two hundred. Perhaps more," Darcy added. "The guest list is still being finalized."

"And," Bingley continued, leaning slightly over the counter, "poultry. Ducks, perhaps. Or game hens. Roberts, what do you think?"

"Game hens would be a fine choice, sir," Roberts replied. "They roast evenly and present well."

The butcher's gaze shifted to Roberts, lingering for a moment on his empty sleeve. "Er... indeed. And will this be for the party at Netherfield, sir?"

"Precisely," Darcy said, his tone brooking no argument. "You have heard of it?"

"Well, there's been talk, certainly," the butcher said hesitantly. "Though I must admit, I hadn't expected..."

"Expected what?" Bingley interjected, all innocence. "That the finest butcher in Meryton would not be involved? Impossible. Your reputation precedes you, sir."

The man flushed slightly under Bingley's praise. "Well, if you insist, sir."

"Good," Darcy said crisply. "We shall expect delivery next week. Roberts will coordinate the details. And, ah... you will come, of course?"

The butcher's eyes widened. "Me, sir?"

"Of course!" Bingley replied. "If you wish, that is. I assume you will want to sample your own meats. It would look rather poorly if we had to say the butcher would not come eat some of his own roast."

The butcher swallowed. "I will... I shall speak to my wife, sir."

"Very good," Darcy answered. "Roberts here will settle the account as soon as you can arrange to have the meats delivered."

As they turned to leave, the butcher's assistant whispered something to her employer, glancing nervously at Roberts. Darcy caught it but gave no outward sign. He simply straightened his shoulders and held the door for his companions. One advantage they had was the weight of consequence, silencing further murmurs.

B Y THE TIME THEY reached the baker's, the sun had begun its slow descent, casting long shadows over the town. Inside, the air was warm and sweet, the scent of fresh bread mingling with spices and sugar.

"Ah, this is where the magic happens," Bingley said as they entered, his voice buoyant. "We shall need an array of cakes, tarts, and puddings. Too much for Cook to manage all on her own, of course, so this will do nicely. Something festive—do you have plum pudding?"

The baker, a thin man with flour-dusted hands, nodded. "I can, sir, though you've almost waited too long to order if you want 'em rightly aged. Will you require a few?"

"A few?" Bingley exclaimed. "We shall need a dozen! Perhaps more. What do you think, Darcy?"

Darcy inclined his head slightly. "A dozen to start. And a centerpiece cake. Something... remarkable."

The baker hesitated, his gaze darting toward Roberts, who stood silently behind the gentlemen.

"Do you take commissions, Mr. Baker?" Bingley pressed. "Something extraordinary to match the grandeur of Netherfield."

"Er... of course, sir. And this is for... the Christmas party?"

"It is indeed," Darcy said. "Sir Thomas will host, but the event will welcome the entire neighborhood."

"The entire neighborhood?" the baker repeated faintly.

"We assumed everyone knew," Bingley said with a slight shrug. "But if not, do spread the word. Sir Thomas insists, and Darcy and I mean to spare no expense."

"No... expense?" The baker swallowed.

"Ah, of course." Darcy withdrew his pocketbook. "You might require some supplies, and I would not have you out of pocket before you have even been paid. Allow me." He dropped a few notes on the desk. "And I trust you will attend as well?"

The baker's hesitation melted under their combined pressure, and by the time they left, he was discussing flour quantities with a one-armed Army veteran and two of London's most wealthiest bachelors as though it were the most natural thing in the world.

As the carriage trundled back toward Netherfield, Darcy glanced at Bingley. "You handled yourself well."

Bingley grinned. "You mean I was useful for once?"

Darcy allowed the faintest smile. "Your charm has its uses."

Roberts cleared his throat softly. "If I may, gentlemen, I believe you have caused quite a stir in town."

"Good," Darcy said firmly. "They *should* be stirred."

And as they passed the edge of Meryton, Darcy caught sight of a group of villagers huddled in conversation, their heads turning toward the carriage as it rolled by. He met their gazes squarely, his purpose set. Whatever prejudices the town harbored, they would not be enough to deter him now.

Seventeen

"MISS ELIZABETH, DO TAKE care!" Darcy's voice carried across the icy expanse, his tone just stern enough to earn an arched brow from Elizabeth.

She pushed off with a confident glide, the frost-bright air biting at her cheeks. "I assure you, Mr. Darcy, I am perfectly capable of maintaining my footing."

Bingley, laughing as he skated past, called back, "Careful, Darcy! Miss Elizabeth might leave you in the dust."

"Quite," Elizabeth quipped, executing a graceful turn. "Though, if Mr. Darcy prefers the safety of solid ground, I would not blame him."

Darcy, clearly unwilling to let her challenge go unanswered, stepped onto the ice. His movements were deliberate but assured, his skates cutting clean arcs across the frozen pond. Elizabeth smirked, admiring his form but unwilling to give him the satisfaction of acknowledgment.

Nearby, Jane clung to Bingley's arm, her laugh soft and delighted as he guided her in slow, careful loops. Elizabeth's heart warmed at the sight of her sister's happiness.

"Lizzy!" Jane called, her voice carrying over the laughter and chatter around them. "Is this not the most splendid morning?"

"It is rather fine," Elizabeth admitted, catching up with her sister with a few brisk strides. "Though I suspect you find it even finer in Mr. Bingley's company."

Jane blushed prettily, and Bingley beamed, looking altogether too pleased with himself. "Miss Elizabeth, you wound me. Surely, the morning's charm extends to all of us."

Elizabeth opened her mouth for a witty retort, but a ripple of laughter from the growing crowd at the edge of the pond drew her attention. Familiar faces from Meryton gathered in clusters, their curiosity outweighing their initial reservations. Mothers stood bundled against the cold, daughters stealing glances at Darcy and Bingley, while the younger children clamored to join the fun.

Darcy glided past Elizabeth, his movements deliberate as he navigated toward Jane and Bingley. His gaze flicked briefly toward the onlookers, his expression composed, though Elizabeth caught a slight tightening at the corner of his mouth.

"Do you think the good people of Meryton will embrace such festivities?" he asked, keeping his eyes on the clusters of townsfolk.

Elizabeth considered the question, watching as Lydia and Kitty skated past, chattering animatedly. A few of the younger Meryton ladies exchanged hesitant smiles with them, their initial stiffness melting under the pull of shared amusement.

"It seems to me they already are," Elizabeth replied, tipping her chin toward the shifting dynamic. "Though I suspect it is less about the skating and more about their curiosity."

"Curiosity can be a powerful motivator," Darcy said, his attention lingering on a group of merchants gesturing toward Bingley.

"And once satisfied?" Elizabeth asked.

Darcy's gaze returned to her, and for a moment, his intensity seemed almost warm. "It depends entirely on what they discover."

Elizabeth held his gaze, her pulse quickening despite herself. "Then I hope, Mr. Darcy, that you are prepared to exceed expectations."

"And again, Miss Elizabeth, that will be a matter of opinion. What is yours?"

She frowned, tilting her head playfully. "Favorable. But my opinion matters little. The rest... it will take time," she said honestly. "But even the coldest ice thaws eventually, Mr. Darcy."

Let us hope you are right, Miss Elizabeth."

Her stomach gave an odd flutter, but she brushed it aside. "Shall we test that theory, sir? Or are you content to let Mr. Bingley steal all the attention?"

Darcy grinned, though he said nothing. He offered Elizabeth his hand and propelled himself toward the far side of the pond. Elizabeth followed, the cool air sharpening her focus as they wove between slower-moving skaters.

Bingley's laughter rang out again, this time drawing Elizabeth's attention to a group of children, squealing with delight as Bingley spun them each in turn in fast circles on the ice. Jane stood nearby, her hands clasped as she watched.

Elizabeth paused, her gaze sweeping over the pond, where activity hummed with a growing vibrancy. Mr. Bingley had moved from playing with children to coaxing a cluster of young men and boys from the town to join him. "Come along, gentlemen! The ice is solid, I promise. Besides, we cannot let the ladies have all the fun!" His goads and dares were apparently infectious enough that one or two reluctantly laced their skates and ventured forth, muttering excuses about boots and cold toes.

Elizabeth's eyes shifted to Mr. Darcy, who had positioned himself near a group of older gentlemen huddled in conversation by the benches. He inclined his head politely. "The conditions could not be better," he said. "Though I confess, I am no expert skater myself. Still, the exercise is bracing, and I find it quite improves one's mood."

One of the men, Mr. Long, rubbed his hands together, eyeing the pond. "I cannot recall the last time I ventured onto skates. My wife claims I am a danger to myself in such conditions."

"Better to be cautious than reckless," Darcy agreed, a faint smile tugging at his lips. "But perhaps your wife might enjoy watching you take to the ice again, if only to prove that she has nothing to fear."

The other men chuckled at this, and Mr. Long gave a mock sigh. "You put me to shame, sir. Very well, I shall give it a go—but if I land on my back, I shall blame you."

Elizabeth found herself suppressing a laugh as Mr. Long shuffled off to fetch his skates. She turned her attention to the ice, where Lydia and Kitty twirled past with a gaggle of Meryton girls, their shrieks of laughter cutting through the frosty air.

A few minutes later, Darcy was guiding a hesitant Violet King onto the ice, his hand extended in silent encouragement. She looked up at him, her nervous smile softening as she let him lead her a few steps forward.

"You see?" Darcy said, his voice calm and steady. "One step at a time. The ice will hold."

Violet wobbled slightly, her grip tightening on his arm, but she nodded as she gazed up at him, her eyes round with awe and some degree of flirtatious longing. "I... I think I might manage it."

"That is the spirit. You need not rush. We are in no competition here."

No competition, indeed. Did Darcy have any idea of how many more of Meryton's single female population were, even now, rushing home to grab their skates? And all for *his* benefit, of course. Bingley was charming, but it was Darcy who seemed to draw the eye of every lady within five miles, whether he liked it or not.

Elizabeth tilted her head, observing him more carefully. There was no showmanship in his actions, no effort to draw attention to himself. Yet he managed, with his quiet confidence, to set others at ease. It was a skill she might not have credited him with until now

.

Beside her, Jane leaned closer. "Mr. Darcy has surprised me," she said softly. "I had not expected him to seem so... forward and inviting."

"Come, Jane, you know as well as I do that it is all an act to benefit Sir Thomas's cause. He has said plainly enough before that he dislikes attention."

"But to pull it off so convincingly—why, he almost has me convinced that he is in his natural element. Indeed, I could *almost* be persuaded that he is naturally a nice man."

"He is not exactly a brute," Elizabeth admitted, her lips curving slightly. "But you are right, about one thing. It seems there is more to him than I imagined."

Bingley skated over just then, beaming as he clapped his gloves together. "Well, this is turning into quite the success, is it not? Miss Bennet, you have been standing here far too long. Come, you must warm up by moving about. I should be honored to escort you, if you would allow me."

Jane's cheeks pinked prettily, and she nodded. "I would be delighted, Mr. Bingley."

Elizabeth watched as the two made their way to the center of the ice. As she turned back toward the crowd, she caught sight of Darcy once more, his gaze sweeping the pond until it briefly met hers. Something flickered in his expression—something that felt so *right* and familiar that she could hardly credit the fact that they had known each other less than a week. Elizabeth felt a strange, bubbly warmth rise in her chest before she looked away.

The barriers between the townsfolk and the residents of Netherfield were softening, if not dissolving entirely. Elizabeth could hear snippets of conversation now—Meryton mothers complimenting the gentlemen from Netherfield on their skating, children calling out to one another as they formed impromptu races. It was, she realized, precisely what Darcy and Bingley had hoped for: a moment of unity, small but significant.

Elizabeth's heart stirred at the sight. For all his aloofness and reserve, Darcy's actions spoke volumes. Perhaps he was not so inscrutable after all.

"Lizzy," Jane said quietly, skating up beside her. "Do you see what they are doing?"

Elizabeth followed her sister's gaze to where Darcy stood, now gesturing toward a small evergreen that someone had decorated with ribbons. And giving his hand to Mr. Jackson as he escorted his wife onto the ice.

She smiled faintly. "Creating a scene no one in Meryton will want to miss, I imagine."

"Do you suppose it will work?"

Elizabeth hesitated, her gaze returning to Darcy. "It already has."

As they returned to Netherfield, the group was met with a lively scene in the entrance hall. Mrs. Bennet, her bonnet adorned with a jaunty sprig of holly, stood in the middle of the ballroom, directing activity with the fervor of a battlefield commander. The beds which had been formerly set along the walls for an infirmary had been temporarily moved to the western wing halls. A handful of footmen carried bundles of greenery and boxes filled with decorations, while Roberts stood stoically nearby, a small notebook in his hand.

"Lizzy! Jane!" Mrs. Bennet exclaimed, waving them over with a gloved hand. "Come here this instant! I was just telling Mr. Roberts that we simply *must* have more ribbons—green and gold, I think, though perhaps a touch of crimson would do nicely for the garlands. What say you?"

Elizabeth exchanged a glance with Jane, who bit back a smile and replied with an appeasing tone. "I am sure whatever you choose will be lovely, Mama."

"Of course it will," Mrs. Bennet said, bustling forward to inspect a bolt of fabric in Roberts's hands. She turned suddenly, her eyes alighting on Mr. Darcy, who had just handed his coat off at the door. "Oh, Mr. Darcy! What a magnificent idea this party is! You are a credit to your sex, truly."

Elizabeth resisted the urge to groan as Mr. Darcy inclined his head with his usual composure. "You are too kind, Mrs. Bennet."

"Not at all, sir, not at all!" Mrs. Bennet continued, clasping her hands together. "Why, I daresay everyone in the neighborhood will be talking of nothing else all winter. Such generosity, such ingenuity—it is almost too much!"

Elizabeth leaned slightly toward Jane, her voice low. "Too much by half, you mean."

Jane's lips curved, but she said nothing. Darcy, however, turned his head just slightly, his expression flat but his eyes flicking toward her. Elizabeth's cheeks burned. Had he heard her? If so, he gave no sign, his attention returning to Roberts, who was now consulting his notebook.

From across the room, her father's voice cut through the chatter. "Really, my dear, if Mr. Darcy is so adept at party planning, perhaps we should recruit him to manage all our family affairs. What do you think, Sir Thomas?"

Sir Thomas, seated in a chair near the hearth, chuckled softly. "I believe Mr. Darcy has quite enough on his plate without taking on the Bennet household, though I am certain he would manage admirably."

Bingley strode in then, his face flushed with cold and good cheer. "Ah, Darcy, good, our little venture into Meryton was a resounding success, was it not?"

Darcy gave a small nod. "Indeed. We have confirmed our orders with all the merchants, the payment arrangements are all settled, and I believe we made an impression on more than a few of the shopkeepers."

"More than a few?" Bingley grinned. "Why, they were practically falling over themselves to see that we had the finest wares. One would think we had single-handedly saved their businesses."

Elizabeth folded her arms, tilting her head with interest. "And here I thought Mr. Bingley was speaking of *today's* 'venture'. I rather thought that bore the earmarks of success as well. What of you, Mr. Darcy?"

"A well-planned strategy," he confessed. "And an excellent suggestion, Miss Elizabeth. I think I met more people today than I even knew lived in Meryton."

"And what of the invitations?" Jane asked. "Did anyone give their reply?"

"Ah, well," Bingley began, casting a sidelong glance at Darcy. "There were, shall we say, some initial hesitations. But once we explained the full scope of the evening—"

"And promised the finest musicians and refreshments," Darcy interjected.

"—they were quite eager to attend," Bingley finished. "I daresay even the most austere matron we ever saw was tempted to send her acceptance after some cajoling."

Elizabeth arched a brow. "Let me guess. Mrs. Purvis? That must have been a sight worth seeing."

"It was indeed," Darcy said, his tone wry. "Though I believe the promise of hothouse flowers from London might have sealed her approval."

"Ah, yes," Sir Thomas chimed in, his gaze thoughtful. "Flowers can do wonders for softening even the hardest of hearts."

At that, Mrs. Bennet clapped her hands together. "Oh, flowers! Yes, we must have them everywhere—on the tables, on the mantels, perhaps even in the chandeliers! Oh, Mr. Darcy, do you think there will be enough for all that?"

"I am certain there will be plenty, Mrs. Bennet," Darcy replied with a slight bow.

Elizabeth stifled a laugh, shaking her head as her mother launched into a detailed list of additional suggestions. Across the room, she caught Darcy's gaze again. This time, he met her eyes fully, his expression calm but unwavering, and Elizabeth felt an odd flutter in her chest. It was a sensation she could not entirely name—but one she found increasingl y difficult to ignore.

T HE MUFFLED SOUND OF voices drifted into the hall as Darcy descended the grand staircase, pulling on his gloves. He had intended to meet Sir Thomas in his study to speak of the temporary relocation of the children's nursery so that the party might not keep the little ones awake and restless all hours of the night. Fortunately, there were, at the moment, only three children under the age of two requiring the care of a nurse, and Darcy meant to propose the large sitting room between his room and Bingley's. It would accommodate them handsomely and afford them privacy, quiet, and a large hearth for warmth.

Yet, as he approached the study door, he caught the sharp, cutting tone of an unfamiliar voice.

"...and I protest again, Sir Thomas, that your efforts are nothing more than a vain attempt to cloak your depravity in the guise of charity."

Darcy stiffened, his steps halting.

"This party, this... *spectacle*, is an insult to the moral order of this community. You cannot buy your way into acceptance, and you cannot cleanse your reputation with ribbons and garlands. Heaven and earth, you have couples living here, right now, as man and wife who are not lawfully wed!"

Darcy's brow furrowed. A glance across the hall revealed young Mrs. Jackson standing stiffly, her hands clasped tightly before her, her face pale as her eyes glittered oddly. The study door was slightly ajar, allowing the words to spill out into the corridor.

"You are so concerned about 'morality'," Sir Thomas's voice replied wearily. "But it was you, Reverend, who refused to marry Mr. and Mrs. Jackson in your church. Was I wrong to purchase a common license and find an officiant willing to unite them?"

"Do not twist the matter, Sir Thomas," the vicar snapped. "A union outside the sanctity of our parish is no union at all. It is your arrogance that leads these people further into sin."

Darcy's jaw tightened. He had heard enough. His hand twisted the latch and stepped into the room. "Sir Thomas," he said smoothly, "you wished to see me?" He glanced at the vicar, his expression one of polite curiosity. "Ah, I did not realize you had company. Should I return later?"

The vicar, a stout man with ruddy cheeks and an ill-concealed sneer, pointed a trembling finger at Darcy. "It is *you* who has emboldened him—this ridiculous party, this show of extravagance. You, with your wealth and influence, have brought this charade upon us!"

Darcy's gaze hardened, though his voice remained calm. "You accuse me, Reverend, of supporting a cause that seeks to uplift those in need. And what, may I ask, is so offensive about that?"

"Offensive?" the vicar sputtered. "Before you arrived, Netherfield was a stain upon this community, yes, but it was contained. The people there knew their place. Now, they dare to walk the streets of Meryton, parading as equals! Have you no decency, no thought for propriety?"

"On the contrary." Darcy crossed his arms. "I hold 'decency' in highest regard. And it is not 'decent' for good men to turn their backs when they have the power to help the less fortunate."

"It is not fortune but depravity which has sunk them so. What place do they have among the good people of Meryton?"

Darcy took a measured step forward. "True religion," he said, his voice lowering to a growl, "is to look after orphans and widows in their distress. Is that not what your own scripture teaches in the book of James?"

"That, sir, is a laughable twisting of the verse."

"Is it?" Darcy tilted his head, his eyes flipping back and forth as if he were reading that same verse in context at that moment. "How else does one interpret the phrase 'orphans and widows'?"

"They are not widows!" the vicar spat. "They are fallen women, and the men they consort with under this very roof are no better than beggars!"

Darcy's jaw clenched, but he did not raise his voice. Instead, he turned and gestured to the door. "I think, Reverend, that you have said quite enough. Sir Thomas is a man of unimpeachable honor, and your accusations do nothing but tarnish your own. Kindly see yourself out."

The vicar stood frozen for a moment, his face reddening with fury, but he seemed to recognize that he was outmatched. He gathered his hat and coat, glaring at Darcy before storming from the room.

Darcy closed the door behind him, the sharp click of the latch echoing in the silence. When he turned back, Sir Thomas sat slumped in his chair, his hands resting heavily on his desk. The firelight cast deep shadows across his face, emphasizing the weariness etched into his features.

"I apologize for the interruption," Darcy said. "I had not intended to intrude."

Sir Thomas lifted his gaze, his eyes filled with quiet resignation. "You need not apologize, Darcy. The vicar's opinions are hardly a secret, though hearing them aloud—in my own home—does little to lessen their sting."

Darcy hesitated, searching for the right words, but none seemed sufficient. Finally, he gave a small nod. "If there is anything more I can do..."

Sir Thomas waved a hand dismissively. "You have done more than most. Let us leave it at that."

Darcy inclined his head and exited the room, his thoughts a maelstrom. As he passed Mrs. Jackson in the hall, her gaze met his, and he offered a small, reassuring nod. Her lips trembled, but she returned the gesture before turning away.

It was then, as Darcy ascended the stairs to his own chambers, that the full weight of the vicar's words struck him. This party was not enough. Goodwill and festivity alone could not undo the damage of years of prejudice and mistrust. Sir Thomas's people needed more than a single night of acceptance—they needed a future.

Darcy's steps quickened as a plan began to take shape in his mind.

Darcy folded the thick paper carefully, the ink barely dry, before placing the letter into the envelope and sealing it with his signet. The faint scent of the wax lingered in the room as he pressed his thumb over the seal, ensuring it was set firmly. The task gave him a moment of pause—a brief chance to consider whether he had chosen his words with the necessary balance of formality and urgency.

It had been a few weeks, at least, since he last wrote to Colonel Fitzwilliam, and while the circumstances of the letter were unusual, he knew his cousin would rise to the occasion. Fitzwilliam always had a knack for knowing when Darcy truly meant more than he admitted in writing.

He rang the bell for Roberts, who appeared a moment later at the door.

"This letter is to be sent at once," Darcy instructed, holding out the sealed missive, along with several coins. "Have it sent express to London. I should like it to reach Colonel Fitzwilliam without delay."

"Very good, sir," Roberts replied, taking the letter with his remaining hand and tucking it carefully into his pocket.

Darcy watched him retreat, a flicker of admiration stirring as the man's determined gait carried him out of the room. Roberts was proof of the resilience Darcy admired in those who resided at Netherfield—proof, too, that Sir Thomas's efforts were far from misplaced.

Indeed, it was not enough, this party. It would create a momentary reprieve, perhaps even kindle some goodwill within the community—but what then? Would the people here look more kindly upon Sir Thomas and his dependents? Or would the party only serve as further fodder for Meryton's relentless gossip?

The townspeople had softened, that much was clear. Whispers of the upcoming Christmas revelry had stirred curiosity where once there had been only disdain. The butcher's hearty assurances, the draper's enthusiasm, and the baker's delighted ambition all hinted that the tide might turn. And that was not even to begin speaking of the local gentry who had tendered their acceptance. Yet, the larger question still loomed.

He paused by the window, looking out over the snow-dappled grounds. The air was still, the house unusually quiet, save for the faint echo of children playing with down the hall. Healthy children—children who were safe, with a roof over their heads and full bellies. Children who were not consigned to the workhouse at age five.

He should have been satisfied. They were doing a good thing here. The preparations were progressing, and the hint of the community's approval seemed just within reach. But approval alone would not sustain what Sir Thomas had built here.

Darcy paced back toward the desk, his eyes dropping to survey the papers scattered before him. Sir Thomas had saved so many—men who had gone on to carve out extraordinary lives, even before this venture at Netherfield. He thought of Watts, the promising solicitor; Pence, now a thriving merchant; and Drummond, who had risen to prominence in the Admiralty. They were but a few of the men who owed their lives to Sir Thomas's daring.

It was time to call in those debts.

Darcy pulled out fresh paper, his pen moving swiftly across the page. Letters of inquiry, requests for support, names and ideas forming in quick succession. And the more he wrote, the brighter his inspiration burned.

Apprenticeships for soldiers. Partnerships with merchants and tradesmen. Opportunities for the women who sought a new start. Each thought took shape with a clarity that had been eluding him since the idea of the party began.

A knock at the door pulled him from his focus. Bingley appeared, his grin as bright as the afternoon sun. "Darcy, are you hiding in here? Sir Thomas has just inspired Roberts to show Mrs. Bennet the plans for the ballroom, and I fear it may be the end of us all."

Darcy set down his pen, looking up with the faintest glimmer of amusement. "Is she staging a coup?"

Bingley laughed. "I would not call it that, but she is certainly campaigning for her own vision of Christmas splendor. It involves far more ribbons than I think Sir Thomas anticipated."

Darcy shook his head, rising. "I shall come at once, if only to prevent utter anarchy."

As they made their way toward the ballroom, Bingley leaned closer, his voice low. "It is working, Darcy. The town is curious, the plans are coming together—and dare I say, even Sir Thomas is starting to look a bit less gloomy."

Darcy nodded, a flicker of satisfaction sparking within him. "It is a start."

Eighteen

FOUR DAYS HAD PASSED since Darcy had sent his letters, and Meryton bustled with midday activity. The grey sky above threatened snow, and the air held the crisp bite of winter. Darcy stood near the market square, adjusting the cuffs of his gloves, his gaze shifting toward the approaching carriage.

At last, the vehicle came to a halt with a creak of wood and jingling harnesses. The door swung open, and Colonel Fitzwilliam descended, his boots striking the snow-dusted cobblestones with purpose.

"Darcy! Greeting me in town instead of at Netherfield, are you? A rather quaint scene you've chosen for this reunion. What happened to my dignified cousin?"

"Needs must," Darcy replied, shaking his cousin's hand. "You are here to assist, not to critique."

Fitzwilliam arched a brow. "Assist with what, exactly? You've been maddeningly vague."

Darcy gestured toward the pub down the street, its windows glowing warmly against the frosty air. "You shall see soon enough."

Fitzwilliam hesitated, a smirk tugging at his lips. "A public house, Darcy? You, willingly stepping into such a den of common conviviality? I should have the apothecary examine you on the way."

"I trust your wit is as sharp as ever," Darcy said, his tone flat but his pace brisk as he led the way toward the pub.

"I am merely trying to imagine what grave calamity has driven you to such measures," Fitzwilliam said, following. "Do tell me you've not taken to rustic indulgences."

"Your imagination," Darcy said over his shoulder, "is both unnecessary and unwelcome."

"And yet, I shall continue imagining all I like."

Darcy shot him a look, sharp enough to warn but lacking the bite to silence him. "If you could temper your sarcasm for five minutes, Fitzwilliam, you might notice that we are being watched."

Fitzwilliam raised an eyebrow, slowing his pace slightly. "Watched? Ah. I see now." His voice dropped, though the smirk remained. "This is theater, then."

"Of a sort." Darcy inclined his head subtly toward a small cluster of shopkeepers standing just outside the draper's, their conversation halting as the two men passed. "And thank you for bringing your father's newest carriage. I wonder that he did not object."

"Who says I asked him?"

"I see. Well, whatever means you employed, I daresay I am grateful. It is important that we be seen."

"Doing what? Strolling with an air of consequence?"

Darcy suppressed a sigh. "Engaging with the community. Showing that Netherfield's occupants—Sir Thomas's people—are not beneath *our* notice, which means they are not beneath *theirs*."

"Fascinating," Fitzwilliam murmured, glancing around at the curious glances they were garnering. "And here I thought your talents lay in accounting figures and brooding."

"Keep your voice down," Darcy muttered, steering him toward the entrance of the inn. The smell of roasting meats and the warm hum of voices greeted them as they stepped inside, the sudden heat brushing the chill from their coats.

"Now you've really lost me," Fitzwilliam said, his tone pitched low. "You hate places like this."

"Yes," Darcy admitted. "But this is where people talk. And I mean for them to talk about the right things."

"Such as?" Fitzwilliam asked, though his gaze wandered to the barmaid who had paused mid-motion, her eyes widening slightly at the sight of them.

Darcy removed his gloves deliberately, meeting Fitzwilliam's gaze with quiet intent. "The party. The preparations. And the fact that we are here, inviting them to attend."

Fitzwilliam chuckled under his breath. "Well, this is unexpected. Very well, Darcy. Let us play our roles."

They approached the Golden Fox, a modest but respectable establishment on Meryton's high street. Darcy stepped inside first, his gaze sweeping the room. The warm hum of conversation buzzed around them as townsfolk sat gathered at tables, their faces lit by the glow of the hearth.

Darcy selected a table near the center of the room and gestured for Fitzwilliam to sit. Fitzwilliam hesitated, clearly nonplussed. "Here? Truly? Not a private alcove?"

"Yes, here," Darcy said evenly. "And keep your voice at a volume the room might appreciate."

Fitzwilliam raised a brow but took his seat, a crooked grin tugging at his lips. "You never fail to amuse, Darcy. First, a public house, now *you* instructing *me* on manners. What next?"

Darcy waved over a serving girl and ordered drinks for them both. As soon as the ale was brought to the table, he lifted his mug and nodded toward Fitzwilliam. "To the season, and to good company."

Fitzwilliam's brow furrowed as he hesitated. Darcy gave him a pointed look, and Fitzwilliam seemed to understand. Lifting his own mug, he mirrored Darcy's toast. "To good company."

Darcy leaned back slightly, his gaze sweeping the room before settling on Fitzwilliam. "This Christmas party we are planning—" he began, deliberately raising his voice a fraction.

"Oh, yes," Fitzwilliam replied, catching on just enough to follow Darcy's lead. "I have heard about this grand affair. Do tell me more."

Darcy nodded as though Fitzwilliam's response was natural. "Sir Thomas has been most generous in offering Netherfield for the occasion. It shall be a truly splendid evening. Music, dancing, a grand supper—every detail carefully considered."

Fitzwilliam took a long sip of his ale, his eyes narrowing slightly at Darcy over the rim of the mug. "And the company, I imagine, will be equally delightful."

"Indeed," Darcy said smoothly. "The ladies of Meryton are quite remarkable."

Fitzwilliam nearly choked on his drink. "Remarkable, are they?"

"The prettiest and most agreeable ladies you ever met." Darcy's eyes met his cousin's, the faintest flicker of warning passing between them. Fitzwilliam cleared his throat and composed himself. "Yes, I suppose they must be."

Darcy tilted his head as though pondering his cousin's words. "You shall see for yourself, Fitzwilliam. I daresay you may find the evening... enlightening."

Fitzwilliam's face warmed with suppressed amusement, but he gave a short nod. "I am sure I shall."

Their conversation continued in this vein, carefully measured yet loud enough to carry to the nearby tables. Darcy noticed the glances exchanged among the other patrons, their curiosity growing with every word. By the time they left the Golden Fox, he felt confident their mission had been successful.

"YOU ARE A PUZZLING creature, Darcy. If I did not know better, I might think you enjoyed our little display."

"Hardly," Darcy replied. "It was necessary."

"Necessary, was it? Well, whatever it was, you should do it more often. It suits you."

Darcy ignored the jibe as they entered Netherfield house. Roberts greeted them in the hall and directed them toward the drawing room where Sir Thomas awaited. Darcy stepped inside first, his gaze immediately seeking the baronet, who sat by the hearth with an open book in his lap.

"Fitzwilliam!" Sir Thomas exclaimed, rising with a broad smile. "It has been far too long. A colonel now, eh? Who the devil thought to promote you?"

"Sir Thomas," Fitzwilliam laughed, stepping forward to clasp the older man's hand. "I would say you are a sight for sore eyes, but I fear my own appearance might be the more pitiable."

"Nonsense," Sir Thomas said with a chuckle. "You look well, my boy. And your presence here is most welcome."

The door opened again, and Bingley strode in, shrugging into his coat as he entered. "Ah, Darcy, there you are! I was beginning to think you two would never return. What, did Fitzwilliam's carriage take a wrong turn?"

"Bingley," Darcy said, his brow furrowing. "What is the rush?"

Bingley paused, a mischievous glint in his eye. "Do not tell me you have forgot."

"Forgot what?"

"Dinner at Longbourn, of course," Bingley said, his grin widening. "We are expected shortly. Do hurry, Darcy—we cannot afford to keep the ladies waiting."

Darcy froze, a mixture of surprise and something perilously close to anticipation washing over him. Dinner at Longbourn? He had not been informed.

Bingley gave him a knowing look, one that seemed to say, *I planned this, and you will thank me later.* Darcy sighed inwardly but reached for his own coat.

"Very well," he said. "Come along, Richard. Let us be off."

ELIZABETH CROSSED THE ROOM in restless strides, her gaze darting toward the window before she turned back to Jane, who sat at the dressing table adjusting the ribbons in her hair.

"Lizzy, if you do not stop pacing, you may find yourself with nothing left to tread on."

Elizabeth paused mid-step and raised a brow. "I had not realized my movements were so disruptive."

"They are not disruptive," Jane replied, her hands stilling for a moment. "They are... telling."

"Telling?" Elizabeth echoed, crossing her arms. "I am merely passing the time until dinner. Shall I sit and wait in silence instead?"

Jane turned to face her, one corner of her mouth lifting ever so slightly. "You are waiting for more than dinner, Lizzy."

Elizabeth blinked. "For the company, perhaps. That is natural."

"For Mr. Darcy," Jane said matter-of-factly.

Elizabeth pressed her lips together, but Jane's knowing look did not waver. With a sigh, she sat down on the edge of her bed. "Is it so obvious?"

"To me? Yes," Jane replied. "But I know you best. So, tell me—are you falling in love with him?"

Elizabeth's cheeks heated. She hesitated, then gave a small, reluctant nod. "I think... perhaps I am."

Jane's face brightened, though she wisely refrained from any exclamation. "And why do you think so?"

She chewed her lower lip as her eyes squinted in thought. "He is kind, though he takes great care to disguise it. Thoughtful, though he says little. And I admire how sure he is, Jane. He knows who he is and what he stands for, and he... well, I suppose he does exactly as he pleases, but what he 'pleases' to do is good."

Jane smiled, leaning forward slightly. "Then you approve of his character as well as his wealth?"

"Oh, bother! You know very well I care nothing for that."

"Well, you should. 'Twould be a fearful shame if you fell for a man who had not two pence to rub together."

Elizabeth sighed. "What I mean, Jane, is that when I first met Mr. Darcy, I had set him far from my mind. He was amusing to flirt with, but it was nothing serious. I thought such a man could have no possible interest in..." She looked down at her hands. "Well. Perhaps he still does not. And I could hardly blame him, of course, but I am gratified that he has taken such an interest in Sir Thomas's predicament."

Jane crossed her legs and leaned back primly against her vanity. "Ah, she finally admits it! I told you, Aunt and I had a terribly useful idea, putting Mr. Bingley and Mr. Darcy in the way of learning about Netherfield. You cannot accuse us of doing anything more than leading the horses to water, Lizzy. It was up to them to drink, and so they did."

Elizabeth rolled her eyes. "I think, rather, that you employed hefty doses of both guilt and temptation, but so far, the gentlemen have made no objection."

"Mark my words; they have no intention of doing so."

"Oh? What makes you so sure?"

Jane blushed and fought back a giggle. "You cannot ask me to say."

Elizabeth arched a brow. "What? Has Mr. Bingley told you something? You *do* appear to be in his confidence."

Jane's mouth dropped open in sheepish denial. "But it was not only what he said, though. I am not blind, Lizzy, and neither is anyone else. It seems to me that Mr. Darcy is rather captivated by you."

Elizabeth blinked, a soft laugh escaping her lips. "Do not be absurd, Jane."

"I am not," Jane insisted. "He watches you, Lizzy. Not in the way some men do, with idle interest or fleeting admiration. He observes you as if he is memorizing everything you do. It is as though he wants to understand every part of you."

Elizabeth's her heart quickened, though she shook her head. "You imagine things."

"I do not," Jane said firmly. "I think Mr. Darcy admires you deeply. And if you would let yourself believe it, you might see it too."

Elizabeth could not bring herself to answer. A quiet thrill ran through her at Jane's words, but she tempered it with caution. Hope, she knew, was a precarious thing.

THE FAINT JINGLE OF carriage bells outside drew Elizabeth's attention from the bouquet she was arranging. Jane, beside her, adjusted a stray ribbon on the mantle garland, pausing when the noise grew closer.

"That must be them," Jane said, smoothing her gown and casting a glance at Elizabeth.

Elizabeth met her sister's gaze with a smile she could hardly restrain before following their mother toward the front door. As the door opened, the sight of Mr. Darcy, Mr. Bingley, and a man Elizabeth had not met filled the threshold.

Darcy inclined his head politely, stepping aside to gesture to his companion. "Mrs. Bennet, Miss Bennet, Miss Elizabeth. Forgive me for the last-minute addition to the party, but may I introduce my cousin, Colonel Fitzwilliam?"

Colonel Fitzwilliam bowed with a warm smile. "It is an honor to make your acquaintance."

Mrs. Bennet curtsied deeply, her face lighting with eagerness. "Oh, a pleasure, Colonel! No surprise, sir, at all, for Mr. Bingley informed us this very morning that you were expected. Oh, my heavens, how *well* you look in your regimentals! I always said it was patriotic—yes, yes, *patriotic* to think a man looks at least ten times handsomer in a red coat."

Oh, good heavens. Elizabeth bit the inside of her cheek as Kitty and Lydia practically spilled forward in unison, their wide eyes fixed on the Colonel. They were about to start drooling.

"Come in, come in!" Mrs. Bennet insisted. "The weather has been so wretched, and you must be chilled. We have a fire in the drawing room—and refreshments, of course."

Mr. Bennet appeared in the hallway, his hand resting on the doorframe as his sharp gaze swept over the new arrival. "Ah, so this is the famous Colonel Fitzwilliam. Welcome, sir. I trust my wife has not overwhelmed you already."

The colonel laughed, his voice rich and warm. "Not in the least, Mr. Bennet. Your hospitality is most appreciated."

Darcy stepped forward then, his eyes flicking to Elizabeth for a fleeting moment before turning to address Mr. Bennet. "I trust we are not arriving too early?"

"Not at all," Mr. Bennet replied. "Though I would suggest you pace yourselves—Mrs. Bennet's enthusiasm knows no bounds."

"Oh, Mr. Bennet! You do tease me so." Mrs. Bennet protested, though her indignation was clearly for show. She turned back to Colonel Fitzwilliam with a dazzling smile. "Please, you must tell us more about your regiment! My daughters have such a keen interest in all matters military."

Colonel Fitzwilliam smiled graciously, though he seemed to sense the trap. "Perhaps after dinner," he said. "I find such tales are best accompanied by good wine."

Elizabeth's gaze shifted to Mr. Darcy, who was studying the exchange with what looked like a faint smile tugging at the corner of his lips. She tilted her head slightly, catching his eye just as he turned toward her.

"Miss Elizabeth," he said, "I trust you have been well since last we met?"

She curtsied lightly. "Quite well, thank you, Mr. Darcy. And you?"

"Perfectly, thank you."

That seemed to be an intimate conversation for Mr. Darcy—at least, as intimate as he would permit in public. His eyes, though—she had learned a little of how to read them now, and there was a sort of sweetness there that she could swear had kindled only when he spoke to her. Perhaps Jane was right...

Before she could say more, Mrs. Bennet clapped her hands, ushering everyone toward the drawing room. "Come, gentlemen, come! There is tea waiting, and we cannot have you standing in the cold hallway like beggars."

Elizabeth lingered a step behind the group, her thoughts catching briefly on Mr. Darcy's expression. It had been so brief, but she could have sworn there was something unspoken in his gaze—something that lingered with her even as they entered the warmth of the drawing room for drinks before dinner.

L ATER, AS THEY WERE called into the dining room, Elizabeth found herself next to Colonel Fitzwilliam. Darcy, she noticed with a pang of sympathy, had escorted her mother to her seat and was now ensnared at the other end of the table. Mama was already chattering at him about goodness-knew-what, but he seemed to bear it all with polite endurance.

"Miss Elizabeth," Colonel Fitzwilliam began, lifting his glass faintly in polite deference. "It must be quite a change, having my cousin and Mr. Bingley descend upon your corner of the world."

Elizabeth glanced toward Mr. Darcy, who appeared entirely absorbed by her mother's detailed account of Mary's musical talents. A faint smile touched her lips. "Change is seldom unwelcome, Colonel, provided it is of a tolerable nature."

Fitzwilliam chuckled. "And has it been tolerable, then? I admit, my cousin can be a difficult man to pin down in unfamiliar surroundings."

"Oh, you do him too little credit. Mr. Darcy has been most obliging. Hosting a Christmas party for the entire neighborhood is no small undertaking. One might almost think him determined to charm all of Hertfordshire."

"Charm?" Fitzwilliam said, raising a brow. "Now, that would be an unexpected endeavor for Darcy."

Elizabeth's smile widened. "Would it? You speak as though you doubt his ability."

"Not his ability," Fitzwilliam corrected with mock seriousness. "Only his inclination. My cousin is rather particular about the company he keeps."

"Then I suppose we should all feel honored by his presence," Elizabeth said lightly, though the glance she cast toward Darcy carried a hint of curiosity.

Fitzwilliam followed her gaze, his expression softening. "Honored, perhaps. But also assured. When Darcy sets his mind to something, you can be certain he will see it through."

Elizabeth tilted her head. "And what might he have set his mind to here, Colonel?"

Fitzwilliam paused, his fingers tracing the rim of his wineglass. "That," he said, his tone thoughtful, "is a question best answered by observing him. Darcy's actions often speak louder than his words, if one knows where to look."

She regarded him for a moment, intrigued despite herself. Before she could respond, Fitzwilliam's smile returned, disarming and warm. "But enough about Darcy. Tell me, Miss Elizabeth—what part do you play in this grand endeavor? From all I have heard, your family has been rather instrumental in its success thus far."

Elizabeth hesitated, caught between amusement and uncertainty. "I would not say instrumental, Colonel. We have merely... lent our assistance where it seemed appropriate."

"Ah," Fitzwilliam said with a knowing nod. "Modesty becomes you, Miss Elizabeth. But I suspect there is more to the story than you let on."

Elizabeth gave a small laugh, shaking her head. "Colonel Fitzwilliam, you are determined to credit me with far more than I deserve. I assure you, my contributions have been quite ordinary."

"Ordinary?" Fitzwilliam said, a glint of mischief in his eye. "I doubt Darcy would see it that way."

Something like butterflies tickled her stomach. "And what makes you think Mr. Darcy has taken notice of anything I have done?"

Fitzwilliam grinned. "Because I know my cousin. He has a way of noticing what others overlook. And if he speaks of something—or *someone*—you can be certain he has considered it carefully."

"High praise," Elizabeth said demurely, though her heart was pattering in her ears. Was the colonel talking about *her*, or his other endeavors? "It is fortunate, then, that he appears to approve of this particular undertaking."

"Oh, he approves, Miss Elizabeth. In fact, I would venture to say he sees it as more than just a party." Fitzwilliam leaned back slightly. "My cousin does not take on causes lightly. When he involves himself, it is often with an eye toward a greater purpose."

Elizabeth's brows knit faintly. "What purpose could he have here, beyond aiding Sir Thomas and his household?"

Fitzwilliam's expression grew thoughtful, the humor in his voice giving way to something more measured. "Darcy has ambitions, Miss Elizabeth—though he does not often speak of them openly. For years, he has considered the possibility of public service. I think Bingley first put the idea in his head, but my father also took up the cause. He has been urging him to consider a seat in the House."

Elizabeth's fork paused midway to her plate. "Yes, he has spoken of it."

"He has? Why, that is very interesting, indeed. He must be thinking on it even more seriously than I had realized."

"Well, I would hardly know, sir. He did speak of it, but with little relish, I thought."

"Aye, that would be Darcy. More natural gifts and endowments than any one man ought rightly to have, and he hardly likes any of them. But he would be a natural fit in politics, even if he did not care for it. His business acumen, his devotion to his tenants and his family duties, and his ability to manage complex affairs... all of these are qualities that would serve him well in such a role."

Elizabeth nodded slowly, her fork resting forgotten on her plate. "And what does he hope to accomplish in Parliament?"

Fitzwilliam smiled faintly, leaning back with a comfortable ease. "Ah, Darcy is always on about inequities—how to address them, how to create opportunities for those who have none. It is why this endeavor at Netherfield matters so much to him. If handled well, it could serve as a model for what might be achieved on a broader scale."

Elizabeth's stomach twisted, though she kept her expression composed. "A model," she said softly. "And does he believe the neighborhood will welcome such... innovation?"

"Public opinion is a curious thing, Miss Elizabeth," Fitzwilliam replied, his tone easy but sharp with meaning. "It can be fickle, certainly, but Darcy has a knack for earning respect where it matters. A man like him does not need universal approval—just enough to tip the scales."

"And those who do not approve?" she asked, her voice quieter now, her thoughts racing.

Fitzwilliam shrugged lightly, the gesture entirely too casual. "They will be won over. Darcy knows how to seize an opportunity, and his name carries weight. His actions speak for themselves."

"Or," Elizabeth pressed, her throat tight, "are they framed to speak for themselves?"

"Ah, framing," Fitzwilliam said, his smile turning wry. "An astute observation, Miss Elizabeth. Humanitarian causes are quite fashionable, you know. They make an excellent platform for a political campaign—provided, to use your own words, they are 'framed' correctly."

Elizabeth's breath caught. "And what exactly does that entail?"

"The public must feel inspired," he said matter-of-factly, as though discussing the weather. "A sense of pity. Perhaps moral superiority. Perception is everything, Miss Elizabeth."

Elizabeth's gaze flicked toward Darcy. He was nodding politely at her mother, his expression open and attentive, entirely unbothered by Mrs. Bennet's effusions. He glanced up at Elizabeth, catching her eye for just a moment, and smiled—genuine, unguarded. To Elizabeth, it felt like the twist of a knife.

She turned back to Colonel Fitzwilliam, forcing her voice to remain steady. "And do you believe Mr. Darcy would... *frame* things correctly?"

Fitzwilliam chuckled lightly. "My cousin is many things, Miss Elizabeth, but he is no fool. He knows how to make an impact."

Elizabeth's stomach churned. Was this what Darcy intended? To turn Sir Thomas and the residents of Netherfield into objects of pity, all to serve his own ambitions? The thought filled her with a cold dread.

Her fork clinked softly against her plate as she set it down. Darcy caught her eye once more, his expression warm and unwittingly disarming. She could not bear to meet it and turned her attention instead to her untouched meal. Fitzwilliam continued speaking, but his words faded into the background, leaving her thoughts to spiral in dismay.

Could she have been so completely wrong about him?

Nineteen

DINNER AT LONGBOURN WAS the sort of loving chaos that seemed to thrive in the Bennet household. Darcy watched it all in a detached sort of awe as Mrs. Bennet presided with gleeful energy, extolling her daughters' virtues to anyone who would listen. Miss Catherine and Miss Lydia hung on Colonel Fitzwilliam's every word, gasping with delight at his tales of military life. And Bennet himself seemed content to listen to everyone else talk while he drank his wine in peace.

There was only one Bennet who actually captured Darcy's notice, and she was trapped on the far side of Richard, at the opposite end of the table. But still, he could feel her warmth and wit, even from that distance. She laughed at her father's quips—when he troubled himself to speak—listened earnestly to her sisters, and even joined Fitzwilliam in a playful exchange about the challenges of military discipline. To the casual observer, she was the very picture of warmth and sociability.

And yet, something felt off.

It wasn't until their eyes met across the table that he truly noticed it. There was no spark, no challenge, no teasing glint in her gaze—just a polite coolness that chilled him all the way to the heart. She glanced away almost immediately, turning her focus to her sister, and Darcy was left to wonder if he had imagined it.

Surely, he had. Why, she was the very picture of grace, smiling like that. And she would be smiling even more when he told her about the idea he had, only this evening, as he glanced around the table.

For each of the Bennet sisters wore some sort of jewelry—some precious trinket that marked them as the daughters of a gentleman of at least modest means. Elizabeth wore her garnet cross—a pretty little thing set with gold and dark-ish stones that dangled just at the creamy notch where her throat met her collarbone. Her elder sister had a pearl pendant. He could not see Miss Mary's beneath her overly-stuffy fichu, but there was a gold chain glinting at her neck, and the younger sisters... well, he did not like to let his gaze rest on their bosoms long enough to study their pendants, lest they feel his gaze and make assumptions, but they had *something*.

And that gave him an idea. One that would help to answer the question of *what next* for the members of Sir Thomas's household. But he would need to go to London for it. He would ask Elizabeth—perhaps she could guide him.

But by the time the party moved to the drawing room, her apparent distraction and his unease had grown. Elizabeth had spoken to everyone with her usual good humor, but to him, she offered only brief, guarded responses. The shift was subtle, but unmistakable.

He lingered by the fire, waiting for the right moment to approach her. Elizabeth had seated herself near Miss Bennet, a book in hand that she barely glanced at. Darcy crossed the room, determined to understand.

"Miss Elizabeth, might I have a word?"

Elizabeth's hand tightened on the book's spine, but her expression remained composed as she looked up. "Certainly, Mr. Darcy," she replied. "What would you like to discuss?"

For a moment, relief flickered in him. Perhaps he had been mistaken about that chill in her demeanor. "I wished to express my gratitude," he said, offering her a faint smile. "Your family's hospitality has been most gracious."

Her lips curved slightly. "I am glad you have found it so."

Encouraged, he continued in a lower voice, so as not to be overheard in case she told him his idea was madness, or misplaced extravagance, or... or anything, really. He wanted *her* to be the first one he spoke to about this. "I had a rather curious notion while we were at dinner. It strikes me that there is... more that could be done. For the people of Netherfield, that is."

Her face lifted swiftly, and it was odd, but there was a tick to her lower left eyelid as she peered up at him. "Such as?"

"Well..." How to put it? He glanced swiftly about the room. Anything he said in this room would be overheard, and his idea... why, it probably *did* sound outlandish. In fact, a rich man like him, buying such articles for other women... good heavens, it could be positively scandalous if rumors spread or the words were not phrased correctly. And that would only make matters worse.

He lowered his voice still more. "It occurs to me that... that much of what we call 'respectability' is in nothing more than favorable appearances."

Her eyes narrowed faintly. "Explain yourself."

Darcy swallowed. Egad, she was rather blunt this evening. Where was his smiling, charming compatriot? "I mean," he murmured in a still-lower voice, "that if one but has the means, dignity can... well, it can almost be bought. Or at least a chance—an opportunity, if you will."

Elizabeth's jaw flexed. "Opportunity?"

"Indeed, for without opportunity, how is one to display the content of their character? The qualities that make them remarkable? I cannot answer all needs, but I think, Miss Elizabeth, I know of a way to open the doors of opportunity."

Her breast—that garnet cross—lowered softly in a long exhale. "And for this, I shall hazard a guess. You mean to go to London to procure this.... opportunity?"

He straightened. Despite all her seeming skepticism tonight, perhaps she was, indeed, following the direction of his thoughts. "Yes, I have... connections there. I shall write letters immediately to begin the arrangements. Something fine and... dare I say it... extravagant? I think Sir Thomas's people deserve nothing less. But we must take care to... to frame our words correctly, so we are not misunderstood."

She blinked, and her lips parted softly as she gaped at him.

Why was she staring like that without speaking? This was not at all like the Elizabeth Bennet he knew—the woman who had stolen his heart already. Perhaps if he explained a little more, she would understand. "A—anyway, I was hoping you might..." He glanced over his shoulder at Mr. Bennet, whose gaze felt like a hot fire poker boring into his back. "That is, if your father approves, I was hoping you and perhaps your sister might also come to London for a few days. I should like to speak with Mrs. Gardiner as well. I could use a lady's advice, and—"

She sucked in a sharp breath and stepped away. "I think I have heard quite enough, sir."

Instinctively, he reached out and caught her elbow before he could examine why he had done so. "Miss Elizabeth," he began cautiously, "have I given you reason for displeasure?"

Her chin lifted. "Not at all, Mr. Darcy. You are always perfectly civil."

The words, though polite, carried a finality that left him momentarily at a loss. Before he could press further, she cut him off with a smile. "If you will excuse me, Mr. Darcy, I find I must see to the tea," she said, gesturing toward the service tray.

He inclined his head, though the unusual formality of her tone stung. "Of... of course. Perhaps we will have an opportunity later for me to explain my idea more fully."

Her smile was thin and entirely insincere. "That will not be necessary, sir. Please excuse me."

Not... not *necessary*? What the devil did she mean by *that*? But he had no choice but to step back, allowing her to move past him.

Darcy remained rooted to the spot, aware of the sudden quiet that seemed to gather around him. Out of the corner of his eye, Fitzwilliam exchanged a glance with Bingley, whose conspiratorial nudge in the colonel's side earned a faint smirk. Darcy ignored them both, his focus drawn entirely to Elizabeth as she busied herself with the teacups, her movements crisp and deliberate. Whatever he had done—or failed to do—it was painfully clear that Elizabeth was in no frame of mind for any flirtations tonight.

Not that... well, not that he usually *flirted*. Just... enjoyed her company. Like that of no other woman he had ever known.

"Well?" Fitzwilliam murmured. "Are you going to stand there like a statue, or will you try again?"

Darcy shot him a warning look but said nothing. Instead, he crossed the room with deliberate steps, joining Mr. Bennet, who was seated comfortably with a book.

"Mr. Bennet," Darcy began, determined to appear composed, "I was hoping to ask your opinion on an aspect of the party preparations."

Mr. Bennet peered over his spectacles, his expression faintly amused. "You are braver than I thought, Mr. Darcy. Few men willingly seek advice from a father with five daughters."

Darcy allowed himself a small smile. "And yet, your household seems well accustomed to managing the unexpected. I thought your insight might be valuable."

Mr. Bennet chuckled, closing his book. "Very well. My advice, Mr. Darcy, is this: let the guests entertain themselves. People are often more agreeable when they believe they are acting of their own accord."

Darcy inclined his head. "Sage advice, Mr. Bennet."

"Though if you are hoping to apply that wisdom to your current predicament," Mr. Bennet added, his tone sharpening slightly, "you may find my Lizzy less easily impressed than the rest of us."

Darcy met Mr. Bennet's gaze. "Your daughter," he said after a measured pause, "is indeed not one to be impressed lightly. It is a quality I admire."

Mr. Bennet leaned back, his expression aloof but his eyes keen. "Admiration is all very well, Mr. Darcy. But admiration alone seldom persuades her."

Darcy allowed a faint smile, though his thoughts churned. "Then I must ask, sir—what does persuade Miss Elizabeth?"

Mr. Bennet's brow rose, the faintest flicker of approval in his expression. "Ah, now that, Mr. Darcy, is a question I believe you must answer for yourself. But I will say this—she values honesty above all else. Not flattery, mind you. Genuine honesty."

Darcy inclined his head. "That much, I believe I already knew."

The older man's gaze lingered for a moment before he returned to his book. "Well, then. Let us see if you can rise to the challenge, Mr. Darcy."

Darcy's response was cut short by Mrs. Bennet bustling toward the tea tray. "Lizzy! My dear, please pour the tea for *all* of us, would you? Mr. Darcy and Colonel Fitzwilliam must be served, and you always make such a fine job of it."

Darcy's gaze snapped up to see Elizabeth's shoulders tightening almost imperceptibly, but she swallowed and bobbed her head. "Of course, Mama."

Darcy couldn't look away as she lifted the teapot, her hands sure, but her movements almost mechanical rather than graceful, lacking the natural ease he had come to associate with her. The room buzzed softly with conversation, but for Darcy, the air between them was thick with the twisting of unspoken feeling.

Mrs. Bennet turned to Darcy with an expectant smile. "Mr. Darcy, do let Lizzy serve you first. She always knows just how much cream to add."

He rose from Mr. Bennet's side and approached slowly. A little caution might be wise this time, giving her space before speaking. "Miss Elizabeth, may I trouble you for a cup?"

Her hands stilled for the briefest moment before she resumed pouring. She placed the cup on its saucer and held it out to him, her gaze fixed on the table.

"Thank you," he said quietly, but she offered no reply.

Across the room, Fitzwilliam leaned back in his chair, his arms crossed over his chest as he raised a brow at Darcy. Bingley cleared his throat loudly and rose, moving toward Miss Bennet with an exaggerated air of cheer.

"Miss Bennet, your mother assures us that your taste in decorations is second to none. Might I trouble you for your opinion on the garlands for the ballroom?"

Miss Bennet's gaze flicked briefly toward Elizabeth, her expression tinged with concern. "I would be happy to assist," she replied to Bingley. "Though I wonder if Mr. Darcy might already have strong preferences. His attention to detail is rather renowned, is it not?"

Bingley laughed, shaking his head. "Darcy? That will be the day. I assure you, Miss Bennet, his tastes are decidedly practical."

"Practical, perhaps," Miss Bennet agreed as she glanced at her sister again. "But even practicality can surprise us now and then. Still," she continued lightly, "I am happy to help. It is not every day one plans a party on such a scale."

"Excellent," Bingley said. "Perhaps Darcy and I should take notes. You seem to have the knack for these things."

Darcy allowed himself the barest tilt of an eyebrow at the comment. His gaze shifted to Elizabeth at the tea tray, her focus fixed on the task as though she were conducting a delicate experiment. She poured with precision, never glancing up, but the tightness in her shoulders gave her away.

Miss Bennet's subtle maneuvering wasn't lost on him. It struck him, not for the first time, that while Elizabeth's wit was razor-sharp, her sister's quieter approach could be just as effective—and often, more disarming.

Darcy's gaze snapped back to Elizabeth as she stepped back from the tea tray, her hands clasped tightly in front of her. "Mama, I am afraid I must excuse myself," she said, her voice low but firm. "I have a headache."

"A headache?" Mrs. Bennet cried. "But Lizzy, Mr. Darcy and Colonel Fitzwilliam—"

"I beg you will excuse me, Mama. I really am feeling quite unwell," Elizabeth said, cutting her off. She glanced once at her elder sister before she started toward the door.

Darcy watched her retreat, unease settling deep in his chest. Elizabeth Bennet, usually so sharp and vibrant, had been distant all evening. The change was undeniable, and it left him searching for answers.

Across the room, Fitzwilliam met his gaze with a subtle but pointed nod, as if urging him to persevere. Bingley, lingering nearby, caught Darcy's eye and gave a fleeting smile before returning to Miss Bennet's side, his posture unusually attentive.

But it was Mr. Bennet who held his attention. The older man was watching him with quiet amusement, his sharp gaze seeming to take the measure of him. Darcy forced a polite smile and moved closer, attempting to engage him in conversation about the party preparations. That was all he could manage tonight.

"MARY, YOU *MUST* WEAR the pink sash!" Lydia declared. "It is festive. It is charming. It is... the only thing that will make you look tolerable at the party."

Elizabeth, seated by the window, kept her gaze on the embroidery in her lap, though her needle hovered motionless above the cloth. She wasn't stitching daisies anymore—she was simply stabbing at the same spot over and over.

"I shall not degrade myself with frivolity," Mary retorted, straightening with an air of self-righteousness. "Or did you forget the very point of this party? A sensible gown and a modest demeanor will suffice."

"You'll look like a governess!" Lydia groaned, flopping onto the floor beside Kitty, who burst into giggles.

Elizabeth's lips twitched despite herself, but her amusement faded as quickly as it had come. Her sisters' chatter about the party only deepened the knot in her chest. Every mention of Netherfield, every speculation about its hosts, brought the evening's dinner to the forefront of her mind. And with it, a pair of dark, questioning eyes.

"Lizzy, do you not agree?" Kitty asked, glancing up from her pile of ribbons. "Mary must at least try to look agreeable. What do you think?"

Elizabeth blinked, dragged from her thoughts. "I think," she said slowly, "that Mary has every right to wear what pleases her."

"Oh, bother, you *would* say that," Lydia huffed, tossing a ribbon over her shoulder. "You are no fun at all today."

Elizabeth's smile was tight. "Am I not?"

"No, you are not," Lydia declared. "You sit there poking holes in that poor daisy as if it has personally offended you. Whatever is the matter, Lizzy? Are you still sulking over the weather?"

Kitty chimed in with a mischievous grin. "Or perhaps it is something—or some-one—else?"

Elizabeth's cheeks warmed, but her expression did not falter. "You are imagining things, Kitty."

"Oh, she's definitely imagining things," Lydia said with a knowing smirk. "And so are we all, but la, it is all true, is it not? Tell me, Lizzy, what does Mr. Darcy think of daisies?"

The room burst into laughter, and Elizabeth, unwilling to grant her sisters the satisfaction of a reaction, kept on sewing... or pretending to, at least.

Mary gave them both a glare before turning her attention to Elizabeth. "Lizzy, do tell them that a lady's true worth is found in her intellect and character, not in fripperies."

Elizabeth blinked. "I believe both intellect and character are better demonstrated by allowing others to wear what they please without censure."

Lydia snorted. "That is Lizzy's way of saying she agrees with me."

Elizabeth forced a small smile before glancing back out the window. The branches of the trees swayed in the wind, casting restless shadows across the lawn. She wished her own thoughts were so easily swept away.

The events of the previous evening had settled heavily in her chest. Colonel Fitzwilliam's words had been an unwelcome revelation. For all Mr. Darcy's grand speeches and evident generosity, Elizabeth now wondered if they had all been carefully calculated. His cousin had all but said so, and Darcy's exceedingly odd questions to her after dinner had confirmed it. This entire effort at Netherfield was meant to be used as a political platform.

Elizabeth stabbed her needle into the fabric, her jaw tightening.

"Lizzy!" Kitty exclaimed, leaning over to peer at her embroidery. "You have made a terrible knot!"

"Oh," Elizabeth said, looking down at her work. "So, I have."

Lydia laughed, tossing a ribbon over her shoulder. "What is wrong with you today, Lizzy? You look as though you have been to a funeral."

"I am simply distracted," Elizabeth said, carefully undoing the knot. "This room is hardly conducive to focus."

"That is no excuse," Mary intoned. "A disciplined mind should be able to concentrate anywhere."

Elizabeth bit back a retort and returned to her stitching, though her mind remained elsewhere. Darcy had seemed so genuine when they spoke in the library. His quiet determination, his reflections on duty and ambition, even his confessions of regrets and mistakes—they had felt real. Yet now, Elizabeth could not help but question everything. Was it all an act? Was he simply using Sir Thomas and the people of Netherfield as pawns in some larger game?

The thought of him standing before Parliament, turning the residents of Netherfield into pitiable figures for his own gain, made her stomach churn. She could almost hear the patronizing tone he might use, the calculated words crafted to inspire both sympathy and scorn. And the people of Netherfield—proud, wounded, rebuilding their lives—would become nothing more than objects of derision.

"Lizzy, you are doing it again," Kitty said, pointing at her fabric. "Another knot!"

Elizabeth sighed and set the embroidery hoop down. "Perhaps needlework is not for me today."

"Perhaps nothing is for you today," Lydia teased, tossing a cushion at her.

Elizabeth caught it and flung it back with far less playfulness. She glanced at Jane, who was quietly hemming a gown across the room. She ought to speak to Jane, to have some way of giving vent to her fears and discovering if they were all for naught. But Jane had been so happy lately, her spirits buoyed by Mr. Bingley's clear attentions. Elizabeth could not bear to darken her sister's mood by voicing her suspicions.

Besides, there was no evidence that Mr. Bingley shared Mr. Darcy's schemes. Mr. Bingley was too guileless, too earnest. His every word and action seemed to come from a place of genuine affection for Jane and goodwill toward others. No, it was Darcy who was the puzzle, Darcy who now seemed a stranger wearing a mask she had been foolish enough to admire.

Elizabeth stood abruptly, smoothing her skirts. "I believe I shall take a turn about the garden."

Mary raised her brow. "In this weather?"

"Perhaps the air will clear my head," Elizabeth replied, already moving toward the door.

The garden path was damp beneath her shoes, and the wind nipped at her cheeks, but Elizabeth welcomed the briskness. It gave her a focus, something sharp and immediate to cut through the haze of doubt and frustration.

She paused by the cut-back and naked rosebushes, her thoughts turning over and over like the leaves caught in the wind. The party was already the talk of the town. People were excited, curious, eager to attend. How could she stop it now? How could she undo what had already been set in motion? And even if she could, did she have the right to take away this opportunity for the people of Netherfield to be seen, to be welcomed—even if only temporarily?

No, she could not stop the party. But she could stop herself. She could leave before Darcy's plans came to fruition, before she had to witness what she feared would unfold. Before she could be any more a part of something she could not countenance.

She would go to London, to Aunt Gardiner. It was the sensible choice, the safe choice.

And yet, the thought of leaving sent a pang through her chest that she could not explain.

Elizabeth shook her head, turning back toward the house. She would write to Aunt Gardiner that very evening.

Twenty

D ARCY SHRUGGED INTO HIS coat, his gaze straying to the frost-covered fields beyond the window. The sunlight caught on the distant trees, glinting like ice-bound jewels, but his thoughts were elsewhere—at Longbourn.

Two days since he had seen *her*. Two days since she had greeted him with that glorious smile, those eyes that flashed like sapphires, and that laugh that made him warm from the inside.

And two days since she had left him standing there with a fresh teacup and a mouth full of questions... and no answers.

Was she ill? Simply overwrought? A family such as hers would do it to the stoutest character. They were... well, they were tolerable. For *her*, he could tolerate anything. And that realization settled into his heart with all the clarity of a promise.

He needed Elizabeth Bennet in his life.

She... she challenged him. Gave him something to aspire to, to look forward to. She made him laugh, made him want to reach beyond the dull monotony of business and the regrets that had kept him from being who he was born to be.

She made him better.

He considered whether propriety might excuse another visit to Longbourn so soon. The party, surely... Perhaps a word with Mr. or Mrs. Bennet about the preparations would suffice as justification.

A sharp knock interrupted his musings. "Come in," he called, stepping away from the window as Roberts entered, a bundle of letters tucked neatly under his arm. "The morning post, sir."

Darcy accepted them with a nod, sorting through the correspondence with practiced efficiency. One envelope stood out—thick, cream-colored paper bearing the unmistakable seal of Matlock. He broke it open and unfolded the letter, his uncle's familiar script unfurling across the page.

My dear nephew,

I confess myself intrigued by the recent news surrounding you and your rather novel undertaking at Netherfield. Sir Thomas's reputation precedes him—whether that is to his credit or his detriment depends entirely upon the circles in which one travels.

It strikes me, Fitzwilliam, that you have stumbled upon an opportunity that, handled correctly, could yield dividends far beyond mere goodwill in the neighborhood. Imagine, for instance, the leverage such a project might lend to a man with aspirations of public office. It is, after all, one thing to speak of compassion and quite another to be seen acting upon it.

I am curious to hear your thoughts. How, precisely, do you intend to align this endeavor with your ambitions? And more importantly, how do you mean to prevent it from appearing... imprudent? You have a rather questionable litany of accomplishments yourself, and though I have spoken favorably of you seeking public office, I have held my reservations about your appeal, for I do not think you would be universally palatable. Indeed, this... project of yours could prove the lynch pin that unites the voters of Derbyshire around a common cause. But it must be done strategically, else you chance appearing as a sentimental fool rather than a beneficent strategist.

I look forward to speaking with you more about this.

The letter was signed with the earls's seal and signet—all the pomp and flair that was to be expected of the man. Darcy read the letter twice, his eyes lingering on the precise, almost detached phrasing.

His uncle's suggestions were laid out like a campaign strategy: exploit Sir Thomas's efforts for public sympathy, position the residents of Netherfield as pitiable beneficiaries of Darcy's intervention, and frame the entire endeavor as a testament to his leadership and moral vision. It was a carefully constructed path to influence—a path that led straight through the lives and dignity of others.

He set the letter aside, his fingers drumming briefly on the desk as his thoughts churned. Once, not so long ago, he might have entertained such a plan. He had been raised to see influence as power and power as duty, with appearances the currency of his world.

And his uncle was right—he did *not* hold universal appeal for the voters of Derbyshire. There were no large industrial cities where the allure of his business acumen would draw support. And the gentlemen farmers, the wealthy and powerful, would be naturally prejudiced against him for blurring the lines between trade and gentility. He *would* need some... some device, as it were, to succeed.

Even now, the temptation lingered. His uncle's argument was persuasive, and Darcy could imagine how easily such a strategy might yield success.

But the cost—it was too clear now. He thought of Sir Thomas, whose work had already been maligned by those who refused to see the value in helping people rebuild their lives. To turn those people into mere symbols, tools for political gain, was not just an insult to Sir Thomas's vision—it was a betrayal.

Darcy leaned back in his chair, his gaze drifting to the window as he imagined what *she* would say. Elizabeth, with her sharp eyes and unwavering principles. She would see through any such maneuver in an instant. Her approval—no, her respect—was something he valued more than he had ever thought possible. And she would never forgive him for such a calculated exploitation of others, nor would he deserve it.

He rose abruptly, pacing the room. His boots barely stirred the thick carpet, but his thoughts were louder than any steps. His uncle's letter had awakened memories he rarely allowed himself to visit: the day he told his father he intended to back Bingley in his ventures. His father's face had been thunderous, the disapproval as cutting as it had been predictable. "*Trade?*" The word had come out like a curse.

Darcy knew even then that his father saw it as a betrayal of everything the Darcy name represented. He could still hear the words ringing in his ears: *"You are the head of Pemberley, Fitzwilliam. Your duties are clear. Or have you forgotten your place entirely?"*

But there had been no forgetting the debt he owed Bingley—a debt no amount of wealth or lands or even family honor could erase. Bingley had pulled Darcy from the wreckage in Paris, risking his own life to save him when all seemed lost. To turn his back on that would have been to turn his back on honor itself. He had chosen loyalty to a friend over obedience to his father, and the price had been estrangement from the home he loved.

Years had passed since then, and in those years, Darcy had seen both the best and worst of his world. He had watched men of standing manipulate their reputations to shield themselves from accountability, using appearances as armor against consequence. He had also seen men of modest means rise above their circumstances, driven by nothing more than grit and character.

And now, his uncle asked him to step back into that gilded cage, to play the game of appearances at the expense of those who needed help most. To use the people of Netherfield as pawns, to turn their struggles into a spectacle for his own benefit—it was a bitter echo of the values he had spent years rejecting.

Darcy exhaled slowly, his decision forming with unshakable clarity. His gaze settled on the letter from his uncle one final time. Indeed, he *had* been thinking, rather recently, too, that politics might be the next logical step for him. Who but he had so utterly bridged both spheres of aristocracy and trade? He could speak to things no other could, and could understand matters that others had never conceived. He knew what must be done, and he knew how to make it happen.

But his uncle's idea of success—prestige, influence, appearances, and all he would have to do to achieve it—felt hollow now. Darcy wanted something better. He wanted something meaningful.

He wanted Elizabeth.

And for the first time, he understood exactly what that meant. It was not about winning her favor with grand gestures or noble intentions—it was about becoming the kind of man who deserved her partnership. A man whose name would stand not for vanity, but for genuine good.

Darcy dipped his pen in ink and began a reply to his uncle. It would be brief, polite, and resolute. There would be no campaign for office, no manipulation of public sentiment. There was work to be done—work that mattered. And Darcy would see it through.

ELIZABETH STOOD AT HER wardrobe, her hands trembling and her throat tight as she folded a wool shawl into her trunk. She refused to let herself falter, though every fold of fabric felt heavier than the last. Jane's quiet footsteps padded across the room behind her, but Elizabeth didn't turn. She knew what was coming—what had been coming since she'd mentioned her plans to leave for London.

"Elizabeth," Jane said, her voice gentle but insistent, "you cannot mean to go now."

"I do mean it. I had a letter from Aunt Gardiner this morning. She wishes for my assistance with their Christmas party, and I agreed to go."

Jane stepped closer. "But why now? What about the *Netherfield* party? You were just as much a part of planning this as anyone else. More so, even. Do you not care how much we all need you? How important this is?"

Elizabeth snapped the trunk lid shut and latched it with finality. "I am certain everything will carry on perfectly well without me. You, Jane, are more than capable of managing it all. Everyone will be just as charmed and delighted as they expect to be."

Jane's brows knit in confusion, her voice tinged with hurt. "Elizabeth, this was partly your idea. You were the one who went to speak with Mr. Darcy and Mr. Bingley—no one else knows that, but I do. You convinced Papa to lend his approval—you know, without you pushing him, he never would have, and Mr. Darcy and Mr. Bingley would have found no other inroad into the neighborhood. And now you are walking away, with no explanation other than... Aunt Gardiner's party?"

Elizabeth froze, her hands on the latch. For a moment, the words she wanted to say surged to the surface. She could not stay here and watch it happen. She could not stand by as *he* turned everything into a spectacle. But she swallowed them down, forcing her voice to work.

"I need to go, Jane. That is all."

Jane's hand closed around Elizabeth's arm, her grip uncharacteristically firm. "No, that is not all. Elizabeth, please—tell me what has happened. Why would you abandon us now, when we need you most?"

Elizabeth turned, her face impassive but her heart aching at the sight of Jane's wounded expression. "Jane, what could you possibly need me for? Everything is going exactly as you hoped, is it not? The party is planned, Mr. Darcy and Mr. Bingley are doing their part, and the town is warming to the idea. It is a triumph. What use am I?"

"Is it Mr. Darcy?"

Elizabeth stiffened, and she could feel the blood draining from her cheeks. "Mr. Darcy..."

"You love him, Lizzy. You love him and you're terrified to admit it."

"I..." Her mouth worked. "Wh... why would I be terrified? When have I *ever* been 'terrified' to confess anything?"

"You said it yourself a few nights ago. You thought he was miles beyond the reach of... well, someone like us. He could crook his finger and have all the wealthiest and most beautiful girls in the country swooning at his feet."

"Well..." Elizabeth turned away to reach for her second-best bonnet on the hook. She did not need another winter bonnet for London, but she could not look Jane in the eye just now. "They are welcome to him."

"They have no chance with him, and you know it. He has set his eyes on you, Lizzy, and that terrifies you, because you know exactly what sort of man he is. He would make you mistress over a vast estate, not to mention a fortune worthy of nobility... an empire, nearly."

Elizabeth popped open the lid of her trunk and tried to find a spot to cram that poor bonnet. "You are imagining things, Jane. If Mr. Darcy proposed right now—and I promise you, he never would—I would refuse him."

Jane's mouth dropped open. "Lizzy, you cannot mean that! I see the way you look at him, the way—"

"It is over, Jane." Elizabeth dropped onto her bed and stared at her hands. "There never was anything between us that I did not imagine myself. Now, I am going to go to London for a month, where I shall not be likely to become fancy's fool."

Jane hesitated, her lips parting as if searching for the right words. And was that a strange sheen over her eyes? Indeed, it was. Jane was trying to choke back tears. "Lizzy, there..." she stammered, her voice cracking. "There... there is something you do not know. M... Mr. Bingley has asked me for a f-formal courtship. He means to speak to Papa this afternoon."

Elizabeth's heart dropped like a stone into her shoes. She stared at her sister, stunned. "Jane, that... why, that is wonderful. Why did you not tell me sooner?"

"I—" Jane flushed, her composure faltering. "I wanted to be sure, but now... now I need you here, Lizzy. I want you by my side in my happiness, just as you have always been. You must stay."

Elizabeth stepped back, shaking her head as she tried to summon a smile. "Jane, you have everything you need. You have Mr. Bingley, you will have Papa's approval, and Mama's delight will surely follow. What more could you possibly require of me?"

Jane's eyes glistened, her grip tightening. "I need you to help manage Mama, to soothe her excitement. I need you to keep Papa from saying something he should not. I need you, Lizzy. Please, do not go."

Elizabeth pulled away gently but firmly. "No, Jane. I cannot manage anyone anymore—not Mama, not Papa, not Mr. Darcy, or Mr. Bingley, or Sir Thomas, or any of it. Look where my meddling has got me. I have no wish to repeat the mistake."

Jane frowned, her brow furrowing in confusion. "What mistake? What are you talking about?"

Elizabeth turned back to her trunk, her throat tight as she tried to flatten the contents enough that the lid would close. "Nothing, Jane. Nothing that matters now."

"It *does* matter," Jane insisted, her voice rising slightly. "Elizabeth, please—what mistake? What has happened to you?"

Elizabeth shook her head, refusing to meet her sister's gaze. "It does not matter. I am leaving in the morning, Jane. That is all there is to say."

Jane stood there, her hands clenching at her sides. "Elizabeth, I do not understand you. I cannot—" She broke off, her voice trembling with frustration. "How can you walk away from everything we have worked for? From me?"

Elizabeth paused, her hands resting on the edge of the trunk. She closed her eyes briefly before turning to face her sister one last time.

"Because, Jane," she said softly, "I know all will be well. You do not need me anymore."

Jane's expression crumpled, but Elizabeth stepped forward and pressed a kiss to her cheek.

"I wish you all the happiness in the world," she said, her voice trembling despite herself. "Truly, I do."

Without waiting for a response, Elizabeth turned back to her trunk, her movements deliberate as she folded the last of her things. She could not let Jane see the tears threatening to spill, nor the way her heart ached at the thought of leaving her sister behind. But she could not stay. Not when the truth shattered her faith in the one man she had thought above reproach.

Twenty-One

D ARCY STOOD BY THE window of his room, his gaze drifting over the snow-covered grounds of Netherfield. He could already imagine the party in full swing: the music, the laughter, the house glowing with warmth and light. The image brightened as his thoughts fixed on Elizabeth Bennet.

He allowed himself a rare indulgence, picturing her beneath the mistletoe, her eyes sparkling with humor and challenge as they so often did. He could almost feel the soft brush of her hand in his, her breath warm against his cheek as he leaned in to...

He stopped himself. His imagination was dangerous territory, but the thought refused to be banished entirely. The vision deepened, becoming more than the fleeting joy of a Christmas kiss.

What if this was not just a moment? What if this was a beginning? The idea stirred something primal, something that had been growing quietly since he first saw her wit flash like lightning across a room. What would it be like to have Elizabeth as a permanent fixture in his life—not just for a night, but for all the nights to come?

It was a notion that had become his muse over the last days—the delirious intoxicant that made his blood heat and his stomach flip in the sort of anticipation he had not known in years. He just needed to speak to her—to learn her feelings and confess his own.

That, however, had been the problem. He could not very well haunt her drawing room. This present circumstance had offered all manner of opportunities to be in company with the Bennets, but over the past days, Darcy had only seen the father. And he had said nothing of his second daughter in Darcy's hearing.

But surely, there was nothing to concern himself about. She was not a fickle woman—of that, he felt sure. Just a matter of poor timing, of too many things happening. He would have the pleasure of her company again soon enough. And hopefully soon, he could speak to her about making that permanent.

His mind turned, almost reflexively, to Georgiana. Would she like Elizabeth? He could not imagine otherwise. Elizabeth's charm and warmth would be the perfect complement to Georgiana's youth and inexperience, drawing her out, encouraging her, making her laugh. The thought made him smile—a rare, unguarded smile—and with it came a sudden resolve.

Georgiana must attend the party.

It was not merely a whim; it was a certainty. Elizabeth must meet Georgiana, and Georgiana must see the woman who had captivated him so thoroughly. But his smile faded as he considered the complications. Georgiana's reputation was delicate, especially with her debut at court looming next year. Would it be unwise to bring her to Netherfield, given the whispers surrounding Sir Thomas's household?

But then again, if this party was not respectable enough for his sister, then it was a sham. Everything he had been working toward would be meaningless. He could write to Georgiana and explain everything, but words on a page would not suffice. No, he would have speak to her in person while he was in London, escort her back himself. She deserved to hear it all in detail from him, and he trusted her judgment enough to let her decide.

The sound of sleigh bells outside broke his reverie. Darcy moved to the window, his breath misting the chilled glass as he watched a sleigh come to a halt in the drive. Mr. Bennet stepped down first, brushing snow from his coat, followed by Miss Bennet, her pale face framed by the fur-trimmed hood of her cloak. Darcy's gaze swept the sleigh once, then again, and his breath hitched—Elizabeth was not there.

His brows drew together. Where was she? A dull weight settled in his stomach, disappointment sharper than he expected. For a moment, he remained by the window, composing himself, before striding purposefully down the stairs and toward the drawing room, his boots echoing softly against the polished floor. Through the open door, he saw Sir Thomas standing near the hearth, flanked by Mr. Bennet and Miss Bennet. A stack of papers rested in Miss Bennet's hands, and she was speaking quietly as he stepped into the room.

"Thank you for bringing the finalized guest list," Sir Thomas said, inclining his head toward Mr. Bennet. "Mrs. Bennet's contributions, I assume, were... enthusiastic?"

Miss Bennet's hands tightened slightly on the papers. "Very much so. She regrets not coming herself. I—I believe she is presently taking tea with my Aunt Philips."

"And no doubt planning all manner of frivolity. You may want to rethink the... er... expenses you had decided to authorize, Mr. Bingley... and Mr. Darcy."

Darcy approached, nodding briefly to the group. "Miss Bennet. Mr. Bennet. I trust the journey was not too uncomfortable?"

Miss Bennet glanced at him, her eyes meeting his for the briefest moment before darting away. "Not at all, Mr. Darcy. Though the roads are still a bit uneven."

Darcy frowned slightly. Her complexion was pale, and her voice—though calm—carried a hint of strain. As she handed the papers to Sir Thomas, Darcy caught Bingley's eye. His friend's usual brightness was muted, his brow furrowed in what Darcy could only describe as concern.

"Have you reviewed the list already?" Bingley asked Miss Bennet, stepping closer. His tone was light, but the way his gaze lingered on her face betrayed his deeper thoughts.

"I have," she replied, offering a faint smile. "I believe it is in good order, though Mama may still try to add a name or two before the day of the party."

Sir Thomas chuckled, though his attention flickered briefly to Darcy. "A list in flux, then. Well, I trust we can accommodate whatever changes come."

Miss Bennet glanced quickly at Bingley, murmuring something Darcy couldn't catch. Bingley's brows lifted slightly, and he turned to Darcy with a deliberate air. "Would you care to review the list, Darcy?" he asked. "Sir Thomas and I could use your input on the final numbers."

"Of course," Darcy said, stepping closer. As Sir Thomas handed him the papers, he noticed Bingley's sidelong glance at Miss Bennet. Darcy's curiosity burned, but propriety held his tongue.

The conversation carried on with details of the party's logistics, but Darcy's thoughts remained elsewhere. Miss Bennet kept avoiding his gaze, her tension evident despite her outward composure. And Elizabeth—her absence loomed over the exchange like a shadow. He forced himself to focus on the task at hand, though the questions churned relentlessly in his mind.

When the discussion concluded, Darcy caught Mr. Bennet watching him again, his gaze sharp but unreadable. Bingley lingered for a moment as the Bennets prepared to leave, his shoulders tight with some sort of anxiousness as he hovered near the lady. Darcy bid them farewell with the requisite politeness but could not bring himself to stand at the door to watch as they plunged into the cold.

Instead, he hurried back into his room and leaned on the window sash, gazing to the north, toward Longbourn. Something was amiss, and every instinct in him screamed that all was not right with Elizabeth.

S CARCELY TEN MINUTES LATER came the knock at the door, and he did not even need to wonder who it was. "Come in," he called.

Bingley entered, his manner roughened by an edge of urgency. "Darcy," he began, running a hand through his hair, "we have a problem."

Darcy straightened, his entire body going rigid. "What is it?"

Bingley's face was a mixture of frustration and guilt. "It's Miss Elizabeth. She's gone to London."

Darcy blinked, the words hitting him like a slap. "London? What do you mean she's gone to London?"

"This morning. Miss Bennet told me. She left rather suddenly, it seems, without much of an explanation."

Darcy stared, his mind refusing to process what he was hearing. "Without—what reason did she give?"

Bingley hesitated, and Darcy had scarcely ever seen his friend looking so pale. "Apparently, none that satisfied her family. Something about the Gardiners hosting a Christmas party for his business partners... you see, nothing so very urgent, but she insisted on going to help. Miss Bennet said they tried every possible measure to convince her to stay."

Darcy's voice sharpened. "Every possible measure? What does that mean?"

"Well..." Bingley looked sheepish. "Miss Bennet even told her sister that we were engaged."

Darcy's head jerked back, his eyes narrowing in disbelief. "Engaged? What nonsense is this, Bingley?"

"No, no, not engaged," Bingley clarified hastily, raising his hands as though warding off an attack. "Not exactly. But she might have implied we were... courting."

"Courting," Darcy repeated flatly. "She *implied* it? To Miss Elizabeth?"

"Yes," Bingley admitted, his face coloring in irregular blotches. "It was a desperate attempt, you see. Miss Bennet thought if Elizabeth saw others embracing happiness, she might reconsider... whatever it is she's trying to run from."

"And..." Darcy stalked closer to Bingley, inspecting his friend closely—every nervous twitch and uneven breath. "... did this supposed announcement come as a surprise to you?"

Bingley swallowed and slipped a finger under the edge of his cravat. "Ah... no. Well, the timing, surely. We had not thought matters would spiral so quickly, but we did speak of... that."

"You spoke of marriage to each other, or simply the prospect of persuading Miss Elizabeth, and..." Darcy arched a brow and pointed at his own chest.

Bingley gulped. "A bit of both, but... m-more the latter."

"More the..." Darcy's outrage surged. "So, let me understand this correctly. You and Miss Bennet devised some scheme to manipulate her sister's feelings—and mine—by fabricating a courtship?"

Bingley flushed deeper, shifting uncomfortably. "It wasn't like that, Darcy. We thought it might encourage her, that's all."

Darcy's laugh was short and humorless. "*Encourage* her? With a lie that could very well damage Miss Bennet's reputation if word got out? Or were you planning to make this pretense a reality?"

Bingley opened his mouth, then closed it again, clearly caught off guard. Finally, he muttered, "I've been considering it."

Darcy's brows shot up. "Considering it? You had bloody well better be doing more than *considering* it!"

"I am!" Bingley snapped, his tone defensive now. "I've thought of little else, in fact! But I hadn't planned to act so soon, and certainly not under these circumstances."

Darcy let out a sharp breath and paced toward the window, his boots thudding against the wooden floor. The snow-covered grounds outside looked pristine, untouched, and offered no solace for the chaos in his mind. He turned back to Bingley, his anger not yet spent.

"And why," Darcy demanded, "were you and Miss Bennet so determined to push Elizabeth toward me? Was it your idea or hers?"

Bingley hesitated, his expression a mix of guilt and defensiveness. "Miss Bennet might have suggested it first. She said her sister has always been difficult to please and that no man she has met has ever measured up. She..." He cleared his throat and shifted uneasily. "She—Miss Bennet, that is—she even said that Miss Elizabeth f-f..."

"Go on. You have got this far," Darcy snapped testily.

Bingley cleared his throat again. "Well, Miss Bennet had a rather serious suitor once. She said she fancied him herself, though it was little more than a girlish intrigue, but—"

"I think I know where this is going, but you are not making a strong case."

"No, no, hang on. This fellow even wrote Miss Bennet some very fine poetry, but Miss Elizabeth thought him a worthless cad, and fairly ran him off before he could declare himself. And since then, she has scarcely let another man near her sister."

Darcy's eyes narrowed. "Either Miss Elizabeth has just risen again in my esteem, or you have just been subject to the worst fleecing I ever heard. You honestly believed the lady when she told you all this?"

"Miss Bennet had nothing to conceal," Bingley retorted hotly. "She wants nothing but happiness, for herself as well as her sister. But knowing her sister as she does, she has come to believe that unless Miss Elizabeth can be induced to fall in love herself, she will never credit that others might do the same. But up until now, no man has ever caught the lady's attention, much less her regard. Miss Bennet thought you might be the one exception."

Darcy's mouth ran dry—not from disbelief, but from the blunt openness of what Bingley was saying. "And you agreed with her?"

"Yes," Bingley said, his tone softening. "Because it's true—for you as well as for her. Darcy, in the weeks we've been here, I've seen you laugh more, smile more, live more than I ever have before. And it's because of her. She's good for you. You know it, and I know it."

Darcy stared at his friend, his emotions warring between indignation and the undeniable truth in Bingley's words. "And what about Elizabeth? Did it occur to either of you that she might not appreciate being maneuvered like a pawn in your matchmaking efforts?"

Bingley winced but did not back down. "We thought she might need a nudge. That's all. But clearly... something went wrong."

Darcy's gaze turned distant as he pieced together the fragments of the puzzle. *Wrong?* That was putting it only mildly. Indeed, something had gone wrong—horribly, painfully wrong—and now Elizabeth was gone. He clenched his fists. "I'm going to London."

Bingley blinked, startled. "To find her?"

"To fix this," Darcy said, his tone clipped and final. "Whatever misunderstanding has driven her away, I will not let it stand."

Bingley let out a breath, relief flickering in his expression. "Then I suppose I'd better wish you luck."

Darcy's lips tightened, but he said nothing more. His thoughts were already in London, with Elizabeth, determined to set things right.

ELIZABETH BENNET BUSTLED ABOUT the Gardiners' drawing room, her hands full with a tangle of ribbons. "Aunt, are you certain we have enough? We could order more before tomorrow."

Mrs. Gardiner glanced up from the sprig of holly she was affixing to a centerpiece. "We are perfectly well-supplied, my dear. And you are entirely too industrious for a girl on holiday. Surely, you ought to rest."

Elizabeth gave a forced laugh, her fingers nimbly arranging the ribbons into a neat bow. "I find I prefer to be busy."

Her aunt's sharp eyes narrowed slightly. "You have not mentioned the Netherfield party once since you arrived. Tell me, is everything in order for it?"

Elizabeth's stomach lurched, but she immediately forced a smile. "Oh, I am sure they have it well in hand. Jane has such a knack for these things, and Mr. Bingley is... quite enthusiastic."

"Only Mr. Bingley?" she asked with a knowing look. "What about—"

Elizabeth was already bracing for her aunt's inevitable question when the butler appeared at the door.

"Forgive me, Mrs. Gardiner, Miss Bennet. A caller has arrived and asking for Miss Bennet."

Elizabeth frowned, setting aside the ribbons. "A caller? For me?"

"Yes, miss. Mr. Darcy."

Elizabeth's heart skipped painfully, her hands freezing mid-motion. She managed a weak "Oh."

Her aunt's brows lifted in surprise, but a sly glint entered her eyes as she rose to her feet. "Well, well. Speak of the devil."

Devil... hardly a devil. But certainly, no angel, either. Elizabeth swallowed and barely had time to swipe trembling hands over her flaming cheeks before the door opened, and there he was. Tall... impeccably dressed, as always, but for that one curl of hair that liked to fall over his forehead... eyes searing and searching, and hands flexing uncomfortably at his sides, but anyone who did not know him well would never be looking at his hands.

Darcy stepped into the room with the kind of quiet authority that seemed to shift the very air around him. His gaze swept the space once before landing back on her, and the weight of it sent a rush of heat to her belly.

He inclined his head, his movements as deliberate and composed, but it was the way he held himself—contained, yet undeniably present—that left Elizabeth's pulse racing. She couldn't have moved if she tried; every muscle seemed caught between the urge to flee and an unfamiliar desire to tumble into his arms and pillow her head on his chest.

"Miss Elizabeth."

"Mr. Darcy." How she managed to keep her voice from cracking was a mystery, for her heart was a riot.

Darcy's eyes seemed to clear all at once, as if he had forgot her aunt was there, too. He drew in a breath and turned. "And Mrs. Gardiner. Thank you for receiving me just now."

Mrs. Gardiner's curious gaze flickered between them. "Mr. Darcy, how lovely to see you again." she said briskly. "But I am afraid I was just stepping out to speak with my cook about an urgent question she had. I shan't be more than a few minutes. Elizabeth, dear, would you entertain Mr. Darcy for a moment?"

Elizabeth turned to her aunt, mortified. "Aunt!"

"I shall not be long," Mrs. Gardiner said with a pointed smile, sweeping out of the room and leaving the door ajar just enough for propriety.

Darcy watched her leave, his brow furrowing slightly before he turned back to Elizabeth. "I apologize for arriving unannounced."

Elizabeth swallowed, willing her voice not to shake. "It is quite unexpected. What brings you to London, Mr. Darcy?"

He hesitated, as though choosing his words carefully. "A number of things, but perhaps first of my concerns is my sister. She is staying with our aunt and uncle for the season. I came to escort her to Netherfield."

Elizabeth's brow arched. "Your aunt and uncle—the Earl and Countess of Matlock?"

"Yes," Darcy said, a note of confusion in his voice. "Why do you ask?"

Elizabeth's pulse hammered in her ears. "No reason," she said tightly, her thoughts spinning. So, this was the uncle in the House of Lords, the one Colonel Fitzwilliam had implied would play a role in Darcy's supposed ambitions. And Darcy had come to town expressly to call at their home.

Darcy went on, his tone casual. "I expect an... interesting conversation with my uncle when I see him. Matters should be settled soon enough. And I had some other arrangements to see to—some of which, I had hoped to discuss with you."

Elizabeth's hands clenched at her sides. Rage and hurt surged through her, sharp and unrelenting. So, it was true. Darcy *did* mean to exploit Netherfield's residents for his political gain. Fitzwilliam's hints had been no exaggeration. And worse, he wanted *her* to be a party to it all!

Her throat felt tight, but she forced her words out. "I am sorry to hear I shall miss the Christmas party. I am sure it will go splendidly."

Darcy's brows drew together in confusion. "Miss it? You cannot mean—"

"I shall be staying in London," Elizabeth interrupted, her voice brittle. "I... expect I shall see you at the wedding."

Darcy's face hardened, dismay flickering briefly before it gave way to something sharper. "The wedding? If you mean your sister's supposed 'engagement' to Bingley, I must correct you. At the time she said it, it was untrue."

Elizabeth stared at him. "'At the time'?"

Darcy's lips pressed into a thin line. "It may not remain untrue for long. I would not be surprised if Bingley proposes any day now. But Miss Bennet only said what she did in the hope of encouraging you toward your own happiness."

Elizabeth's heart gave a great pang, her anger mingling with something more complicated—something she did not want to name. Darcy's gaze pinned her in place, and for a moment, she thought she might drown in the intensity of it.

"I..." she stammered, searching for something, anything, to say. But all that came was a whispered, "*Why?*"

His expression softened, the harsh edges of his features melting into something achingly sincere. "Because, Miss Elizabeth, your happiness matters."

Her breath faltered, his words piercing through the guarded thoughts she clung to. His gaze held hers with a quiet force, as if he were reaching out to touch something deeper within her—something that had broken that night at dinner, over Colonel Fitzwilliam's boasts.

She turned away abruptly, her hands trembling. "I... wish you success with the party, Mr. Darcy. And with all your other... endeavors. Now, if you will excuse me."

"So..." She heard him sigh so deeply that she could almost swear the buttons on his waistcoat were straining. "You will say nothing? No acknowledgment, no recriminations? We were friends, I thought."

Elizabeth squeezed her eyes shut until a tear leaked out. "Yes," she whispered.

"And was I imagining it, or could we have been... something more?"

Her throat ached, and her chest trembled. She dared not speak—she could only clap a hand to her mouth as her head bowed and her shoulders quaked.

"I see." Another heavy sigh. "May I ask, Miss Elizabeth, what has changed? Have I offended you somehow? Please, tell me so that I may put it right."

She opened her mouth and had to force the sound out. "I—I would not have you alter... anything, sir. You must do as you feel fitting, and I must do the same."

There was a pause, during which Elizabeth could no longer avoid looking at him. She risked a glance over her shoulder, and his face... it was stricken. Ghostly and agonized, with tears glittering just at the corners of his eyes. She looked swiftly away.

"I... I do not understand. Elizabeth, please, I—"

She turned back, pasting a smile on her face. "You should go, sir. I would hate for you to miss your appointment with the Earl of Matlock."

Darcy said nothing for a long moment. Then, softly, "Of course. Good day, Miss Elizabeth."

She did not look back as he left, but the sound of his retreating footsteps echoed long after he had gone.

Twenty-Two

T HE CARRIAGE RATTLED TO a halt outside Matlock House, its grand facade rising
against the bleak London sky and its stately windows gleaming in the gray light.
He stared out the window, his thoughts a tangled, oppressive web.

What had he done wrong?

Darcy stepped down before the footman could offer assistance, his boots striking
the pavement with a resolute thud. The crisp air stung his cheeks, but it was nothing
compared to the sharp ache in his chest.

Elizabeth's voice played in his mind, each clipped word and guarded look a dagger
twisting deeper. He adjusted his coat as he ascended the steps, the bitter taste of failure
lashing at his mind. Where had everything gone so wrong? He had thought—foolishly,
perhaps—that they had begun to understand one another. More than understood—that
they just might be two halves of the same whole.

But her withdrawal, her coldness... it was as if a door had been slammed in his face, and
he could not see how to open it again.

He hesitated at the door, his gloved hand hovering over the knocker. For a fleeting
moment, he considered turning back, coming again another day. What could he possibly
say to his uncle or his sister when his thoughts were so wholly consumed by her? But
retreating now was unthinkable. He took a breath and knocked firmly.

The butler opened the door, bowing slightly. "Mr. Darcy. Welcome."

Darcy nodded curtly, stepping inside. The warmth of the grand entry hall did little to
thaw the cold knot in his chest. His uncle's townhouse was immaculate, as always, but

the opulence grated on him today. The world of polished marble and gilded mirrors felt shallow, false, after the authentic sense of *home* he had found in Hertfordshire.

Or thought he had found.

As the butler took his hat and coat, Darcy cast a glance toward the staircase. He could already hear voices drifting from the drawing room. One of them—his aunt's familiar tones—carried an unmistakable note of inquiry. He squared his shoulders and followed the butler toward the sound.

"Darcy," Lady Matlock said as she rose from the settee, her tone clipped, her keen gaze sweeping over him. "You look thinner. Are you eating properly?"

Darcy inclined his head politely. "Aunt."

Lady Matlock gestured for Darcy to take a seat, her sharp gaze fixed on him as though trying to uncover his purpose. "We were not expecting you. I trust this is not merely a social call."

Darcy inclined his head, settling into the chair opposite her. "It is not. I came to speak with Georgiana—and with you, Aunt."

Her brows lifted faintly, though her expression remained imperious. "Georgiana? What could be so pressing that it requires you to appear unannounced? We heard you were in Hertfordshire at... some house." The curl of her lip was impossible to miss.

Darcy hesitated, briefly running a hand along the armrest as he considered his words. "I was, and I am returning as soon as I have finished some other business here in Town. I wish to invite her to join me in Hertfordshire for the rest of the festive season."

Lady Matlock's lips thinned, and she straightened in her seat. "Hertfordshire? Whatever for? I have heard whispers about this Netherfield—what on earth are you doing there?"

Darcy met her gaze. "I am hosting a Christmas gathering. It is an endeavor involving Sir Thomas and his household. I suppose you *do* remember Sir Thomas."

She released a sigh. "I remember what Richard told me of him."

"He may have saved your son's life, and mine. At the very least, he spared us months of imprisonment in a French gaol—a penalty he bore, himself, in our place."

"You needn't belabor the point, Darcy. We sent him a handsome gift, but that was eight years ago. What shall we do now? Laud every odd whim the man takes upon himself? This... this scandal—"

"—Is nothing more than the world turning its back. But Sir Thomas did not. I believe what he is doing to be worthwhile, and I would like Georgiana to be part of it."

Her silence stretched for a moment before she leaned back slightly, one hand lifting to adjust a fold of her sleeve. "And you imagine it is appropriate for a girl of Georgiana's standing, on the cusp of her presentation, to immerse herself in such... peculiar company?"

Darcy's jaw tightened. "If this gathering is unfit for Georgiana, then it is unfit for anyone. I would not ask her to come if I believed it would harm her in any way. On the contrary, I think it will be good for her—to see such kindness and resilience firsthand, and to take part in something meaningful."

Lady Matlock's gaze narrowed. "And you have decided all of this without so much as a letter to inform me? You might at least have spared me the shock."

"I thought it best to speak in person. I wanted to explain my reasoning and ensure Georgiana has a choice in the matter."

Lady Matlock studied him. "A choice, is it? You think a girl of her age would refuse her brother when he appears so set on this whim of his? And what of her reputation, Fitzwilliam? Have you considered the scrutiny she might face?"

"I have," Darcy replied firmly. "And I trust Georgiana's strength of character to rise above it."

"Rise above it? That scandal-ridden den of misfortune?" Her voice dropped as if the very word might summon some dreadful specter. "Your uncle is appalled, and I cannot say I disagree. You risk your reputation—*and* our reputation—with this folly."

Darcy stood taller, his voice measured. "What I risk, Aunt, is my own. Not yours, nor my uncle's."

"Is that so?" she shot back. "Do you truly believe you can shield this family from the consequences of your actions? You have always been stubborn, Fitzwilliam, but this... this is madness. If you have any sense left, you will leave the whole wretched business behind and focus on your future."

"My future is precisely what concerns me," Darcy replied. "And I intend to shape it with purpose."

Her jaw hardened. "I can hardly refuse you, Darcy, but I must demand that you reconsider."

"Ask her," he insisted, "to speak with me privately, Aunt. I have considered, and I find this to be in her best interests."

"A fine sentiment, but how does this reflect on Georgiana? You are asking her to mingle with these... projects of Sir Thomas, while risking the opinions of any reputable families present. She is to make her debut next year, Fitzwilliam. This could very well tarnish her standing."

Darcy's jaw tightened, but he did not rise to the bait. "It is Christmas. And they are but people, Aunt, just as you and I are. People who have been dealt harsh blows and deserve compassion, not judgment."

"Compassion," she echoed dryly. "A sentiment best saved for decent people who will actually feel the honor of it."

Darcy's blood heated. After the confusion with Elizabeth, the crushing of the only hope that had inspired his heart in... well, in far too long... this was all too much. "Aunt, I will brook no disputes on the matter. Please ask my sister to come down."

Lady Matlock's ample breast rose in a resigned sigh. "You are your father's son in all the ways I least expected, Fitzwilliam. He would never have dreamed of such... audacity. Very well, speak to her. But do not say I did not warn you."

Darcy turned at the sound of footsteps, and a flicker of warmth crossed his face as Georgiana entered. She hesitated on the threshold, her hands loosely clasped, her expression an uncertain mix of curiosity and delight.

"Brother?" she said, her voice lifting slightly. "I did not know you were here!"

Darcy rose, crossing the room to greet her. "Georgiana. I came because I have a matter to discuss with you." He glanced toward Lady Matlock, who watched with narrowed eyes, then back at his sister. "Would you sit with me?"

Georgiana's brows knit slightly, but she nodded and took a place on the settee. Darcy sat beside her, his posture relaxed yet deliberate, as if willing her to feel at ease.

"Bingley and I have been staying in Hertfordshire, at Netherfield Park, for some weeks now," he began, choosing his words carefully. "It is a house with an unusual history—one tied to a man whose courage and selflessness have saved lives, including my own."

Georgiana's eyes widened slightly. "Yes, you wrote something of that. You met Sir Thomas again?"

"Yes." Darcy inclined his head. "He has taken in people in need, offering them safety and a chance to rebuild. Bingley and I have been assisting him with an effort to unite his household with the surrounding community." He paused. "And I would like you to join me there for Christmas."

Georgiana's lips parted in surprise. "Join you? At Netherfield?" She glanced at her aunt, who was already stiffening in her chair. Then she turned back to him, her expression guarded. "But why me? What could I possibly contribute?"

"Your presence, for one," Darcy said gently. "You have a gift for making people feel at ease, Georgiana. And I believe you would find it as enriching as I have."

Lady Matlock let out a derisive sniff. "Enriching? Georgiana, I must remind you that you are to make your debut next year. Fitzwilliam, desist from this nonsense. Do you honestly think mingling with such company will elevate her standing?"

Darcy's gaze hardened, but his voice remained even. "If Georgiana wishes to decline, she is free to do so. But I will not have her pressured into a decision by fear of appearances."

Georgiana hesitated, her eyes darting between them. "Will it... will it cause harm to your plans if I refuse?" she asked, her voice soft.

Darcy leaned forward, meeting her gaze. "Not harm, no. But your presence would mean a great deal—to me and to others."

Georgiana studied his face for a moment, her expression searching. Slowly, she nodded. "If you believe it is right, then I will come."

Lady Matlock's chair creaked as she shifted. "You are making a mistake, Fitzwilliam. Mark my words."

Darcy stood, offering Georgiana his hand. "Thank you, Aunt. Your hospitality, as always, has been most illuminating."

Lady Matlock's lips pursed. "If this folly casts a shadow over her prospects, Fitzwilliam, you will have only yourself to blame."

Darcy inclined his head, his tone calm but final. "If it does, Aunt, then I will answer for it." Turning to Georgiana, he added gently, "We will stay at our townhouse for tonight, and possibly tomorrow—depending on how long my other business takes. You will need to have your trunk packed. Ask the maid to assist you. I will wait."

Georgiana nodded, her eyes flitting nervously between her aunt and her brother before she disappeared down the hall.

Lady Matlock's gaze bored into Darcy. "This is reckless, even for you."

"Reckless? No, Lady Matlock. It is deliberate, and not without cause for hope."

The silence stretched until Georgiana returned, two footmen trailing behind with a heavily laden trunk. Darcy stood, fixing his aunt with a calm but unyielding gaze. "Thank you for your hospitality, Aunt. Please extend my regards to Uncle. I will not be troubling him in his study today."

Her mouth opened, no doubt to launch another protest, but Darcy's resolve was set. He took Georgiana's arm and led her toward the door, their footsteps echoing in the grand hall.

An icy wind was now bristling its way through the London streets, but it was a welcome reprieve from the oppressive stuffiness of Matlock House. He helped Georgiana into the carriage, her fingers trembling lightly against his. Once she was seated, he turned to direct the footman to secure the trunk before climbing in beside her.

He should have spoken to Lord Matlock. Any other day, he would have, but today, he had no words for his uncle. No heart for arguments. All he wanted now was to finish his remaining tasks in London and return to Netherfield. To put things right, if it were even possible.

But as the carriage rolled away, Darcy could not shake the hollow ache that followed him. Without Elizabeth waiting for him when he got back, even his greatest efforts felt incomplete—like the hollow shell of a dream that might never be whole.

E LIZABETH FUMBLED WITH THE teapot, the lid slipping from her fingers and clattering onto the tray. She hissed under her breath, quickly righting it before any tea spilled. Her hands trembled slightly as she reached for her cup, but even that small motion felt futile. She sank back into the chair by the window, her fingers gripping the fabric of her skirt as if anchoring herself to something solid. Beyond the narrow street below, the world moved on without her, but she could barely make sense of it. Her throat ached, tight with the tears she refused to let fall.

She had barely slept the last two days. Every time she closed her eyes, she saw Mr. Darcy standing in the Gardiners' parlor, his expression so open, so wounded, as though her coldness had struck him like a blow. Could she have been so mistaken in him? Her mind churned. She had always prided herself on her ability to read people, to discern their true natures, but with Darcy...

It did not add up. Everything about his demeanor, his words, his actions—they had all seemed so genuine. And yet... how could a man so accustomed to power and privilege truly understand the feelings of those less fortunate? The temptation of using and manipulating—it had to be second nature to someone like him, as natural as breathing. A man who had never lacked for anything might not even realize how his actions could harm others.

That had to be it. His charm, his gentleness—they were merely tools of a man who always got what he wanted.

But her heart rebelled against her reasoning, whispering that Darcy was different. He had shown her consideration, vulnerability, and even respect. Her! A country girl of small dowry with a family that was sometimes... embarrassing... and an uncle in trade. Most gentlemen of wealth and connections would never even bother to learn her name, but Darcy had sought her out. Seemed to have permitted himself to develop feelings for her.

And now... she might never see him again.

A tear slipped free before she could catch it, and she dashed it away hastily as her aunt entered the room.

Mrs. Gardiner stopped short, her perceptive eyes narrowing as she took in Elizabeth's forlorn posture. "Lizzy," she said gently, crossing the room to sit beside her. "What is the matter? Are you unwell?"

Elizabeth shook her head quickly. "No, Aunt. I am quite well."

Mrs. Gardiner tilted her head, her tone softening. "This would not have anything to do with Mr. Darcy, would it?"

Elizabeth's breath caught, but she looked away, attempting a laugh. "Mr. Darcy? Why, do I look angry?"

Her aunt reached out, laying a hand over Elizabeth's. "You cannot fool me, Lizzy. I saw the way he looked at you when he was here. And I saw the way you looked at him. Did something happen?"

Elizabeth shook her head again, this time more forcefully, though her voice trembled. "Sometimes people... they simply change their minds. That is all."

Mrs. Gardiner regarded her for a long moment, her brows knitting together, but when it became clear Elizabeth would not say more, she sighed and straightened. "Speaking of changing minds..." She hesitated, then added, "Your uncle and I have decided not to host our Christmas party after all."

Elizabeth turned to her in dismay. "What? Why not?"

Mrs. Gardiner folded her hands in her lap. "Several of Mr. Gardiner's business partners sent their regrets just yesterday. They have suddenly decided on journeying to the country rather than remaining in London. Without them, the party would feel quite diminished."

Elizabeth bit her lip. She had been relying on the party as a distraction, something to fill the gaping void in her thoughts where Mr. Darcy had firmly lodged himself. "I see."

Her aunt gave her a small, apologetic smile. "Do not fret. We have another invitation that promises to be even more festive."

Elizabeth frowned slightly. "Another invitation?"

Mrs. Gardiner nodded. "A gentleman from the North, a Mr. Broadmere, is presently in London and hosting a ball. Rather suddenly, or so it seems. Your uncle only received the invitation yesterday."

"Mr. Broadmere?" Elizabeth repeated slowly. "Who is he?"

"His name is familiar, but I confess I do not know him," her aunt admitted. "I believe he is running as MP for Derbyshire."

Elizabeth's heart gave a sudden, uncomfortable flip. "For Derbyshire? Does he mean to challenge Mr. Darcy?"

Mrs. Gardiner blinked in surprise. "Mr. Darcy? Was he planning to run for MP?"

Elizabeth nodded stiffly, her pulse quickening. "He told me so."

Her aunt frowned thoughtfully. "That would certainly bode ill for Mr. Broadmere. The Darcy name carries considerable weight, and with the Earl of Matlock's influence as well, it would be a daunting challenge. I wonder why Mr. Broadmere would even consider it. Surely, he must know his chances are slim."

Elizabeth's mind raced. "When did Mr. Broadmere announce his candidacy?"

"I believe this ball is his official announcement," Mrs. Gardiner replied. "As far as I know, it is a recent development."

The pieces clicked together with startling clarity. Elizabeth's skin shivered with a deep thrill as realization dawned. If Mr. Broadmere was only now announcing his intentions, it could only mean one thing.

Darcy had withdrawn.

That had to be it! The cryptic visit to his uncle, the darkened sorrow in his eyes when he spoke to her, when he begged for her understanding. Why, she... she *had* misjudged him!

And she was never so delighted to be wrong in all her life.

She rose quickly, her chair scraping against the floor. "Aunt," she said, her voice tight, "I need to go home."

Mrs. Gardiner looked up at her in alarm. "Home? To Longbourn? Lizzy, whatever for?"

Elizabeth's hands trembled as she reached for the back of her chair to steady herself. "I cannot explain, not yet. Please, Aunt... I must go. Today. Right now!"

Twenty-Three

D ARCY STEPPED DOWN FROM the carriage, his boots striking the sanded ice in the drive with deliberate precision. Georgiana followed, her gloved hands clutching her cloak as her eyes widened at the sight of Netherfield's grand facade.

"Brother, it is even lovelier than you described," she sighed.

Darcy forced a smile in return. "It has its charms."

The doors opened before they reached the steps, and Bingley bounded out. "Darcy! Miss Darcy! Welcome back! Good heavens, man, we feared you might have got lost in your ledgers, and I would have to send an express to Wilson to evict you from your own study. And you have brought Miss Darcy! Why, this is, indeed, a pleasure!"

Georgiana smiled warmly. "Mr. Bingley, it is wonderful to see you again. My brother told me of everything you were doing here, though I suspect he understated it."

Bingley's grin widened. "A pleasure indeed, Miss Darcy. And I'll take that as a challenge to exceed my already glowing reputation. Come along—there's enough bustle inside to rival an assembly at Almack's!"

As they entered the drawing room, Colonel Fitzwilliam rose from the sofa where he had been conversing with Sir Thomas. His face lit up as he strode toward Georgiana. "Georgie! Look at you—have you grown taller since I last saw you? Or is it just that Darcy's sour face makes you seem taller by comparison?"

Georgiana giggled, curtseying slightly. "Cousin Richard. I am glad to find you in good humor."

"It is my natural state," Fitzwilliam said with a wink. "Especially now that we have reinforcements to wrangle this lot into shape."

Sir Thomas stepped forward next, his expression warm but reserved. "Miss Darcy, it is a pleasure to meet you at last. Your brother has spoken very highly of you."

Georgiana blushed faintly and dipped another curtsey. "Thank you, Sir Thomas. I am honored to be here."

Sir Thomas gestured toward the room. "Your timing is fortuitous. There is still much to do before tomorrow's gathering."

Bingley clapped his hands together. "Indeed! Miss Darcy, I wonder if you might assist the ladies with preparations. Miss Flora and Mrs. Jackson have been juggling details all day. They could use your insight."

"Of course!" Georgiana replied eagerly. "I mean, I have never planned anything like this, but I would be glad to help."

Bingley grinned. "Excellent. And tomorrow morning, Miss Bennet and her younger sisters will be arriving to assist Sir Thomas's household in dressing for the party. They are lending gowns from their own collections, but Darcy and I sent for more from Town—you did bring them back with you, did you not, Darcy?"

Darcy nodded. "If you look behind my carriage, you will see a drayage cart loaded with trunks to that purpose."

"Excellent! Every lady is meant to feel beautiful tomorrow night."

Georgiana's eyes lit up. "How thoughtful! I would love to meet them and help."

Darcy's stomach twisted. An army of Bennet sisters, come to array the ladies of Netherfield in splendor... but Elizabeth would not be among them. Egad, how *was* he to survive the next couple of days?

He forced a nod and turned toward Fitzwilliam, grasping for a distraction. "Richard, what else remains to be arranged?"

"Plenty, though we've made progress. Bingley and I have been attempting to teach some of the chaps to dance. A noble effort, but one that's mostly ended in bruised toes."

Bingley chuckled ruefully. "The men are willing, but the coordination is... lacking."

Darcy grunted. "Well, this is not a ball, for a mercy. There will be no dancing."

Fitzwilliam's expression sobered. "Just a bit of a jest, Darcy. Criminy, where has your humor gone? I know as well as you do that some of those fellows have peg legs or injuries that make dancing impossible. Watching others enjoy it might only remind them of what they've lost. But we did have a bit of fun in between hanging greenery and new drapes, eh, Bingley?"

"Indeed." Darcy looked away, his thoughts drifting to Elizabeth. A good thing there was to be no formal dancing. The very idea of dancing without her felt hollow. It was not just the soldiers who would find no joy in it.

Georgiana touched his arm lightly. "Brother, shall I begin with Miss Flora and Mrs. Jackson?"

"Yes," Darcy replied, more quickly than he intended. "Of course, though I am sure you want to refresh yourself first. But I think they will be grateful for your help."

She smiled, but the question in her eyes overshadowed any pleasure in her face. She had sensed his mood since London—how could she not? Thus far, he had tried to shield her from his bitter disappointment, but it would become more difficult now, with the loss of Elizabeth creating a gaping hole where once joy had taken root. He squeezed her hand, and she followed the maid out of the room.

Fitzwilliam glanced at Darcy, his brow furrowed. "Rough travels? You look worse than some of those poor devils in the ballroom."

Darcy exhaled sharply, shaking his head. "It is nothing. Let us ensure tomorrow's gathering meets its purpose."

Fitzwilliam watched him for a beat longer before nodding. "Whatever you say, Darcy."

But Darcy's mind remained elsewhere, the ache of Elizabeth's absence gnawing at him. He had envisioned this moment—the introduction of Georgiana to Elizabeth—countless times. Now, it felt like a shadow of what it could have been. Without her, even his best efforts seemed to falter.

MRS. BENNET BURST THROUGH the front door, her shawl trailing behind her as she waved both arms in the air. "Lizzy! Is it really you?" Kitty and Lydia followed on her heels, their skirts tangling as they raced each other to the coach. "What a surprise! We had no notion you would return so soon!"

Kitty and Lydia darted forward, almost colliding with each other in their haste. "Lizzy! Oh, what timing!" Kitty started, her breath coming fast. "You'll never believe the arrangements."

Lydia cut in, barely waiting for Kitty to finish. "Mama and Mrs. Philips have been working endlessly. You should see the decorations!"

"And Mr. Darcy and Mr. Bingley sent crates of things from Town," Kitty added. "You should see the trimmings! Ribbons, lace, everything!"

Mrs. Bennet fanned herself with her apron, beaming. "Oh, it's been a flurry of work, but we've prevailed. The neighborhood is positively abuzz, and it's all thanks to our efforts! Even Mrs. Long had to admit—"

Kitty broke in again, barely pausing to breathe. "Oh, and the gowns! Jane and I just came back from Netherfield. Lizzy, wait until you see them. Dozens of them, all sent straight from Town."

"They're perfect!" Lydia crowed. "And we're going to help the Netherfield ladies dress tomorrow. We'll be arranging their hair, styling them—it's like something from a novel!"

Elizabeth laughed, almost lost in the swirl. "You've all been very industrious. I shall have to see what wonders you've accomplished."

Mrs. Bennet looped her arm through Elizabeth's, drawing her toward the house. "Oh, Lizzy, you cannot imagine the work we've had convincing the entire neighborhood to attend! Mrs. Philips and I have all but pleaded with Mrs. Dunning and Mrs. Goulding, but what finally got them is hearing that Mrs. Purvis and Lady Lucas will have the pleasure of seeing their daughters with so many beaux and Netherfield all beautiful with candles. Oh, and the musicians! Did you hear about the musicians? And now everyone is coming! It will be the grandest affair Hertfordshire has ever seen, I daresay."

Elizabeth's feet barely touched the ground as they dragged her inside. Jane appeared at the doorway, her calm presence a stark contrast to the bustle. "Lizzy," she said with a conspiratorial smile, "it is so good to have you home."

Elizabeth returned the smile, though she felt her sister's assessing gaze. *Jane knew.* Of course, Jane knew. She always did.

As soon as they were fully inside, Elizabeth turned toward the stairs, but Jane caught her arm. "We must speak," she said, her voice low. "Come upstairs with me."

"In a moment," Elizabeth replied, gently extracting herself. "I should like to speak with Papa first."

Jane's brow lifted, and a knowing look flickered across her face. "Very well. But do not think you will escape me, Lizzy."

"I know better than that." She made her way to her father's library and found him seated comfortably with a book, his glasses perched low on his nose. He glanced up as she entered, his expression both pleased and amused.

"Ah, my prodigal daughter returns," he said, setting his book aside. "I trust your sojourn in London was not entirely unpleasant?"

Elizabeth smiled faintly, closing the door behind her. "It was... enlightening."

Mr. Bennet gestured toward the chair opposite him. "Come, sit. I have missed our conversations, and I suspect you have something to say."

Elizabeth hesitated before sitting, folding her hands tightly in her lap. "Papa," she began, "I returned because I needed to know the truth."

"About what, my dear?" he asked, though his tone suggested he already had some inkling.

"About Mr. Darcy," she began hesitantly, her hands fidgeting with the folds of her skirt.

Mr. Bennet raised an eyebrow, though his expression remained mild. "Ah, the man who so recently turned our neighborhood into a flurry of lace and ribbons. You know how I love lace and ribbons. Go on."

Elizabeth drew in a breath, then let it out slowly. "I thought I understood him. I thought I saw his character clearly, and... I admired it."

"That sounds like the beginning of a glowing recommendation. But I suspect you are about to temper it with a sharp critique."

She shook her head, frowning. "No, it isn't that. I—" She paused, pressing her lips together before continuing. "I allowed myself to be swayed by hearsay. By gossip I should have known better than to trust."

Mr. Bennet tilted his head, watching her closely. "Hearsay, is it? From a reliable source, I presume?"

Elizabeth gave a soft, humorless laugh. "I thought so at the time. Colonel Fitzwilliam is his cousin, after all."

"Ah, cousins," he mused, a faint smile tugging at his lips. "Always the keepers of our deepest truths—or so they claim."

She couldn't help but smile faintly at his tone, but quickly sobered. "I was too quick to believe the worst of him. His cousin spoke of ambition, of plans that seemed so...

calculated. And I let myself think it meant Mr. Darcy was using everyone at Netherfield as pawns."

"But since you are here, should I assume that opinion has changed?"

Elizabeth hesitated. "New information, I suppose, and… Oh, no, that will not do. The more I thought on it, the more I decided what I had believed did not align with the man I had come to know. The man who has shown care and respect—to Sir Thomas, to the people under his roof. To my family. To me."

He nodded slowly, his expression thoughtful. "And what does this realization mean to you, Lizzy?"

She looked down at her hands, then back up at her father, her voice trembling slightly. "It means I was wrong, Papa. It means I judged him unfairly based on hearsay. And now… I don't know if I have ruined everything."

He snorted. "Ruined everything, you say? Come, Lizzy, I had persuaded myself that you were the least silly of all my girls. Do not go and prove me wrong with some histrionic exaggeration."

"But I have! I as good as spat on his shoes, Papa. What man would be fool enough to let me near him again?"

Her father waved dismissively. "I daresay, Lizzy, you know little enough about men if you think that. I never saw a man so heartbroken that he would not burn up the soles of his boots running back to the object of his affection if she but smiled at him once more."

She dashed a tear from her cheek. "I think you overestimate—"

"I overestimate nothing." Her father gave her a wry look and crossed his arms. "The man has had stars in his eyes since the first time I ever saw him—odd, though. He only looked that way when you were in the room."

Elizabeth looked up, her breath catching slightly. "Are you… sure of that, Papa?"

He rolled his eyes and pinched the bridge of his nose. "Lizzy, how do you feel about *him?*"

She gulped. Could she say it out loud? "I think… I think he might be the best man I have ever known. But I need to be sure."

He raised a single brow.

"Indeed, it is true, Papa. That is why I came back in such a hurry. I had to see for myself if it is true."

Mr. Bennet studied her for a long moment. "Well, Lizzy, I cannot say I am surprised. You have always had an inconvenient fondness for discovering the truth, even when it disrupts your peace."

She laughed softly, a tear slipping down her cheek. "Do you think I am wrong, Papa?"

He shook his head. "No, my dear. But whether you are right or not, I think you will never forgive yourself if you do not find out."

Elizabeth smiled, feeling something like a vise easing its grip on her heart. "Thank you, Papa."

He nodded, reaching for his book again. "Now, off with you before your sisters come battering down the door. You have a great deal of prying to endure upstairs, I am sure."

Elizabeth rose, a small laugh escaping her. "Indeed, I do."

"BLAST IT, DARCY, is this table made of lead?" Fitzwilliam grunted as they maneuvered the unwieldy trestle toward its designated spot.

Darcy adjusted his grip. "Perhaps you have spent too much time in drawing rooms and not enough in the field, Cousin."

Fitzwilliam let out a sharp breath, dropping his end onto the floor with a dull thud. "And here I thought being a soldier was strenuous. Remind me not to assist with your next party."

Darcy straightened, his gaze sweeping the bustling room. Soldiers shuffled chairs into rows, Bingley was directing the butcher's delivery boy near the door, and Sir Thomas calmly orchestrated the chaos with an encouraging word here and a steadying hand there.

"Nor is it my usual occupation, I assure you."

Fitzwilliam leaned against the table, surveying the scene. "I imagine at Pemberley, the servants do all this before you even blink. Admit it, Darcy—you are enjoying this."

Darcy glanced around the room, the makeshift crew hauling decorations and aligning chairs. There was an honesty to the effort, a shared sense of purpose he had not experienced in years. "There is something refreshing about this," he admitted. "A man takes pride in a task when he must do it himself."

Fitzwilliam's grin widened. "Refreshing? I shall remind you of that when we are moving the next table."

Before Darcy could reply, Bingley's voice rang out from the doorway. "The Bennets are here!" And then he was bounding out the door to greet them. Naturally.

Darcy's pulse quickened, his first thought unbidden: *Elizabeth*. He turned slightly toward the door but caught himself.

What was the point? He already knew she would not be with them. She had gone to London, far removed from this moment, from this place—and from him.

Fitzwilliam raised an eyebrow. "Not going to greet them, Darcy? That is rather unsociable, even for you."

Darcy turned back to the trestle, gripping its edge as if it required his undivided attention. "I am occupied," he replied brusquely. "Besides, Bingley is more than capable of seeing the ladies and all their trunks and so on upstairs."

Fitzwilliam gave a knowing hum, but he said nothing further. Darcy bent to his work, the murmurs of greetings and laughter filtering in from the entry hall as the Bennets were welcomed. Each sound grated against his composure, a stark reminder of what—of *who*—was missing.

"Richard, are you going to help or just stand there like a bleeding stump?" he growled.

Richard gave him a sidelong glance, then cleared his throat as he set back to work. "Yes, yes, let us get on with it. I say, ah... How did you find my father when you were in London, Darcy?"

Darcy tightened his jaw and reached for another table, unwilling to meet his cousin's gaze. "I did not see him."

"You didn't see him? Why ever not? You went all the way to London, turned up in Mother's drawing room to collect Georgiana, and you never greeted my father? I thought you would have a dozen things to discuss with him."

"I did not feel equal to the conversation."

Fitzwilliam chuckled, hoisting his end of the table as Darcy moved the other side into place. "I can only imagine. What would the Earl of Matlock think of all *this*? A Darcy of Pemberley, carrying tables and playing host to ex-soldiers and tradesmen alike? I hope you did not tell him I was here."

Darcy's hands tightened on the edge of the table. "He would think precisely what I told him to think."

Richard squinted at him. "Eh? You just said you did not see him. How…?"

"I said all that was needed in the letter I wrote to him last week. He and I took opposing views of the purpose of this party. Where I saw a chance to help someone, he saw… other opportunities. Considering the realization that our opinions differed so wildly, I have withdrawn my intentions to run for office."

Fitzwilliam froze mid-motion, the corner of the table nearly slipping from his grip. "What?" He set it down abruptly, staring at Darcy in open disbelief. "You're serious?"

"I am. I have given the matter due consideration. The compromises required for a career in politics would have rendered the position meaningless to me."

"But you—you've been preparing for this for years! It was the logical next move."

Darcy straightened. "It was never what I wanted. I only thought it would be expected. Useful. But I have no interest in living a life dictated by the expectations of others."

Still gaping, Fitzwilliam muttered, "Well, don't I look the fool? I've been telling everyone what a fine statesman you'd make. Including Miss Elizabeth."

Darcy's head snapped up, his expression hardening. "Miss Elizabeth?"

"Indeed, who else? I thought she, of all people, would fancy hearing—"

"*What* did you say to her?"

Richard blinked. "I only said that this party was a fine endeavor, and it could serve your political career well. I thought I was helping to talk you up, Darcy."

A surge of anger rose in his chest. "You thought—" He let out a sharp breath, pacing a few steps away. "You thought you were *helping*? You've undone everything, Richard!"

"What?" Richard looked genuinely confused. "I say, what the devil do you mean?"

"You have made me look like an opportunist! Like I am exploiting this entire effort for my own gain." Darcy's voice rose, his frustration spilling over. "She must have believed every word you said!"

Richard stepped back, his face falling in realization. "Darcy, I swear, I didn't mean—"

"This is why she left for London! She thinks I am exactly the man I've worked so hard *not* to be! Egad, who could blame her for washing her hands of me?"

"Oh, come. Surely it had nothing to do with—"

"It had *everything* to do with it! Little wonder she could hardly stand the sight of me." He lurched for the door. "I'll call for my horse. I'll ride to London now and—"

Richard grabbed his arm, halting him. "Darcy, stop. Think."

Darcy spun to face him, his expression fierce. "*What* am I to think, Richard? That you've cost me the only woman I have ever—" He broke off, his voice snagging on the words.

Richard held up his hands in apology. "I'm sorry, Darcy. Truly, I am. I really thought it sounded fine—responsible and benevolent and all that, but taken a certain way..."

"What sort of woman did you think she was?" Darcy raged. "The sort to lust for power and wealth? The sort I have spent years avoiding?"

Richard's Adam's apple bobbed. "You are right. She is not at all like that—I am heartily sorry, Darcy. But you cannot leave now. The party is in a few hours. If you abandon this, all of it will have been for nothing."

Darcy's shoulders sagged. His breath came hard and fast, the effort to restrain himself almost as taxing as his earlier labors. He glared at Richard, fists clenched at his sides. "You are right," he bit out, his voice low and tight. "But do not think for a moment that this is over. When this party is done, you and I will have a reckoning."

Richard offered a faint, nervous smile. "I'll even confess it all to her myself, if it helps. When this is done, you can take a swing at me. Break my nose, bust my jaw—whatever you like."

Darcy's lips twitched despite himself, though his voice remained hard. "You deserve worse."

Richard chuckled weakly. "Probably. But first, let's see this party through. Then, first thing tomorrow, we will go to London together and bring your lady home."

Twenty-Four

Elizabeth's foot landed on the first step, and her eyes immediately swept upward.

"It is beautiful, is it not?" Jane murmured, stepping into the house beside her.

Elizabeth nodded, her gaze drifting from banisters to ceiling—to the new rugs gracing the entry and the hothouse flowers brightening every corner and wall. "They've outdone themselves. It feels as though the entire house has come alive."

From somewhere down the hall, a burst of laughter and the murmur of voices reached her ears. The commotion seemed to come from the direction of the ballroom. Elizabeth's head turned instinctively, her gaze drifting toward the partially open door at the far end of the corridor.

Bingley, who was directing footmen with the Bennet sisters' trunks of gowns toward the staircase, caught the movement and smiled broadly. "Ah, that would be Darcy and Fitzwilliam," he said, gesturing with one hand. "They're in the ballroom making final arrangements. I think Darcy's taken it upon himself to ensure the orchestra's placement is flawless—or at least that's what he claims. Likely, he just needs something to keep him busy."

Elizabeth's pulse quickened. Her gaze lingered on the door, and she thought she caught a faint, familiar cadence to the voices within. Darcy's voice, surely! The words were indistinct, muffled by distance, but the sound tugged at something deep within her.

For a fleeting moment, she imagined slipping away, finding an excuse to venture into the ballroom. What would he say if she walked in? What would *she* say? Her fingers curled lightly around the banister, her resolve teetering.

If she could speak to him alone—even for just a few minutes—it might ease the desperate ache that had followed her since London. Her hand twitched as though to take a step, but Jane's gentle touch on her arm stopped her.

"Come, Lizzy," Jane said, linking their arms. "The ladies are all taking turns upstairs to dress, and we've all so much to do before the evening begins."

Ahead of them, Kitty and Lydia were already halfway up the staircase, their laughter echoing through the hall as they chattered about ribbons and shoe roses. Elizabeth glanced back toward the ballroom door, the temptation still pulling at her. But Jane was right—tonight, there were no "lessers and betters." There was no one to trim the candles and sweep the floors while others loitered upstairs. Everyone had a role to play, and she had come to make herself useful.

Besides, Darcy was busy, too. The thought of the embarrassment she might cause him with such a poorly timed intrusion was enough to stop her.

"Yes, of course," she said softly, allowing Jane to guide her toward the stairs. "There will be time enough later."

As they ascended, the faint sounds of the ballroom faded, replaced by the bustling commotion of the upstairs rooms. Here, the air was charged with nervous energy. Young women—Sir Thomas's household—stood in clusters, fidgeting with borrowed gowns, smoothing skirts, and anxiously adjusting their hair.

Elizabeth took it all in with a pang. These women, more than anyone, deserved to feel radiant tonight. Whatever their pasts, tonight they would be honored guests, and she was determined to help them shine.

"Lizzy?" Kitty called from across the room. She was trying to untangle a knot in Mrs. Jackson's hair, and it looked as though the knot was prevailing. "Would you come help me? I tried to pin it, but I cannot manage her curls, but your hair is a little similar, so perhaps you know better how to manage."

"Let us have a look." Elizabeth took the brush from Kitty's hand and shook her head with a tsk. "Here is your first problem. This brush is all wrong for curls. Mrs. Jackson, what sort of style do you fancy? I think a high twist, with your curls loose to frame your face would look terribly fetching."

Mrs. Jackson turned her head from side to side, inspecting her reflection. "My husband likes my curls."

"I think they all do," Elizabeth chuckled. "That settles it. Oh! We have some primroses here. They would look lovely with your eyes and complexion. What do you think?"

At Mrs. Jackson's blushing agreement, Elizabeth set to work.

As the sisters moved from one young woman to another, lending combs and sashes and words of encouragement and praise, the atmosphere began to shift. Nervous glances turned into tentative smiles. Lydia was offering ribbons from her own collection, exclaiming, "This blue will be perfect for you! You must wear it!"

"Perfectly chaotic," Mary muttered as she hemmed a gown for yet another girl. "But there, I daresay you will not trip."

Elizabeth laughed lightly, pressing a hand to her cheek as she finished pinning another girl's hair. It was good to see her sisters pitching in, however clumsily. For once, they felt like a true family—a united front determined to make this evening as magical as it deserved to be.

Behind her, Jane was trying to take in the bodice of Elizabeth's own plum-colored gown for a freckled girl named Clara, who stood uncertainly near a dressing table, her trembling fingers struggling with the buttons so Jane could fit it properly.

"Here, allow me," Elizabeth said, taking the task into her own hands, since Jane was busy with the needle.

The girl glanced up in surprise. "Thank you, Miss Lizzy. I was afraid I might tear it."

Elizabeth smiled as she worked the buttons, smoothing the back of the gown once it was secured. "Nonsense. This color suits you beautifully—truly! You shall be the envy of everyone in the ballroom."

The girl blushed and glanced shyly toward the mirror, as though daring to believe Elizabeth's words.

A moment later, Elizabeth was tightening the last ribbon on Miss Flora's gown and stepped back, admiring her handiwork. "There," she said, smiling. "It fits you perfectly."

"Miss Elizabeth, is this too much?" a shy voice asked. Elizabeth turned to see Maryanne, a dark-haired young woman holding up a string of pearls with trembling hands. "I have never worn anything so fine."

Elizabeth smiled warmly, crossing the room to take the necklace from her. "It is perfect, Maryanne. Here, let me."

As she fastened the pearls around the girl's neck, Maryanne glanced at her reflection, her face a mixture of awe and disbelief. "Mr. Darcy insisted I wear it," she murmured. "I told him it was too grand, but he said... he said everyone deserves to feel beautiful tonight."

Elizabeth's fingers stilled briefly before she gave the clasp a final turn. "Did he?" she asked softly, her voice carefully even.

Maryanne nodded, her cheeks pinkening. "I... I always thought him so stern. But then he came to the kitchens last evening and spoke to all of us. And he gave each of us a necklace, brought new from London. Every one of us, miss!"

Elizabeth tilted her head to have a better look at the necklace in the mirror. "Did he? That was very sweet of him."

"Aye, miss. He asked about my family, my hopes... no one ever asks those things."

Elizabeth stepped back, her throat tight as she took in the girl's expression—an odd mixture of joy and gratitude that spoke volumes. How many lives had Mr. Darcy touched in ways she had not imagined?

Maryanne caught her lower lip in her teeth. "I picked the pearls. There were others, you know—gold pendants, some with jewels—but I liked these..." She brushed her fingertips over the pearls. "Pearls are for tears, but they don't have to be for sad tears, do they?"

Elizabeth smiled. "No, they do not. They can just as well be for happy tears."

Maryanne sighed. "I'll have to sell them eventually. Mr. Darcy said we might—he said it was to be our dowries, if we wished. I know, it... it seems rather cold to sell a gift."

"He gave you something beautiful," Elizabeth replied. "And the beauty is not simply in the vanity of the thing. The beauty is also in the caring—in seeing a kindness to be done and doing it."

"Aye, miss."

"Lizzy," Jane called from across the room, drawing her attention. "Could you help with this bow? Clara keeps turning."

"Only because I am nervous!" Clara protested with a laugh.

Elizabeth sniffed and squeezed Maryanne's shoulder as she stepped away. And it was then that she noticed how all the girls were, indeed, wearing some sort of jewelry. More sets of pearls, several crosses set with rubies or amber or other stones. Each necklace was unique, each precious... just like the girls who wore them.

She sighed, her heart full of pride and joy in this man who had showered sweetness on so many who had probably seldom known a kind word in their lives. She crossed the room and joined her sister, and her hands fell to deftly fixing the satin ribbon.

"You have no need to be nervous, Clara. You look glorious."

"Lizzy is right, Clara," Jane agreed. "I think I have never seen anyone look so well in that shade, but with your auburn hair, gold makes you look so warm and radiant!"

"Oh, it's not the gown, Miss Bennet. I'm so worried my Daniel might set up a fuss and refuse to stay in his crib and... oh, miss, who will be watching the children?"

"Ah," Jane mused with a gentle smile. "Well, as to that, you will hardly believe it, but the vicar's own wife said she would lend a hand in the nursery. Along with my sister Mary, who found that to be far more agreeable than wearing a ball gown. Is that not right, Mary?" Jane called.

Mary looked up from the lace she was trying to mend for a girl Elizabeth did not know. "Much more rational, and a goodly task for a virtuous person."

Jane laughed. "There, you see? I daresay even our good vicar could not prevail on his lady to stay away from this evening. And I believe Colonel Fitzwilliam had a rather rousing game of Blind Man's Bluff organized for the older children—before they are sent to bed for the night with all the sweeties Mr. Darcy brought for them from London, of course. Not to worry, Clara. I think everything is well in hand."

"Well, that... that is a right treat, miss." As Clara turned to inspect herself in the mirror once more, the door opened, and a new voice greeted the room. "Oh, my! This is where the magic is happening, I see."

Elizabeth turned to find another young woman entering, but she was not one of the Netherfield girls. She was tall and possessed of a willowy sort of grace, but her cheekbones still bore the softness of youth. Her morning gown was of expensive make, with soft amber curls framing a delicate face that bore an unmistakable resemblance to... to Mr. Darcy.

"Mr. Bingley said I should come up," she declared. "He said I might help. Where shall I start?"

Elizabeth tilted her head and stepped closer, a smile teasing her lips. "Wherever you like. Have you much skill with a needle?"

The girl's eyes widened. "I am *very* good," she replied with frank honesty, and very little humility.

"Good!" Elizabeth laughed and leaned forward with a conspiratorial whisper. "Because Lydia is trying to help fit Miss Sophie's gown, and I'm afraid poor Sophie might become a pincushion."

The girl giggled. "You must be Miss Elizabeth Bennet. My brother has spoken of you."

Elizabeth blinked, her composure faltering slightly. "Brother?" She sucked in a gasp. "You are Miss Darcy."

"Georgiana," she said brightly. "My brother and I arrived from London yesterday."

"He, ah…" Elizabeth eased closer, her brow furrowed. "He wanted you to attend the party, did he?"

"Oh, yes. And he wanted me to meet you."

Elizabeth blinked. "Me?"

"Of course. He said you are most kind and clever. And now I see he was quite right."

Elizabeth flushed and glanced down, uncertain of how to reply. Jane stepped in, extending her hand. "Miss Darcy, it is lovely to meet you. I am Jane Bennet, Elizabeth's elder sister."

Georgiana's face brightened further as she took Jane's hand. "It is a pleasure, Miss Bennet."

Elizabeth recovered herself and gestured toward the table cluttered with brushes and ornaments. "Well, shall we, Miss Darcy? Let us see if we can relieve Lydia of that needle."

E LIZABETH ADJUSTED THE LACE fichu on the young woman in front of her, tucking it gently into the top her bodice before stepping back with a satisfied nod. "There. Perfect."

The girl blushed, her fingers brushing over the delicate fabric. "Thank you, Miss Lizzy." She dipped into an awkward curtsey before hurrying out to join the others. The door closed behind her, and the room erupted into a brief, shared sigh of relief.

Georgiana, perched by the vanity, turned toward Elizabeth and Jane, a bright smile lighting her face. "Well! That must mean it is our turn. Come with me—I shall lend you my room to dress. It is the least I can do."

Elizabeth blinked, brushing a stray hair from her cheek. "Georgiana, you are too generous. We could not—"

"Not at all," Georgiana interrupted, rising to her feet. "I insist." Her tone held a note of steel that was probably a family trait, and she took Elizabeth's hand as if to pull her along.

Jane laughed softly, looping her arm through Elizabeth's. "It seems we have no choice, Lizzy. Come, let us not keep her waiting."

Elizabeth hesitated, her gaze sweeping the room. The hum of activity had quieted, and the last few ladies were gathering their courage before moving downstairs.

"Very well," Elizabeth said, allowing herself a small smile. "Lead the way."

Elizabeth stepped inside Georgiana's room and paused. There, laid out on the bed with careful precision, were the new gowns Aunt Gardiner had bought for them last month—Jane's rose chiffon and Elizabeth's moonlight blue silk.

"Flora and Mary brought them up and got all the creases out of them," Georgiana explained, moving to the vanity where a small assortment of pins and ribbons had been arranged, along with some of the prettiest roses and lilies for their hair. "They wanted to help you, too—they insisted everything be perfect."

Jane smiled warmly as she stepped to the bed, smoothing her hand over her gown. "It's as though they knew we would be the last to make our preparations."

"They do seem to have thought of everything," Elizabeth said softly.

Jane picked up her gown and swept behind the dressing screen, while Elizabeth stared at her blue gown. Tonight, Darcy would see her in it... and she hoped it would give him as much pleasure as he had given so many others this day.

"Well," Georgiana replied with a playful twinkle in her eye. "Shall I fix your hair?"

Elizabeth laughed softly, finally lifting the gown from the bed. "If you insist."

"L IZZY, WAIT FOR A moment."

Elizabeth tucked a stray curl behind her ear as they started for the stairs in their evening gowns. "Is something the matter?"

"No, not at all." Jane fidgeted with her hands. "In fact, it is... the opposite."

Elizabeth tilted her head and drifted down the first step. "Go on."

"Mr. Bingley... he has asked me to enter into a formal courtship."

Elizabeth froze on the step and whirled on her sister. "Jane! He—he has? You are not just easing me this time, are you? This is real?"

"It is! He intends to speak to Papa tonight."

"Oh, Jane," Elizabeth breathed, her hands flying to her sister's. "That is wonderful! I could not be happier for you."

"You mean that this time?" Jane asked, her eyes searching Elizabeth's. "You did not seem very happy before."

"Of course I do, and I am! You deserve all the happiness in the world, and I have no doubt Mr. Bingley will do everything in his power to give it to you."

"Oh, I hoped you might feel that way. I know you have been... uncertain about Mr. Darcy, and I thought—"

Elizabeth shook her head quickly. "No, Jane. I am not at all uncertain about Mr. Darcy. But anyway, this is not about me. You and Mr. Bingley are perfectly matched, Jane. You have my full blessing."

Jane reached out, clasping Elizabeth's hands. "I wish you could feel the same joy for yourself, Lizzy. I have seen how Mr. Darcy looks at you. He cares for you, I am certain of it."

Elizabeth's heart squeezed, but she shook her head, her voice faltering. "Jane... I shall not speculate—"

"Why not? You are worth everything he has to offer, and I believe he sees it."

Elizabeth swallowed hard. "Well. Let us think only on the pleasant things for now. Tonight is about Christmas and joy and caring for others. I shall not attempt to manipulate that poor man again."

"Oh, quite right, as you should not," Jane agreed. "But I am not without hope that you, too, will receive a Christmas gift, Lizzy, from someone who seems to care very much f or *you*."

Twenty-Five

D ARCY SQUARED HIS SHOULDERS and looked to the door as the sound of sleigh bells echoed through the crisp evening air, the latest guests arriving in a flurry of muffled laughter and swirling cloaks. He extended a hand to Sir William Lucas, whose rosy cheeks betrayed the chill outside.

"Welcome, sir, and Merry Christmas! Do, come warm yourself by the fire," Darcy said with a slight nod, gesturing toward the warmth of the house.

Sir William nodded in return. "Thank you, Mr. Darcy. Quite the gathering you have here."

"Indeed," added Lady. Lucas, unbuttoning her cloak as she scanned the crowd with wide eyes. "The *entire* neighborhood seems to be here. Even those who swore they would never set foot in Netherfield."

Darcy allowed himself a faint smile. "That was the hope."

He turned as Roberts escorted another group inside, their voices overlapping with the strains of a lively violin tune spilling from the ballroom. Darcy moved to greet them, shaking hands and exchanging polite words. Each new arrival brought a fresh wave of skepticism that gradually melted as the festive atmosphere worked its charm. The scent of spiced punch and roasting meats wafted through the air, and the warm glow of candlelight reflected in the polished floors and gleaming mirrors.

"Darcy," Richard greeted, appearing at his side with a glass in hand. "I have never seen you in such a state. You are practically the spirit of the evening."

Darcy glanced at him, arching a brow. "I would not go that far."

Fitzwilliam chuckled. "Oh, come now. Look at you—shaking hands, exchanging pleasantries, even smiling occasionally."

Darcy resisted the urge to roll his eyes. "If you have something to say, Fitzwilliam, say it."

"I already have." Fitzwilliam sipped his drink, his smirk widening. "You're enjoying yourself."

"Perhaps." Darcy turned his gaze back to the crowd, his expression neutral, though a flicker of truth danced in his cousin's words. This evening was not the usual tedious affair of London society. It was different. Purposeful.

His eyes tracked Watts, one of the men Sir Thomas had saved from a French gaol, who was holding court near the refreshment table. Watts's deep voice carried over the hum of conversation as he shared stories of the trials Sir Thomas had endured for his men. The gentlemen around him were joining in with similar tales.

"You chose well in inviting them," Fitzwilliam remarked, following Darcy's gaze. "Watts, Pence, and Drummond, and I think I also spotted Michaels, Anderson, Williams... egad, is that Pierce and Tollman? Our entire rooming house from Paris seems to be here tonight! Solid men, the lot of them."

"They were Sir Thomas's men first," Darcy replied. "It is only right they should be here to speak on his behalf."

Fitzwilliam tilted his head. "And here *you* are, orchestrating the grand event as if it were your life's calling. Are you sure you're not seeking public office?"

Darcy gave him a sharp look. "I assure you, I am not."

Fitzwilliam held up a hand in mock surrender. "Easy, Cousin. Only teasing." He gestured toward the ballroom, where music swelled, and voices grew louder. "Though I must say, you've created something remarkable here. Even the matrons of Meryton seem to be reconsidering their initial reservations."

Darcy followed his cousin's gaze to the far side of the room. The older women of Meryton clustered together, their heads bent in conversation, their glances darting toward the women from Netherfield. They were split along clear lines, but Darcy noted a few tentative smiles and nods exchanged between the groups.

"It will take time," Darcy said. "But the first steps are being taken."

Fitzwilliam grinned. "First steps, indeed. Though you might find the second steps more challenging—especially with so many eyes watching."

Darcy did not reply, his focus shifting to the door as Roberts admitted yet another group of guests. He straightened slightly, his pulse quickening as he scanned the arrivals. But the familiar figure he hoped to see was not among them. Of course, she was not.

"Still waiting for someone?" Fitzwilliam asked.

Waiting... No, he was not waiting. She knew all about this party. She could have come back if she had wanted... if she could find it in her to change her mind, to give him a chance...

But the rest of the Bennets were all here—Miss Catherine sitting by the fireplace, Miss Lydia already laughing by the punch bowl, and Miss Bennet was probably on Bingley's arm somewhere. Elizabeth... was not here.

Darcy sighed and turned back to the crowd. "This is going well. But it is not enough yet," he said quietly. He handed his glass to a passing footman and crossed the room.

The colonel followed. "What are you planning now?"

Darcy ignored him. Instead, he stopped near Mrs. Long and her niece. "Mrs. Long, how wonderful to see you this evening," he said warmly.

Mrs. Long blinked at him, clearly taken aback. "Mr. Darcy," she said, her voice wary.

He gestured toward the women from Netherfield. "I wonder if I might introduce you to Miss Maryanne? She has an eye for embroidery that rivals anything I have seen from London."

Mrs. Long hesitated, glancing toward the younger woman. But Darcy would brook no hesitation, and she seemed reluctant to defy him. In this, his experience brokering business deals and carrying his way served him well.

"Well," she said finally, "if you think so highly of her..."

"I do," Darcy said firmly. "I am certain you shall find her delightful."

Mrs. Long allowed herself to be drawn into conversation, and Darcy moved on, repeating the process with another guest, then another. Soon, the lines between groups began to blur. The music swelled, and laughter rose above the murmur of conversation.

Fitzwilliam shook his head in disbelief as Darcy returned to his side. "You are a marvel. I half expect you to start matchmaking next."

Darcy gave him a sharp look. "Do not tempt me."

The colonel laughed, clapping him on the shoulder. "Whatever has come over you, Cousin, I approve. If only London could see this side of you."

Darcy allowed himself a faint smile. "Perhaps London underestimates what is possible when people are treated with dignity."

The colonel tilted his glass in a mock salute. "Well said. Now, do tell me, are you pacing yourself, or do you plan to collapse before midnight?"

Darcy ignored him, his attention drawn to a cluster of women standing near the far end of the room. The women of Netherfield; their gowns might be borrowed, but the joy in their eyes tonight—that was all their own. Slowly, they were being drawn into the crowd, thanks in no small part to Sir Thomas, who had stationed himself near the dance floor.

Darcy crossed the room, pausing to speak with Mr. Drummond, who was laughing with a young shopkeeper. "It seems you are already making friends, Drummond."

The man chuckled. "It is easy enough when there is good company and better punch. Do you know, I felt rather badly sending my regrets to Gardiner on such short notice, but he was all for it."

"Yes, I sent him a note of apology when I realized I was stealing some of his guests. He wrote back that he quite understood and wished us merry."

"Very jolly of him! Good show, Darcy. Excellent wine, bit of good meat. Not sorry I left London, my good man, not one bit."

Darcy glanced around, taking in the mingling guests, the growing ease between groups that had once seemed insurmountable. "Well, do enjoy yourself. Excuse me, please."

He had just rejoined Richard in the hall when a sudden burst of laughter—familiar laughter—drew his attention. He turned—and froze when he saw *her*.

The world shifted beneath him. Elizabeth Bennet stood near the far edge of the crowd, speaking with one of Sir Thomas's former soldiers. The starry blue of her gown caught the light with every movement as if it had been made to reflect the brilliance of her eyes. Her dark hair, arranged in soft curls, framed her face with an elegance that struck him like a physical blow. She laughed at something her companion said—lightly, warmly—and the sound sent a jolt through him, a sound he had feared he might never hear again.

And then, as if sensing him, she turned.

Their eyes met, and Darcy's heart stopped. For a fleeting moment, he could not breathe, could not think. There was only her, standing there as if conjured by some unspoken prayer. The tension that had gripped him since London unraveled in an instant, replaced by an astonishment so raw it nearly staggered him.

She had come back. And she was smiling... at him.

A quiet stillness seeped into his soul, as though the world had paused for just a moment, leaving him with nothing but the undeniable clarity of what he felt. Everything—the music, the hum of voices, the careful arrangements he had labored over for weeks—receded into the background. The world narrowed until it held only her.

Beside him, Richard gave a low, amused whistle. "Well," the colonel murmured, "I think I've just gained an answer to a question I hadn't even asked."

Darcy barely heard him. His gaze never left Elizabeth as he started forward, his steps slow but deliberate. Each movement felt like a promise, the weight of every unspoken word driving him toward her. The world might crumble around him, but in this moment, none of it mattered.

She was here—the best Christmas gift he could have ever asked for. Elizabeth Bennet, smiling and laughing and looking as though she had been waiting, just to speak to him.

And tonight—tonight—he would ask for next Christmas, too. And all the ones after that.

T HERE HE WAS.

Mr. Darcy stood near the entryway, his dark coat and perfectly tailored attire cutting him out from the haze that went unfocused behind him. The flickering candle-light danced over his face, and his gaze found hers with an intensity that seemed to make the air between them hum. Elizabeth's steps faltered, her heart thudding unevenly as her breath faltered.

He moved toward her, weaving through the crowd as if they were not even there. "Miss Elizabeth."

"Mr. Darcy."

His gaze swept over her, lingering on the sweep of her blue gown and then rising to her eyes. "You look..." He hesitated, the corners of his mouth softening. "You look stunning."

Warmth bloomed in her cheeks, but she refused to drop her gaze. "Very kind of you, sir."

He stepped closer, lowering his voice to something meant only for her. "I am not nearly kind enough to do you justice."

Elizabeth's breath hitched again, but this time, she did not hide it. Her hands fidgeted briefly at her sides before she clasped them to still their movement. "Mr. Darcy," she began, her voice softening, "there is something I must say."

He stiffened slightly, his posture becoming more formal. "Of course."

Her gaze flicked toward the glittering ballroom, where laughter and music spilled out, before she brought it back to his. "I owe you an apology."

His brow furrowed, confusion flickering across his face. "An apology?"

"Yes." She swallowed hard, her voice trembling just slightly. "I was wrong about you. About... so much. We had so many plans, talked of so many things, but then I just left it all—left you for London, because I believed—I feared..." She stopped, her courage faltering momentarily under the weight of her own words. "I—I was unfair to you."

Darcy's expression darkened slightly, though not with anger. "Fitzwilliam," he muttered under his breath. "He told me that he spoke to you at dinner. What did he say?"

Elizabeth's lips twitched in a fleeting smile. "Nothing that he did not believe to be in your favor, I think. The fault is mine, entirely."

He shook his head, his hands flexing at his sides. "No. My cousin is too often clumsy with his good intentions. And I... I should have made myself clearer. I should have spoken sooner."

"Perhaps." Her voice softened as she met his eyes. "But it does not excuse me. I doubted your character when I should not have. And, for that, I am truly sorry."

For a moment, Darcy said nothing. Then, quietly, he asked, "Do you still?"

Her heart twisted, her breath leaving her in a rush. "No," she said simply. "No, Mr. Darcy. I do not, and I never shall again."

His shoulders loosened just slightly as his eyes searched hers for something deeper. "You cannot know what it means to hear you say that."

Elizabeth allowed herself to smile now, a small but genuine curve of her lips. "Perhaps I do."

The strains of a Christmas hymn floated through the air, mingling with the chatter of guests and the clink of glasses. Elizabeth glanced toward the sound, and Darcy followed her gaze, his expression softening further.

"Would you walk with me?" he asked, his tone hesitant but hopeful. "There is something *I* would very much like to say now."

Elizabeth nodded, the warmth in her chest blooming fully. "I would like that."

As they moved toward the edge of the room, Darcy offered his arm, and she took it without hesitation. And finally, the heavy clouds of doubt begin to lift, and in their place came something lighter, brighter—something that felt remarkably like hope.

Twenty-Six

E LIZABETH LINKED HER ARM with Darcy's as they strolled toward the ballroom, the murmur of voices and strains of music growing louder with each step. Just as they reached the arched entryway, a flurry of motion nearly collided with them—Lydia, darting past with a shoe rose in one hand and a glass of punch in the other.

"Lydia!" Elizabeth exclaimed, instinctively pulling Darcy to the side. "Must you charge about like a startled goose?"

Lydia whirled, grinning unapologetically. "They're starting carols, Lizzy! You'll miss it if you don't hurry!"

Darcy arched a brow, adjusting his coat as if it had been personally affronted by Lydia's exuberance. "Is this a common occurrence?"

Elizabeth stifled a laugh. "Only when Lydia has been left unchecked for more than five minutes."

"I see."

She stood on her toes, bringing her mouth near his cheek. "I fear you will get used to her, sooner or later. Whether *she* will ever be corrected remains to be seen."

Darcy's cheek had darkened hues, and the smile he gave her then was almost bashful. "Is that a test, Elizabeth?"

She grinned. "What do you think?"

He closed his other hand over hers where it rested in the crook of his elbow. "I have never liked failing tests, so I do not mean to fail this one."

Elizabeth squeezed his arm. "Good answer."

They entered the ballroom, where the chandeliers glowed warmly, their light reflecting off polished floors and gleaming decorations. Elizabeth let her gaze sweep the room. Groups of guests mingled near the refreshment tables, some laughing and gesturing, while others stood stiffly, their faces betraying their unease. The ladies of Sir Thomas's household lingered at the edges, their borrowed gowns beautifully fitted but their smiles hesitant.

"Do you see Mrs. Long?" Jane's voice came from just behind them, her tone both hopeful and wary. "She promised to bring her niece, but I cannot find her anywhere."

Elizabeth turned, her brows lifting as she spotted the older woman by the punch bowl, clutching her cup as if it might ward off any overly friendly advances. "There she is. Though I suspect her niece has fled to a safer distance."

Darcy followed her gaze, a faint curve appearing at the corner of his mouth. "Your neighbors are... reserved."

Elizabeth tilted her head, suppressing a smirk. "Reserved is a generous term."

Across the room, Mr. Bingley leaped onto a small platform, narrowly avoiding knocking over a harpist's music stand. He clapped his hands together, his voice booming. "Ladies and gentlemen, it's time to raise our voices in some Christmas cheer!"

A ripple of laughter spread through the crowd, though some guests exchanged uncertain glances. The matrons of Meryton had broken off from their daring socializing of earlier, and now clustered like wary hens, their eyes darting toward the residents of Netherfield with a mix of curiosity and disdain.

Elizabeth squeezed Darcy's arm lightly. "Do you think your friend can charm them into song?"

"If anyone can, it is Bingley. Though I doubt even he can break through Mrs. Long's fortress of propriety."

As if in answer, Bingley gestured grandly to the musicians, who began the opening notes of God Rest Ye Merry, Gentlemen. His enthusiasm was contagious, and soon, a few brave voices joined in.

A particularly spirited rendition from Colonel Fitzwilliam, who was standing at the front of the room, caught Elizabeth's attention. His deep baritone was unexpectedly robust—and a little off-key.

Elizabeth laughed softly. "Your cousin appears determined to lead the charge."

Darcy glanced at Fitzwilliam, whose arms were now gesturing dramatically to encourage others. "Determined, yes. Tuneful, no."

Their shared laughter felt like a balm, and Elizabeth found herself leaning just slightly closer to Darcy. "Do you sing, Mr. Darcy?"

"Not in public," he said firmly, though his expression softened as he glanced down at her. "But I will gladly accompany you if you wish."

The warmth in his voice stirred something in her, and for a moment, she forgot the hum of the crowd or the music filling the room. It was just him—steady, certain, and looking at her as though no one else in the world mattered.

By the time they reached the final verse, the entire room was singing, even the most skeptical of Meryton's matrons. Elizabeth glanced across the room and saw Sir Thomas standing near the doorway, his expression awash in gratitude and relief as he watched the transformation unfolding before him.

"Excellent!" Bingley exclaimed as the song ended, his face alight with pleasure. "Now, let us try something a bit livelier! How about 'Hark! The Herald Angels Sing'?"

The musicians obliged, launching into a sprightly rendition, complete with several comical "mistakes and interruptions"—probably staged ahead of time by Mr. Bingley—that had several younger guests laughing and clapping along.

"You sing beautifully, Miss Elizabeth," Darcy said, his voice low enough that only she could hear.

Elizabeth felt her cheeks warm under his steady gaze. "Thank you, Mr. Darcy. You sing rather well yourself."

"I cannot promise to join the choir, but I shall do my best to support the effort."

Elizabeth opened her mouth to reply, but Bingley's voice called from across the room, drawing Darcy's attention. He turned, his expression shifting into something sharper, more focused.

"Forgive me, Miss Elizabeth," he said, inclining his head. "Bingley appears to need me for something. I will return shortly."

Elizabeth nodded, her pulse fluttering as his gaze lingered on hers for just a moment longer before he turned and strode toward Bingley. She watched him weave through the gathering, his tall figure effortlessly commanding the space. When she finally looked away, Jane was beside her, her gaze sweeping the room.

"A promising start, do you not think?" Jane murmured, her tone as light as her teasing glance.

Elizabeth smiled, but kept her eyes trained on Darcy's retreating figure. "It seems so," she said, though her thoughts were already following him.

There was something about the way he moved through the room, his interactions measured but sincere, that seemed to draw others to him despite his usual reserve. It was a side of him she had not fully seen before—she doubted anyone had.

The caroling continued, each song weaving a thread of unity among the guests. By the time the musicians played the final notes of "We Wish You a Merry Christmas," the earlier tension in the room had all but melted away, leaving only warmth and good cheer... and several jests from slightly inebriated gentlemen asking where the figgy pudding was.

Elizabeth glanced toward Darcy once more, only to find his gaze already on her. For a fleeting moment, the room seemed to quiet, the hum of voices fading into the distance. She inclined her head slightly, a silent acknowledgment of something unspoken between them, before turning back to Jane.

As the singing broke up, guests clustered into groups for parlor games. A table near the center was surrounded by animated players engaged in Spillikins, while another corner hosted a spirited round of charades. Elizabeth lingered near the refreshments, watching Jane and Bingley as they enthusiastically explained the rules of Snapdragon to a curious onlooker.

"Miss Elizabeth, you're looking entirely too peaceful. This must be remedied."

Elizabeth turned to find Colonel Fitzwilliam approaching, his grin rakish as he held up a deck of cards. "Do you know Commerce, Miss Elizabeth? It seems we are short one player, and I believe you would elevate our little group significantly."

"You flatter me, Colonel. Are you sure you are not simply desperate for another victim?"

"Desperate? Never," he replied smoothly. "But I will admit my cousin suggested you might enjoy a game."

Her gaze flickered across the room to where Darcy stood near the musicians, deep in conversation with Sir Thomas. Despite the serious set of his brow, she could feel his attention on her—whether real or imagined, it was difficult to say.

"And what role do you play in this scheme of his, Colonel?" she asked, folding her arms.

"I, Miss Elizabeth, am but a humble facilitator." Fitzwilliam extended a hand with exaggerated gallantry. "Allow me to 'facilitate' your victory."

Elizabeth hesitated for only a moment before placing her hand lightly in his. "Very well, but I warn you, Colonel—I am fiercely competitive."

"I would expect nothing less," he replied, leading her toward a table where a small group awaited.

As Elizabeth took her seat, she could not resist a glance toward Darcy. He was watching them now, his dark gaze steady and unflinching. Colonel Fitzwilliam leaned closer, his voice low enough for only her to hear.

"Ah, yes," he murmured, "there it is. That look could burn through stone. If I am not careful, I shall be asked to duel by morning."

Elizabeth bit back a laugh. "You are imagining things, Colonel."

"Am I?" Fitzwilliam straightened with a wink, turning his attention to the cards. "Let us see if I survive the evening."

The game began, and Elizabeth quickly became absorbed in the play, her competitive streak ignited by Fitzwilliam's relentless teasing. Yet even as laughter rang out around her, she could not ignore the steady pull of Darcy's gaze from across the room.

"SIR THOMAS!" A HEARTY voice rang out as Watts, one of Sir Thomas's former comrades, strode through the crowd, his steps purposeful and his hand outstretched. "It's been far too long."

Darcy stepped aside as Watts reached Sir Thomas, clasping his hand firmly. The man's voice carried across the room, drawing attention from nearby guests. "I owe you more than my life, sir. It's an honor to stand here tonight and say it face-to-face."

Darcy noted the way Sir Thomas's shoulders stiffened, as though the praise was too much to bear. He didn't miss the way Sir Thomas's other hand trembled slightly as it gripped the edge of his coat.

"You owe me nothing, Watts," Sir Thomas replied, his voice rough. "It was a duty. Nothing more."

"A duty that cost you years," Pence chimed in, stepping forward with Drummond at his side. "You gave us the chance to come home. Without you, we might have been rotting in that prison for years—or worse."

Sir Thomas shook his head, his gaze dropping for a moment as if to collect himself. "What any man would have done."

"Not any man," Watts pressed. "You went back for us when no one else would. You showed us what it means to fight for more than survival."

Darcy could see the conflict etched in Sir Thomas's face—gratitude mingled with a humility so deeply rooted it bordered on disbelief. Sir Thomas finally spoke, his voice tight with emotion. "And you've all come so far. Watts, Pence, Drummond... it's good to see you thriving."

Darcy's own throat threatened to close up—not with self-reflection this time, but with pride. These were the men he had invited, the ones he'd written to, because Sir Thomas deserved this moment. A public acknowledgment of the sacrifices he'd made, of the lives he'd changed, even if it left him uncomfortable.

Watts glanced around the bustling ballroom, a faint smile on his lips. "And this?" He gestured to the vibrant crowd. "You've done more than save lives, Sir Thomas. You've built something lasting. And tonight... you've brought people together who'd never have stood in the same room otherwise."

Sir Thomas's voice faltered. "I... I never imagined..."

Darcy, standing beside him, placed a hand on the older man's shoulder. "You may not have imagined it, Sir Thomas, but you inspired it. Bingley and I merely gave shape to what you have already built."

Sir Thomas's gaze darted to Darcy, then to the crowded ballroom. His weathered face softened, his eyes glistening with unshed tears. "I scarcely dared to hope for a moment like this," he murmured. "To see them—everyone—together, as equals."

Darcy gave Sir Thomas's shoulder a squeeze. "Every handshake, every kind word tonight—those are the echoes of your own actions, the lives you've saved, and the chances you've given. Merry Christmas, Sir Thomas."

Sir Thomas's breath hitched as he turned fully to face Darcy, his voice trembling. "This... this is the greatest gift I've ever received. You and Bingley—this evening—what you've done here, it's beyond what I could have hoped."

Darcy inclined his head, his grip tightening once more on Sir Thomas's shoulder before stepping back. He glanced across the room, where Bingley was engaged in a lively conversation with a group of local tradesmen, his natural charm bridging gaps that might otherwise have remained insurmountable. For all his friend's easy laughter, Darcy knew how deeply Bingley believed in the importance of this night—and how much of its success was due to his unwavering enthusiasm.

As Sir Thomas turned to greet another well-wisher, Darcy allowed himself a rare moment of satisfaction. Tonight was a triumph, not for appearances or social niceties, but for something real—something that mattered.

But the triumph faded quickly for him—meaningless, almost, until his gaze chanced across the one who had inspired him. Across the room, seated at a card table, was Elizabeth. Her dark curls gleamed in the candlelight, perfectly framing the sharp curve of her cheek and the vibrant blue of her gown. She laughed—bright, unrestrained—and for a moment, he was utterly frozen, his entire world narrowing to that sound, that vision.

Fitzwilliam, seated across from her, was gesturing with a theatrical flourish at his cards, clearly losing but playing the fool to draw another laugh from her. Darcy's stomach twisted—not with jealousy, but with an undeniable need to be the one seated across from her, to hear her laughter directed at him.

He barely registered Sir Thomas's murmured thanks to another well-wisher as he excused himself. Darcy was already moving, his steps purposeful, his focus unshakable. Elizabeth Bennet had captured his heart, and tonight, he would not let her slip away again.

He hardly recalled walking across the room, but a moment later, he was standing behind her chair, watching her claim another victory over his cousin. "Miss Elizabeth," he said, his voice carrying just enough weight to turn her gaze. "Would you join me in a different sort of game?"

She looked up at him. "Oh? What sort of game are you leading, Mr. Darcy?"

"Oh, do tell us, Darcy," Fitzwilliam asked. "Are you about to demonstrate your skill at card tricks? Or perhaps an old hunting game you believe we country folk would find fascinating?"

Darcy did not even glance at him. "No cards, no hunting. But I do believe Snapdragon is the game of the hour."

Elizabeth tilted her head, interest sparking in her eyes. "Snapdragon? I have heard of it but never had the opportunity to play."

Fitzwilliam gave a theatrical groan. "Darcy, you are as full of surprises as a Christmas pudding. Very well, steal her away if you must. But be warned, I shall win her back at the next opportunity."

Darcy turned to his cousin, his response dry. "Your chances are as promising as they ever were."

Elizabeth's soft laugh was... well, it was everything. He extended his arm to her, and she placed her hand lightly on his sleeve, her warmth seeping through the fabric. "I hope you have quick fingers, Mr. Darcy," she said. "Lead on."

As they entered the parlor, the faint scent of brandy greeted them, mingling with the warmth of the crackling fire. A shallow dish of raisins floated in the center of the table, and Darcy went to the fire, bringing back a glowing stick to ignite the brandy. Blue flames danced across the surface, casting flickering shadows that played against the walls.

Elizabeth's eyes widened as she watched the fire's hypnotic glow. "It is beautiful," she murmured.

Darcy turned slightly toward her, the faintest smile touching his lips. "It is also unforgiving. Are you prepared for the challenge?"

Her gaze snapped to his, a flicker of determination sparking in her expression. "I am not one to back away from a test, Mr. Darcy."

"Nor would I expect you to."

He motioned to the flames and reached in, his movements swift and precise. A raisin appeared between his fingers, and without hesitation, he popped it into his mouth. He stepped back with a nod. "Your turn, Miss Elizabeth."

She hesitated for only a moment before stepping forward. The fire's heat kissed her skin, and Darcy noted the slight curl of her fingers as she reached into the flames. She emerged victorious, holding the raisin aloft with a triumphant glint in her eyes.

"Well done," Darcy said.

She returned to his side, her cheeks faintly flushed. "I believe you underestimated me."

"On the contrary, I expected nothing less."

"Truly?" Her brows arched wickedly, and she held the raisin aloft between them as though she were offering it to him. In public? Darcy shot a quick glance over his shoulder, wondering if anyone was looking at them just now. Did he dare?

Elizabeth's smile widened as she tempted him with that raisin, and just as he was dipping his head down to let her drop it in his mouth, she changed course and slipped it into her own mouth.

And Darcy nearly crashed forward, just barely stopping himself from following that raisin's path to her lips. And any hope he might have ever entertained of keeping his composure around her was shattered.

They were not left alone for long once others saw the flames had been lit. Kitty Bennet was the next challenger, with Maria Lucas and Mrs. Jackson following. Laughter spilled into the room as guests tested their courage. Fitzwilliam, predictably, yelped when he "misjudged" the flames, earning a round of good-natured jeers. Even Sir William Lucas joined in, his booming laugh filling the space as he reached into the fire with the gusto of a man who had nothing left to fear.

As the flames dwindled, Darcy turned to Elizabeth. "You are rather daring, you know."

"Did you expect otherwise?"

"Not at all," he said. "I merely think most would hesitate before reaching into the fire."

"No point in hesitating when I can clearly see what I want," she said, tilting her head with a mischievous smile. "But then, I do not fear a little heat."

His gaze flared, and he was suddenly having some trouble swallowing. "Clearly not."

Before either could speak again, Sir Thomas called from the doorway. "Enough Snapdragon! Who dares to test their skill at Blindman's Bluff next?"

Darcy glanced toward the doorway and then back to Elizabeth. "Shall we avoid the blindfolds and find somewhere quieter to talk?"

Elizabeth hesitated for the briefest moment before nodding. "Lead the way, Mr. Darcy."

Twenty-Seven

A RIPPLE OF LAUGHTER swept through the crowd near the punch bowl as Mr. and Mrs. Jackson found themselves paused beneath the mistletoe. Jackson must have missed seeing it, for it had been on his blind side, but his young wife did not. She covered her mouth with her hand and giggled, pointing upward when she discovered that their friends had suddenly cleared a space around them and were cheering them on. A quick peck—perhaps a little braver than others might have been—and the game was on as others "accidentally" wandered beneath its white berries.

The sprig of greenery dangled gently on its red ribbon, a quiet invitation more than a formal demand. Some guests lingered nearby, feigning casual interest, while others drifted past, their gazes flickering to the mistletoe with varying degrees of curiosity or amusement.

Elizabeth found herself at the edge of the gathering, Darcy still at her side. His expression was rather more composed than hers, though his gaze seemed fixed on the sprig of mistletoe swaying gently above the punch bowl... where practically everyone would stray under its intoxicating powers at some point during the night.

"Do you think Sir Thomas deliberately placed it there to cause a riot?" Elizabeth asked, tilting her head toward the mistletoe.

"If he did, he has been remarkably successful. It seems to have become the centerpiece of the evening."

"Would you say the same if you were standing under it?"

He glanced at her, his eyes glinting with something almost teasing. "Perhaps you should test the theory."

Elizabeth raised a brow. "That sounds suspiciously like a challenge, Mr. Darcy."

"Not at all. Merely an observation."

She turned to him, her cheeks warming at the intensity of his look. "Do you intend to join the spectacle, Mr. Darcy?"

"Only if you wish it."

Elizabeth opened her mouth to respond, but before she could find the words, Colonel Fitzwilliam appeared, his grin as mischievous as ever.

"Cousin!" he exclaimed. "It seems you are the only one who has not yet participated in this grand tradition. What an oversight!"

Darcy's expression shifted into one of mild annoyance. "I am not certain that I—"

"Oh, nonsense," Fitzwilliam interrupted, grabbing his arm. "Come, come! Miss Elizabeth, surely you agree that 'mingling' is the point of the evening, and Mr. Darcy ought to set an example for the rest of us?"

Elizabeth glanced at Darcy, who was already looking at her. "Well," she said lightly, trying to ignore the sudden quickening of her pulse, "it seems we have little choice."

Darcy's lips curved into the faintest of smiles. "It would appear so."

He offered his hand, and she took it, allowing him to guide her toward the mistletoe. The crowd parted for them, their whispers and murmurs creating a hum of anticipation. Elizabeth's heart was pounding so loudly that she was certain everyone could hear it.

They stopped beneath the sprig, its green leaves and white berries casting a shadow over their heads. Darcy turned to face her fully, his gaze steady and unwavering. Elizabeth's breath caught as the room seemed to fade, leaving only him.

"For tradition's sake," he said softly, his voice low enough that only she could hear.

Elizabeth nodded, unable to speak. Her eyes darted to his lips, then back to his eyes. He leaned in slowly, giving her every chance to step away.

She did not.

The brush of his lips against her cheek was feather-light, yet it sent a warmth spiraling through her that felt a great deal like an inferno. When he pulled back, his gaze held hers, and the faintest curve of his lips hinted at something *more*. Gone were the daring taunts she had leveled at him over a game of Snapdragon. This was real, this... this could be forever.

The crowd erupted into cheers and applause, but Elizabeth barely noticed. Her cheeks burned, her heart hammering in a way that had nothing to do with the attention around them. Instead of stepping back, she stayed where she was, her eyes searching his.

Darcy inclined his head slightly, his voice low but carrying an unmistakable warmth. "Thank you, Miss Elizabeth."

"For what?" she asked, her voice sounding somewhat even, though her pulse was anything but.

"For giving me the honor," he replied, his tone edged with something almost teasing, though his sincerity was clear.

Before she could reply, Colonel Fitzwilliam's laughter bellowed behind them. "Bravo, Darcy! A true masterclass in Christmas decorum." He clapped his cousin on the shoulder, his grin unabashed. "Perhaps you could leave some of the mistletoe for the rest of us."

Darcy gave a faint smile but didn't look away from Elizabeth. His gaze, steady and intent, made her feel as though the crowd had melted into nothing more than background noise.

Elizabeth's lips twitched. "I believe, Colonel, that the mistletoe is for everyone. No one has claimed exclusive rights."

Darcy's brow lifted. "Perhaps some traditions deserve a second indulgence."

Elizabeth tilted her head, her smile daring. "Perhaps."

And, so he indulged. Goodness, the man tasted like mulled wine and honey, and she could have lost herself there. They stayed like that for a moment longer, the room's hum of voices and music fading into the periphery. Whatever had fractured their understanding before seemed, in that instant, to begin mending.

She was not sure her heart would ever stop racing.

DARCY AND ELIZABETH HAD only just rejoined the flow of the party, their quiet smiles lingering from the tender moment beneath the mistletoe when Georgiana appeared at Elizabeth's side. Her cheeks were flushed with excitement, her eyes bright as she approached them.

"Miss Elizabeth! We have gathered a group in the drawing room for some Christmas fun, and your presence is absolutely required."

Elizabeth glanced up at Darcy, clearly reluctant to let go of his hand, but the warmth in Georgiana's invitation was undeniable. Darcy felt the faintest twinge of disappointment as she turned to his sister, her easy laugh answering Georgiana's plea.

"Required, you say?" Elizabeth teased. "I suppose I must not disappoint."

Darcy tightened his hold on her hand for a moment, his voice low as he said, "You will come back, will you not?"

Elizabeth tilted her head, her smile softening. "Of course," she said. Rising onto her toes, she pressed a kiss to his cheek—light as a snowflake, yet it left him frozen in place.

Georgiana blinked, her gaze darting between them before she quickly collected herself. "Do not let me interrupt," she murmured, though her tone carried the faintest hint of amusement.

Darcy reluctantly released Elizabeth's hand, and Georgiana linked arms with her, guiding her away into the lively throng. Darcy stood rooted for a moment, watching as the two women dearest to him in the whole world disappeared into the drawing room. His fingers flexed at his side, aching to hold Elizabeth's again, but he let her go, for now.

Because for now, Georgiana needed this moment with Elizabeth—needed a sister, a friend, and though Elizabeth probably did not know it yet, she needed Georgiana. There were still things Elizabeth could not see, things he wanted her to understand. And if anyone could bring Elizabeth into the fold of his world, it would be his sister.

But still, her absence left him feeling... incomplete.

"Darcy," Colonel Fitzwilliam's voice interrupted his thoughts, accompanied by a hand clapping his shoulder. "If you stare any harder, you will frighten the poor girl away."

Darcy straightened, his expression carefully neutral. "I have no idea what you mean."

"Of course, you do not," Fitzwilliam replied dryly. "But if you are not going to do something about it, perhaps I should take my chances."

Darcy turned sharply, fixing Fitzwilliam with a glare that could have silenced Parliament. "You will do no such thing."

Fitzwilliam grinned, entirely undeterred. "Ah, so you *do* intend to do something! Glad to hear it. I was beginning to worry you had resigned yourself to kissing her once, then admiring her from a distance for the rest of your days."

Darcy glanced toward the drawing room, where Elizabeth's laughter carried faintly through the open doorway. A warmth spread through his chest at the sound, steadying him even as it unsettled him. "I kissed her twice, in case you were not counting, and I have not resigned myself to anything, Fitzwilliam."

"Good," Fitzwilliam said, leaning slightly closer. "Because if you have been waiting for the perfect moment, Cousin, it is here. If I were you, I would make sure this night ends with her knowing exactly where you stand."

Darcy's jaw tightened, but he gave a curt nod. Fitzwilliam, infuriating as he could be, was not wrong. For weeks, he had grappled with his feelings, balancing his longing against his uncertainty. But Elizabeth was here, in his world, laughing with his sister, standing with him under the mistletoe. And though the memory of her impulsive kiss still tingled on his cheek, it was not enough.

It would never be enough.

"Excuse me," he said briskly, stepping away from Fitzwilliam's amused gaze. He needed time to think, to gather the right words—not to sway Elizabeth, but to give her the truth she deserved.

Darcy stopped just outside the drawing room, drawn by the lively chatter spilling into the hall. Georgiana sat beside Elizabeth at the center of a circle of women, her hands gesturing wildly as laughter rippled around her. The game was in full swing, the circle of women volleying adjectives with growing creativity. "The Minister's cat is mischievous!" Charlotte Lucas declared, prompting a ripple of approving laughter.

"The Minister's cat is melancholy!" another added, her tone so exaggeratedly somber that even Georgiana doubled over with laughter.

The turn passed to one of Sir Thomas's younger residents—a petite girl with auburn hair who wrung her hands nervously. She opened her mouth, then closed it, her cheeks turning scarlet as the silence stretched. The group stilled, waiting with kind but expectant smiles.

Elizabeth leaned toward the girl, her voice low and soothing. "Why not 'magnificent'?" she suggested, her tone as light as a secret shared between friends.

The girl's lips twitched into a tentative smile. "The Minister's cat is... magnificent!" she said, her voice gaining confidence as the word tumbled out.

The circle erupted into applause, clapping and laughing as the girl sat back with a relieved grin. Georgiana gave her an encouraging squeeze on the arm, and Elizabeth beamed at her, her delight as radiant as if she'd been the one to win the moment.

Darcy's fingers flexed against the doorframe. She belonged to no circle, yet she brought life to every one she entered. How did she always know exactly what to say?

There was something magnetic about Elizabeth in moments like this, her natural warmth drawing people toward her. She was central to every moment of magic that had unfurled itself here this night. Not because she belonged to Netherfield, or even to him, but because she had a rare and undeniable gift for making any space feel brighter, more alive.

He could not—would not—let this slip away. Not again. By the end of this night, he would find the right moment to speak to her, to lay bare everything he had been holding back. Elizabeth deserved nothing less.

By the end of this night, he resolved, he would offer everything he was... to her.

THE PARLOR AT NETHERFIELD was a scene of quiet, cheerful chaos. Chairs were being set to rights, trays of empty glasses gathered, and bits of greenery and ribbon swept into piles. Elizabeth bent to pick up a fallen sprig of holly, the scent of pine and lingering candle smoke still heavy in the air. Around her, the hum of voices filled the room—not the usual noise of her neighbors mingling in polite gossip, but the camaraderie of people working together.

Her mother was flitting from corner to wall to window and back again, direct-ing a cluster of younger girls—Kitty, Lydia, Maria Lucas, and several of Sir Thomas's charges—toward the next room to retrieve the last of the discarded linens. Nearby, Mr. Bennet leaned against the mantel, his face a mask of wry bemusement as he observed the unlikely spectacle of gentry and tradespeople working side by side.

Elizabeth glanced across the room. Jane was deep in conversation with Mr. Bingley, their heads close together, the air between them alive with the ease of shared understand-ing. Even Mary had been coaxed into assisting, her determined frown softening as she sorted a stack of empty dishes beside Sir Thomas himself, who looked as if he might burst with gratitude and pride.

"Miss Elizabeth," Darcy's voice came from behind her, sending a shiver of prickles racing over her skin. She turned to find him standing just a step away, his dark eyes warm in the flickering firelight. He had shed his coat and rolled his shirtsleeves back, his waistcoat slightly askew—a rare and disarming sight.

"I thought you were in some serious conversation with your friends from London before their carriages whisked them away," Elizabeth said, arching a brow as she stood with the holly in hand. "Yet here you are in your shirtsleeves as though you are ready to move tables. It hardly suits our Master of Ceremonies to be cleaning up after the party."

"On the contrary," he replied with a faint smile, "it suits me well enough tonight. And what do you mean by calling me the Master of Ceremonies? I think we both know that I did nothing tonight that Bingley did not put me up to."

Elizabeth laughed. "Do you always make a habit of cleaning up after your guests?"

"Only when the guests are worth the effort," he said lightly, though there was a depth to his gaze that made her heart flutter.

They fell into step together, weaving through the room as they gathered stray ribbons and candlesticks. The shared work brought a gentle closeness to their conversation

"It is remarkable," Elizabeth said after a moment. "The way everyone has stayed. I cannot imagine it happening again, and yet... tonight, it feels right."

"It does," Darcy agreed. "Though I suspect the credit lies with you."

Elizabeth blinked at him, surprised. "Me?"

"You brought them together," he said simply. "Your warmth, your generosity... why, it was even your idea. Bingley and I may have done our part, but without you, none of this would have been possible."

Elizabeth opened her mouth to reply, but the words faltered. She glanced away, unsure how to respond to the intensity of his compliment. The gentle brush of his fingers against hers as they both reached for the same ribbon made her heart stand still.

"Will you walk with me?" he asked.

She nodded.

He guided her from the parlor, and they passed the threshold into a quieter corridor. Behind them, laughter rose and fell, faint now, like music heard from another room. The air felt thinner here, sharp with the cold that seeped through the old walls. Her pulse thrummed louder with each step. She told herself it was the exertion of the evening, her head light and bones heavy with fatigue and too much punch. Yet her thoughts spun around him, his nearness, the gravity he carried so effortlessly.

They stopped near the staircase, where the shadows from the banister danced on the walls in the firelight from the hall. He let go of her hand, only to turn toward her fully. He stood straight, no hesitation in his frame. She could not look away.

"Elizabeth," he said. Her name, so simple, yet transformed in his voice. "I must speak plainly."

She nodded again. Her throat was dry.

"I have spent years," he said, "believing my life was already determined. My duty was clear, my course set, and anything beyond it was folly." He paused, and there was that little smile—the one that made the faintest dimple appear in his cheek, that dimple that most people probably never knew he had. "But I see I was wrong. You have shown me what life could be," he said. "With you, I can see more than duty. More than ambition. With you, there is meaning."

He lowered himself to one knee. She stared at him, and for a moment, the world held still. His words hung in the air between them, not like questions but truths waiting for her answer. Her chest squeezed, as though all the air had been knocked out of her. She tried to draw a breath, but instead hiccupped—a small, undignified sound that startled them both.

She pressed her fingers to her lips, horrified, but Darcy's smile widened, with a brilliance that made her heart lurch.

"I have known you but a few weeks, but there is nothing sudden or uncertain about my feelings. Almost from the first moments of our acquaintance, my affections have been fixed. Elizabeth Bennet, will you do me the honor of becoming my wife?"

Well... for such a question there was only one way she could answer.

She ought to have smiled demurely, offered some polite excuse for her feminine charms or blushed prettily at his compliments. But that was not her way. No, no, if he wanted her, he would have all of her, from this moment forth.

Elizabeth laughed and leaped into his waiting arms. "Y-yes, you... you impossibly wonderful man!"

Darcy yelped in surprise and caught her with a sharp intake of breath, his hold tightening instinctively as he steadied them both. Her arms looped around his neck, and he lifted her from the ground. Elizabeth laughed again, giddy and unrestrained, as Darcy spun her in a wide circle. His laughter joint hers, and the world blurred around them, the corridor and the snow-dusted windows fading into nothing. It was only when he slowed, lowering her gently back to her feet, that she realized how wildly her heart was pounding.

He kissed her then, a bold, claiming kiss that felt like a vow. Her fingers curled into the back of his shirt as if to anchor herself, but she had never felt so free. When they finally parted, her breath came in quick gasps, and her cheeks burned—not from embarrassment but from the kind of joy that left no room for restraint.

As she tilted her head back to look at him, her eyes caught on a movement over his shoulder. Beyond the staircase, just visible through the archway, stood Jane and Mr. Bingley. They were holding hands, watching with undisguised amusement. Jane's smile was soft but knowing, her eyes sparkling with sisterly triumph. Bingley, meanwhile, was grinning broadly, his expression as bright and open as ever.

"Well, Darcy," Bingley called out, "I must say, you have surpassed even my highest expectations. I had no idea you remembered how to smile!"

"More than that," Jane added, glancing at Elizabeth. "I have never seen my sister so thoroughly silenced. It seems you have achieved the impossible, Mr. Darcy."

Darcy turned his head slightly, casting them a glance that was both indulgent and faintly exasperated. "Thank you for your insights," he said dryly. "However, I am afraid I must ask you to excuse us. I have important business to attend to."

Before either could respond, he turned back to Elizabeth and claimed her lips again. This time, the kiss was slower, deeper, and so thoroughly consuming that Elizabeth felt herself tip forward into him, her laughter muffled by the warmth of his embrace.

When at last they broke apart, Elizabeth caught her breath and pressed her forehead against his chest, shaking her head as she smiled. "You are impossible," she whispered.

"And you," he murmured against her hair, his voice low and full of warmth, "are everything."

Epilogue

Christmas 1812
Pemberley

Pemberley was alive.

Darcy stood at the edge of the drawing room, his hand resting lightly on the doorframe as he watched the room hum with life. Laughter rose and fell, echoing against the high ceilings that had too often amplified silence. But Darcy's eyes were not fixed on the people—welcome as they were to him—but rather on the grand fir tree that had once stood in the wood behind the house. It now graced the center of the ballroom, trimmed with ribbons and fruits and carefully guarded candles, its boughs stretching nearly to the chandelier.

They would be lucky if the bloody thing did not burn the house down. Elizabeth had insisted on the tree, smiling mischievously as she told him all about this outrageous German custom she had read about. Did they really bring a tree into the house every winter? Probably not, but she said they did, and that she thought it was a fine new tradition to begin for their first Christmas at Pemberley.

He had indulged her, of course. He always would.

Across the room, Elizabeth was speaking with Mrs. Gardiner, her hands dancing as she described some small, clever detail of the evening. She had always spoken with her hands, though it had taken him months to notice. Probably because he had been lost in her eyes, in her smile. Now, he saw it in every gesture. He had memorized every detail of her, and it had been some while since he had confessed to himself that the greatest pleasure and conquest of his life was the year he had spent glorying in the company and companionship of his wife.

And Pemberley... good heavens, but it was good to be *home* again. It had seemed so empty to him before, but bringing Elizabeth into its halls as its mistress had *made* it his home once more. She belonged here, even more than he did—belonged in every corner of this house, her presence weaving itself into the fabric of Pemberley as if she had always been a part of it.

His throat tightened. For years, he had avoided this place, letting his promise to Bingley and the weight of old arguments push him toward London, toward "greatness," toward something he had believed might ease the ache of his father's disapproval or repay the "debt" he felt he still owed.

Instead, he had found purpose. And now, with Elizabeth at his side, he had found balance.

"Penny for your thoughts, Darcy."

Darcy turned as Mr. Bennet passed him, a book in his hand, as he moved toward the hearth to settle into a chair. "You look positively burdened by sentiment. Do not let it overpower you; I am told it is not becoming."

Darcy followed his father-in-law, easing into another chair as he allowed himself a small smile. "Sentiment does not often get the better of me, sir."

"Ah, but marriage does strange things to a man, does it not? Though I daresay Elizabeth has done you good." Bennet leaned back, settling deeper into the leather as he opened his book. "She has done good for Pemberley too. Perhaps you have even begun to see what all the fuss was about when you brought her here."

Darcy inclined his head, unwilling to argue. "Pemberley is better for her presence. I would not deny it."

"Wise of you." Bennet's eyes gleamed with satisfaction. "My favorite son-in-law—er, that would be Bingley, you understand—"

Darcy coughed, and Bennet only grinned unrepentantly.

"Anyway," he continued, "I daresay Bingley is well pleased to see you looking so settled. Says he never had a holiday in eight years until you found 'something else' to distract you. And in the last year, he has had three—one to Scotland for his honeymoon, one to Bath for yet another honeymoon, and... good heavens, where was that last one?"

"Portugal," Darcy said with a chuckle. "He claimed he was inspecting a new wine merchant for a prospective contract, but I think they spent the entire holiday sea bathing. Perhaps he did *sample* a bit more of that wine than was necessary, but I have seen no new contract."

Bennet chuckled. "Well, well, that is all very fine. As for me, well—I will rest easy knowing that my Lizzy has found a man who can *almost* meet her expectations."

Darcy's lips twitched. "High praise."

"Make of it what you will." Bennet tipped his head in a mock salute before turning his attention back to his book.

Darcy's gaze shifted to where Bingley and Mr. Gardiner stood in quiet conversation near the windows. He would get no more out of Bennet just now, so he rose and joined them, noting the open ledger resting on the table between them. Bingley looked up, his face brightening with a grin.

"Darcy, come—Gardiner has just suggested an addition to the plan for the new estate. We are still calling it Ashford House, are we not? Anyway, take a look at this. I think it is a brilliant idea."

Mr. Gardiner chuckled softly. "Your friend is too kind. I merely observed that the grounds might support both a workshop and a small school. It would allow the children to continue their learning alongside practical work."

Darcy considered this. The Yorkshire estate Bingley spoke of was newly purchased and still unoccupied. He and Bingley had envisioned it as a place of refuge and education, modeled after Sir Thomas Ashford's efforts at Netherfield. It was meant to honor the man who had given them so much, even if Sir Thomas himself could not be persuaded to leave his own Christmas traditions to come advise them on this new venture.

"Practical and aspirational," Darcy said after a moment. "It fits the vision well."

Gardiner smiled, clearly pleased. "And I must commend you both. It is no small thing to dedicate such a property to this work. Sir Thomas would be proud."

Bingley laughed. "Sir Thomas would insist on touring the grounds himself before offering an opinion, but I like to think he would approve."

Darcy allowed himself a rare smile. "He would. And he would not hesitate to suggest improvements."

"Then, if you like this notion, I will go and write some letters at once. I assume you will want to begin work as soon as the ground thaws?"

"The sooner, the better," Darcy said.

"I thought you would say that." Gardiner excused himself, leaving Darcy and Bingley alone by the window. For a moment, they stood in comfortable silence, gazing out at the snow-covered grounds of Pemberley.

"You have done well, Darcy," Bingley said finally, his voice thoughtful. "Pemberley suits you."

Darcy glanced at his friend. "It has always been home."

"Perhaps," Bingley said, turning to face him fully. "But now it feels like you are truly *here*."

"You mean, rather than managing our affairs as I should be?"

Bingley shrugged. "We have enough money. But life, Darcy—you cannot buy the sort of contentment I see on your face these days."

Darcy huffed in silent agreement. For years, Pemberley had been a place of memory and obligation. Now, with Elizabeth, it was something more.

"I believe, Mr. Darcy, that you are shirking your duties as host."

Darcy turned to see Elizabeth standing just a few steps away, her expression bright with teasing.

"I was engaged in business of great importance. But I find myself inclined to address more pressing matters."

Elizabeth raised a brow. "And what pressing matters are those?"

He stepped closer, reaching for her hand. "You, of course." Bingley cleared his throat behind them, but Darcy did not look back.

"Excuse us, Bingley," he said. "I have *very* important business to attend to."

Elizabeth's eyes sparkled as he led her from the room. When they reached the quiet of the hall, he turned to her, his hand still wrapped around hers.

"Elizabeth," he began softly, "thank you for bringing life back to this house. And to me."

She smiled up at him. "It is Christmas, Mr. Darcy. It is what the season does best."

K EEP READING FOR MORE of Darcy and Elizabeth's Christmas adventures in *How to Get Caught Under the Mistletoe* and *The Scotsman's Ghost*!

From Alix

T HANK YOU FOR INDULGING with me and spending a little time with Darcy and Elizabeth.

I hope you've had a delightful escape to Pemberley. I'd love it if you would share this family with your friends so they can experience a love to last for the ages. As with all my books, I have enabled lending to make it easier to share. If you leave a review for *Mr. Darcy's Christmas Kiss* on Amazon, Goodreads, Book Bub or your own blog, I would love to read it! Email me the link at **Author@AlixJames.com.**

Would you like to read more of Darcy and Elizabeth's romance? I have a fun Darcy and Elizabeth Memoir for you to try next! Dive into *How to Get Caught Under the Mistletoe* and laugh along with our favorite couple's letters as they find the love they were destined for!

And if you're hungry for more, including a free ebook of satisfying short tales, stay up to date on upcoming releases and sales by joining my newsletter: https://dashboard.mailerlite.com/forms/249660/73866370936211000/share

<u>Free for new newsletter subscribers!</u>

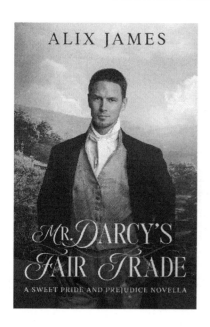

Also By Alix James

The First Impressions Collection:

All Bets Are Off

The Measure of a Man Collection:

The Measure of Love
The Measure of Trust
The Measure of Honor

The Measure of a Man Box Set (Coming December 2024)

The Mr. Darcy Collection:

Mr. Darcy Steals a Kiss
Mr. Darcy and the Governess
Mr. Darcy and the Girl Next Door

Mr. Darcy: Swoonworthy Collection

The Heart to Heart Collection

These Dreams

Nefarious

Tempted

Darcy and Elizabeth: Heart to Heart Box Set

The Sweet Escapes Collection

The Rogue's Widow

The Courtship of Edward Gardiner

London Holiday

Rumours and Recklessness

Darcy and Elizabeth: Sweet Escapes Box Set

The Sweet Sentiments Collection:

When the Sun Sleeps

Queen of Winter

A Fine Mind

Elizabeth Bennet: Sweet Sentiments Box Set

The Frolic and Romance Collection:

A Proper Introduction
A Good Memory is Unpardonable
Along for the Ride

Elizabeth Bennet: Frolic & Romance Box Set

The Short and Sassy Collection:

Unintended
Spirited Away
Indisposed
Love and Other Machines

Elizabeth Bennet: Short and Sassy Compilation

Christmas With Darcy and Elizabeth

How to Get Caught Under the Mistletoe: A Lady's Guide
The Scotsman's Ghost: Or How to Wreck a Yule Party
Mr, Darcy's Christmas Kiss

North and South Variations

Nowhere but North
Northern Rain
No Such Thing as Luck

John and Margaret: Coming Home Collection

Anthologies

Rational Creatures
Falling for Mr Thornton

Spanish Translations

Rumores e Imprudencias
Vacaciones en Londres
Nefasto
Un Compromiso Accidental
Reina del Invierno
Una Mente Noble
Cuando el Sol se Duerm
A lo largo del Camino
Reina del Invierno
Una Mente Noble
El señor Darcy se roba un beso
Cómo quedar atrapado debajo del muérdago

Italian Translations

Una Vacanza a Londra

About Alix James

Short and satisfying romance for busy readers.

Alix James is an alternate pen name for best-selling Regency author Nicole Clarkston.

Always on the go as a wife, mom, and small business owner, she rarely has time to read a whole novel. She loves coffee with the sunrise and being outdoors. When she does get free time, she likes to read, camp, dream up romantic adventures, and tries to avoid housework.

Each Alix James story is a clean Regency Variation of Darcy and Elizabeth's romance. Visit her website and sign up for her newsletter at AlixJames.com

How to Get Caught Under the Mistletoe

Twenty-Six November

In my defense, Charlotte kicked me.

Oh, very well, perhaps it was not a kick. Charlotte is too civilized for that, but it was a very firm nudge. The sort of nudge that will probably leave a bruise.

I recovered myself somewhat and blurted out the first words to tumble into my mouth. "I thank you, yes." And then I died a little.

Mr. Darcy bowed. "I look forward to it, Miss Elizabeth."

As the gentleman walked away, I groaned and rolled my eyes to the ceiling. "Why did you do that?" I whispered to Charlotte.

Charlotte smothered a smug little grin. "I daresay you will find him very agreeable, Lizzy."

"More would be the pity! Tragic indeed to be forced to admit that I enjoyed dancing with a man I swore to despise."

"Despise! Do not let your fondness for Mr. Wickham let you make yourself disagreeable to a man of ten times his consequence. Every lady in the room is pining for a set with Mr. Darcy."

"Well, how unfortunate for him that he chose to ask the one woman who is not." I sighed and drew back my shoulders. "I require a little more punch before I stand up with him. Charlotte, are you well? You are looking somewhat out of breath."

She fanned her face, and indeed, she did seem paler than usual. "Oh, 'tis nothing, Lizzy. I should like to sit for a few moments, though. You know, I do not dance as often as I used to, and I suppose the exertion..."

Movement just beyond Charlotte caught my eye, and I gave her a tug at the elbow. "Yes, yes, keep on with that. You are frightfully out of breath, and your feet hurt and you require some time in the ladies' retiring room. Repeat after me."

She gave me a quizzical look as I rushed her toward the door. "But Lizzy, I said nothing about my feet hurting. It is only that I feel rather faint just now, and—"

"Faint, yes, that is very good. Say something about feeling feverish, too. Oh!" We stopped short as my cousin, Mr. Collins, deposited himself in our path. "Excuse us, cousin. I was just escorting Miss Lucas out for a respite."

He bowed deeply, sweeping his hand from his chest to the air in a ridiculous flourish. "Forgive me, fair cousin. I had hoped to beg a set of Miss Lucas, and, dare I hope, another from you before the evening is complete?"

Charlotte opened her mouth, but I gave her a little push in the shoulder, propelling her forward. "I fear now is not an opportune time, Mr. Collins. My friend is feeling unwell, and I have only a few moments before I must return for my set with Mr. Darcy. Some other time, I hope."

His disappointment was keen, and he was still lamenting about it as I dragged Charlotte from the room. "Lizzy, I would have said yes," she chided me.

"Charlotte, even *your* kindness can extend only so far. My toes are still tender from my set with him, and truly, you do not look like you can sustain half an hour of his conversation." I dragged her away. "There are far more agreeable men."

"But Lizzy, what if none of them mean to ask me? I do not entertain as many offers as you or Jane."

I stopped. "Jane and I only danced with him because we had no choice."

She put a hand on her hip. "You are purposely missing my point."

"Indeed, I am, and I still say you ought to count yourself fortunate that you were spared the trouble. The very idea! It is not as if you would consider anything else with the man."

"Well..."

"Come. Here is a nice seat, and let me fetch you a glass." I swiped one from the tray of a passing footman and placed it in her hand. "There. I shall return straightaway to tell you how odious a half hour I passed."

"Be careful not to accidentally enjoy yourself, Lizzy."

E VERYONE WAS STARING AT me. I swallowed and lifted my chin against the aghast expressions all around—all my neighbors who either knew of my dislike of the gentleman or thought me so far beneath him that they must have assumed it all a good joke. I drew back my shoulders and hoped Mr. Darcy didn't have sweaty palms or clammy fingers.

In point of fact, his hands were quite nice. Just what I might expect from the rogue. And he seemed to know his way about the dance floor, for which my toes blessed him. But he was excruciatingly silent all the while, and the way he stared at me did nothing to settle the flutter of nerves that suddenly tickled my stomach. Why would the man just gape blankly into my eyes, with no thought for conversation or admiration or even a jolly good row? Terribly disconcerting.

Very well, if he would not say something, I would do it. I waited until he stepped forward to lead me down the set. "Mr. Walton's fingers have recovered admirably."

Mr. Darcy's face jerked down to me as we stepped apart. "What?"

"Mr. Walton. He is the violinist, do you see? There. Bitten by a horse last week, I'm afraid. One would never know by his enthusiasm for the piece this evening."

"Er..." Mr. Darcy adjusted his cufflinks. "Indeed. He plays very well."

"There. Now we may be silent until we must step together again." I turned my head to watch a servant replacing a set of nearly guttered candles at the edge of the room, but when I looked back, Mr. Darcy was still staring at me. Oh, bother.

"Do you find the tempo a little fast this evening, Mr. Darcy?"

He looked at me strangely. "I find it precisely as it should be. Do you not?"

"Oh, no, I think it accurate in every way. For, you see, it took us exactly one measure to traverse the line, just as it ought. I only wondered because you look displeased by something."

"Nothing at all, Miss Elizabeth."

"That is very fine. Now, it is your turn to think of something to speak of, Mr. Darcy. Might I suggest observing something about how much pleasanter it is to attend a private ball than a public one? Or perhaps you could comment on the flavor of the soup."

He stepped forward and took my hand to lead me around the next couple. "The soup?"

"Just as you please. The pheasant was done to a turn. Do you not agree?"

"Indeed."

"Oh, come, Mr. Darcy! You must give me something better than one-word answers."

A ghost of a smile touched his lips. "I would be happy to discuss anything you prefer. Pray, tell me what you would most like to speak of."

I considered his question as he marched me around, then returned me to my place. "It must be difficult to settle on a topic, is it not? For I have noted that you, like myself, are usually unwilling to speak at all unless you can say something profound indeed."

"I would argue that *you* possess no such difficulty," was his dry retort. "And I cannot control how my own words are perceived."

"There, an answer that I must think on for a moment. That will do for the present."

He stepped back, but his face did not look so grave as it had. In fact, he almost appeared to be amused, and searching for something to say. "Do you often walk toward Meryton?" he ventured.

That was a piteous attempt. But at least it was a question that evoked a response, so I smiled. "Yes, often. In fact, we had just been meeting a new friend yesterday when you happened upon us."

My heavens! I did not know Mr. Darcy possessed so many feelings, but a great cascade of them blasted over his face all at once. His jaw rippled, his throat bobbed, and his eyes glittered to a fearsome black. "I do not wonder that Mr. Wickham was able to *make* a friend of you. Whether he deserves to *keep* your friendship is another matter."

"A friend is a valuable thing to have, would you not agree?"

His nostrils flared slightly. "I would."

"Then you must also agree that the loss of a friendship is a tragic thing, indeed. The material harm in such a loss cannot be measured."

He moved toward me and caught my hand for another march, and his voice dropped to a low growl. "Unless the 'friend' is shown to be deficient in character, in which case, the loss ought to be his burden to bear, not mine to regret."

I stopped mid-step. "You are very hard, Mr. Darcy. With such high standards, it must be difficult, indeed, for anyone to win *your* friendship."

He tightened his grip on my hand and pulled me out of the way of the next dancers. "Not so difficult as you might imagine. I believe the fault you would assign to me is not lack of civility, but an unwillingness to revise my opinions once they are fixed."

I pivoted into my place. "One must wonder what measure you use. I trust you are exceedingly careful in the forming of these opinions?"

"Exceedingly."

And with that one word, our conversation was done. I fell to silent fuming, and he to dark brooding. The very cheek of the man! To stand here with me and all but tell me to my face that I was being deceived in Mr. Wickham's character, when *he* was the disagreeable one and everyone knew it! For surely, it was for *his* pleasure that Mr. Wickham had been excluded from this evening's enjoyment. And not because the rest of the neighborhood liked Mr. Darcy, but because he was Mr. Bingley's friend, while the other was not.

I was too practical to think myself in love with Mr. Wickham after only two meetings, but I will own that his happy manners and the hope of a dance with such an amiable man had been my balm since Mr. Collins demanded the first set. And now, because of Mr. Darcy, I was to be denied the pleasure of a cheerful man's company.

But there was always tomorrow. Surely, we would see him walking up the lane with Denny, and he would humbly describe some perfectly acceptable excuse for his absence. And then, he would ask to walk our party to Meryton, or call on us again in the following days.

It was only a pity that for nearly every amusement to be had in the neighborhood for the foreseeable future, Mr. Darcy's glowering face would be my company instead. For surely, *he* would be invited everywhere, and Mr. Wickham nowhere. Such a disappointment! For a lady likes to think that as the season approaches for stealing kisses under the mistletoe, she might look forward to an agreeable partner.

Mr. Darcy was not so ungentlemanly as to neglect to escort me from the floor, but it was not with a happy countenance that he did so. I matched his curt bow with an equally impudent curtsey, and finally let go a breath as he turned away. There! That unpleasantness was done for the evening. I spun round to find Charlotte before Mr. Collins could make his way across the room to ask for my hand once more.

"Did you enjoy yourself, Lizzy?" she asked from her chair.

"If I did, you ought to see it in my face. There, what do you think?" I turned my cheek from one side to the other, framing my chin with my hands and fluttering my lashes. "Do I look like a girl who just relished her dance with the most valuable bachelor in the room?"

"Not a bit of it. I hope you did not tease him, Lizzy."

I sank into the chair beside her with a sigh. "No, we argued instead."

"Oh, Lizzy!" Charlotte shook her head and rested a hand on her stomach. "You would do better to keep quiet altogether than to provoke such a man as Mr. Darcy."

"Come, Charlotte, you know I might as well try to stop the sun in its tracks as my mouth. But do not worry—I said nothing he did not deserve, and richly."

She sighed and brushed her forehead with the back of her hand. "Just be careful not to make an enemy of Mr. Darcy. I should think his regard to be something worth having."

I snorted rudely into my glass.

Twenty-Seven November

I have always admired the notion of love. Romance to sigh over, devotion to curl a girl's toes, and passion enough to shatter a heart in two. The sort that is not even spoken about in polite company because it might cause a lady to sweat inconveniently. Perhaps I had read too many novels, but a gallant sir knight to sweep away the princess and promise to spend the rest of his days making all her dreams come true—that was *my* idea of a romantic proposal.

This, however... no.

"My fairest cousin, allow me to protest the sincerity of my feelings, the ardency of my devotion, the depth of my affection—"

I pressed my fingers into my temples. "Mr. Collins, you are simply repeating yourself. I have declined your offer as many times as you have tendered it, and I mean to continue doing so, as long as you keep drawing breath. There is no possible scenario where we would suit one another. In fact, I am quite certain that your esteemed Lady Catherine would be appalled by me."

He clasped his hand over his chest. "Oh, not so, cousin! Why, she is eminently gracious and welcoming. Her condescension is everything magnanimous and splendid, and the advantages of her friendship are too numerous to be counted. I flatter myself, any young lady would—"

"Any young lady but this one. I am sorry, Mr. Collins, but my answer remains unchanged."

I pushed up from the sofa, nearly knocking him backward as I did so—for keeping a polite distance was not something he seemed to understand—and marched out of the room.

It was no mystery what would happen next. He would apply to Mama to try to make me see reason. Mama would weep and mourn about what a foolish, headstrong girl I was, and she would batter the door of Papa's study until he grew tired of the hullabaloo and heard her out.

I would be forced to stand by while Mama sobbed she would never speak to me again unless Papa made me marry Mr. Collins, while Mr. Collins continued with his delusions about his passionate romance and how insensitive I was to the delicacy of my own position. Papa would roll his eyes and declare he would have nothing to do with the matter. And...

That was why I was already on my way out the door toward Lucas Lodge, still buttoning my pelisse and tying my bonnet as I scampered away from the house.

"WHY, Lizzy! WHAT BRINGS you so early?"

Maria Lucas was the only one in the drawing room, and I looked round as I let her take my hat and gloves. "Oh, nothing, I... I wanted to ask how Charlotte was this morning. She seemed rather worn last night."

Maria frowned. "Why, I suppose she is well enough. But now that you mention it, she has been rather late to rise. Shall I call for her?"

"No, no, that will not be necessary. I will call again later." I turned back for my gloves once more, but the memory of what no doubt awaited me at home gave me pause. "You don't suppose I could look in on her myself, do you?"

"Oh, I don't... why, she probably would not mind. Shall I...?" She gestured up the stairs, offering to lead me.

"Thank you. No, that is not necessary. I will show myself up."

Charlotte was slow to answer my knock. Perhaps she had a little too much punch last night. I waited for a moment, then tried again. "Charlotte? It's Lizzy."

Her voice sounded rather thin when she called, "Come in, Lizzy." *Odd.*

I pushed the door open and nearly gasped. Charlotte, usually so robust and cheerful, reclined on her bed, her nightgown rumpled and her face unnaturally pale. The sunlight filtering through the windows cast a warm glow on her, but it couldn't mask the weary shadows beneath her eyes.

"Charlotte?" I moved to her bedside and brushed her forehead. "Are you ill? Was it something you ate last night?"

She managed a feeble smile, her hand gesturing for me to sit beside her. "I am just... not feeling well, Lizzy."

I sat on the edge of the bed and took her hand into mine, feeling the coolness of her skin. "You are more than 'not well,' Charlotte. You look... positively ill."

Charlotte sighed, her eyes drifting towards the window. "I've not been strong for some time now. I've tried to hide it, but I fear after last night, it's caught up with me."

"Some time now?" I repeated. "Why did you not say anything?"

She shrugged weakly. "What would it have done but worry my family? Besides, I did see Mr. Jones."

"And?"

Her eyes met mine, and there was a depth of sadness there that I'd never seen before. "He was concerned. Very concerned."

"Charlotte, no..." My voice was barely above a whisper.

"Headaches, stomachaches, dizziness," she listed off, her voice oddly detached. "I often feel as though I can't catch my breath. And there are some other things I'd... rather not mention."

"But you'll get better," I insisted. "Surely, you only want rest. You must take care to eat properly and not overtax yourself."

She shook her head and looked away. "It's more than that. Mr. Jones thinks I have a wasting disease, Lizzy. There's nothing he can do."

The world seemed to tilt beneath me, and blood pounded in my ears. "No," I whispered. "That can't be right."

Charlotte rested a hand on my arm. "I'm not afraid, Lizzy. Well, perhaps a little. It's not as if I had grand prospects awaiting me."

I couldn't hold back the tears. "Charlotte!"

"I know it's hard, Lizzy. I didn't want to say anything. Please don't tell Mama!"

"But she ought to know! And Jane and Maria... they should all know."

"Oh, yes, do tell Jane. She could keep it to herself, but please, don't tell my family. They don't need that sort of burden." She sighed, her eyes wistful. "Truly, Lizzy, it will be all right. I did wish for a bit of romance, though. Just a taste."

My throat tightened. "Charlotte, you deserve so much more than just a 'taste'."

She chuckled. "I always said I did not care about such a thing, but after watching Jane with Mr. Bingley, I think it would be very fine indeed just to sample a little. That would be enough for me."

I shook my head. "No, it isn't. It's not right, Charlotte."

She thinned her lips and sighed. "Well, I suppose it's not up to us to decide that, is it? Now, why did you rush over here so early the morning after a ball? Don't tell me Mr. Darcy presented himself on your doorstep this morning with an offer of marriage."

I sniffed and blubbered a laugh, then wiped my nose. "Mr. Collins, actually."

"And what did you say?"

I scoffed. "Well... I refused him! What else could I do?"

Charlotte shrugged. "I suppose that is a matter of opinion."

"And I made mine known." I laced my hand in hers. "What can I do for *you*, Charlotte? Shall I bring a book up and read to you?"

She smiled and shook her head on the pillow. "I will be well enough later, Lizzy. These bad spells come and go. I just need a little rest, and I will be downstairs by the time Mama begins to look for me. Go on—I am sure your mother is searching for you, too."

I huffed and shook my head. "That is precisely why I came here. Are you sure you will be well?"

Charlotte tightened her grip on my hand. "Well enough."

T HE MOMENT I ENTERED Longbourn, Mama's familiar wails echoed from the drawing room, louder and more harrowing than any I'd heard before. She was inside Papa's study with the door open, but I managed to slip past without either of them seeing me. What had become of Mr. Collins? I knew not, nor did I mean to stop and ask. It all felt distant, secondary to the fears turning in my stomach after my visit with Charlotte.

"Lizzy!" Lydia's voice called out as I passed the drawing room, but I had no patience for her now. I clutched my skirts and ran up the stairs to Jane's door, and pushed it open without pause. "Jane, I've just come from Charlotte. You'll never believe what I…"

I stopped. Jane sat on her bed, a letter in hand, her face a study of distress. And when she looked up at me, she was blinking away tears.

"Jane?" Could this day take more frustrations or grief? I glanced at the letter, then examined her face. "What is it?"

"Lizzy," she choked. "It's from Miss Bingley. They…" She stopped, closed her eyes, and blew out a slow, shaky breath. "Oh, I am sure it is nothing, truly, but she says that by the time I receive this letter, they will already be on their way to London. Mr. Bingley departed at first light, but the rest of them have decided to follow."

"What?" I took it from her and scanned Miss Bingley's fine script. "For how long?"

Jane sniffed. "She does not say. Only that she is most eager to see Mr. Darcy's sister in London, and that she was pleased to make my acquaintance while they remained in the neighborhood. That does not sound like a farewell to you, does it?"

My lip curled as I read. "It sounds to me like Miss Bingley did not like her brother's fondness for you, and she meant to whisk him away."

"Oh, Lizzy, you do not know that. I am sure he only left on business, but it does seem odd that the rest of the party went after him. London must be so much more diverting at this time of year, but he will come back."

I handed the letter to her. "Yes, with a bride, no doubt. I understand Miss Darcy is a perfect peacock."

Jane's eyes widened. "How did you hear that?"

"Mr. Wickham."

She shook her head and folded her letter, then opened it again to re-read Miss Bingley's words. "No, I am sure you are wrong. The way I read this, she says only that she and Mr. Darcy are eager to see Miss Darcy again. She says nothing about..." She sagged, and her breath left her. "Oh, dear. Lizzy, can it be true?"

"You can count on it. And I think she is doing her brother a tremendous disservice, taking him from a lady he loves and forcing another upon him."

"Oh, Lizzy. Mr. Bingley was never... well, he was friendly. Kind." She looked up to the ceiling, her shoulders slumping and the letter falling to her lap. "I did fancy one or two times there that he might kiss me—you know, when he would escort me for a walk or when Mama would leave us alone in the drawing room. Is that not silly? He never did, of course. He is too much the gentleman for that."

"He is still a man, and a man in violent love, if I ever saw it. Would you truly let Miss Bingley take that away from you?"

"But what am I to do about it?" She tossed her hands, then swiped at a tear. "He is gone, and I cannot know when he will come back."

I frowned and sank onto the bed beside her. "It is not fair, you know. I mean, not fair to him. To have to leave behind a lady he clearly loves, and be forced to make himself amiable to a snobbish bore of a girl just to please his sister and Mr. Darcy."

Jane bit her lip and looked at me, her brow crumpled with hurt. "What do you mean?"

I just lifted my shoulders. "Only that Mr. Bingley seemed quite happy as he was. What a shame to have his hopes stolen, because they did not please someone else."

She dashed another tear from her face. "Oh, Lizzy, to hear you talk, one would think you want me to chase after him. Go to London and seek him out!"

"I suppose that it is very much what I am saying."

Jane shook her head. "No. It seems likely that I was simply misled. If he cares for me, he will come back. I am sure of it."

I thinned my lips and sighed. "Let us hope. Does Mama know about this yet?"

"Oh." Jane clapped a hand over her face. "Did you not hear all the crying downstairs?"

"Yes, but I thought I occasioned that by refusing Mr. Collins. Poor Mama! She truly is having a day of it."

"Indeed."

G ET CAUGHT UP IN this delicious Christmas Romp! Unwrap your copy of *How to Get Caught Under the Mistletoe* today!

The Scotsman's Ghost

Chapter One

Darcy

I loathed country assemblies.

The room was stifling—far too small for the number of people packed in there. And yet, I could not find it in myself to make an excuse and leave, though I had conjured no fewer than six in the last ten minutes. My patience had already been tested beyond its limits. The heat, the noise, the suffocating stench of roast meats and cheap perfume—it was a kind of assault on the senses that made one question why one agreed to leave London at all.

I stole a glance toward Bingley. He was entirely absorbed in some light conversation with a local family, his smile bright, his eyes alight with the easy charm that always seemed to work for him, no matter the company. Charles Bingley could find something to admire in the plainest of towns or the most vapid company, and somehow, he could not seem to find a single word of criticism for any of it.

This was Meryton. A provincial town with provincial people, where the height of entertainment was watching people humiliate themselves at one of these so-called "gatherings." It was an absurd spectacle—overly bright dresses, all lace and ruffles in colors so garish it was as if the entire countryside had turned out to celebrate a jest only they found amusing.

I shifted my weight uncomfortably, the polished leather of my boots catching on the worn floorboards, and resisted the urge to roll my eyes. This was beneath me. And yet, here I was.

It wouldn't do to abandon Bingley, of course. He was far too kind for his own good, and I doubted the poor fool would know what to do with himself without a steady hand guiding him through these situations. He saw good in everything—and everyone, apparently. It was charming in its own way, but also reckless. He refused to acknowledge how deeply out of his element he truly was here.

Across the room, Caroline Bingley stood with the practiced air of someone who believed she was above it all. Which, frankly, she was—though she took every opportunity to remind others of it. She cast her icy gaze across the room, scanning it like a hawk searching for prey, while tossing yet another veiled insult toward her brother.

"These assemblies are so very... quaint, Charles. One must admire the simplicity of country life, of course. Simple amusements for simple people, wouldn't you agree?"

I almost pitied Bingley for the way his smile faltered, but he caught himself before the comment could do any real damage. That was the way of it with Caroline. Her insults came wrapped in fine lace, soft enough to seem like compliments unless one truly listened. Bingley, as ever, did not listen.

I caught his eye, and he shot me a pleading glance—a silent request to engage with the locals or, at the very least, offer him some kind of escape from his sister's barbs.

Not tonight.

I had had my fill of shallow conversations with people who only wished to know me for my fortune or name. I hadn't come to Meryton to mingle with the locals—I had come because Bingley was too easily charmed by novelty and needed someone with sense to keep him grounded. Now, I wondered if it was too late.

Still, I could not leave. Not without appearing rude, though I do not know why it bothered me that I might make enemies in this town. It was not as if I would be staying long.

It was then that I noticed Bingley moving toward me, his eyes bright with excitement as he seemed to sweep through the crowd with ease. I should have known he was plotting something. Bingley was like that—he would make twenty new acquaintances in a matter of minutes and somehow remember them all the next day. I could already sense where this was going, and it filled me with dread.

"Darcy!" he called, a bit too loud for my taste, though no one else seemed to notice. "You've been standing here long enough. I've someone I want you to meet."

I glanced around, hoping he might mean anyone other than that brunette I had spotted earlier this evening. She had been laughing with her sister—the blonde Bingley had danced with... twice. Surely not *her*, of all people. The last thing I wanted was to be used as a sort of fourth for some misguided double-matchmaking endeavors this evening.

But no. Bingley was already steering me through the crowd, and there was no mistaking the direction we were headed.

My stomach clenched as we approached. The lady stood near the refreshments table, her eyes sparkling with laughter as she spoke to her companions. Indeed, there was an ease about her that I could not ignore, no matter how hard I tried. She seemed utterly at home in this room full of people I could barely stand to be near.

Bingley was grinning like a schoolboy as he approached her, oblivious to the tightening of my jaw.

"Miss Elizabeth Bennet," Bingley said cheerfully, "may I present my friend, Mr. Fitzwilliam Darcy?"

Miss Elizabeth turned toward us, her gaze flicking to mine with an unreadable expression. If she was surprised or displeased by the introduction, she hid it well, offering a small curtsey and a polite smile.

"Mr. Darcy," she said pleasantly, though I could detect the slightest hint of irony in her tone. "We are already acquainted."

Her gaze settled on me, and I felt a sharpness there that was unmistakable, even as she kept her expression demure. She was judging me. Again.

I returned her polite nod. "Indeed, we are." In fact, I was acquainted with the lady, her preposterous mother, her gossipy aunt, her uncle the solicitor, all *four* of her sisters, and sadly, not her brother. Because... ah, that was right. She did not have one, which meant the daughters were scouring the landscape for loose males all the more diligently.

Bingley clapped his hands with pleasure. "I thought as much! Well, no harm in reintroducing friends, eh?"

I resisted the urge to contradict him, though I knew any attempt would fall on deaf ears. Instead, I kept my expression neutral, doing my best to ignore the increasingly satisfied look Miss Elizabeth was casting in my direction.

"I hope you are enjoying the evening, Mr. Darcy," she said, almost as if she were preparing to dismiss me. "Assemblies such as these must be quite the novelty for you."

Ah, there it was. The needle, subtle but unmistakable. I had known this was coming from the moment Bingley dragged me over. In fact, I had noted a glint in the lady's eye earlier this evening when we were introduced, and my guess was right. She was the village wit.

Perfect.

I gave a small, tight smile. "They are certainly... lively."

Her brow lifted in response, the corner of her mouth twitching as though she were trying very hard not to laugh. "Indeed," she murmured. "I suppose one could call it lively. Though you do not appear to be enjoying it overmuch."

"I assure you," I replied, keeping my voice flat, "I am tolerating it with perfect equanimity."

That seemed to amuse her even more. Her eyes danced with something I could only interpret as triumph, as though she had expected exactly that answer. "Well, I am pleased to hear it. I should hate to think you find our company wanting."

"Miss Elizabeth," I said stiffly, "you should not presume my thoughts."

"Oh, I wouldn't dream of it, Mr. Darcy."

There was a brief, awkward silence before Bingley cleared his throat. Apparently, this conversation was not going as he had envisioned.

"Well, Darcy," he said, clapping a hand on my shoulder with a force that nearly made me wince, "I shall leave you to it, then. Miss Elizabeth, I hope you'll save me a dance later."

She smiled at him, genuinely this time. "Of course, Mr. Bingley."

And then he was gone, leaving me alone with her, standing awkwardly by the refreshment table as the conversation—and my discomfort—lingered in the air.

Miss Elizabeth's smile faded slightly as she glanced toward the dancers. I should have taken the opportunity to excuse myself, but curse it all, I couldn't think of another place in the room to stand that would not be worse.

"Do you not dance, Mr. Darcy?" she asked suddenly, breaking the silence.

I blinked, caught off guard by the question. "I do," I answered curtly, "though I find it more agreeable in certain settings."

Her lips quirked. "Certain settings?"

I gestured vaguely toward the crowded dance floor, where couples were stumbling through the movements with varying degrees of success. "A room less crowded. More... select company."

Her eyes narrowed, and I immediately regretted my words.

"I see," she said slowly. "Then I suppose you find our company here somewhat lacking in refinement."

"That is not what I meant," I said quickly, though the damage was done. She knew exactly what I meant. Of course, she did.

"No?" she asked, her voice light but her gaze sharp. "Then what did you mean, Mr. Darcy?"

I had no answer that would satisfy her. So, I did what any sensible man would do in such a situation. "Miss Elizabeth," I said, bowing stiffly, "if you will excuse me."

I didn't wait for her reply.

Elizabeth

I suppose it would have been too much to hope that Mr. Darcy might find some excuse to leave early.

I had noticed him, of course. How could I not? He loomed near the back of the room, his expression inscrutable but distinctly unwelcoming. His eyes scanned the assembly as though he were cataloging every last one of us—and finding us all thoroughly beneath his notice. He stood apart from the merriment, barely engaging with those around him, though all evening, Mr. Bingley had been attempting, with almost painful determination, to pull him into the fold.

It wasn't working.

I turned away from the sight of Mr. Darcy, letting my attention drift back to the more pleasant scene unfolding before me. Mr. Bingley was dancing with Jane, and she looked beautiful—flushed and smiling, though I could see the tension in her posture whenever Lydia's giggles rose above the music. My youngest sister had already made quite the spectacle of herself this evening—laughing too loudly, flirting too boldly—and Jane was doing her best to ignore it.

I felt my own face heating at the memory of Mama's remarks earlier. She had practically thrown Jane at Mr. Bingley, as if that would secure him for more than just a dance. It was mortifying, and Jane, bless her, had simply smiled through it all.

Mr. Darcy's disapproval had been written all over his face. He hadn't said a word, but I'd caught him watching us, his brow slightly furrowed, his gaze drifting over my family as if weighing each of us in turn. I supposed he found us lacking. I couldn't fault him for that entirely. The way Lydia was carrying on—and Mama, for that matter—I could hardly deny we were putting on quite the performance.

Still, Mr. Darcy's quiet disdain rankled. He seemed to think himself above the room. Above us. Above everything.

And yet... for all his superiority, I couldn't help but notice that he never once allowed himself to truly slip. His posture was impeccable, his coat perfectly tailored, his expression carefully neutral, no matter how ridiculous the evening became. While others flitted about the room, laughing too loudly or stumbling through a dance, he remained still.

Controlled.

Almost unnervingly so.

It made him all the more absurd, really. To stand so stiffly amidst such chaos, to guard himself so carefully against the prospect of enjoyment. How exhausting it must be, to never allow oneself a moment's unguarded amusement.

As I wandered toward the refreshment table, I caught a glimpse of Kitty and Lydia at the other end of the room, practically hanging off the arms of two soldiers, their laughter ringing out above the music. I winced, glancing toward Jane, who was clearly doing her best to ignore the spectacle. If she was embarrassed, she would never show it.

But I wasn't quite as patient. I could only imagine what Mr. Darcy made of the scene. Why I cared, I had no idea. What did it matter to me if he was a prig? But I still noticed.

He was near the fireplace now, standing perfectly still, his eyes flicking across the room as though cataloging every flaw in the evening. And yet, something about him remained so... steady. I found myself studying him in spite of myself. He was so unlike any man I had ever met—so fastidious, so very controlled, even in a setting like this where most men would have grown frustrated or bored.

My father, for instance, had long since retreated to a corner of the room, where he could sit in peace, nursing a glass of wine and casting the occasional amused glance at Mama's efforts to herd my sisters like a determined sheepdog. But Mr. Darcy? He remained in the thick of it, though he hardly participated. He was like a marble statue, observing, never reacting.

I supposed I should find it irritating—his insistence on remaining aloof. And yet, there was something strangely fascinating about it.

"Lizzy!"

I turned just in time to see Charlotte approaching, her face flushed with exertion from her recent dance. She smiled as she reached my side, following my gaze toward the refreshment table, then across the room to where Mr. Darcy stood, still glowering at the crowd.

"He doesn't look as though he's enjoying himself," Charlotte remarked quietly, her smile fading.

"No," I said, unable to suppress a smile of my own. "I don't think Mr. Darcy was made for country assemblies."

Charlotte shook her head. "Or any sort of assembly at all. How can a man be so disagreeable? And with Mr. Bingley as his friend, no less!"

"Perhaps that is why Mr. Bingley is so eager to befriend everyone else. He must balance out the company he keeps."

Charlotte chuckled at that, though her eyes flicked back toward Mr. Darcy, her expression thoughtful. "Still, there's something about him, isn't there?"

"Something unpleasant, you mean?"

"No, something... steady. You can't quite shake the feeling that he's always in control."

I raised a brow at her. "You find that appealing?"

"Not appealing, exactly." She frowned, considering. "But intriguing. He doesn't seem the type to let anything get the better of him, does he?"

I glanced back toward Mr. Darcy. He was watching Mr. Bingley and Jane dance, his expression as impassive as ever.

"He doesn't," I admitted. "But he also doesn't seem the type to enjoy anything either. Where's the fun in that?"

Charlotte shrugged, her smile returning. "Perhaps he finds enjoyment in other things."

I doubted that very much, but I kept the thought to myself. We had spent enough time analyzing Mr. Darcy for one evening. Whatever his faults—and there were many—I could at least be grateful that he was no threat to Jane's happiness. Mr. Bingley, for all his good nature, seemed unlikely to be swayed by the opinions of his stiff-necked friend.

The evening wore on, and the room grew even more crowded, the air thick with the mingled scents of sweat, perfume, and the increasingly warm bodies pressing closer together. I stayed by Charlotte's side for much of the night, grateful for her company—and her good humor, which made it far easier to ignore the more embarrassing behaviors of my family.

At one point, Jane and Mr. Bingley passed by us, both of them glowing from their second dance, and I smiled at the sight of my sister so obviously happy. If only we could escape Mama's loud declarations long enough to let Jane's natural grace shine through.

And if only Mr. Darcy weren't there to witness the whole evening.

I glanced back toward him one last time just as he turned away from the dance floor. Our eyes met briefly—his expression as hooded as ever—but there was something in his gaze that made me pause.

For a moment, I thought he looked almost... tired. Not the disdain I had seen earlier, but something far more ordinary.

I quickly looked away, unsure what to make of it.

Chapter Two

Darcy

"You know," Bingley said, staring at his plate with a dreamy smile, "I believe I have never met a more amiable woman than Miss Bennet."

I nearly choked on my tea. Amiable was one word for it. Passive might have been another. But before I could remark on his absurd infatuation, Caroline Bingley swept in to fill the gap.

"Yes, Miss Bennet is charming, of course," she purred, carefully buttering a piece of toast as though she hadn't been rolling her eyes the entire night before. "So elegant, so composed."

Composed? I glanced at Bingley, half-expecting him to challenge the blatant exaggeration, but he just nodded, eyes shining like a schoolboy. Nothing about that entire family was *composed*. Apparently, he and I had been at two entirely different assemblies.

Louisa Hurst hummed in agreement, adding, "It is unfortunate, though, about the rest of her family."

Caroline Bingley's knife clattered to the plate with a bit too much enthusiasm. "Yes, it is rather difficult to overlook their... boisterous nature. And that mother of hers—dear me, you could hear her voice echoing across the room like a town crier."

I could feel Bingley's distress rising beside me, so I stared harder at my plate and let the sisters continue. There was no need for me to interject. They would do enough damage on their own.

"And those sisters!" Miss Bingley's voice had dropped to a scandalized whisper, though we were hardly in the company of anyone who cared. "That youngest! Lydia, was it? Absolutely wild. Flirting with every man in uniform—"

"Young girls are lively," Bingley interrupted. He was grasping at straws now. "Miss Lydia was just... youthful enthusiasm. It's perfectly harmless."

I nearly rolled my eyes. One more assembly like that, and Miss Lydia Bennet would likely be causing a scandal that would be heard of from here to London.

"Harmless," Miss Bingley repeated with a delicate sniff. "Well, I suppose you're more forgiving than I, dear brother. I only wonder how Miss Bennet can manage to stand out amidst such a... lively family."

I let Caroline Bingley's words hang in the air and pretended not to hear them. Bingley sighed, looking mournfully at his plate as if it might offer him a solution.

"Darcy," he said suddenly, turning to me as though I could save him from the conversation, "you must have noticed Miss Bennet. Was she not the very picture of elegance last night?"

I looked up from my cup, slowly. The cold tea wasn't going to save me from this, apparently. "She was pleasant."

"Pleasant?" Bingley echoed, looking at me as if I'd said fire was hot. "Well, of course. More than that, though. She's delightful."

Miss Bingley's smile tightened. "Delightful, yes... as long as you can overlook the rest of Meryton's rather provincial charms."

"Provincial charms," I muttered under my breath, eyeing Caroline across the table. I wasn't sure whether I was impressed or irritated by her ability to turn snobbery into an art form.

But before anyone could continue the debate over Miss Bennet's superiority despite her family, the door creaked open, and a servant entered, carrying a letter on a silver tray. He crossed the room with the expression of someone who had interrupted one too many of these charming breakfasts and handed it to me.

I frowned, unfolding the letter and reading it over, my mood shifting from mild irritation to outright confusion.

Fitzwilliam Darcy, Esq.

Darcy House, London and Pemberley House, Derbyshire

Dear Mr. Darcy,

I write to inform you of an unexpected development regarding the estate of an elderly widow, one Miss Isobel McLean, with whom you may not be acquainted. Her passing last month has brought to light a connection to your family, and as such, you have been named the beneficiary of certain assets and properties under her estate.

This matter requires your immediate attention, and I urge you to travel to London as soon as you may to review the legal documents and finalize the transfer of inheritance. Please come at your earliest convenience so that we may discuss the particulars.

Yours faithfully,

John ArthursonSolicitorArthurson & Wilkes, London

I flipped the letter over as if the back of it might contain further enlightenment, but alas, it was as blank as it was when I broke the seal. A relative I had never heard of? No... I squinted at the letter again. It only said she had a "connection" to my family, which could mean anything under the sun. What in the world...?

"Bad news?" Bingley asked, leaning forward with the kind of wide-eyed curiosity I found mildly alarming.

I folded the letter slowly and placed it next to my plate. "It seems I'm required in London."

Bingley blinked. "London? Whatever for?"

"A matter of inheritance," I said. "From a connection I was not even aware of."

Caroline Bingley raised a brow. "A relative you didn't know? How... strange."

Strange didn't even begin to cover it. McLean? That sounded Scottish, but I had no Scottish relations. That I knew of. But I wasn't about to launch into the complexities of my family tree over breakfast, especially not in the company of Caroline Bingley, who had made it clear that she wished to become a branch in said tree.

"It seems the situation demands my attention," I continued, doing my best to sound as though the whole thing didn't perplex me as much as it did. "I will send for my carriage and leave at once."

Bingley's face fell, and for a moment, I wondered if he might actually pout. "But Darcy, you'll miss the shooting! We've been planning it for weeks!"

I glanced toward the window, where the grey sky had taken a distinctly menacing turn. "The weather promises rain," I said, more to save myself than to comfort him. "I doubt there will be much sport today."

Bingley looked as though he might argue, but one glance outside and his shoulders sagged. "Well, still. It's only a passing shower, I'm sure. You won't be gone too long, will you?"

I took another sip of coffee, considering the letter that lay neatly folded beside me. "I should return by tomorrow, or perhaps the day after next."

Caroline Bingley sighed. "I do hope your business will not detain you too long, Mr. Darcy. We should all feel terribly bereft without your company."

"I'm sure you'll manage," I said, allowing myself the smallest flicker of a smile.

Louisa Hurst laughed lightly. "At least you'll be spared any further... local amusements today."

I couldn't argue with that. The thought of escaping Meryton, if only briefly, was one small consolation.

"Well," Bingley mused, "at least we'll have calls to look forward to, eh? I daresay we shall be full of visiting neighbors, and we shall start calling on our new acquaintances."

A pity I was going to miss that. I stood, pushing my chair back with deliberate calm. "I will prepare for my departure."

Bingley mumbled something about bad timing and poor luck as I excused myself, but my thoughts were already elsewhere. As the door clicked shut behind me, I couldn't help but glance once more at the letter in my hand.

A connection I'd never heard of. Inheritance matters that couldn't wait.

London called, and for once, I was glad of it.

Elizabeth

"I don't know why you insist on rifling through these old things, Lizzy," my father's voice sounded from the doorway, sounding half-amused and half-exasperated.

I looked up from where I sat cross-legged on the floor of his library, surrounded by books and a few scattered papers I had pulled from the shelf.

"I like history," I replied, without any real guilt. "And you hide all the interesting things in here."

He raised an eyebrow. "It's not hiding. It's *my* library, and I would rather it stay that way."

I grinned, holding up a dusty old book I had just uncovered. "Is this a personal favorite? 'A Complete Account of the Families of Hertfordshire'—sounds positively riveting."

"Thrilling, I assure you," he said dryly, stepping further into the room. "If you enjoy reading about long-dead people with too much land and too little sense."

"I do enjoy that, actually," I said, flipping through the brittle pages with care. "Though I must say, your taste in reading is a bit... practical. You don't have any scandalous letters tucked away in here, do you?"

Father gave me a look over his spectacles. "If I did, I certainly wouldn't tell you."

I let out a mock sigh of disappointment and set the book aside, reaching for another stack of papers. "You must have something of interest to hide in here. Some secret will? A forgotten fortune?"

"What I have in here," he said pointedly, "are old estate records and documents you likely have no business reading."

"That's what makes them interesting," I said with a grin, holding up a particularly aged-looking paper. "Look at this—it's from the year 1700! I'm practically touching history."

"You're touching something dusty," he corrected, stepping closer to peer at the paper in my hand. "And most likely irrelevant."

"Is it?" I squinted at the document, trying to make sense of the elaborate script. "What is it, then? Some kind of land agreement?"

Father sighed. "That, my dear, is a very old lease agreement for a tenant farmer. Hardly riveting."

"Maybe not to you," I said, glancing at it again. "But I find it fascinating how everything is so... connected. The land, the families, the history of it all."

"If you'd been born a son, you'd have made an excellent steward, but a rather useless master. Far too inquisitive for your own good."

"I'll take that as a compliment," I said brightly, rolling up the paper and setting it aside.

Father moved to sit at his desk, shuffling some of the papers I had displaced. "You know, Lizzy, not everything in this library is meant for idle curiosity."

I shrugged, unrepentant. "Perhaps not. But you leave it all lying about as if you're waiting for someone to discover it."

"I leave it all lying about because no one else is usually fool enough to wade through these old ledgers and documents."

"Foolishness or curiosity?" I asked, smiling at him. "There's a fine line between the two."

He chuckled softly, shaking his head. "One you seem determined to dance upon."

I reached for another book, my fingers brushing the worn leather cover. "There's so much history in these pages," I murmured. "All these names and events, shaping everything around us, even now."

Father leaned back in his chair, watching me with an indulgent expression. "And what is it you hope to find in all this history, Lizzy?"

I paused, thinking about it. "Maybe I just want to understand how things work. The estate, the land... why we're all tied to it the way we are."

"And here I thought you only cared for novels."

"I'm more complicated than you give me credit for," I said with a smirk, turning the page in the ancient book I had picked up.

"So you keep reminding me." Eventually, he sighed again, a long-suffering sound I'd heard many times before.

"You really should leave these things alone, you know."

I grinned. "I'll take it under advisement."

G ET READY FOR THE wildest Christmas Ball ever! Dive into _The Scotsman's Ghost_ today!

Printed in Great Britain
by Amazon

54607303R00166